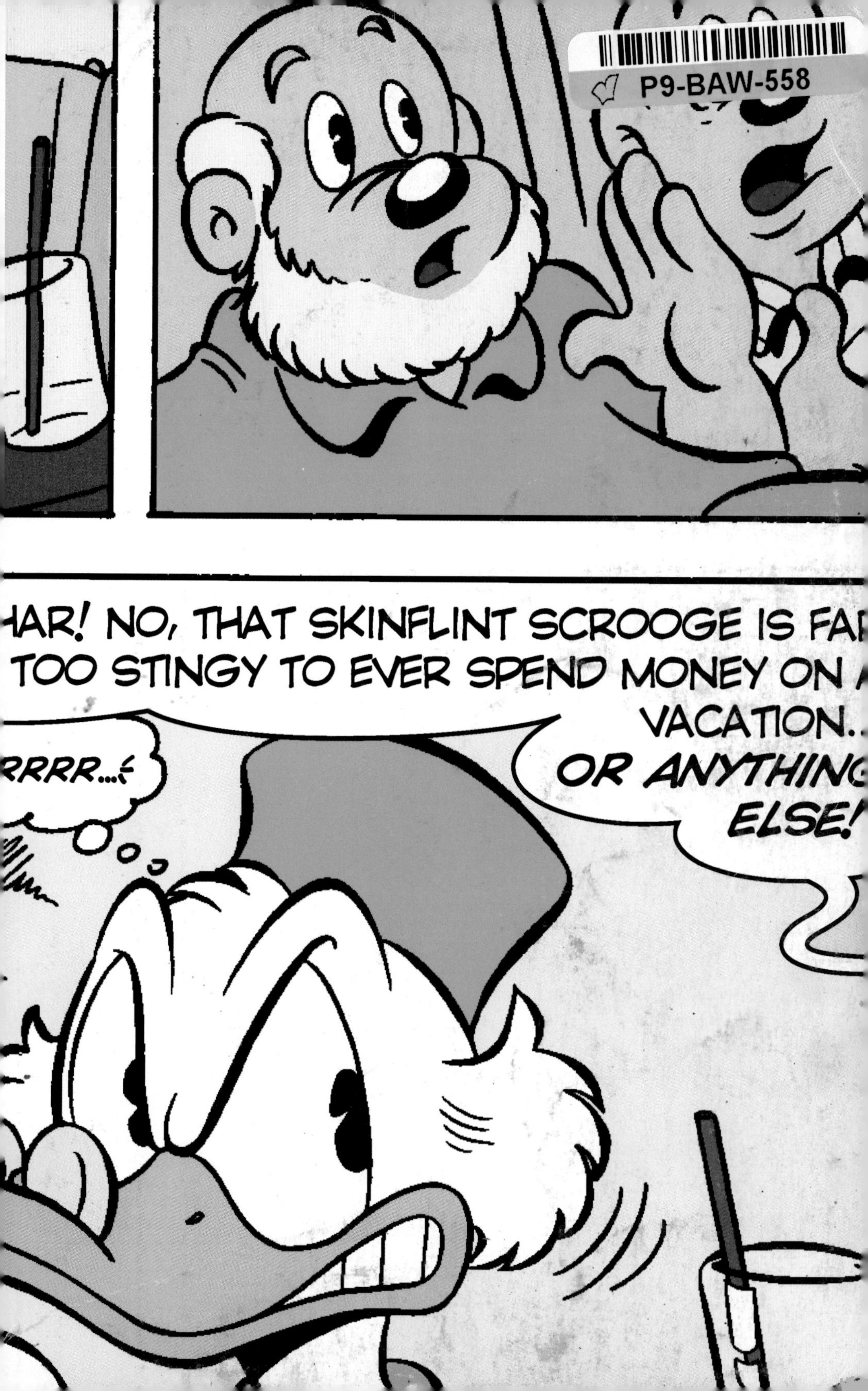
HAR! NO, THAT SKINFLINT SCROOGE IS FAR TOO STINGY TO EVER SPEND MONEY ON A VACATION... OR ANYTHING ELSE!
RRRR...!

# WALT DISNEY'S UNCLE $CROOGE

BOOM KIDS!

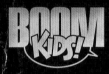

ROSS RICHIE
chief executive officer

MARK WAID
editor-in-chief

ADAM FORTIER
vice president,
new business

WES HARRIS
vice president,
publishing

LANCE KREITER
vice president,
licensing & merchandising

CHIP MOSHER
marketing director

MATT GAGNON
managing editor

FIRST EDITION: JUNE 2010

10 9 8 7 6 5 4 3 2 1
FOR INFORMATION REGARDING THE CPSIA ON THIS PRINTED MATERIAL
CALL: 203-595-3636 AND PROVIDE REFERENCE # EAST – 67004



Office of publication: 6310 San Vicente Blvd Ste 404, Los Angeles, CA 90048-5457.

A catalog record for this book is available from OCLC and on our website www.boom-kids.com on the Librarians page.

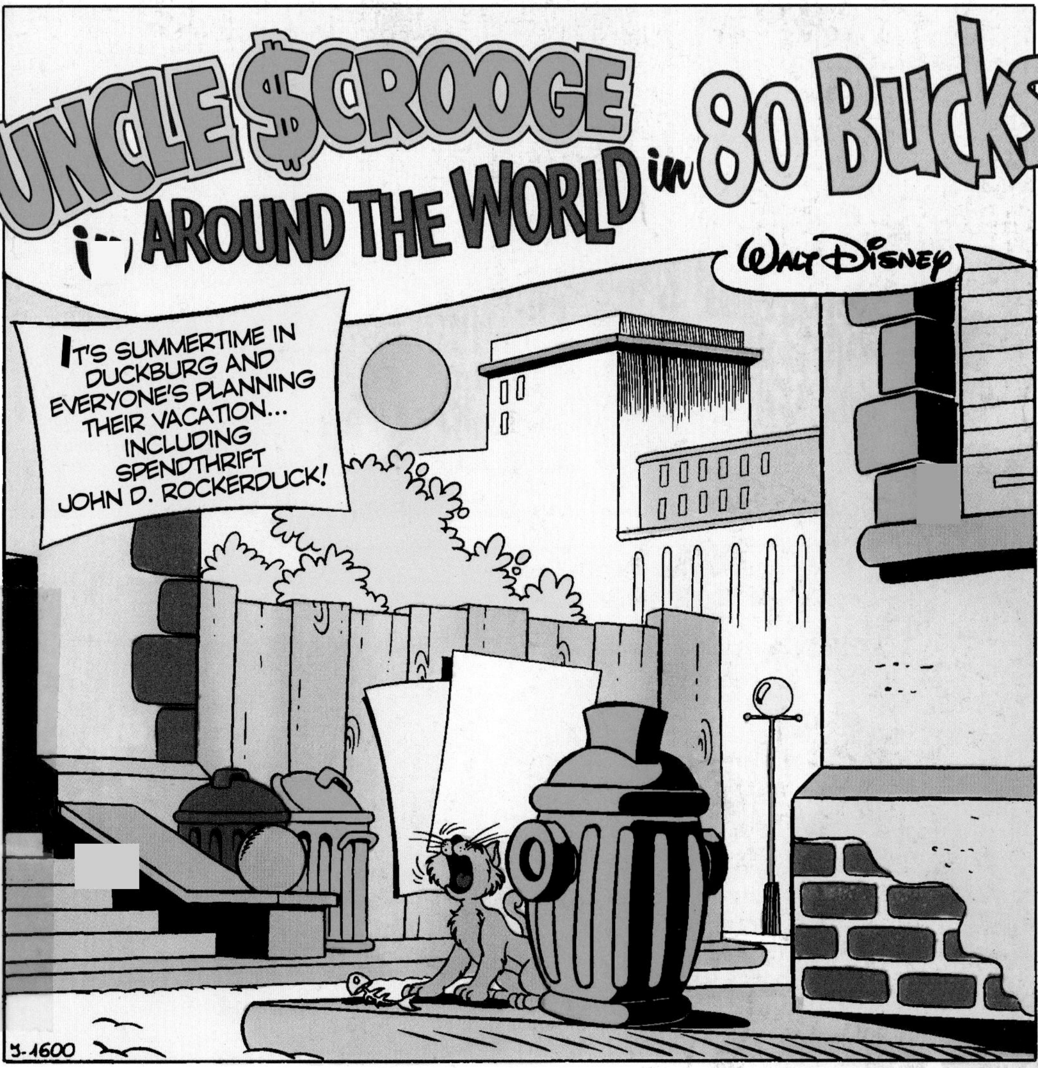
UNCLE $CROOGE
AROUND THE WORLD in 80 Bucks
WALT DISNEY
IT'S SUMMERTIME IN DUCKBURG AND EVERYONE'S PLANNING THEIR VACATION... INCLUDING SPENDTHRIFT JOHN D. ROCKERDUCK!
J-1600

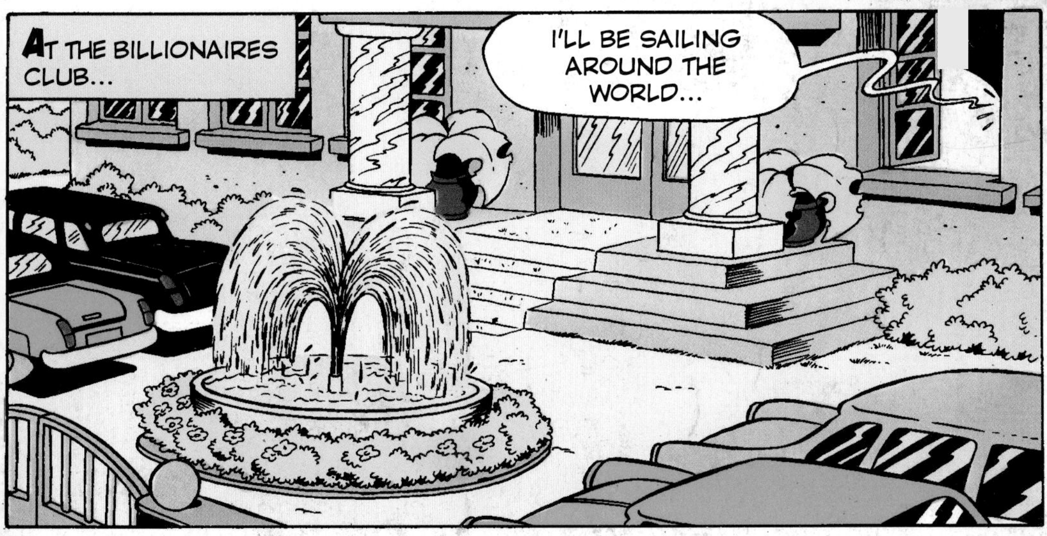
AT THE BILLIONAIRES CLUB...
I'LL BE SAILING AROUND THE WORLD...

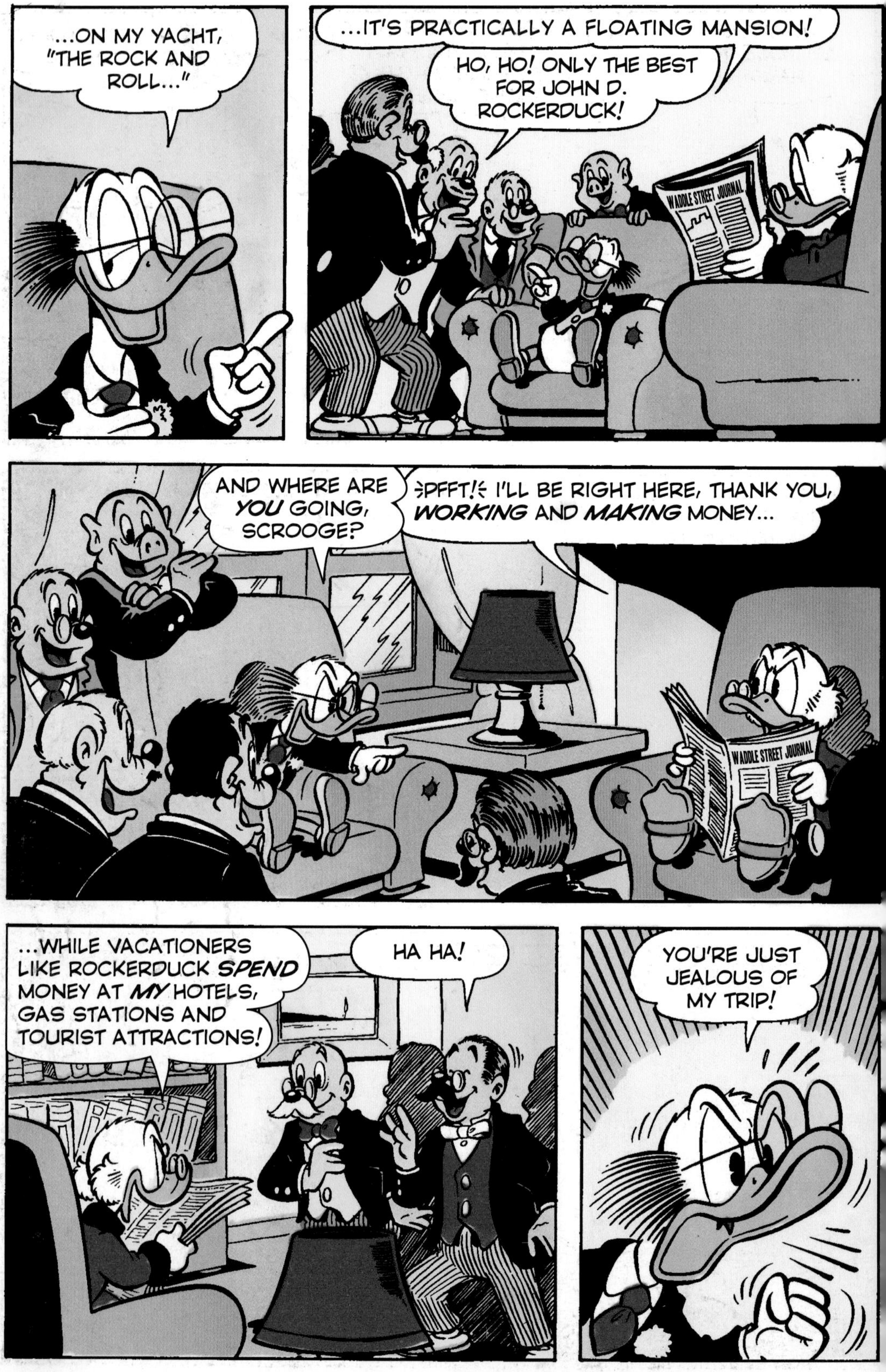
...ON MY YACHT, "THE ROCK AND ROLL..."
...IT'S PRACTICALLY A FLOATING MANSION!
HO, HO! ONLY THE BEST FOR JOHN D. ROCKERDUCK!
WADDLE STREET JOURNAL
AND WHERE ARE YOU GOING, SCROOGE?
PFFT! I'LL BE RIGHT HERE, THANK YOU, WORKING AND MAKING MONEY...
WADDLE STREET JOURNAL
...WHILE VACATIONERS LIKE ROCKERDUCK SPEND MONEY AT MY HOTELS, GAS STATIONS AND TOURIST ATTRACTIONS!
HA HA!
YOU'RE JUST JEALOUS OF MY TRIP!

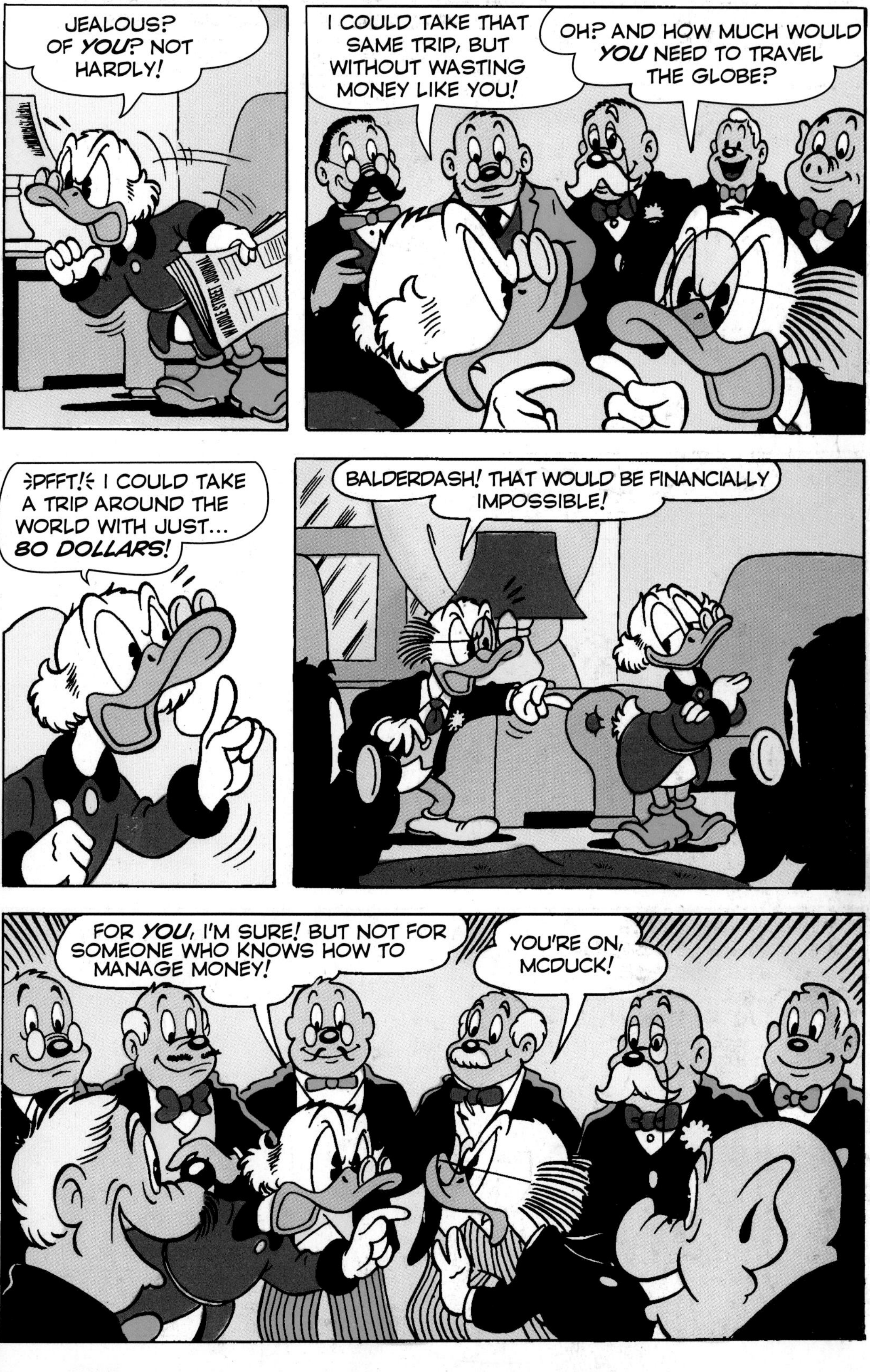
JEALOUS? OF *YOU*? NOT HARDLY!
I COULD TAKE THAT SAME TRIP, BUT WITHOUT WASTING MONEY LIKE YOU!
OH? AND HOW MUCH WOULD *YOU* NEED TO TRAVEL THE GLOBE?
*PFFT!* I COULD TAKE A TRIP AROUND THE WORLD WITH JUST... *80 DOLLARS!*
BALDERDASH! THAT WOULD BE FINANCIALLY IMPOSSIBLE!
FOR *YOU*, I'M SURE! BUT NOT FOR SOMEONE WHO KNOWS HOW TO MANAGE MONEY!
YOU'RE ON, MCDUCK!
WALL STREET JOURNAL

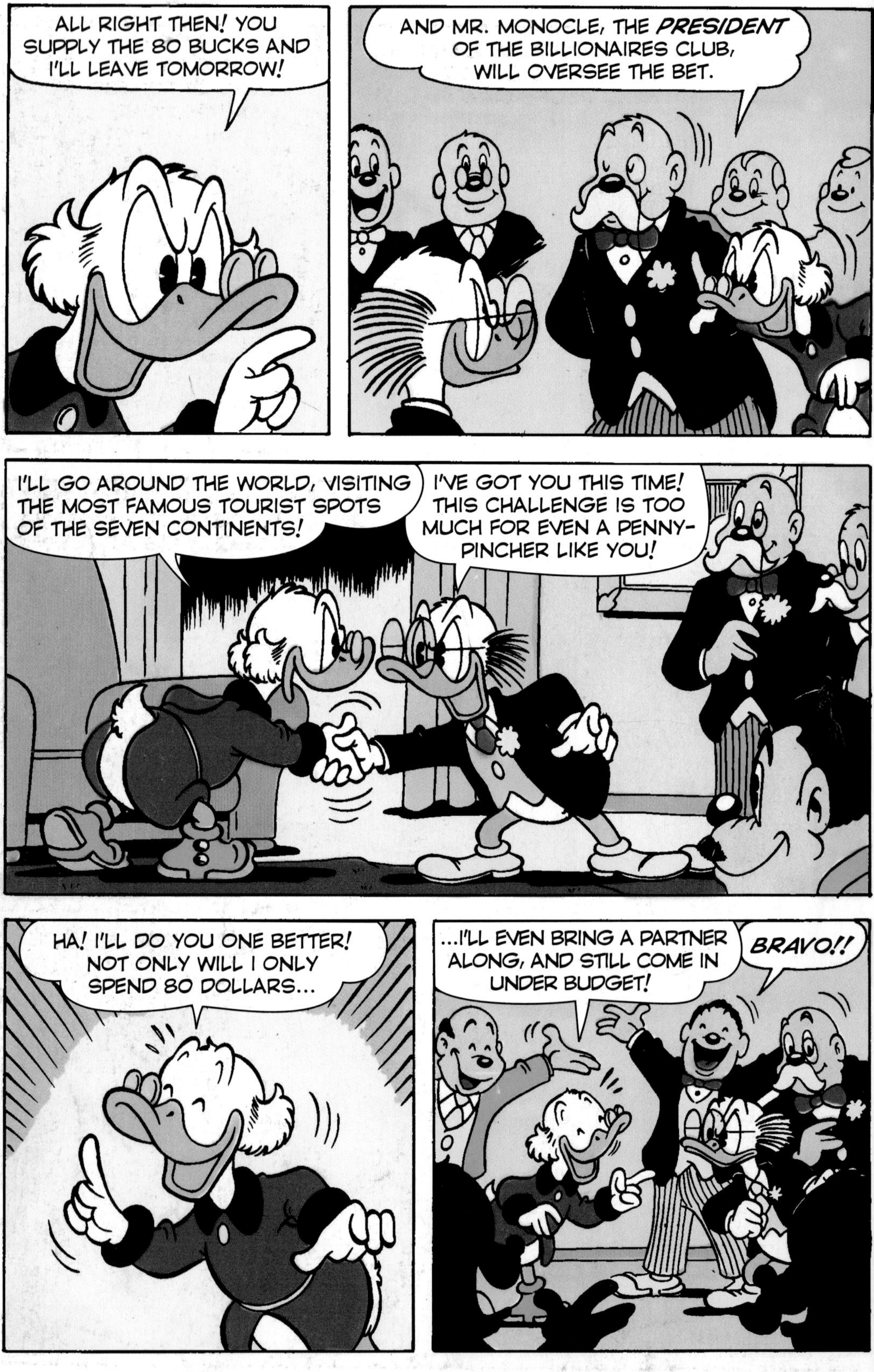
ALL RIGHT THEN! YOU SUPPLY THE 80 BUCKS AND I'LL LEAVE TOMORROW!
AND MR. MONOCLE, THE *PRESIDENT* OF THE BILLIONAIRES CLUB, WILL OVERSEE THE BET.
I'LL GO AROUND THE WORLD, VISITING THE MOST FAMOUS TOURIST SPOTS OF THE SEVEN CONTINENTS!
I'VE GOT YOU THIS TIME! THIS CHALLENGE IS TOO MUCH FOR EVEN A PENNY-PINCHER LIKE YOU!
HA! I'LL DO YOU ONE BETTER! NOT ONLY WILL I ONLY SPEND 80 DOLLARS...
...I'LL EVEN BRING A PARTNER ALONG, AND STILL COME IN UNDER BUDGET!
*BRAVO!!*

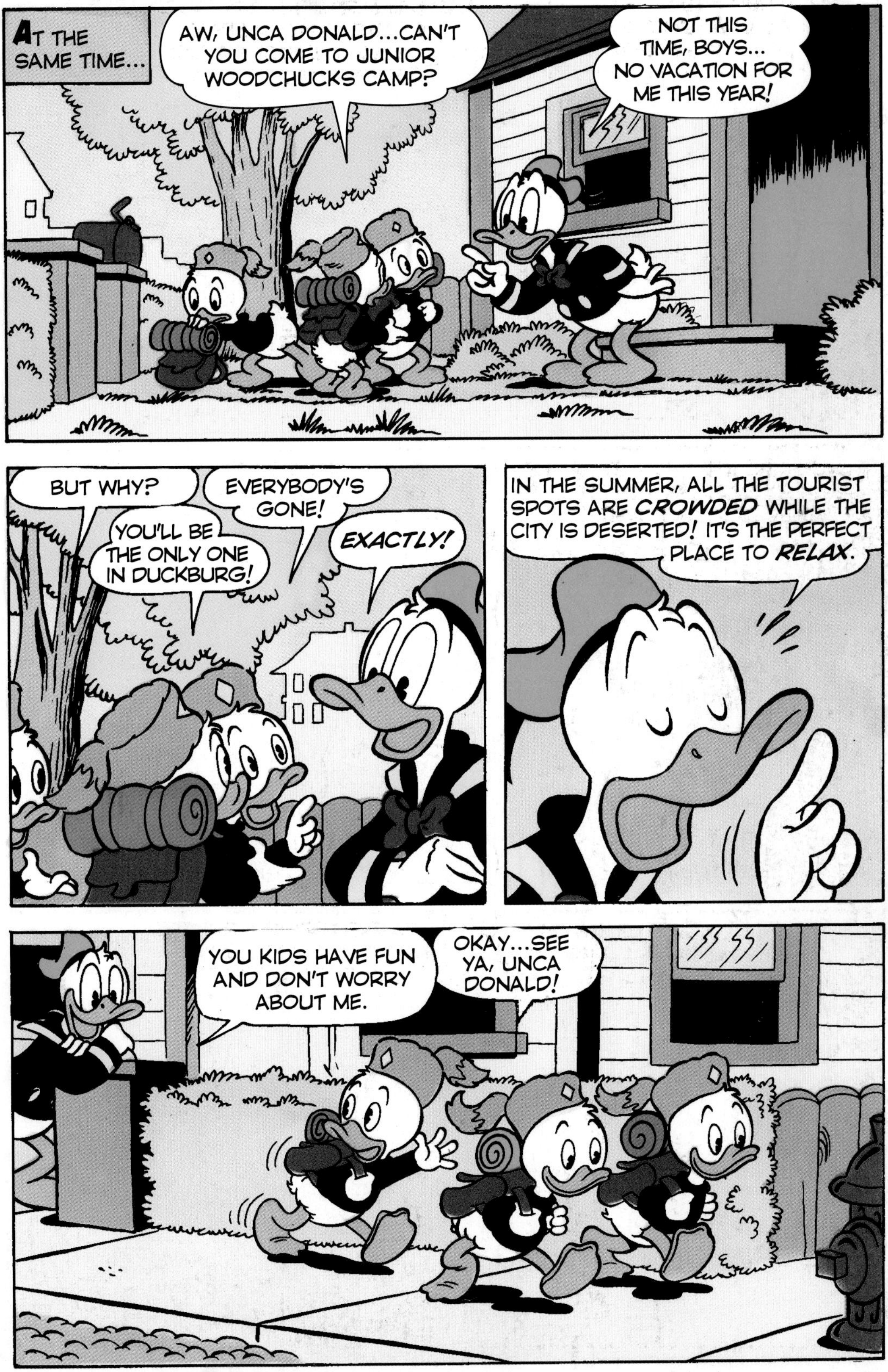
AT THE SAME TIME...
AW, UNCA DONALD...CAN'T YOU COME TO JUNIOR WOODCHUCKS CAMP?
NOT THIS TIME, BOYS... NO VACATION FOR ME THIS YEAR!
BUT WHY?
EVERYBODY'S GONE!
YOU'LL BE THE ONLY ONE IN DUCKBURG!
EXACTLY!
IN THE SUMMER, ALL THE TOURIST SPOTS ARE CROWDED WHILE THE CITY IS DESERTED! IT'S THE PERFECT PLACE TO RELAX.
YOU KIDS HAVE FUN AND DON'T WORRY ABOUT ME.
OKAY...SEE YA, UNCA DONALD!

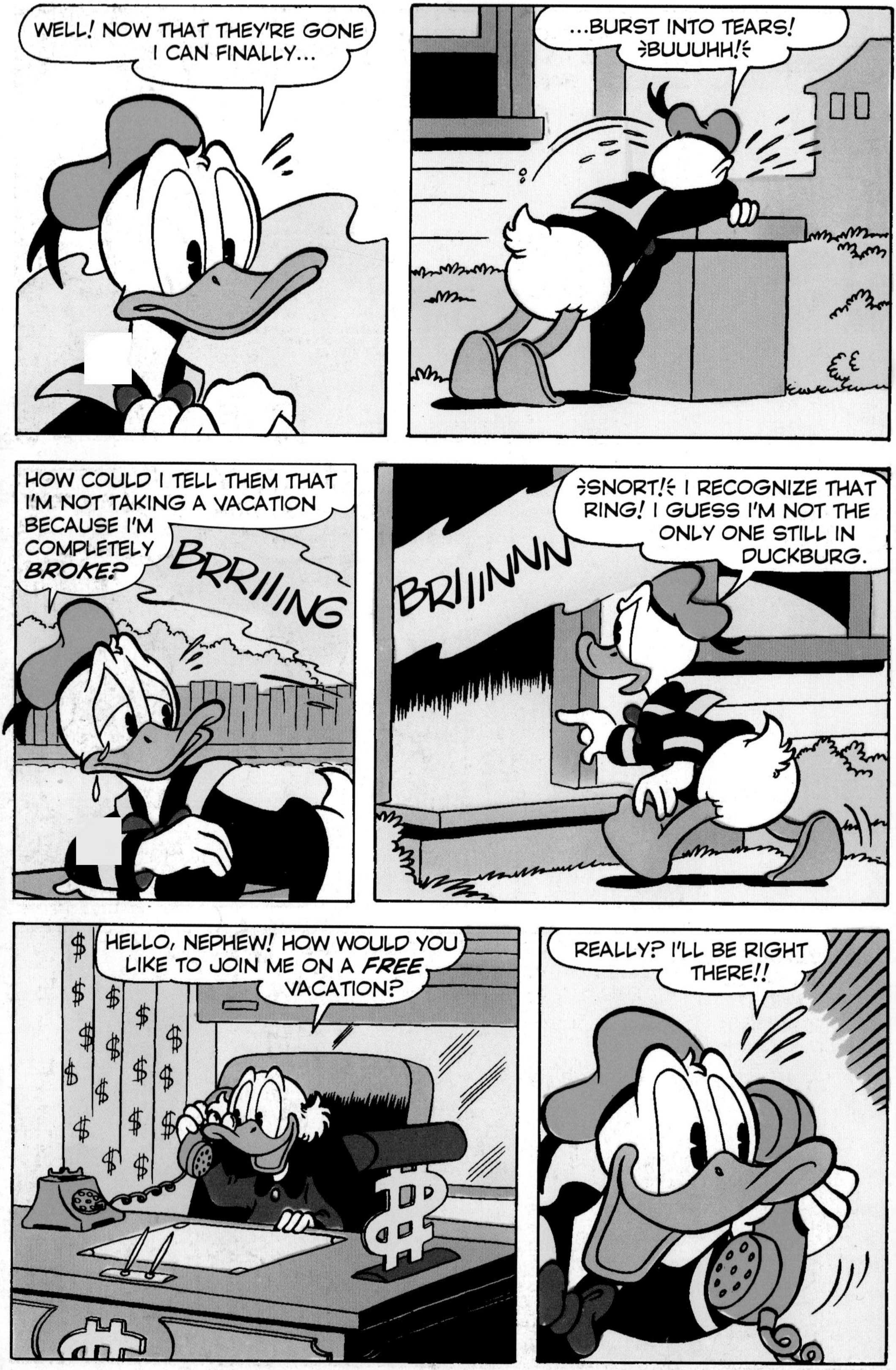
WELL! NOW THAT THEY'RE GONE I CAN FINALLY...
...BURST INTO TEARS! BUUUHH!
HOW COULD I TELL THEM THAT I'M NOT TAKING A VACATION BECAUSE I'M COMPLETELY BROKE?
BRRIIIING
BRIIINNN
SNORT! I RECOGNIZE THAT RING! I GUESS I'M NOT THE ONLY ONE STILL IN DUCKBURG.
HELLO, NEPHEW! HOW WOULD YOU LIKE TO JOIN ME ON A FREE VACATION?
REALLY? I'LL BE RIGHT THERE!!

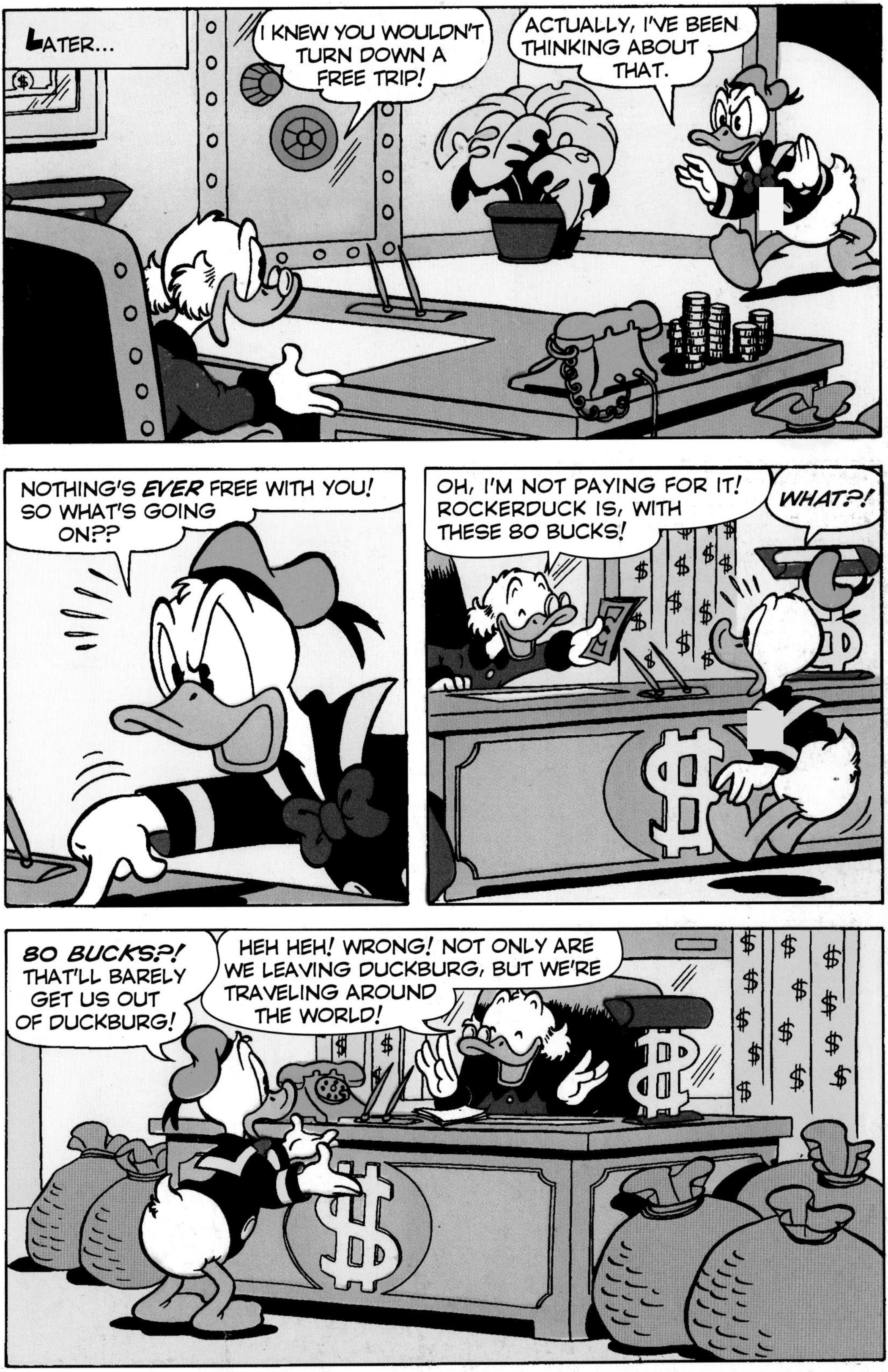
LATER...
I KNEW YOU WOULDN'T TURN DOWN A FREE TRIP!
ACTUALLY, I'VE BEEN THINKING ABOUT THAT.
NOTHING'S EVER FREE WITH YOU! SO WHAT'S GOING ON??
OH, I'M NOT PAYING FOR IT! ROCKERDUCK IS, WITH THESE 80 BUCKS!
WHAT?!
80 BUCKS?! THAT'LL BARELY GET US OUT OF DUCKBURG!
HEH HEH! WRONG! NOT ONLY ARE WE LEAVING DUCKBURG, BUT WE'RE TRAVELING AROUND THE WORLD!

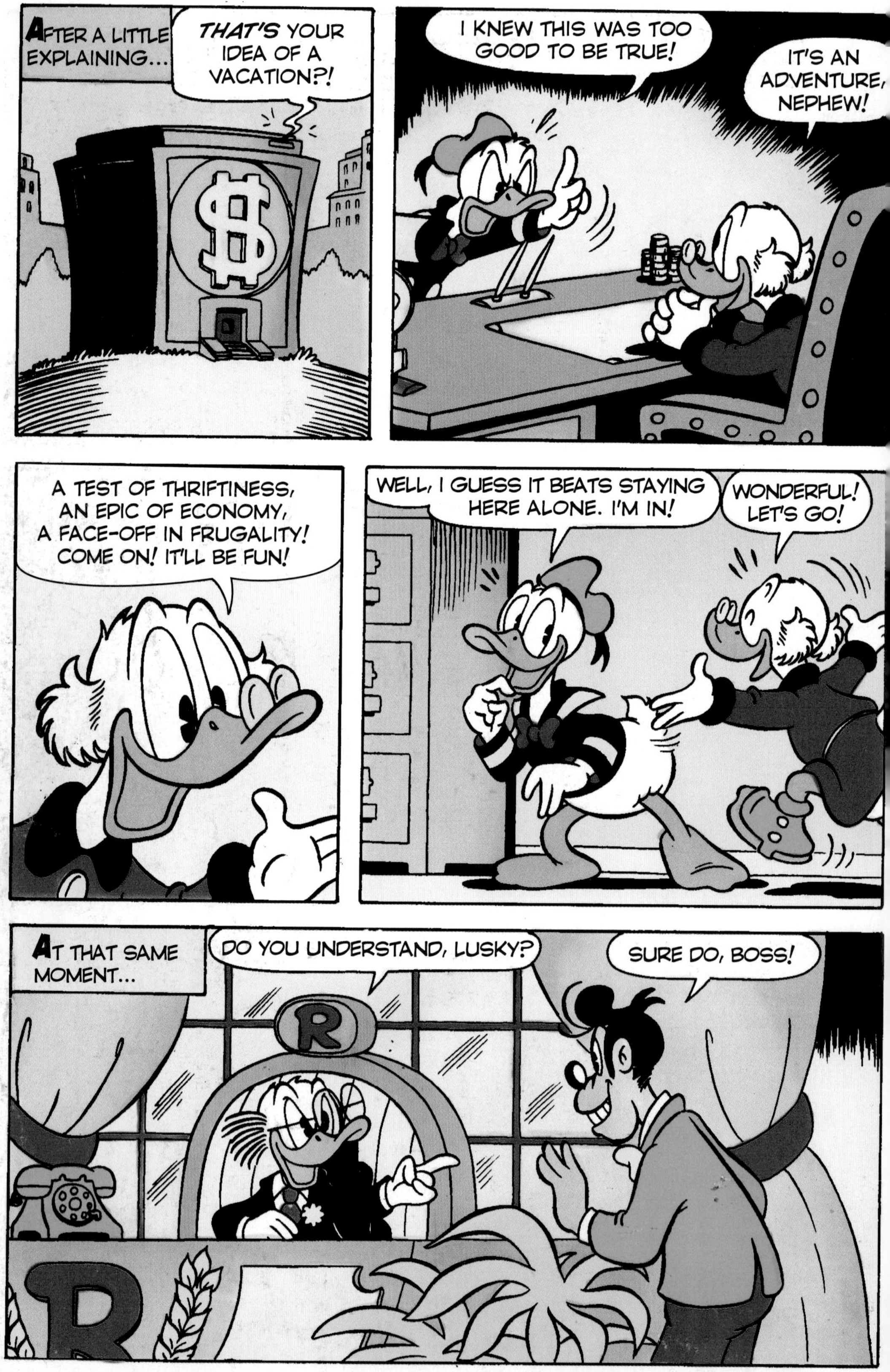
AFTER A LITTLE EXPLAINING...
THAT'S YOUR IDEA OF A VACATION?!
I KNEW THIS WAS TOO GOOD TO BE TRUE!
IT'S AN ADVENTURE, NEPHEW!
A TEST OF THRIFTINESS, AN EPIC OF ECONOMY, A FACE-OFF IN FRUGALITY! COME ON! IT'LL BE FUN!
WELL, I GUESS IT BEATS STAYING HERE ALONE. I'M IN!
WONDERFUL! LET'S GO!
AT THAT SAME MOMENT...
DO YOU UNDERSTAND, LUSKY?
SURE DO, BOSS!

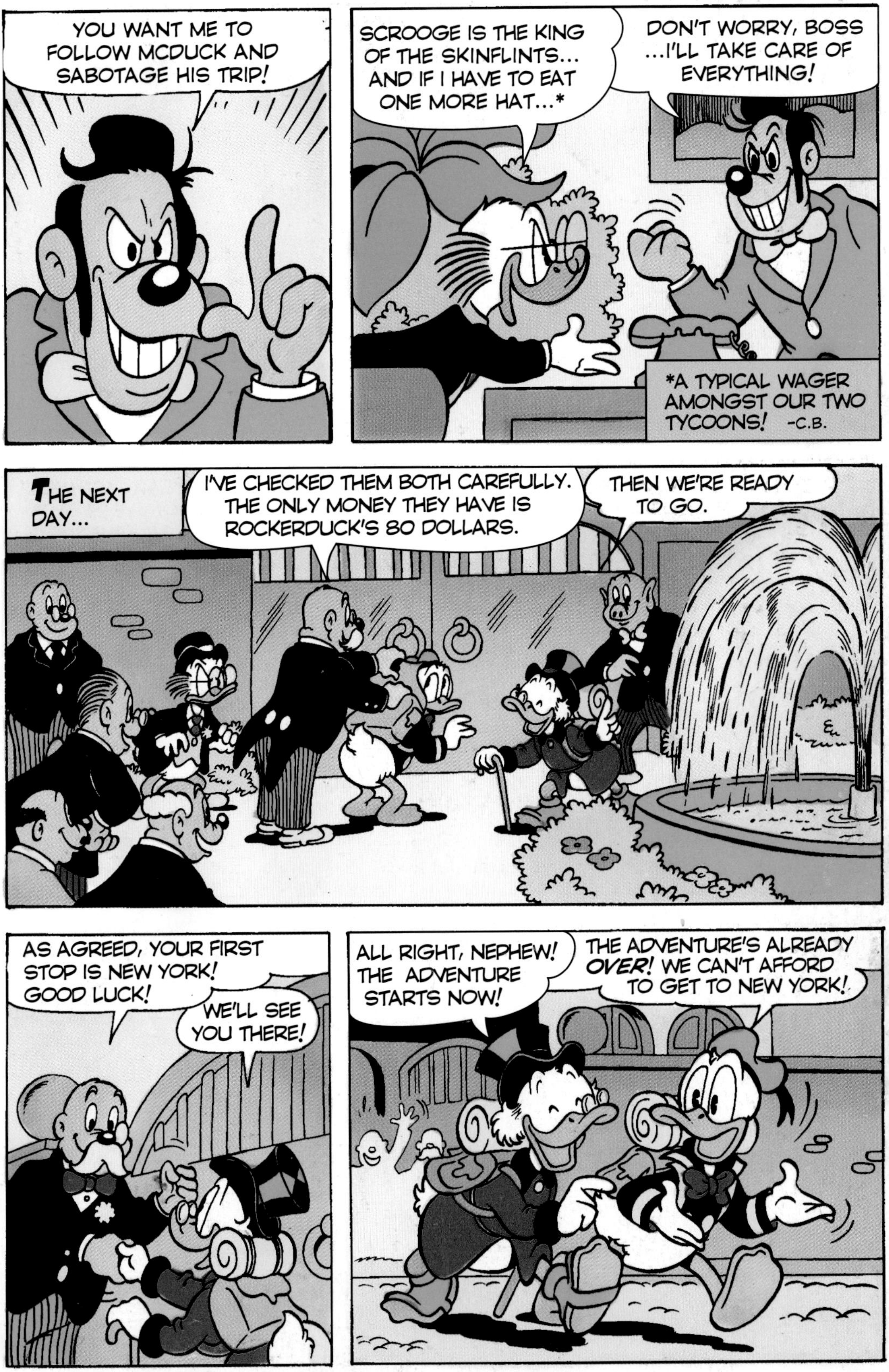
YOU WANT ME TO FOLLOW MCDUCK AND SABOTAGE HIS TRIP!
SCROOGE IS THE KING OF THE SKINFLINTS... AND IF I HAVE TO EAT ONE MORE HAT...*
DON'T WORRY, BOSS ...I'LL TAKE CARE OF EVERYTHING!
*A TYPICAL WAGER AMONGST OUR TWO TYCOONS! -C.B.
THE NEXT DAY...
I'VE CHECKED THEM BOTH CAREFULLY. THE ONLY MONEY THEY HAVE IS ROCKERDUCK'S 80 DOLLARS.
THEN WE'RE READY TO GO.
AS AGREED, YOUR FIRST STOP IS NEW YORK! GOOD LUCK!
WE'LL SEE YOU THERE!
ALL RIGHT, NEPHEW! THE ADVENTURE STARTS NOW!
THE ADVENTURE'S ALREADY OVER! WE CAN'T AFFORD TO GET TO NEW YORK!

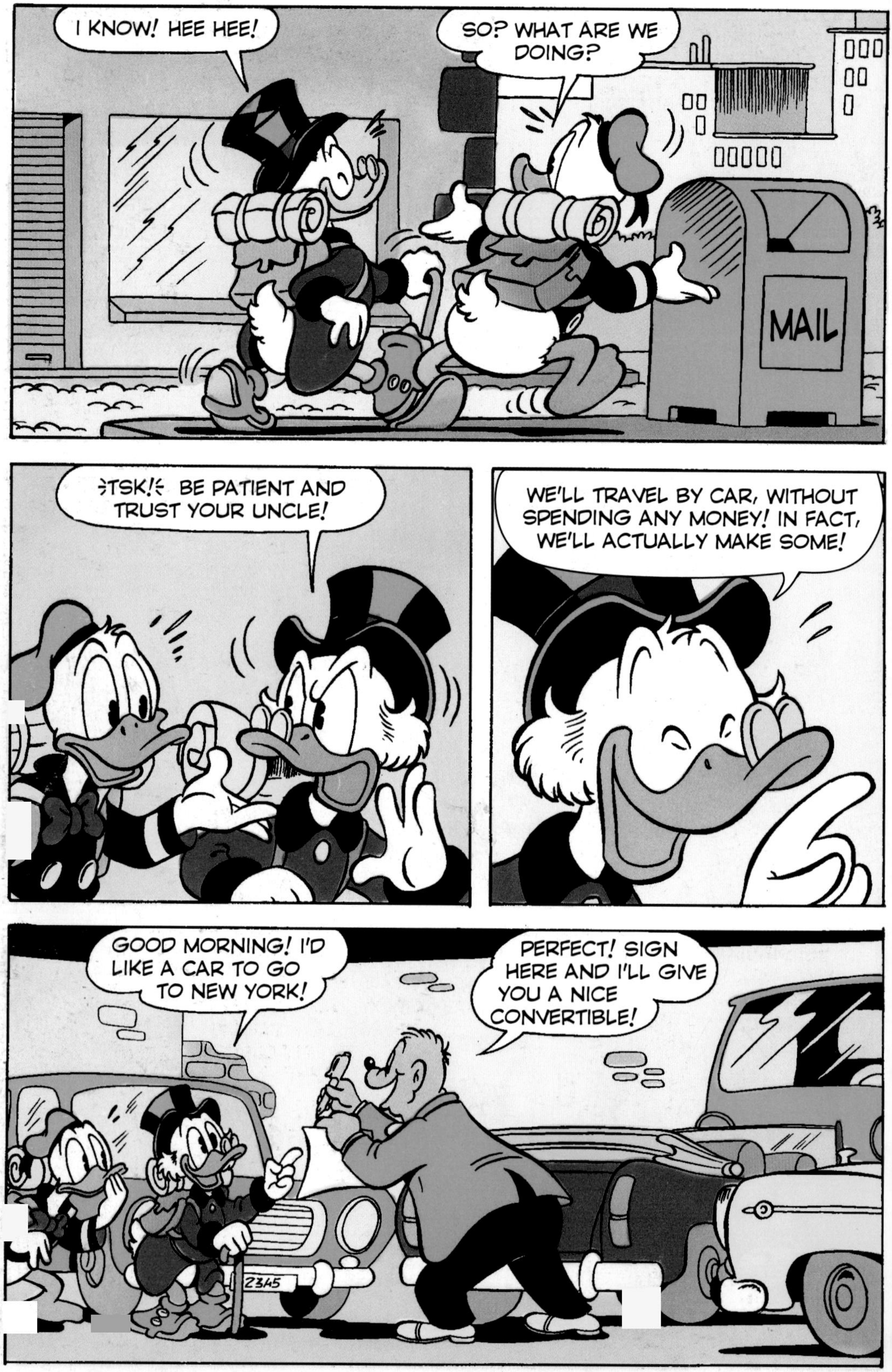
I KNOW! HEE HEE!
SO? WHAT ARE WE DOING?
MAIL
TSK! BE PATIENT AND TRUST YOUR UNCLE!
WE'LL TRAVEL BY CAR, WITHOUT SPENDING ANY MONEY! IN FACT, WE'LL ACTUALLY MAKE SOME!
GOOD MORNING! I'D LIKE A CAR TO GO TO NEW YORK!
PERFECT! SIGN HERE AND I'LL GIVE YOU A NICE CONVERTIBLE!
2345

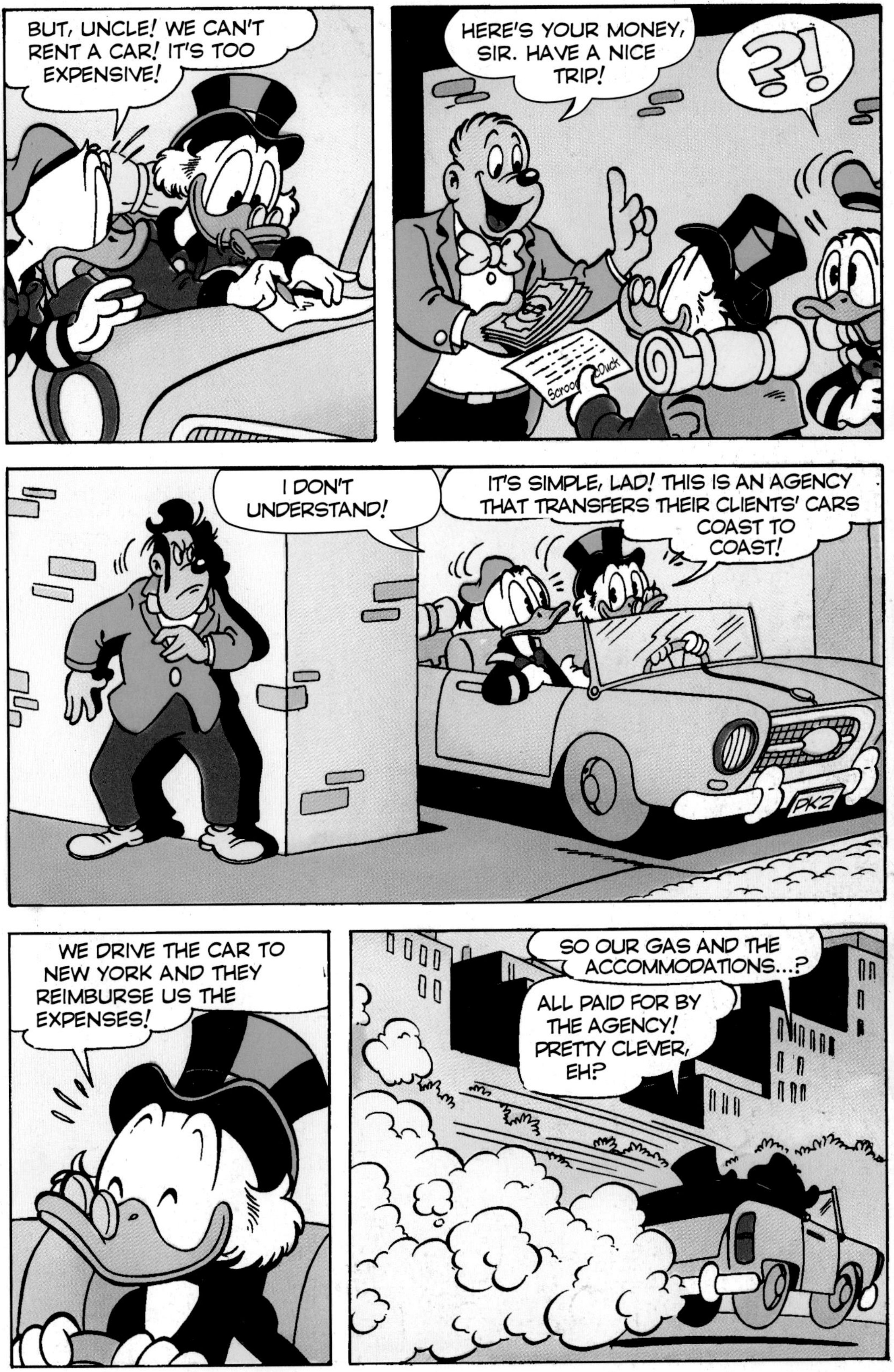
BUT, UNCLE! WE CAN'T RENT A CAR! IT'S TOO EXPENSIVE!
HERE'S YOUR MONEY, SIR. HAVE A NICE TRIP!
?!
I DON'T UNDERSTAND!
IT'S SIMPLE, LAD! THIS IS AN AGENCY THAT TRANSFERS THEIR CLIENTS' CARS COAST TO COAST!
PK2
WE DRIVE THE CAR TO NEW YORK AND THEY REIMBURSE US THE EXPENSES!
SO OUR GAS AND THE ACCOMMODATIONS...?
ALL PAID FOR BY THE AGENCY! PRETTY CLEVER, EH?

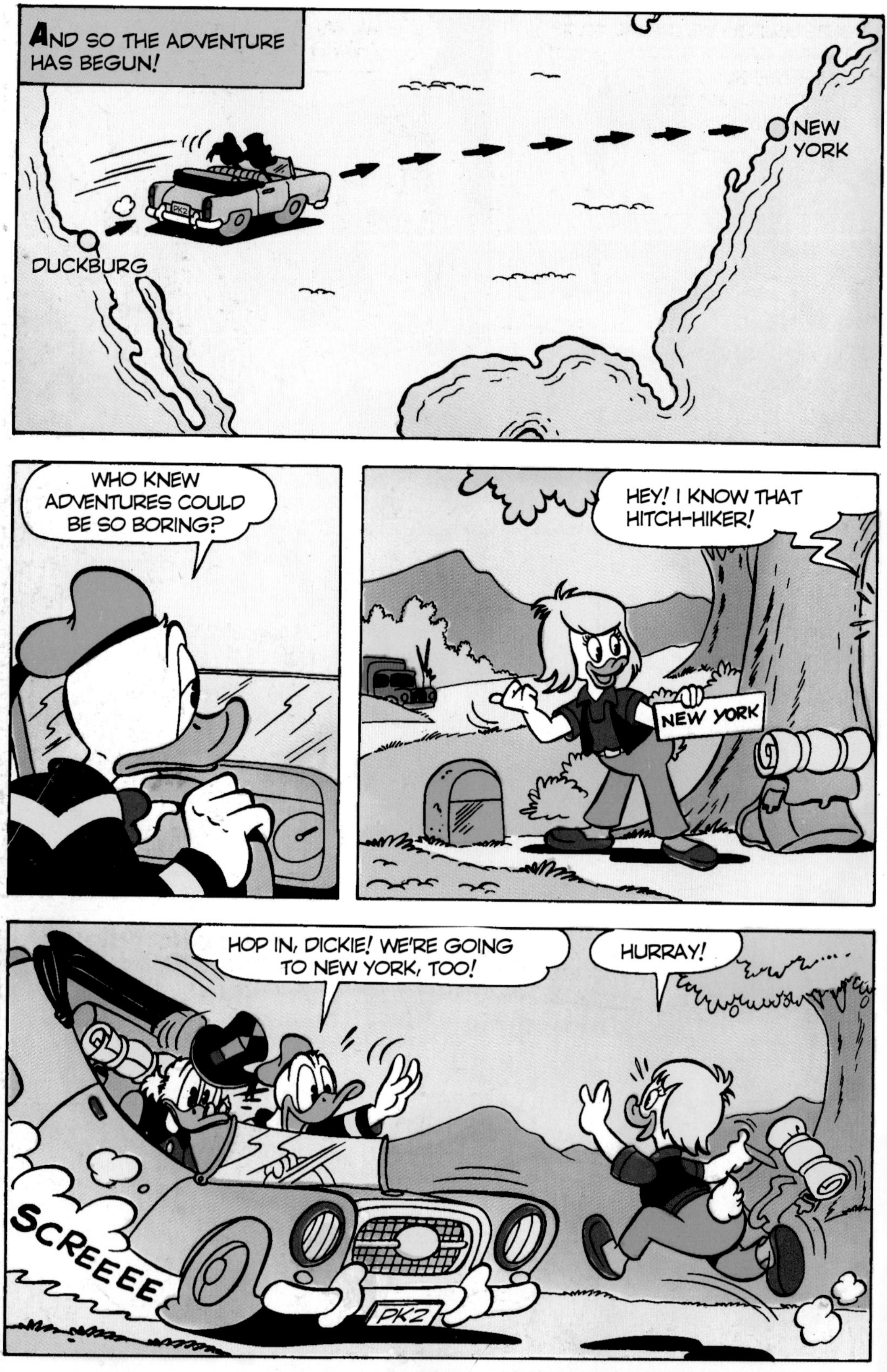

AND SO THE ADVENTURE HAS BEGUN!
PK2
DUCKBURG
NEW YORK
WHO KNEW ADVENTURES COULD BE SO BORING?
HEY! I KNOW THAT HITCH-HIKER!
NEW YORK
HOP IN, DICKIE! WE'RE GOING TO NEW YORK, TOO!
HURRAY!
SCREEEEE
PK2

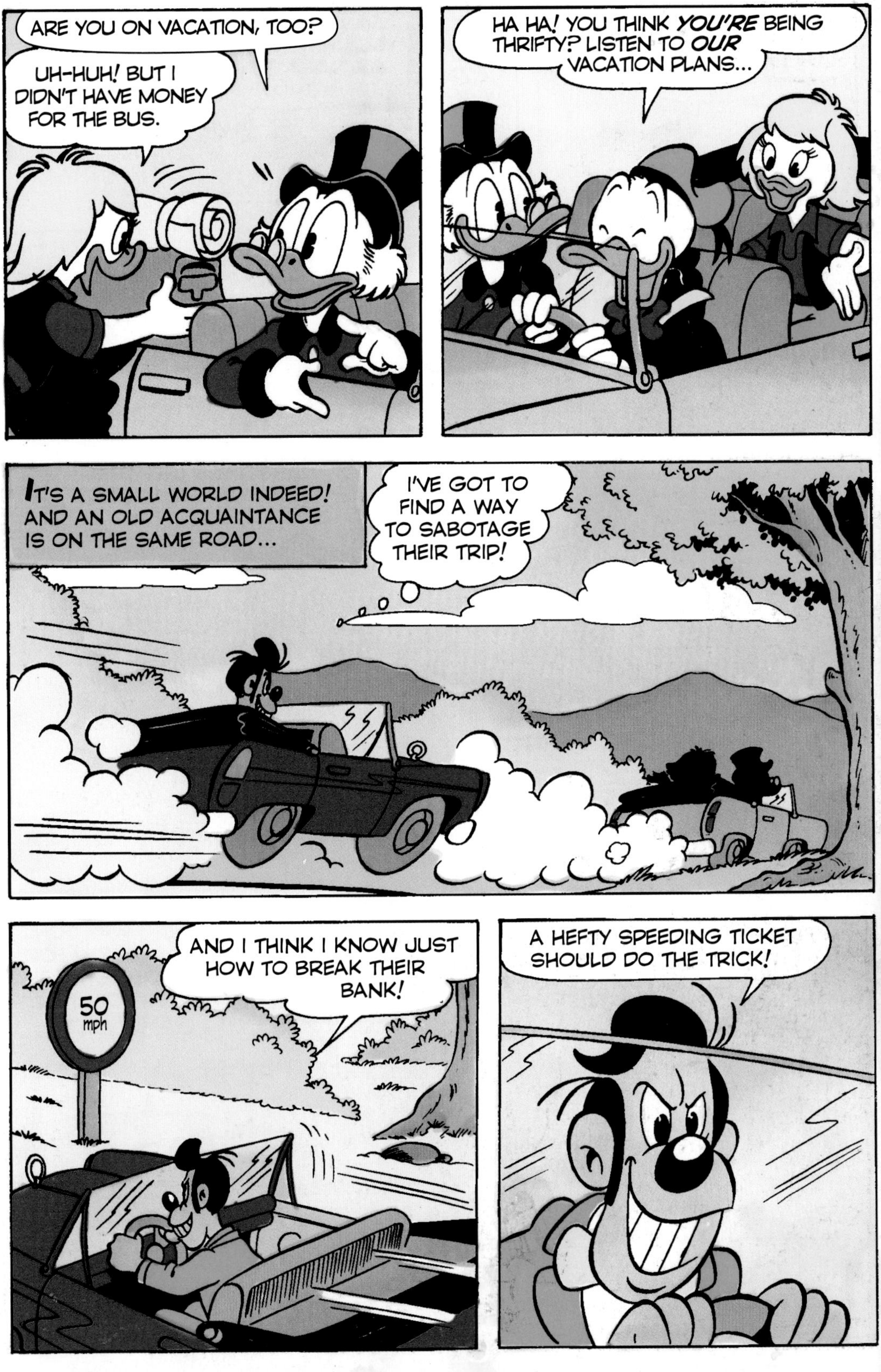
ARE YOU ON VACATION, TOO?
UH-HUH! BUT I DIDN'T HAVE MONEY FOR THE BUS.
HA HA! YOU THINK *YOU'RE* BEING THRIFTY? LISTEN TO *OUR* VACATION PLANS...
IT'S A SMALL WORLD INDEED! AND AN OLD ACQUAINTANCE IS ON THE SAME ROAD...
I'VE GOT TO FIND A WAY TO SABOTAGE THEIR TRIP!
50 mph
AND I THINK I KNOW JUST HOW TO BREAK THEIR BANK!
A HEFTY SPEEDING TICKET SHOULD DO THE TRICK!

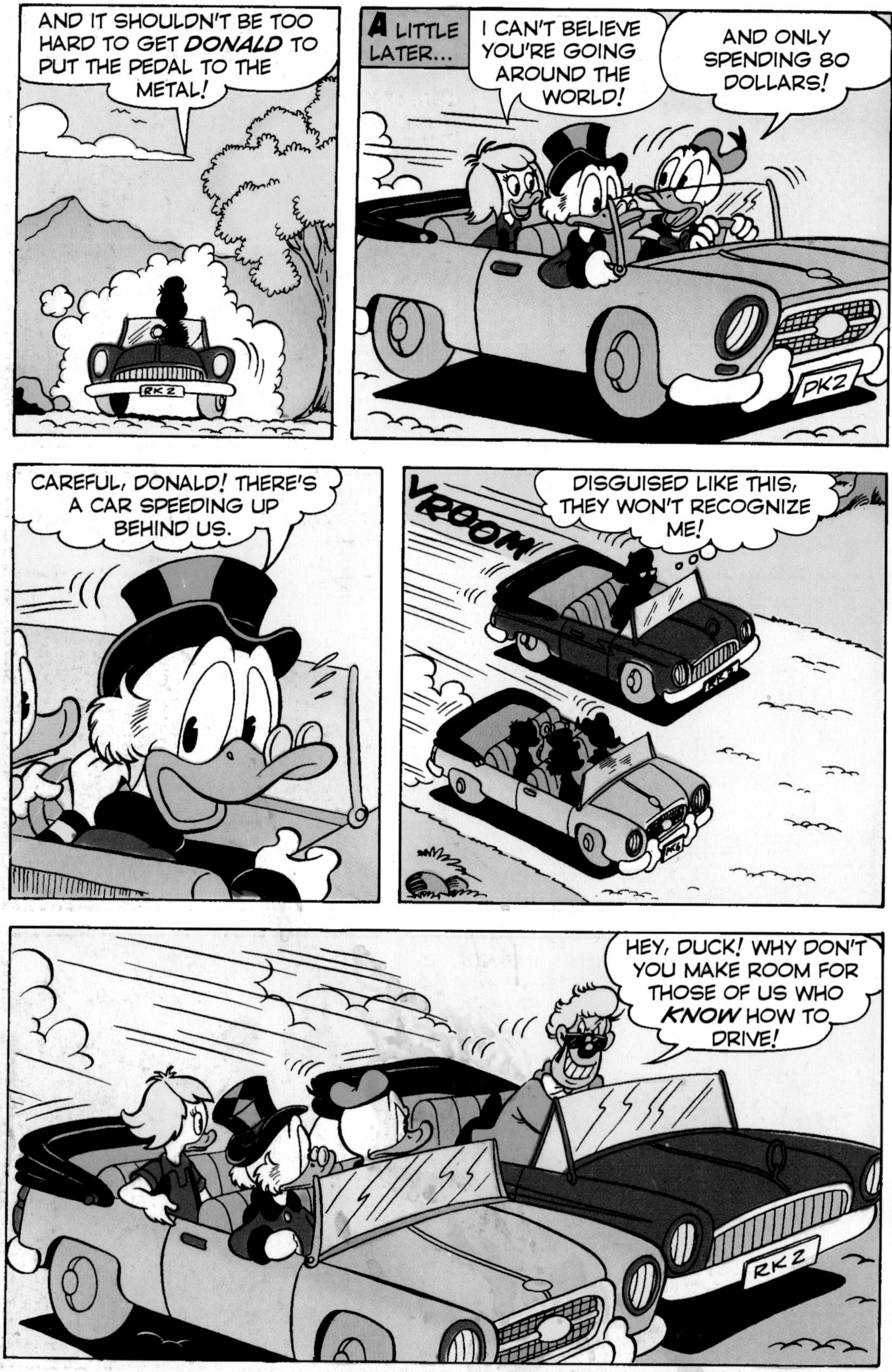
AND IT SHOULDN'T BE TOO HARD TO GET DONALD TO PUT THE PEDAL TO THE METAL!
RK 2
A LITTLE LATER...
I CAN'T BELIEVE YOU'RE GOING AROUND THE WORLD!
AND ONLY SPENDING 80 DOLLARS!
DK2
CAREFUL, DONALD! THERE'S A CAR SPEEDING UP BEHIND US.
VROOOM
DISGUISED LIKE THIS, THEY WON'T RECOGNIZE ME!
HEY, DUCK! WHY DON'T YOU MAKE ROOM FOR THOSE OF US WHO KNOW HOW TO DRIVE!
RK 2

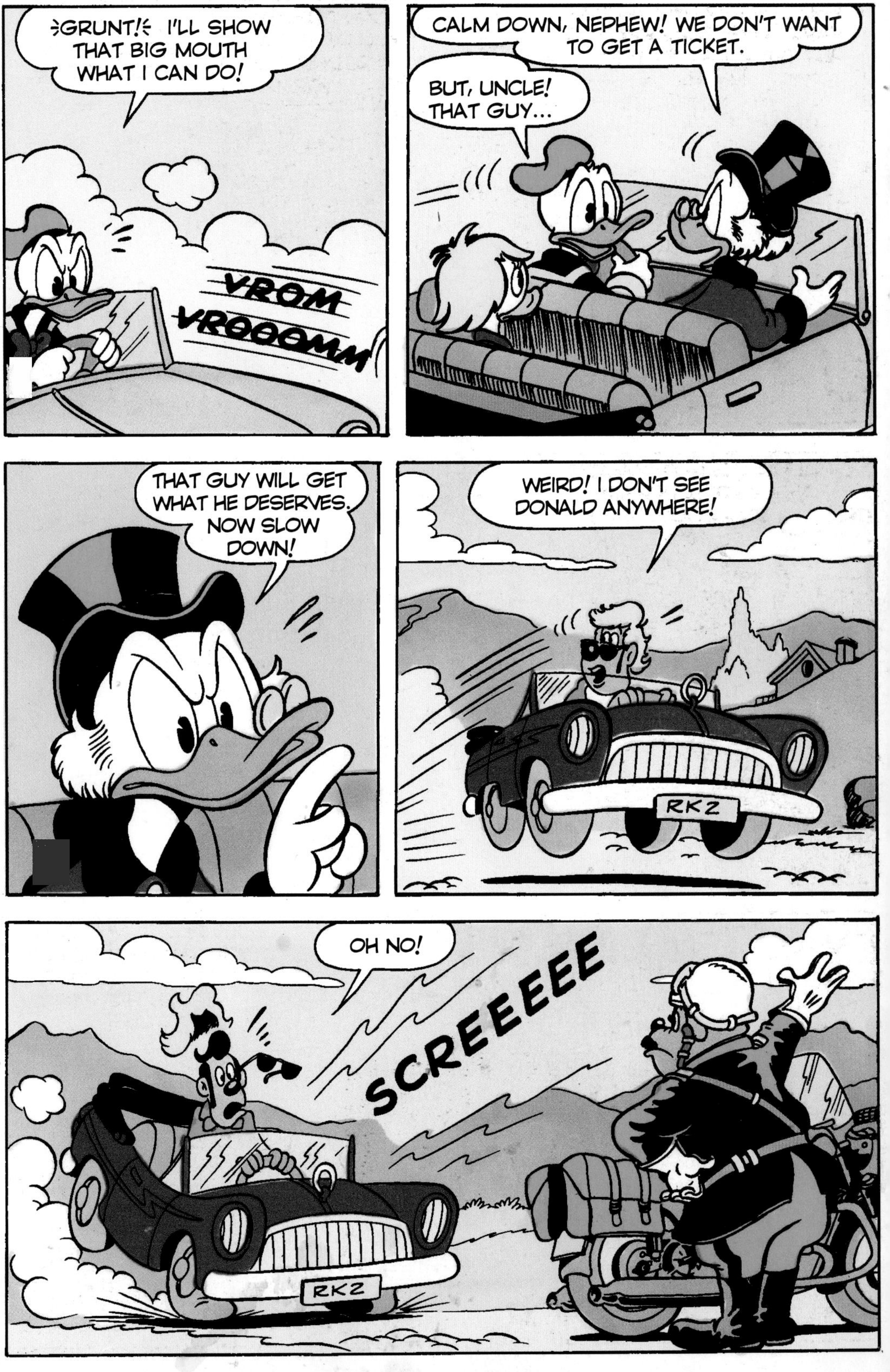

GRUNT! I'LL SHOW THAT BIG MOUTH WHAT I CAN DO!
VROM
VROOOMM
CALM DOWN, NEPHEW! WE DON'T WANT TO GET A TICKET.
BUT, UNCLE! THAT GUY...
THAT GUY WILL GET WHAT HE DESERVES. NOW SLOW DOWN!
WEIRD! I DON'T SEE DONALD ANYWHERE!
RK2
OH NO!
SCREEEEEE
RK2

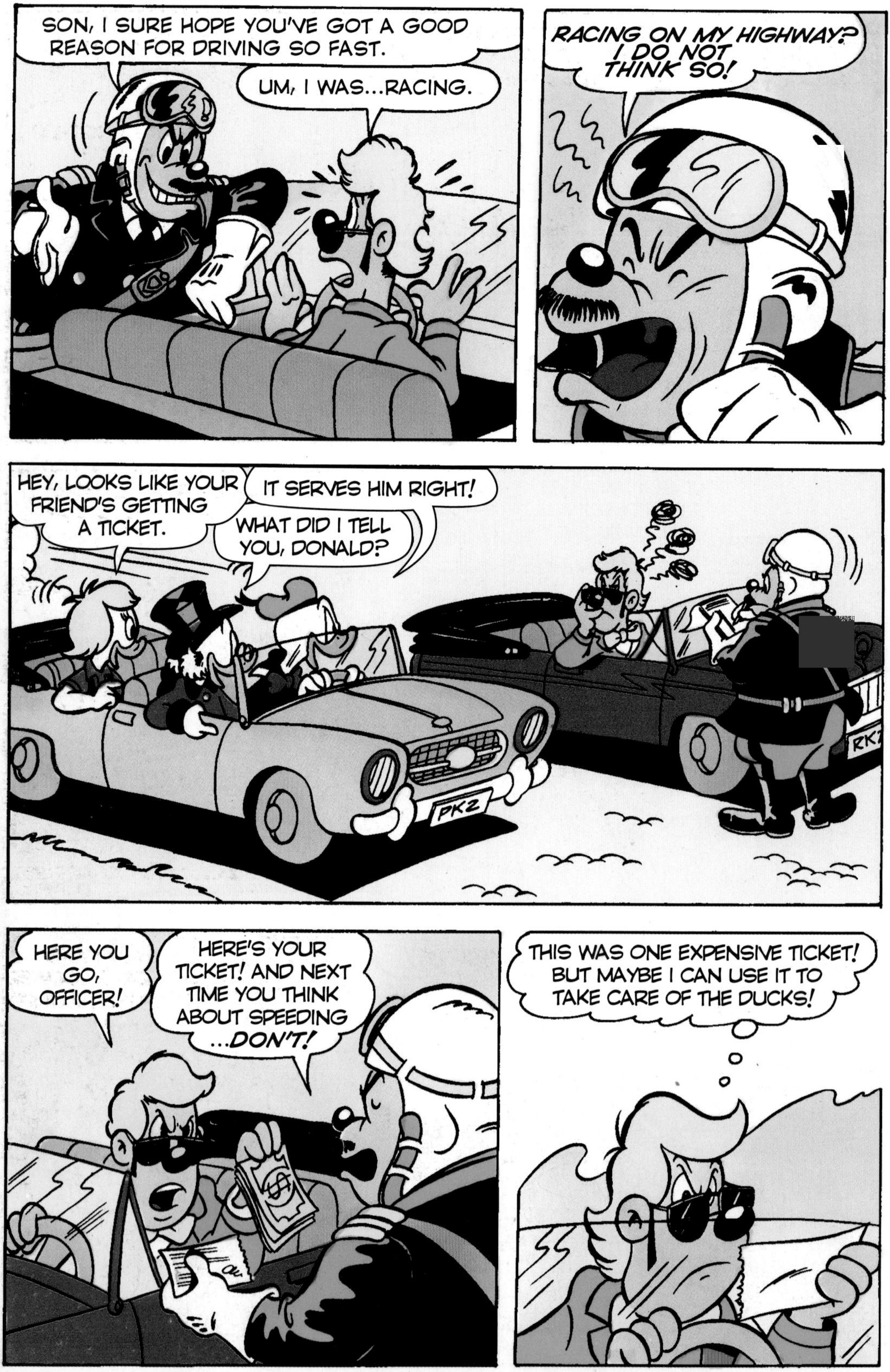
SON, I SURE HOPE YOU'VE GOT A GOOD REASON FOR DRIVING SO FAST.
UM, I WAS...RACING.
RACING ON MY HIGHWAY? I DO NOT THINK SO!
HEY, LOOKS LIKE YOUR FRIEND'S GETTING A TICKET.
IT SERVES HIM RIGHT!
WHAT DID I TELL YOU, DONALD?
PK2
RK
HERE YOU GO, OFFICER!
HERE'S YOUR TICKET! AND NEXT TIME YOU THINK ABOUT SPEEDING ...DON'T!
THIS WAS ONE EXPENSIVE TICKET! BUT MAYBE I CAN USE IT TO TAKE CARE OF THE DUCKS!

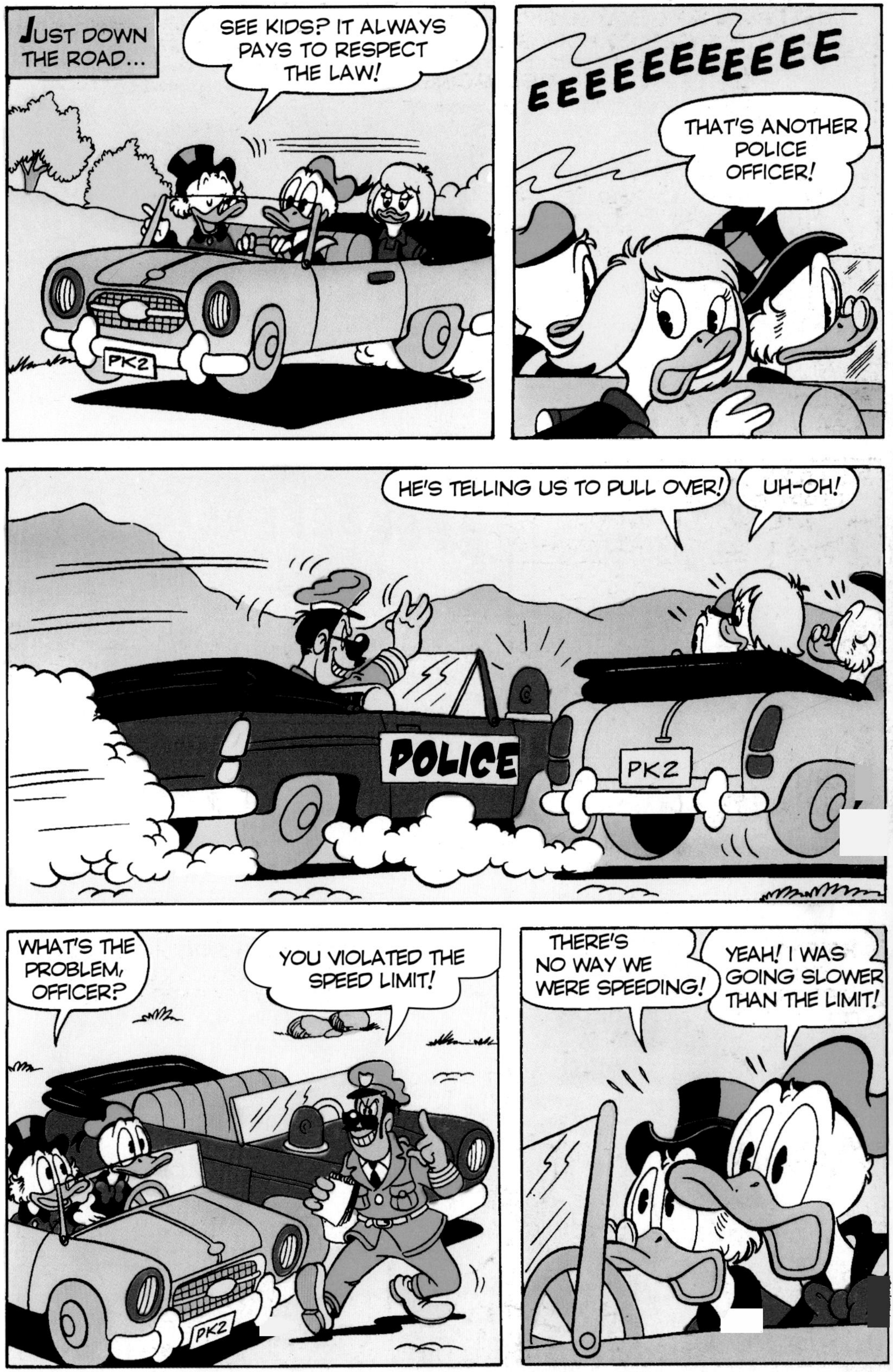
JUST DOWN THE ROAD...
SEE KIDS? IT ALWAYS PAYS TO RESPECT THE LAW!
PK2
EEEEEEEEEEEE
THAT'S ANOTHER POLICE OFFICER!
HE'S TELLING US TO PULL OVER!
UH-OH!
POLICE
PK2
WHAT'S THE PROBLEM, OFFICER?
YOU VIOLATED THE SPEED LIMIT!
PK2
THERE'S NO WAY WE WERE SPEEDING!
YEAH! I WAS GOING SLOWER THAN THE LIMIT!

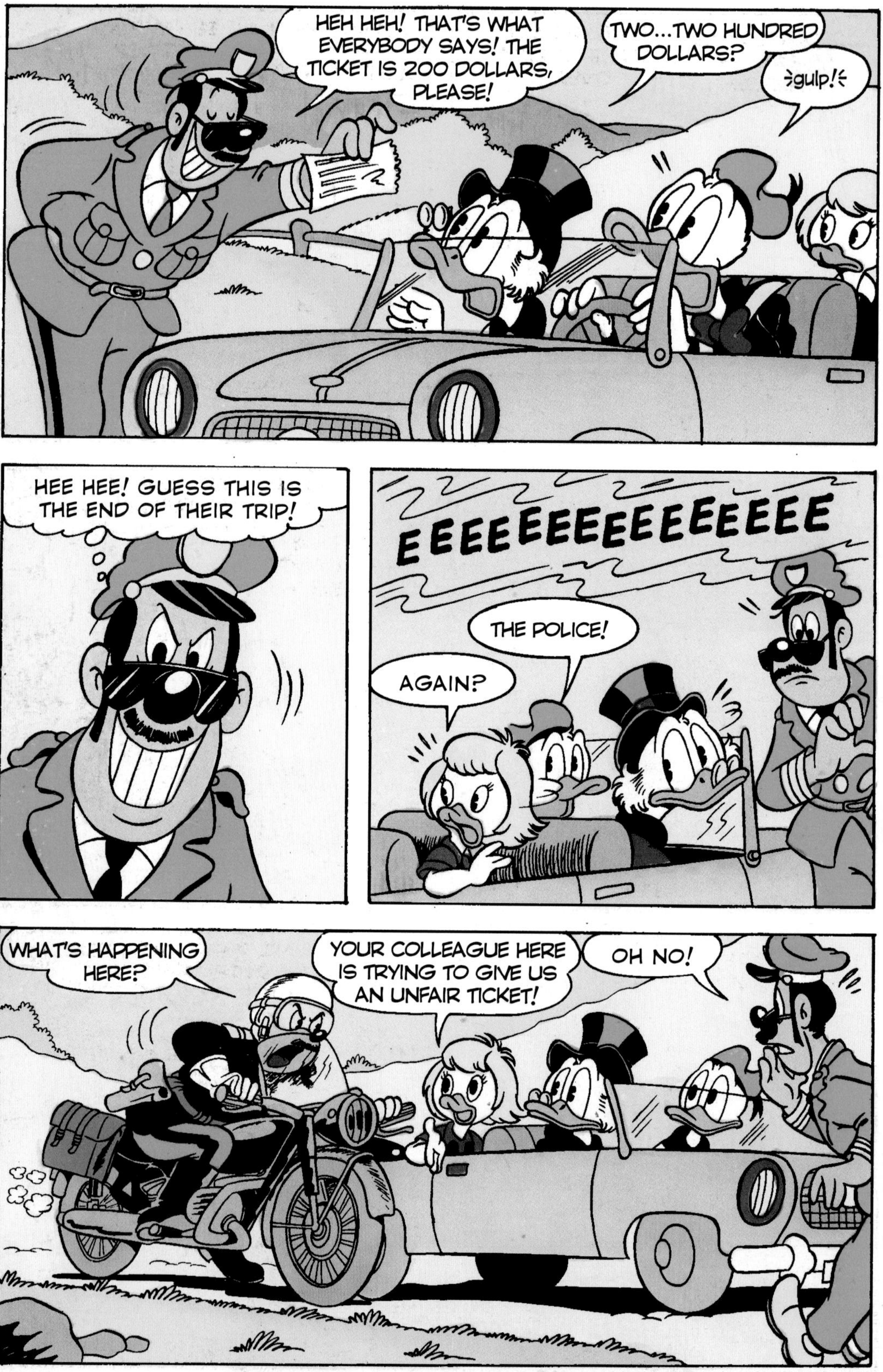
HEH HEH! THAT'S WHAT EVERYBODY SAYS! THE TICKET IS 200 DOLLARS, PLEASE!
TWO...TWO HUNDRED DOLLARS?
gulp!
HEE HEE! GUESS THIS IS THE END OF THEIR TRIP!
EEEEEEEEEEEEEEE
THE POLICE!
AGAIN?
WHAT'S HAPPENING HERE?
YOUR COLLEAGUE HERE IS TRYING TO GIVE US AN UNFAIR TICKET!
OH NO!

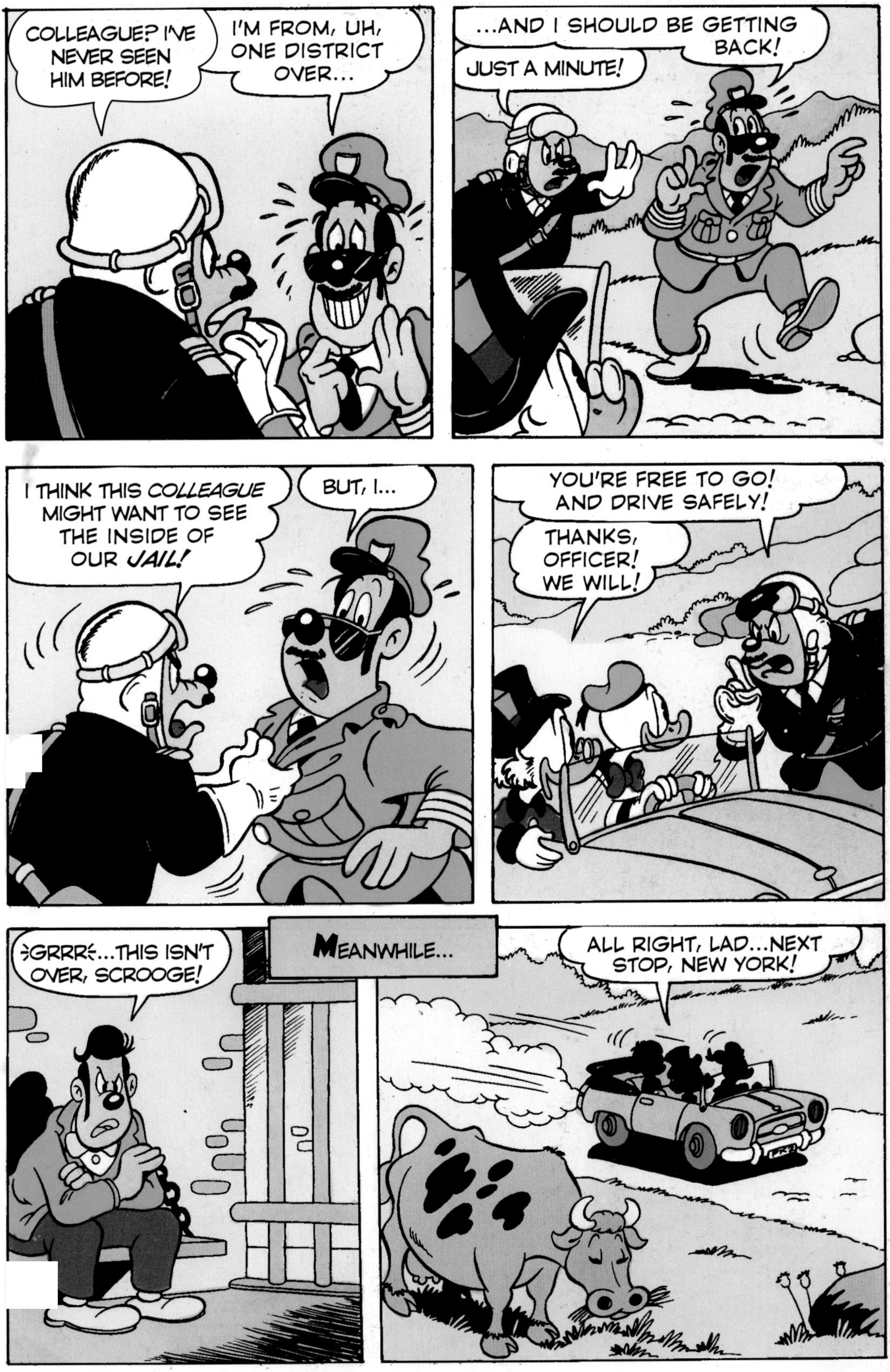
COLLEAGUE? I'VE NEVER SEEN HIM BEFORE!
I'M FROM, UH, ONE DISTRICT OVER...
...AND I SHOULD BE GETTING BACK!
JUST A MINUTE!
I THINK THIS COLLEAGUE MIGHT WANT TO SEE THE INSIDE OF OUR JAIL!
BUT, I...
YOU'RE FREE TO GO! AND DRIVE SAFELY!
THANKS, OFFICER! WE WILL!
GRRR...THIS ISN'T OVER, SCROOGE!
MEANWHILE...
ALL RIGHT, LAD...NEXT STOP, NEW YORK!

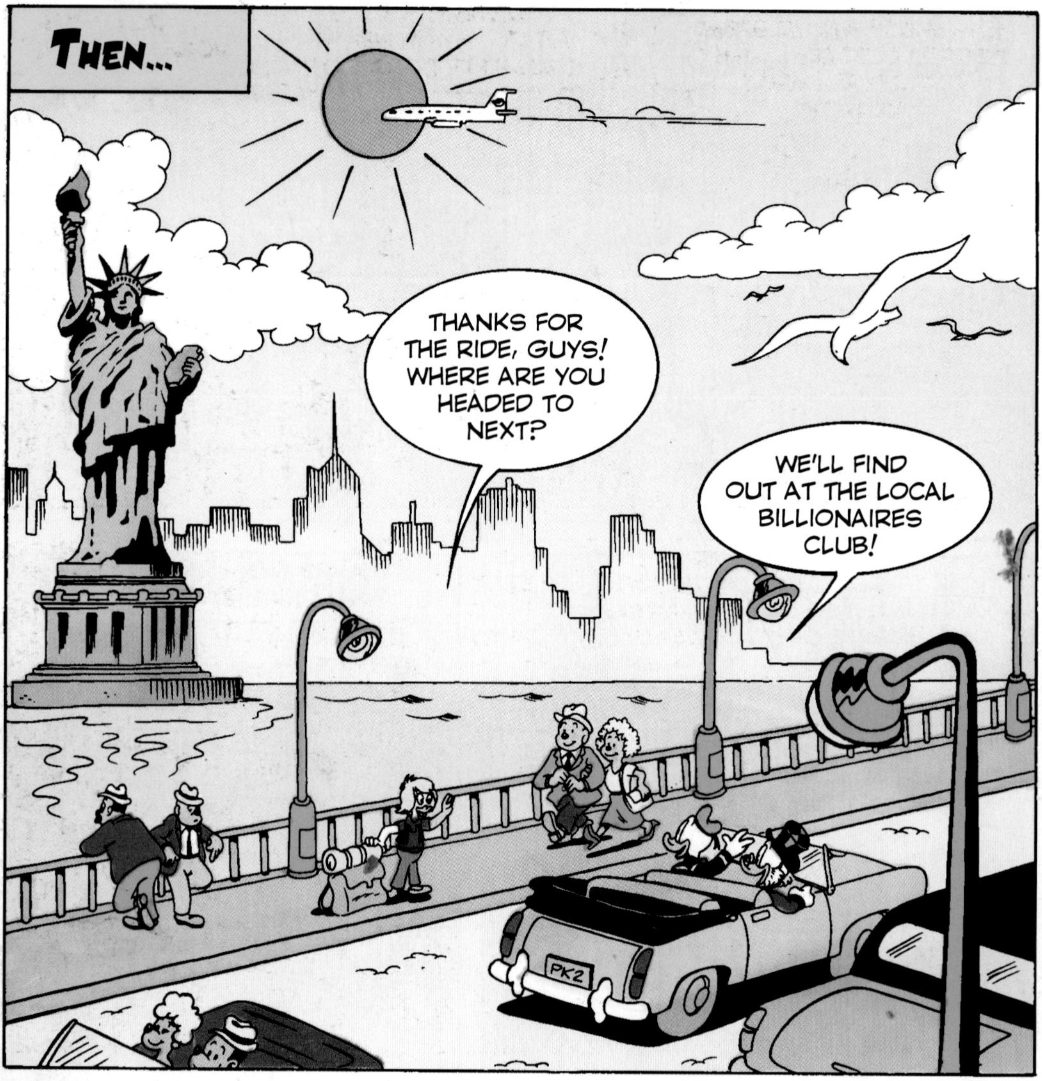
THEN...
THANKS FOR THE RIDE, GUYS! WHERE ARE YOU HEADED TO NEXT?
WE'LL FIND OUT AT THE LOCAL BILLIONAIRES CLUB!
PK2

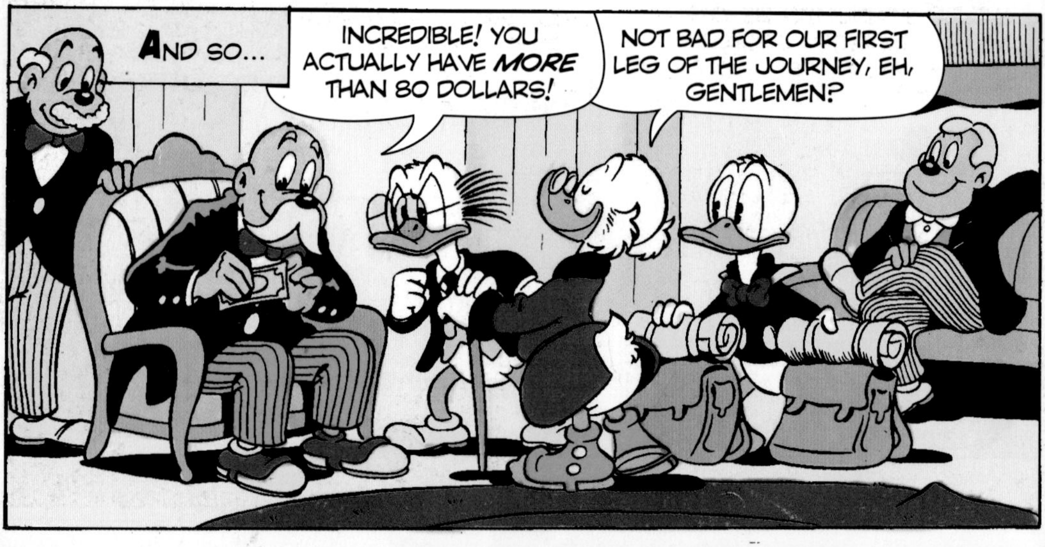
AND SO...
INCREDIBLE! YOU ACTUALLY HAVE *MORE* THAN 80 DOLLARS!
NOT BAD FOR OUR FIRST LEG OF THE JOURNEY, EH, GENTLEMEN?

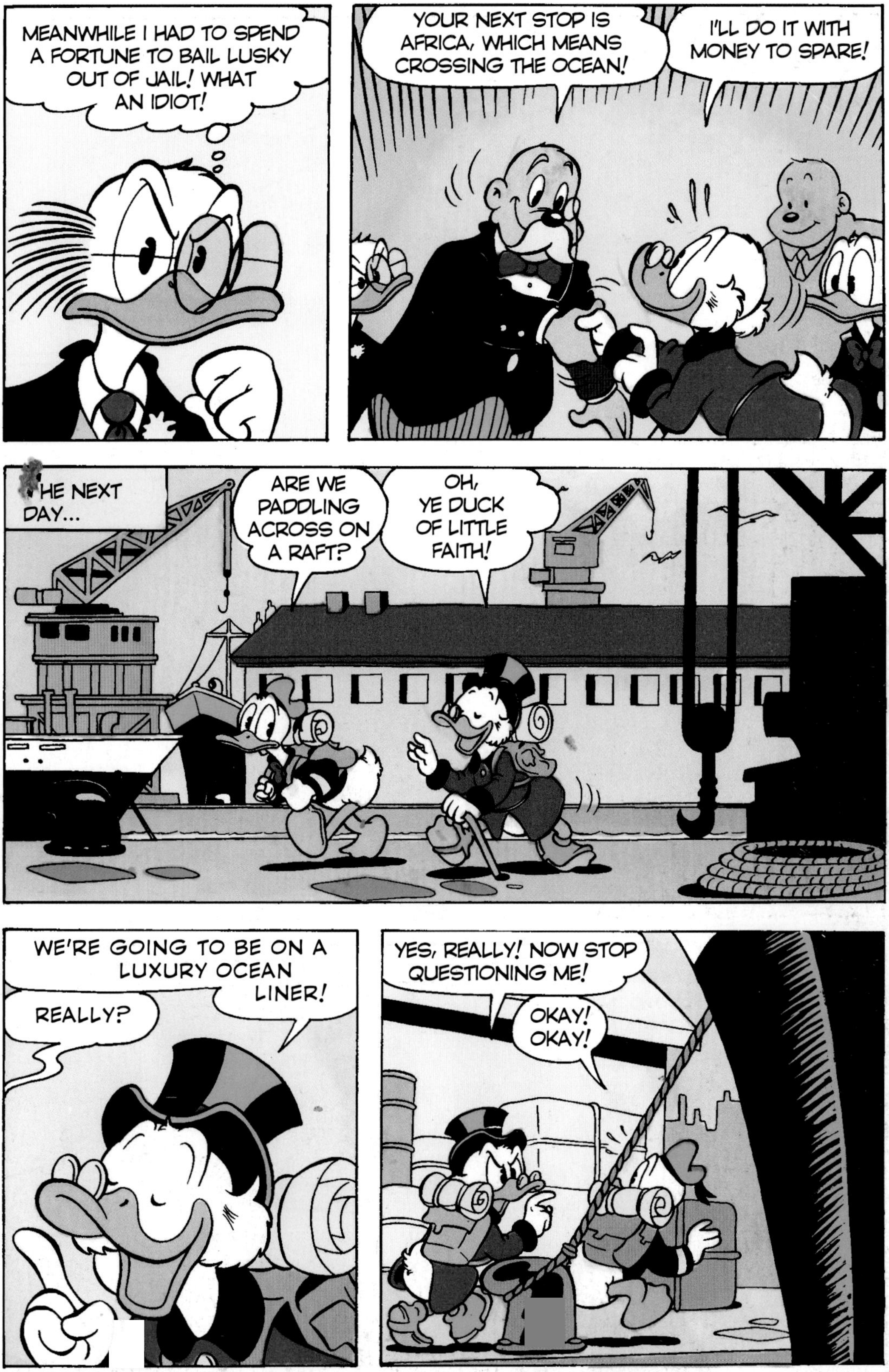
MEANWHILE I HAD TO SPEND A FORTUNE TO BAIL LUSKY OUT OF JAIL! WHAT AN IDIOT!
YOUR NEXT STOP IS AFRICA, WHICH MEANS CROSSING THE OCEAN!
I'LL DO IT WITH MONEY TO SPARE!
HE NEXT DAY...
ARE WE PADDLING ACROSS ON A RAFT?
OH, YE DUCK OF LITTLE FAITH!
WE'RE GOING TO BE ON A LUXURY OCEAN LINER!
REALLY?
YES, REALLY! NOW STOP QUESTIONING ME!
OKAY! OKAY!

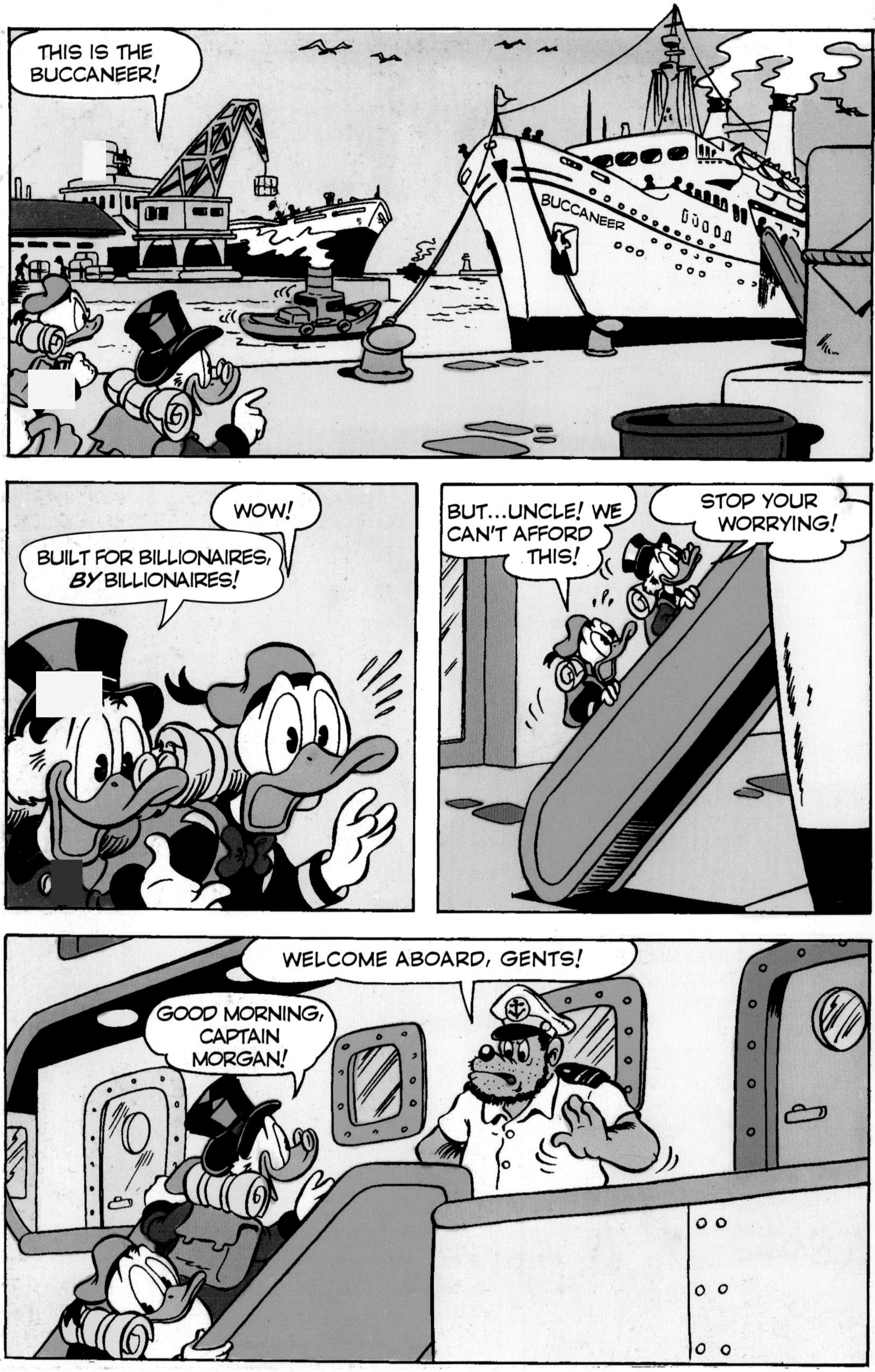
THIS IS THE BUCCANEER!
BUCCANEER
WOW!
BUILT FOR BILLIONAIRES, BY BILLIONAIRES!
BUT...UNCLE! WE CAN'T AFFORD THIS!
STOP YOUR WORRYING!
WELCOME ABOARD, GENTS!
GOOD MORNING, CAPTAIN MORGAN!

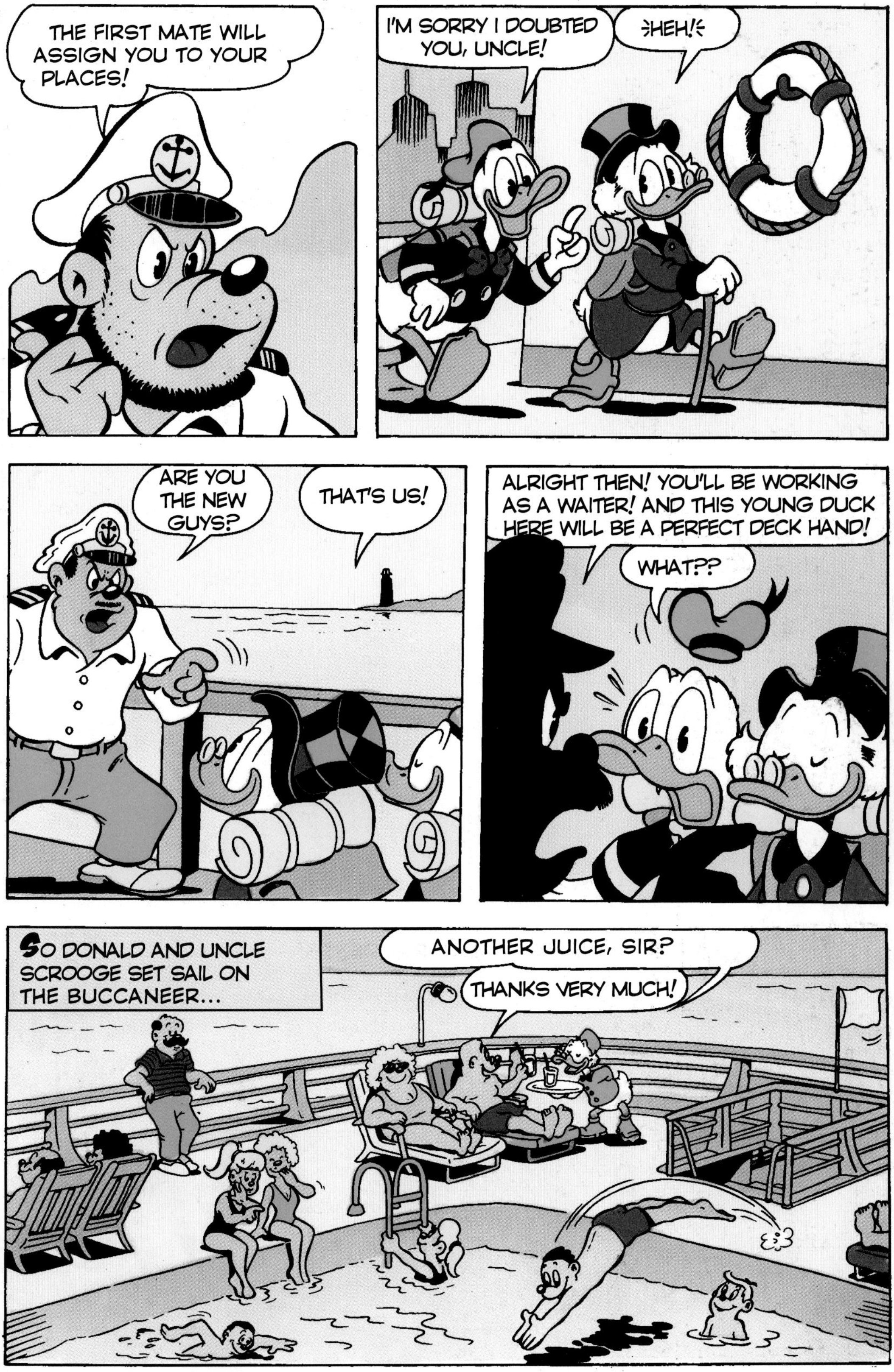
THE FIRST MATE WILL ASSIGN YOU TO YOUR PLACES!
I'M SORRY I DOUBTED YOU, UNCLE!
HEH!
ARE YOU THE NEW GUYS?
THAT'S US!
ALRIGHT THEN! YOU'LL BE WORKING AS A WAITER! AND THIS YOUNG DUCK HERE WILL BE A PERFECT DECK HAND!
WHAT??
SO DONALD AND UNCLE SCROOGE SET SAIL ON THE BUCCANEER...
ANOTHER JUICE, SIR?
THANKS VERY MUCH!

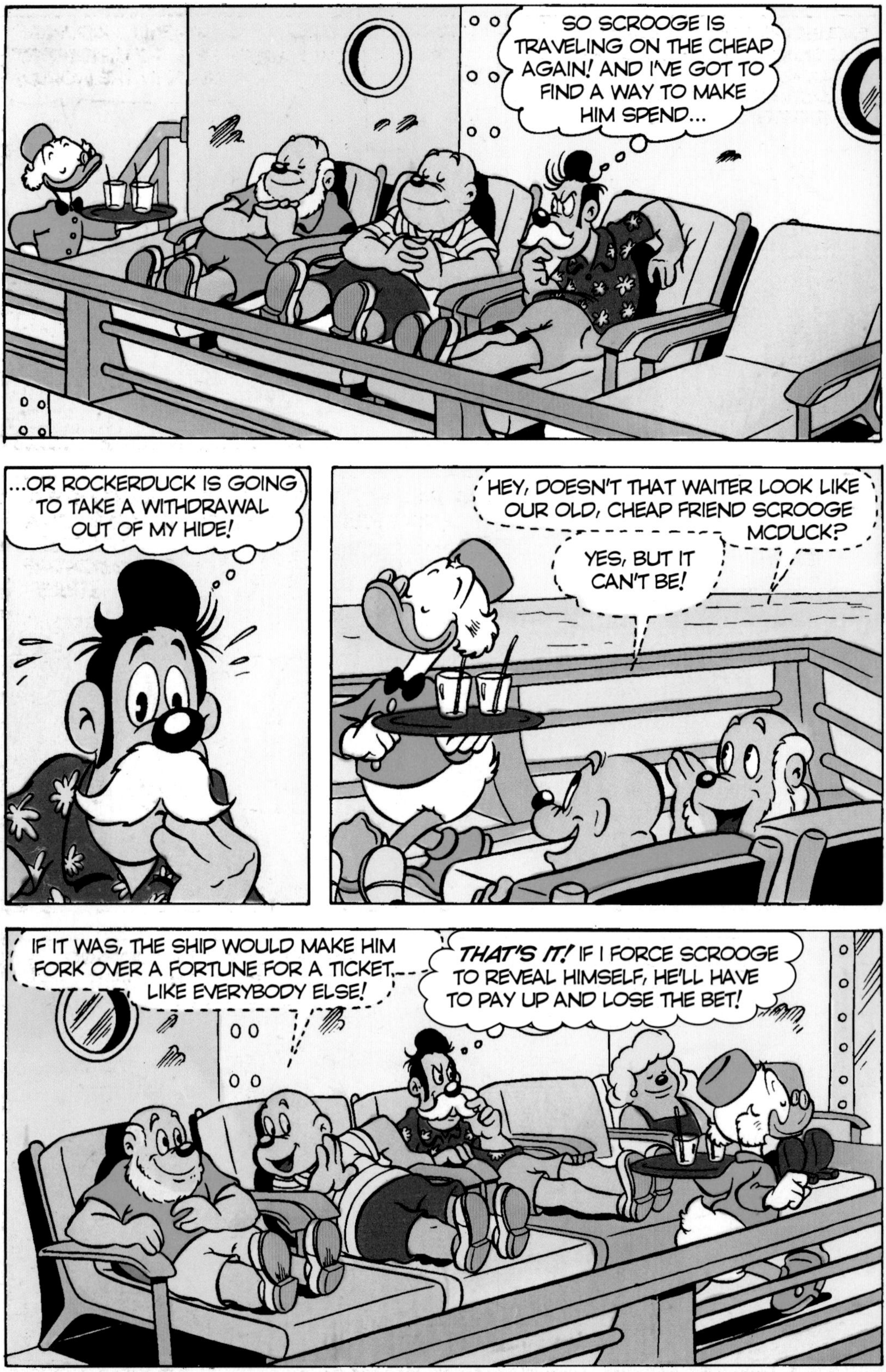
SO SCROOGE IS TRAVELING ON THE CHEAP AGAIN! AND I'VE GOT TO FIND A WAY TO MAKE HIM SPEND...
...OR ROCKERDUCK IS GOING TO TAKE A WITHDRAWAL OUT OF MY HIDE!
HEY, DOESN'T THAT WAITER LOOK LIKE OUR OLD, CHEAP FRIEND SCROOGE MCDUCK?
YES, BUT IT CAN'T BE!
IF IT WAS, THE SHIP WOULD MAKE HIM FORK OVER A FORTUNE FOR A TICKET, LIKE EVERYBODY ELSE!
THAT'S IT! IF I FORCE SCROOGE TO REVEAL HIMSELF, HE'LL HAVE TO PAY UP AND LOSE THE BET!

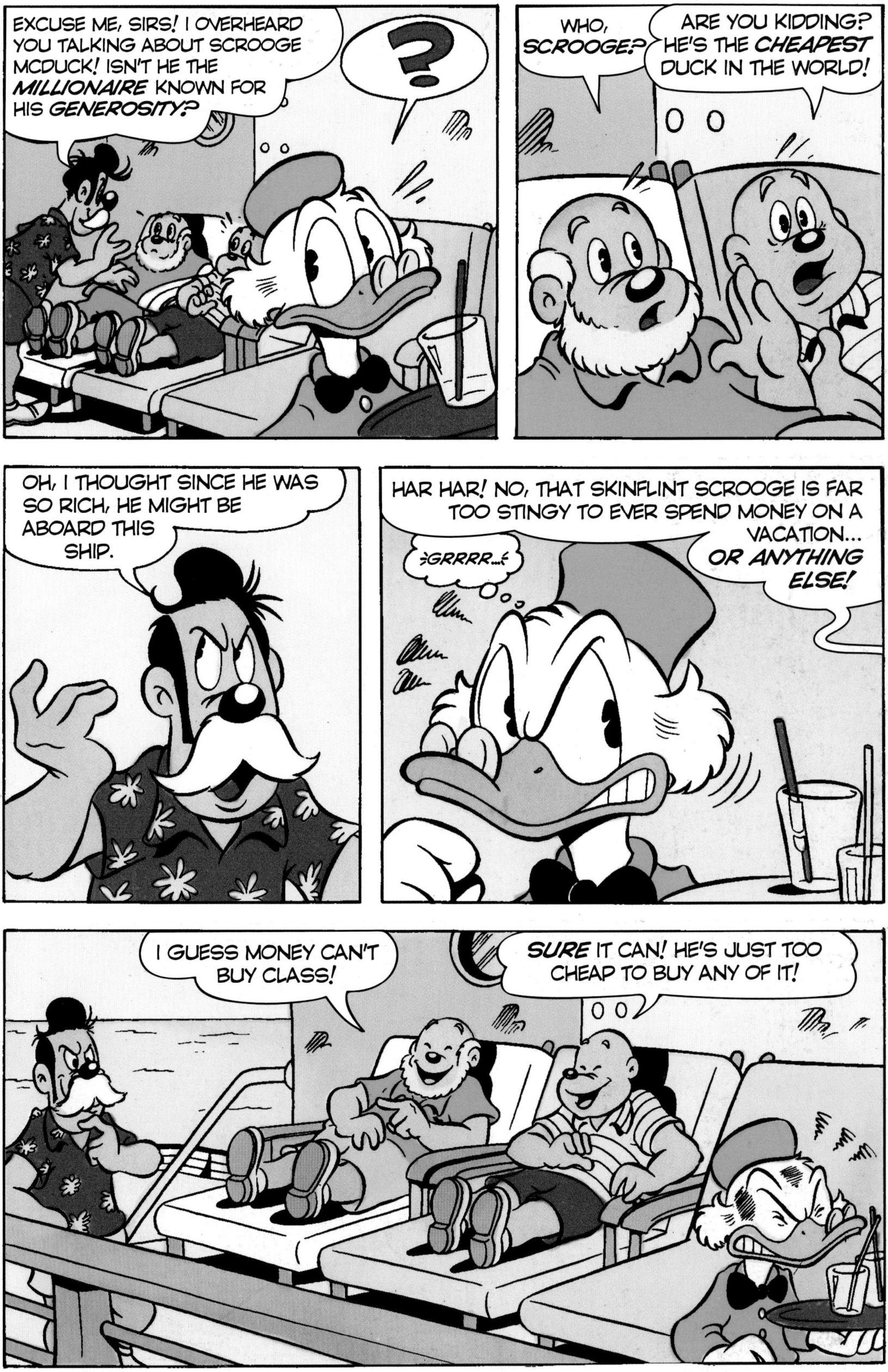
EXCUSE ME, SIRS! I OVERHEARD YOU TALKING ABOUT SCROOGE MCDUCK! ISN'T HE THE MILLIONAIRE KNOWN FOR HIS GENEROSITY?
?
WHO, SCROOGE?
ARE YOU KIDDING? HE'S THE CHEAPEST DUCK IN THE WORLD!
OH, I THOUGHT SINCE HE WAS SO RICH, HE MIGHT BE ABOARD THIS SHIP.
HAR HAR! NO, THAT SKINFLINT SCROOGE IS FAR TOO STINGY TO EVER SPEND MONEY ON A VACATION... OR ANYTHING ELSE!
GRRRR...
I GUESS MONEY CAN'T BUY CLASS!
SURE IT CAN! HE'S JUST TOO CHEAP TO BUY ANY OF IT!

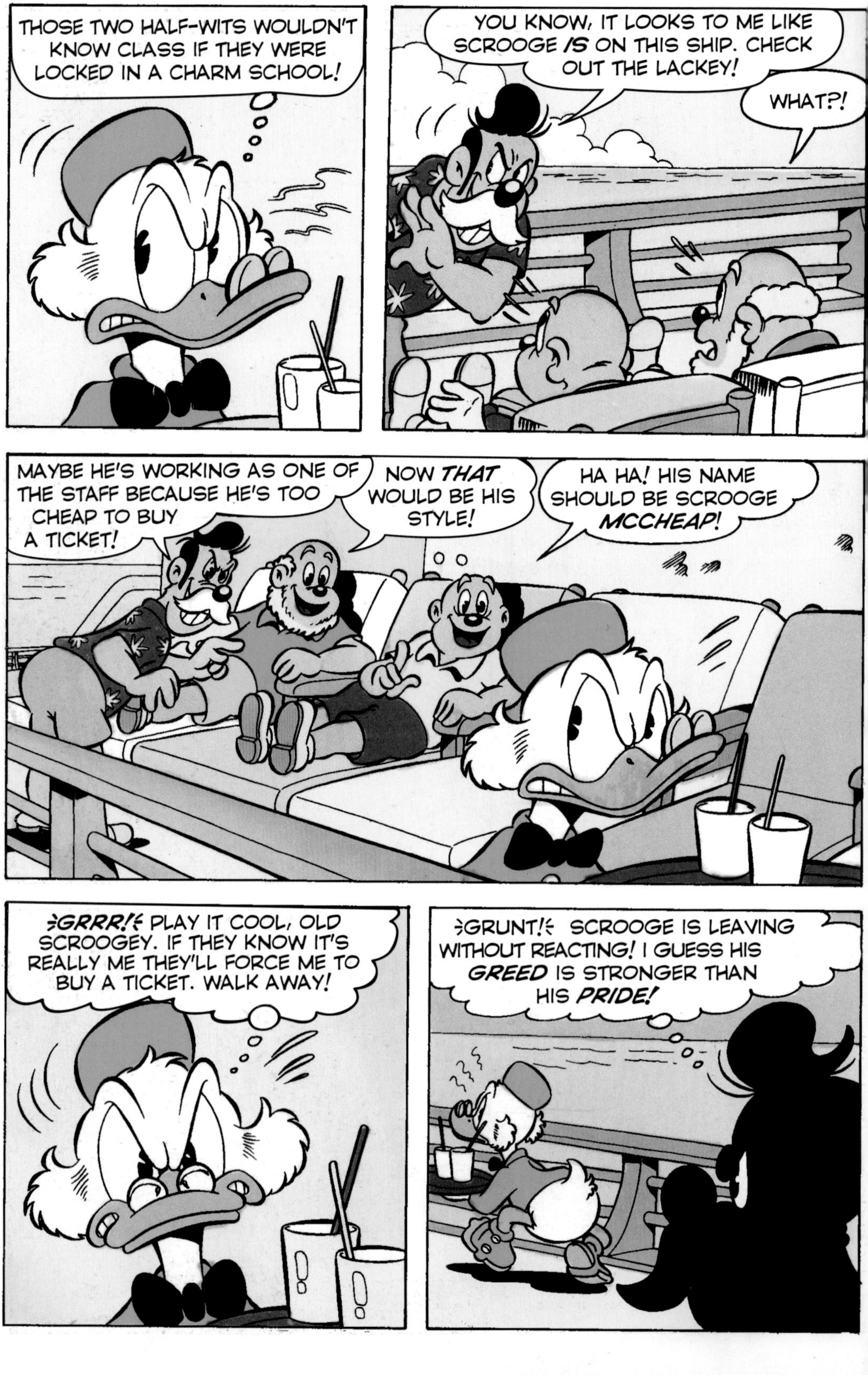
THOSE TWO HALF-WITS WOULDN'T KNOW CLASS IF THEY WERE LOCKED IN A CHARM SCHOOL!
YOU KNOW, IT LOOKS TO ME LIKE SCROOGE *IS* ON THIS SHIP. CHECK OUT THE LACKEY!
WHAT?!
MAYBE HE'S WORKING AS ONE OF THE STAFF BECAUSE HE'S TOO CHEAP TO BUY A TICKET!
NOW *THAT* WOULD BE HIS STYLE!
HA HA! HIS NAME SHOULD BE SCROOGE *MCCHEAP!*
*GRRR!* PLAY IT COOL, OLD SCROOGEY. IF THEY KNOW IT'S REALLY ME THEY'LL FORCE ME TO BUY A TICKET. WALK AWAY!
GRUNT! SCROOGE IS LEAVING WITHOUT REACTING! I GUESS HIS *GREED* IS STRONGER THAN HIS *PRIDE!*

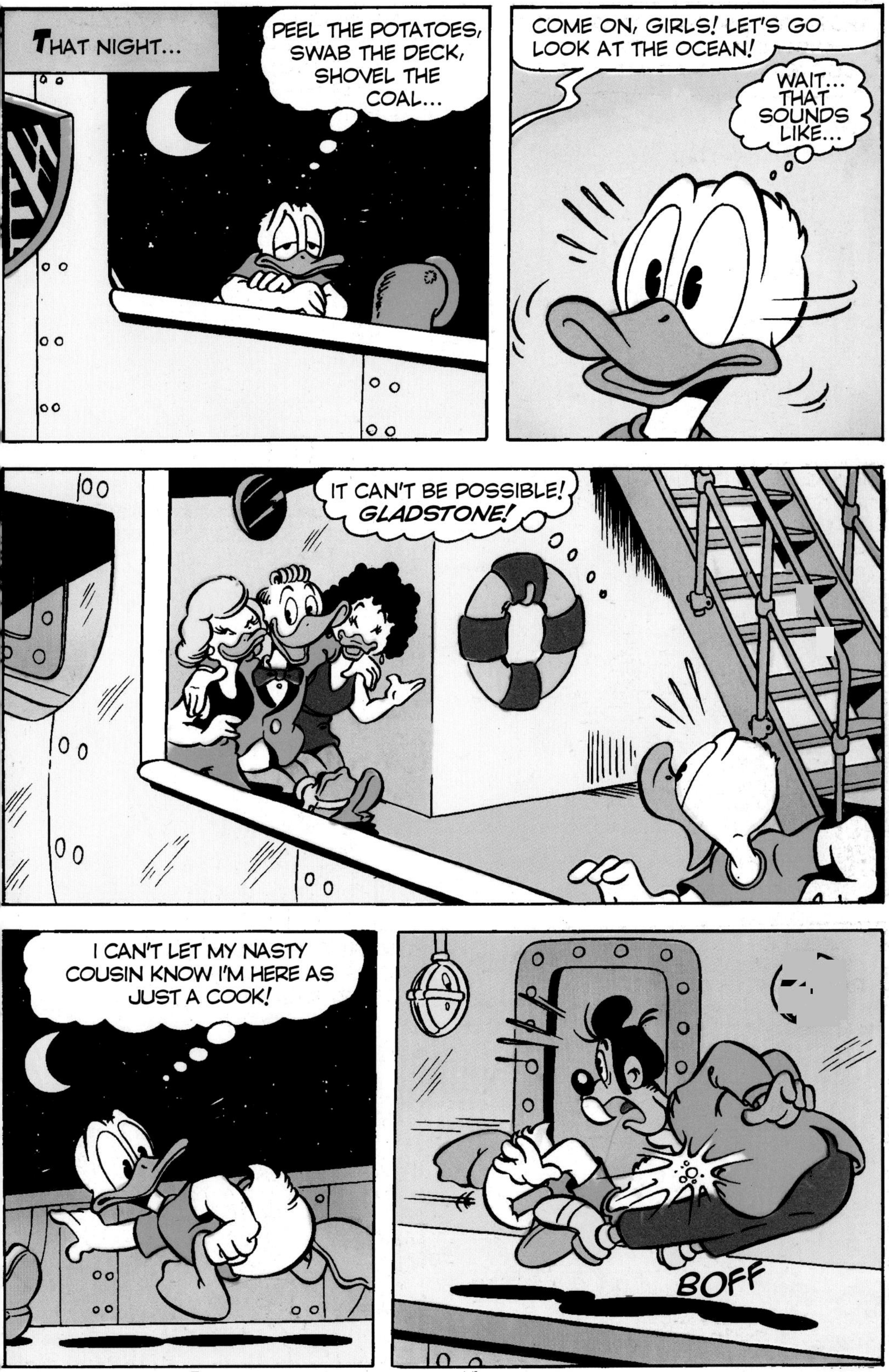

THAT NIGHT...
PEEL THE POTATOES, SWAB THE DECK, SHOVEL THE COAL...
COME ON, GIRLS! LET'S GO LOOK AT THE OCEAN!
WAIT... THAT SOUNDS LIKE...
IT CAN'T BE POSSIBLE! GLADSTONE!
I CAN'T LET MY NASTY COUSIN KNOW I'M HERE AS JUST A COOK!
BOFF

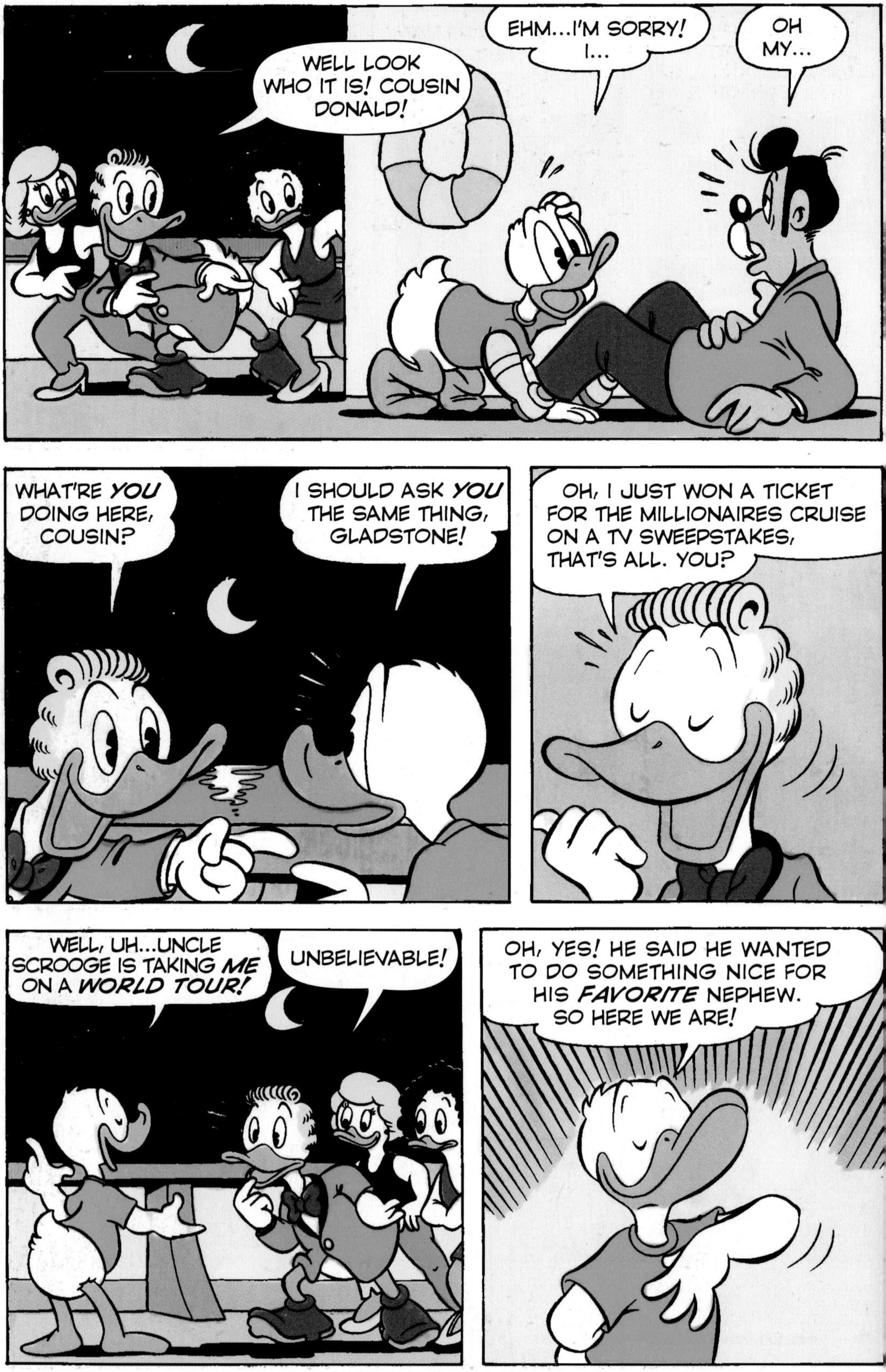
WELL LOOK WHO IT IS! COUSIN DONALD!
EHM...I'M SORRY! I...
OH MY...
WHAT'RE YOU DOING HERE, COUSIN?
I SHOULD ASK YOU THE SAME THING, GLADSTONE!
OH, I JUST WON A TICKET FOR THE MILLIONAIRES CRUISE ON A TV SWEEPSTAKES, THAT'S ALL. YOU?
WELL, UH...UNCLE SCROOGE IS TAKING ME ON A WORLD TOUR!
UNBELIEVABLE!
OH, YES! HE SAID HE WANTED TO DO SOMETHING NICE FOR HIS FAVORITE NEPHEW. SO HERE WE ARE!

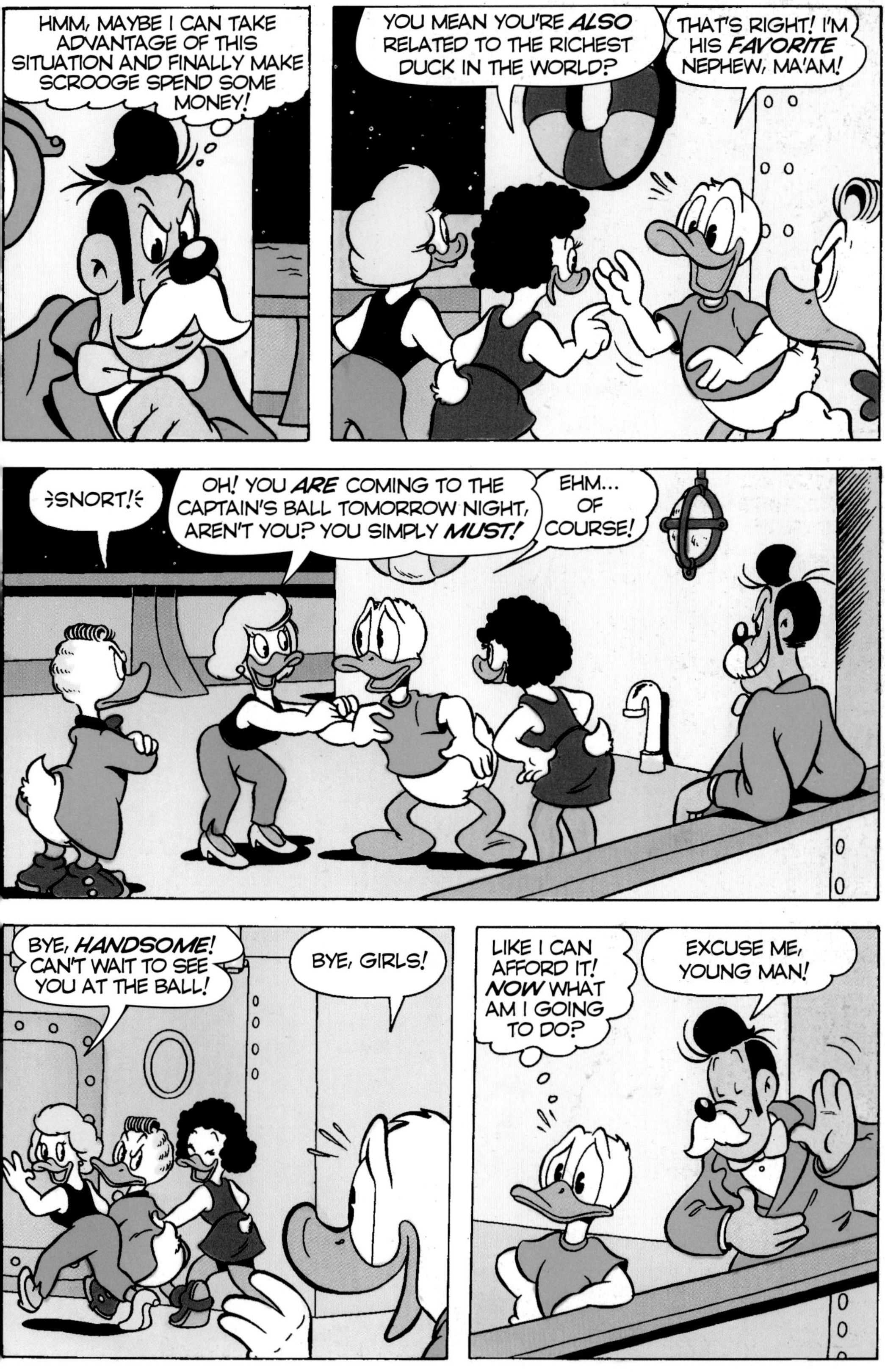
HMM, MAYBE I CAN TAKE ADVANTAGE OF THIS SITUATION AND FINALLY MAKE SCROOGE SPEND SOME MONEY!
YOU MEAN YOU'RE *ALSO* RELATED TO THE RICHEST DUCK IN THE WORLD?
THAT'S RIGHT! I'M HIS *FAVORITE* NEPHEW, MA'AM!
SNORT!
OH! YOU *ARE* COMING TO THE CAPTAIN'S BALL TOMORROW NIGHT, AREN'T YOU? YOU SIMPLY *MUST!*
EHM... OF COURSE!
BYE, *HANDSOME!* CAN'T WAIT TO SEE YOU AT THE BALL!
BYE, GIRLS!
LIKE I CAN AFFORD IT! *NOW* WHAT AM I GOING TO DO?
EXCUSE ME, YOUNG MAN!

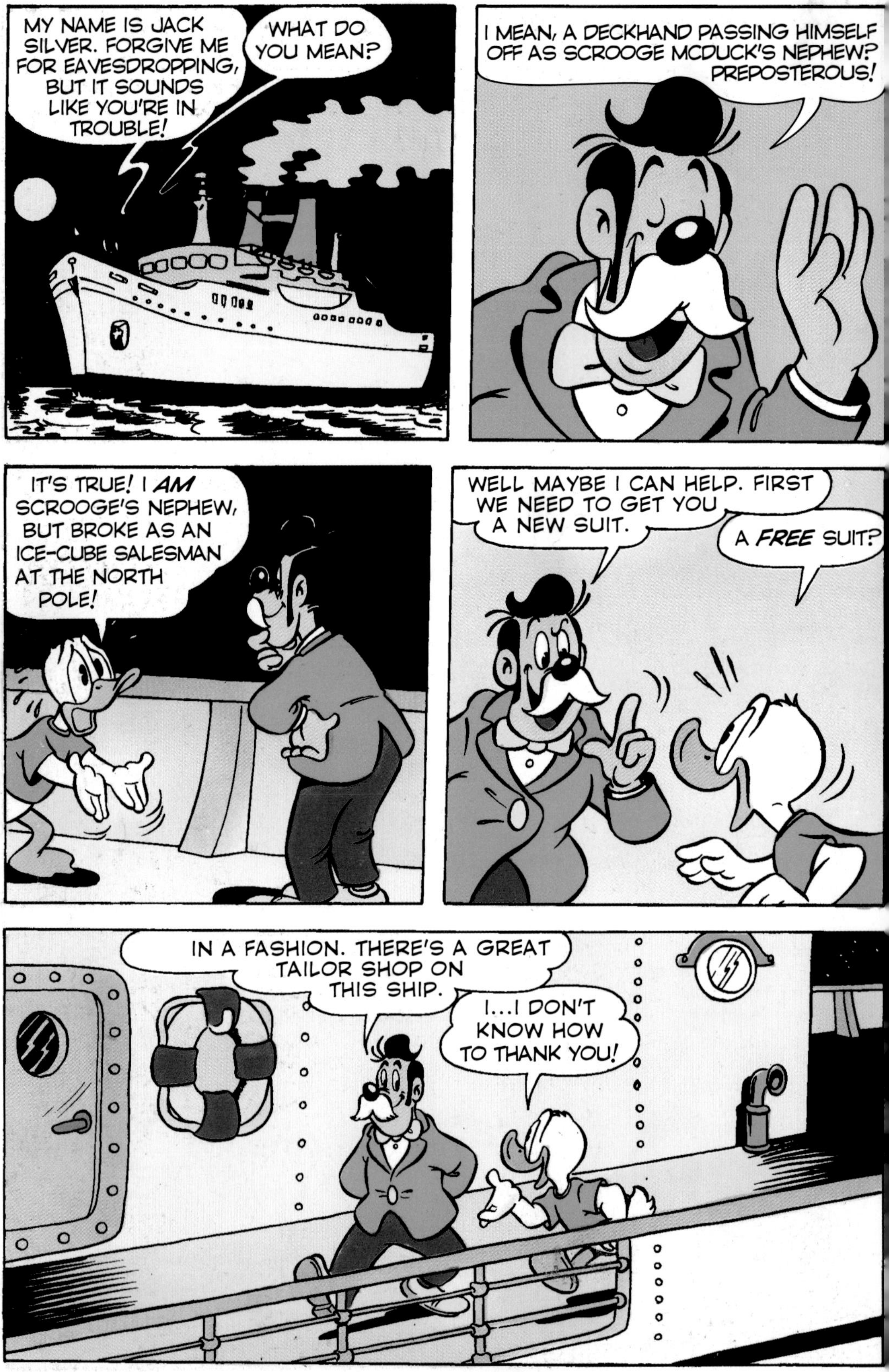
MY NAME IS JACK SILVER. FORGIVE ME FOR EAVESDROPPING, BUT IT SOUNDS LIKE YOU'RE IN TROUBLE!
WHAT DO YOU MEAN?
I MEAN, A DECKHAND PASSING HIMSELF OFF AS SCROOGE McDUCK'S NEPHEW? PREPOSTEROUS!
IT'S TRUE! I AM SCROOGE'S NEPHEW, BUT BROKE AS AN ICE-CUBE SALESMAN AT THE NORTH POLE!
WELL MAYBE I CAN HELP. FIRST WE NEED TO GET YOU A NEW SUIT.
A FREE SUIT?
IN A FASHION. THERE'S A GREAT TAILOR SHOP ON THIS SHIP.
I...I DON'T KNOW HOW TO THANK YOU!

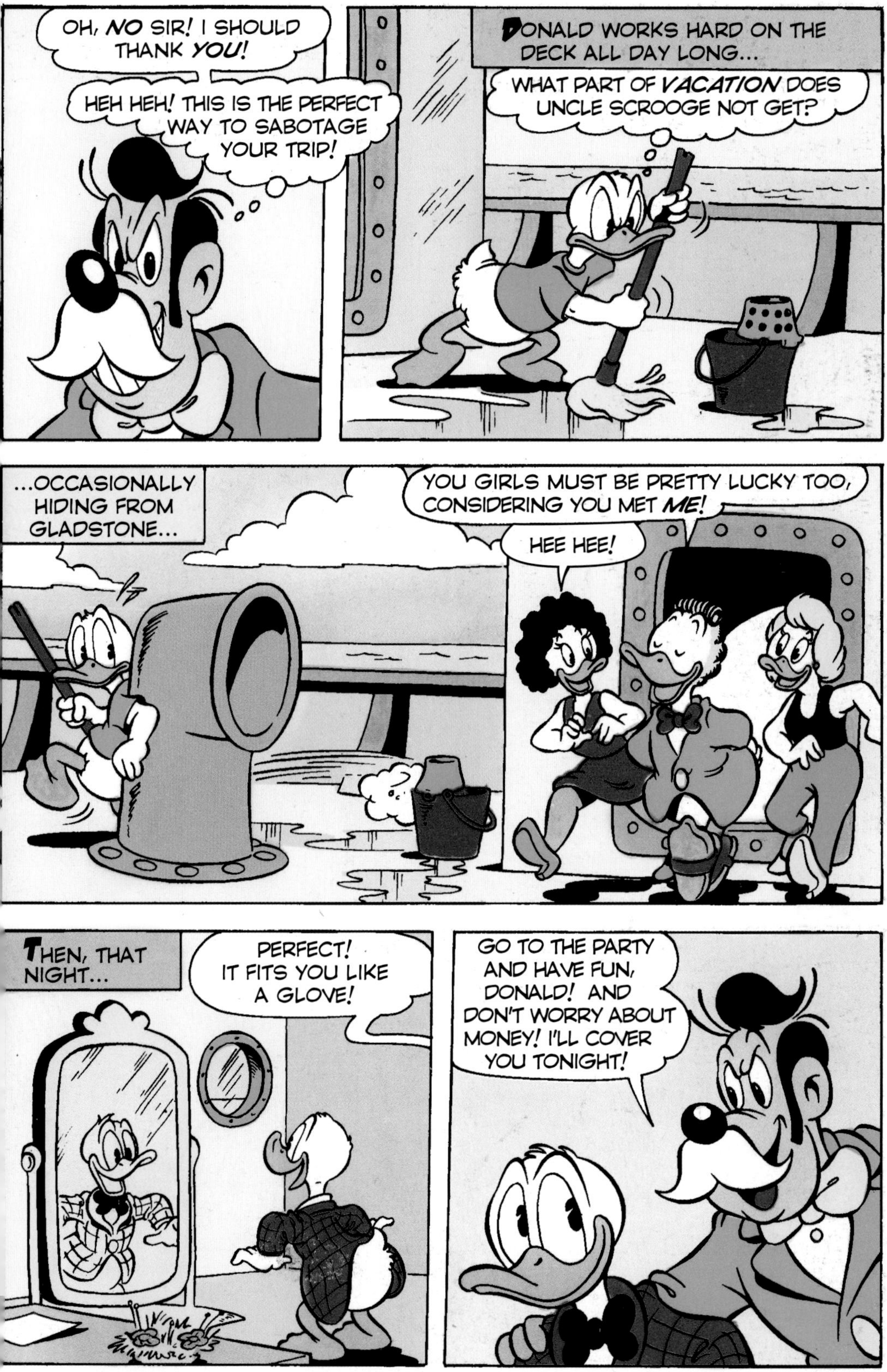
OH, NO SIR! I SHOULD THANK YOU!
HEH HEH! THIS IS THE PERFECT WAY TO SABOTAGE YOUR TRIP!
DONALD WORKS HARD ON THE DECK ALL DAY LONG...
WHAT PART OF VACATION DOES UNCLE SCROOGE NOT GET?
...OCCASIONALLY HIDING FROM GLADSTONE...
YOU GIRLS MUST BE PRETTY LUCKY TOO, CONSIDERING YOU MET ME!
HEE HEE!
THEN, THAT NIGHT...
PERFECT! IT FITS YOU LIKE A GLOVE!
GO TO THE PARTY AND HAVE FUN, DONALD! AND DON'T WORRY ABOUT MONEY! I'LL COVER YOU TONIGHT!

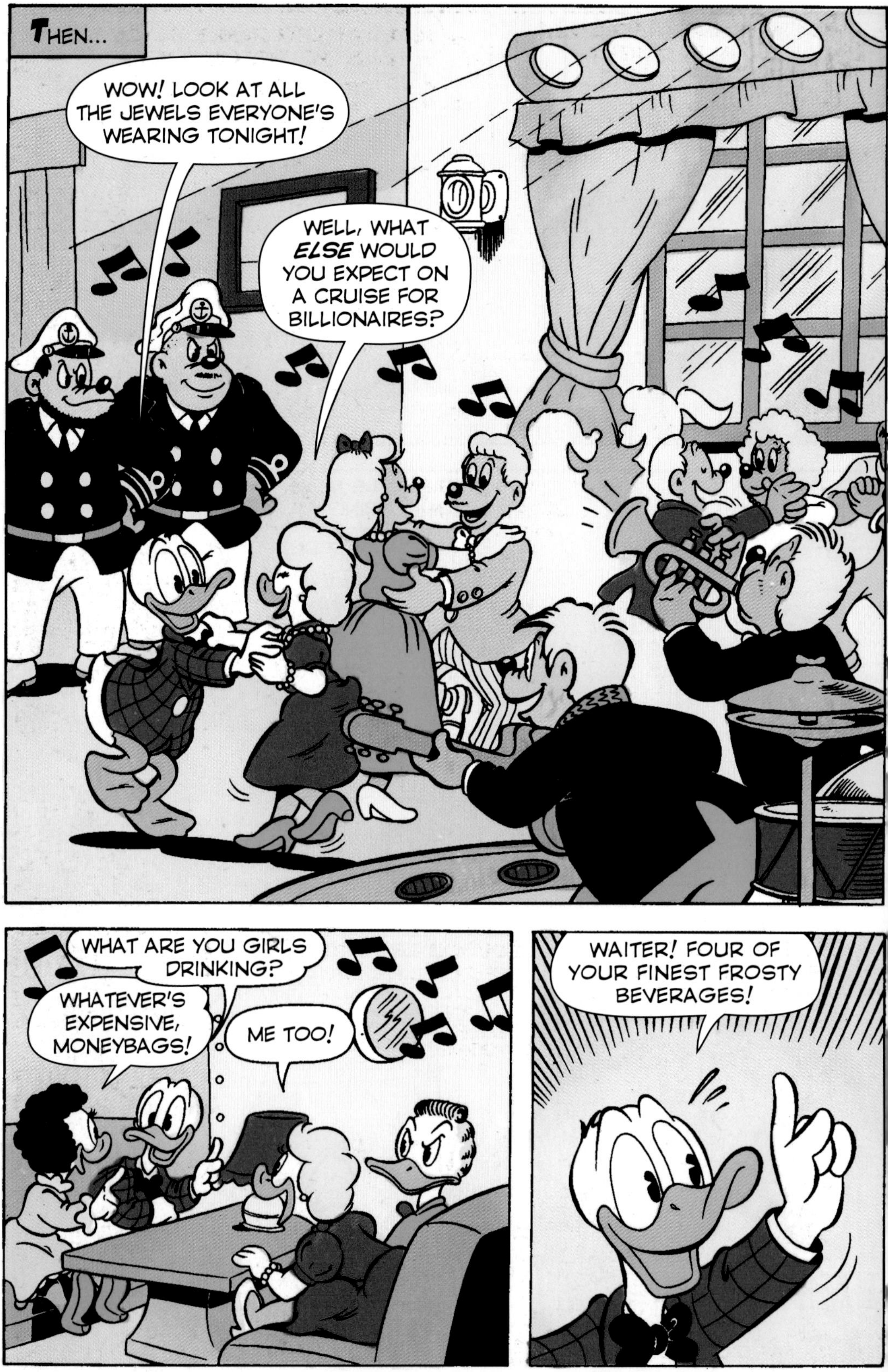
THEN...
WOW! LOOK AT ALL THE JEWELS EVERYONE'S WEARING TONIGHT!
WELL, WHAT *ELSE* WOULD YOU EXPECT ON A CRUISE FOR BILLIONAIRES?
WHAT ARE YOU GIRLS DRINKING?
WHATEVER'S EXPENSIVE, MONEYBAGS!
ME TOO!
WAITER! FOUR OF YOUR FINEST FROSTY BEVERAGES!

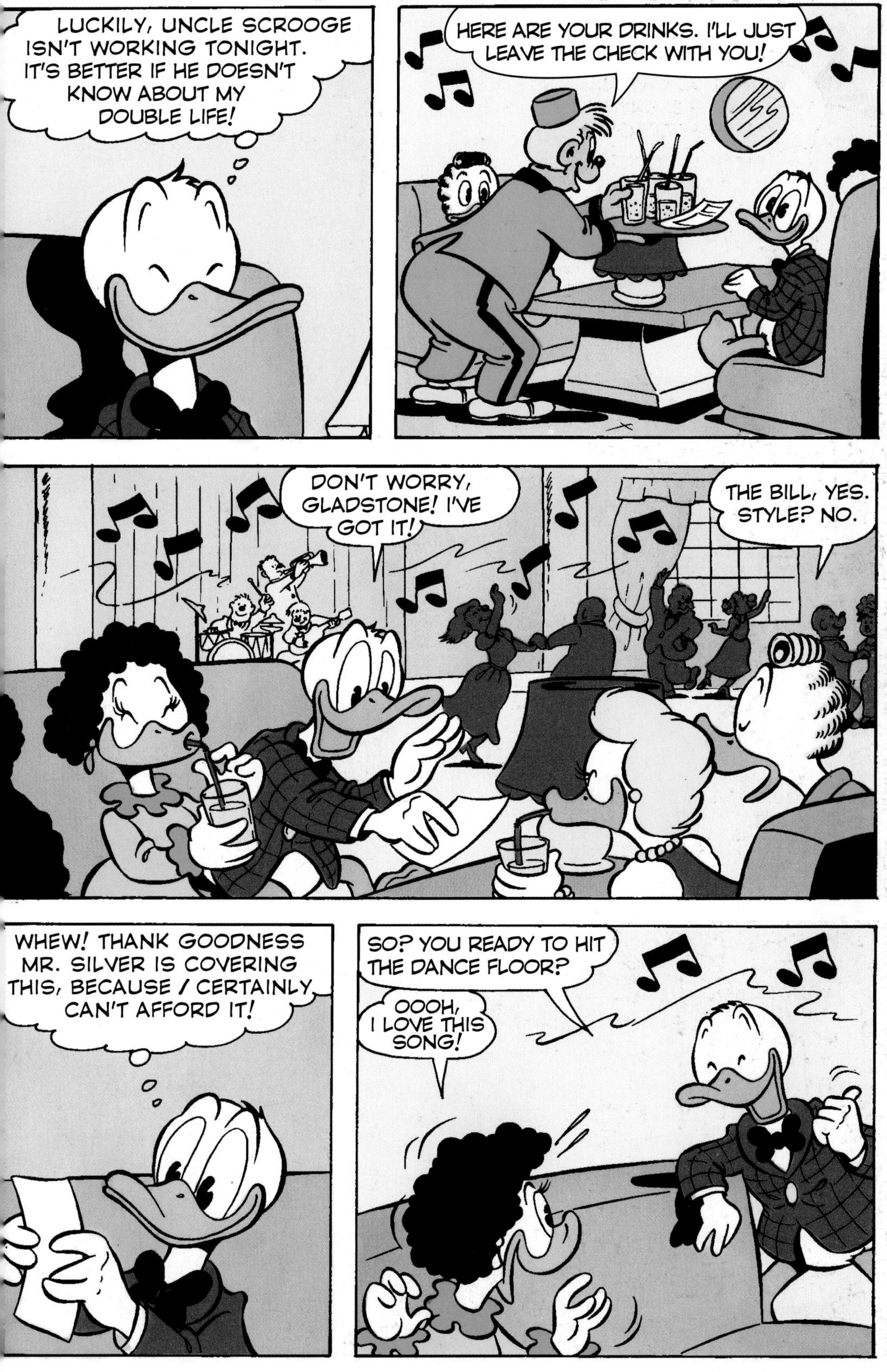
LUCKILY, UNCLE SCROOGE ISN'T WORKING TONIGHT. IT'S BETTER IF HE DOESN'T KNOW ABOUT MY DOUBLE LIFE!
HERE ARE YOUR DRINKS. I'LL JUST LEAVE THE CHECK WITH YOU!
DON'T WORRY, GLADSTONE! I'VE GOT IT!
THE BILL, YES. STYLE? NO.
WHEW! THANK GOODNESS MR. SILVER IS COVERING THIS, BECAUSE I CERTAINLY CAN'T AFFORD IT!
SO? YOU READY TO HIT THE DANCE FLOOR?
OOOH, I LOVE THIS SONG!

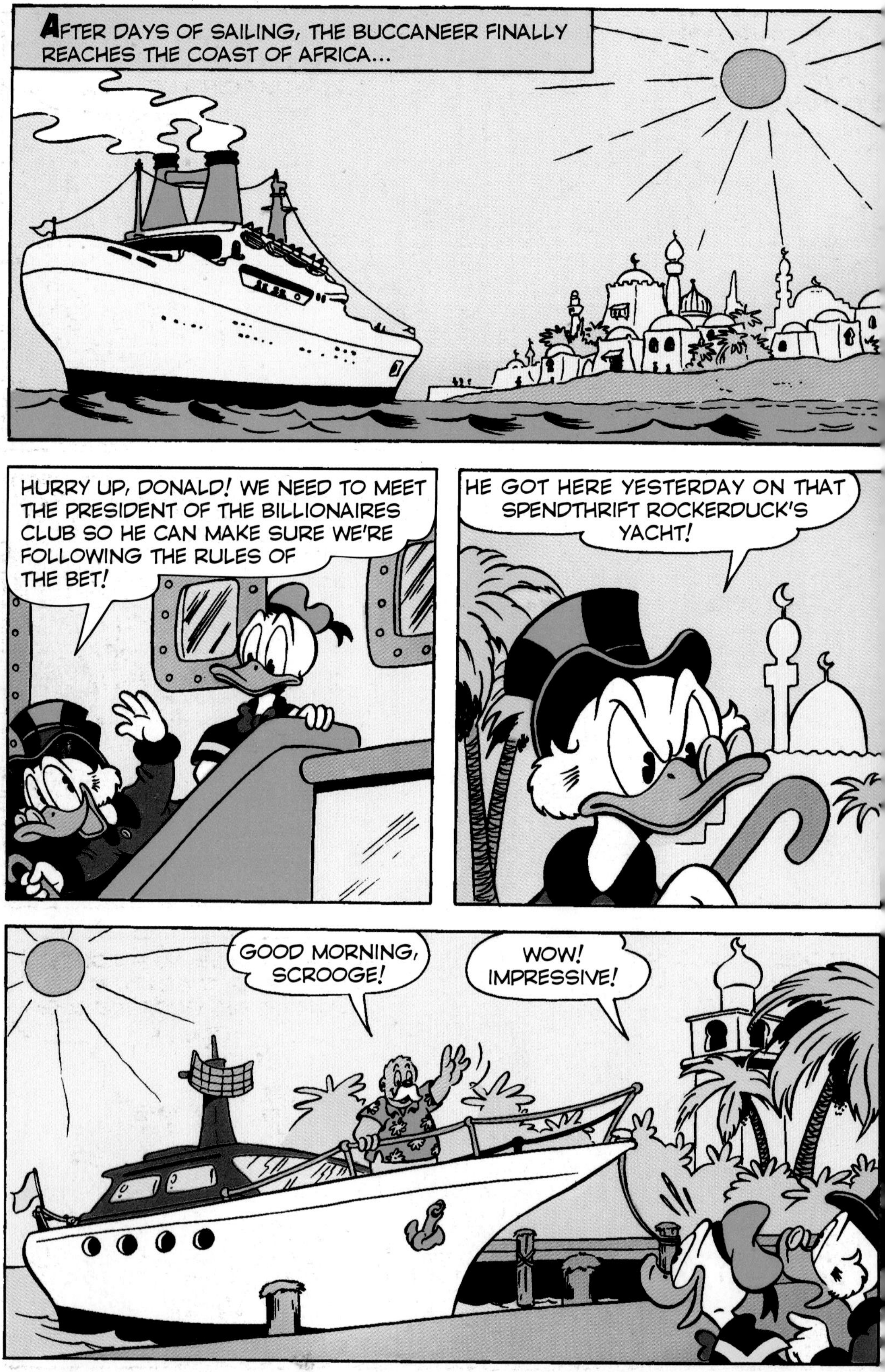
AFTER DAYS OF SAILING, THE BUCCANEER FINALLY REACHES THE COAST OF AFRICA...
HURRY UP, DONALD! WE NEED TO MEET THE PRESIDENT OF THE BILLIONAIRES CLUB SO HE CAN MAKE SURE WE'RE FOLLOWING THE RULES OF THE BET!
HE GOT HERE YESTERDAY ON THAT SPENDTHRIFT ROCKERDUCK'S YACHT!
GOOD MORNING, SCROOGE!
WOW! IMPRESSIVE!

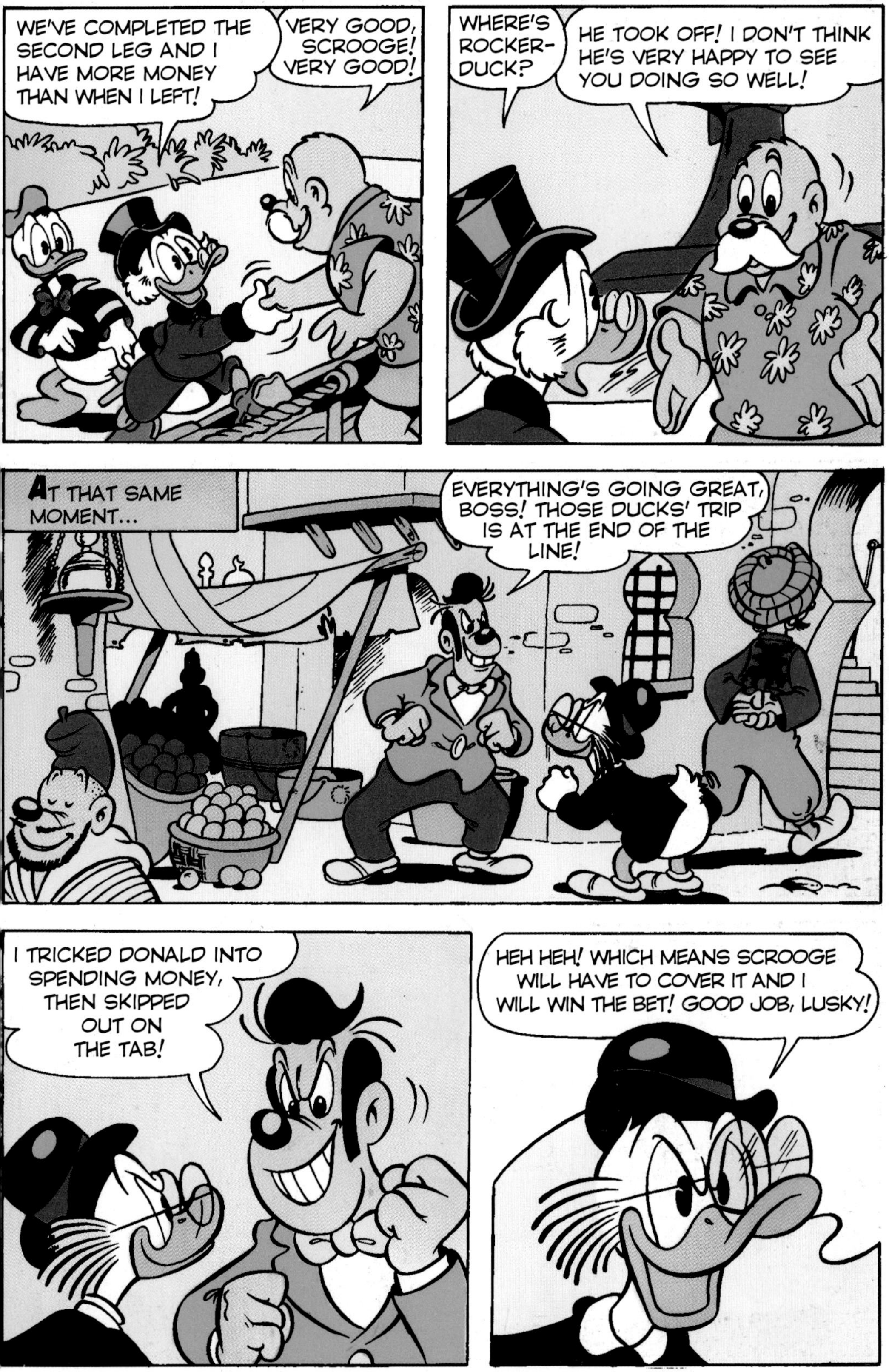
WE'VE COMPLETED THE SECOND LEG AND I HAVE MORE MONEY THAN WHEN I LEFT!
VERY GOOD, SCROOGE! VERY GOOD!
WHERE'S ROCKER-DUCK?
HE TOOK OFF! I DON'T THINK HE'S VERY HAPPY TO SEE YOU DOING SO WELL!
AT THAT SAME MOMENT...
EVERYTHING'S GOING GREAT, BOSS! THOSE DUCKS' TRIP IS AT THE END OF THE LINE!
I TRICKED DONALD INTO SPENDING MONEY, THEN SKIPPED OUT ON THE TAB!
HEH HEH! WHICH MEANS SCROOGE WILL HAVE TO COVER IT AND I WILL WIN THE BET! GOOD JOB, LUSKY!

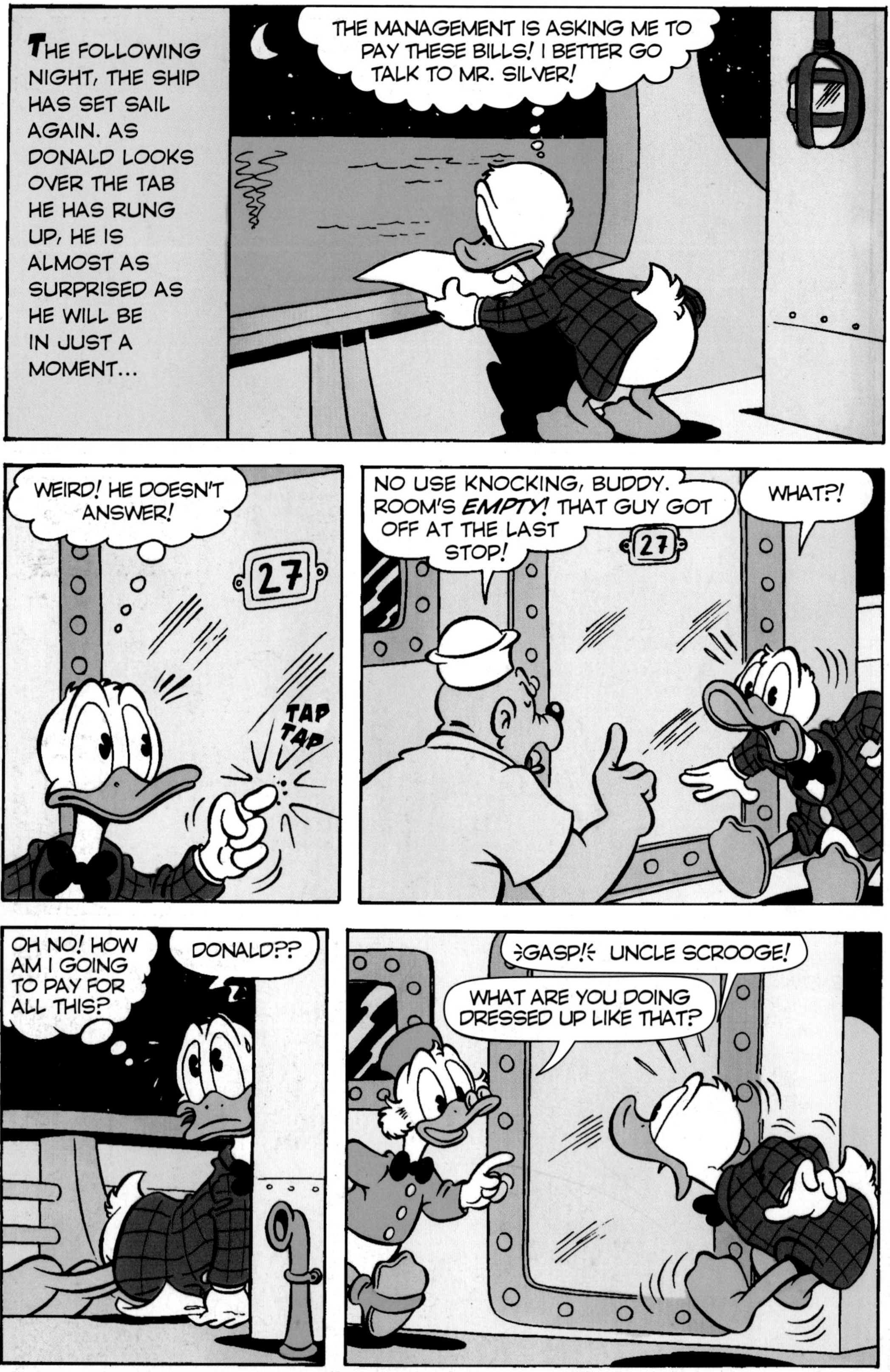
THE FOLLOWING NIGHT, THE SHIP HAS SET SAIL AGAIN. AS DONALD LOOKS OVER THE TAB HE HAS RUNG UP, HE IS ALMOST AS SURPRISED AS HE WILL BE IN JUST A MOMENT...
THE MANAGEMENT IS ASKING ME TO PAY THESE BILLS! I BETTER GO TALK TO MR. SILVER!
WEIRD! HE DOESN'T ANSWER!
27
TAP TAP
NO USE KNOCKING, BUDDY. ROOM'S EMPTY! THAT GUY GOT OFF AT THE LAST STOP!
WHAT?!
27
OH NO! HOW AM I GOING TO PAY FOR ALL THIS?
DONALD??
GASP! UNCLE SCROOGE!
WHAT ARE YOU DOING DRESSED UP LIKE THAT?

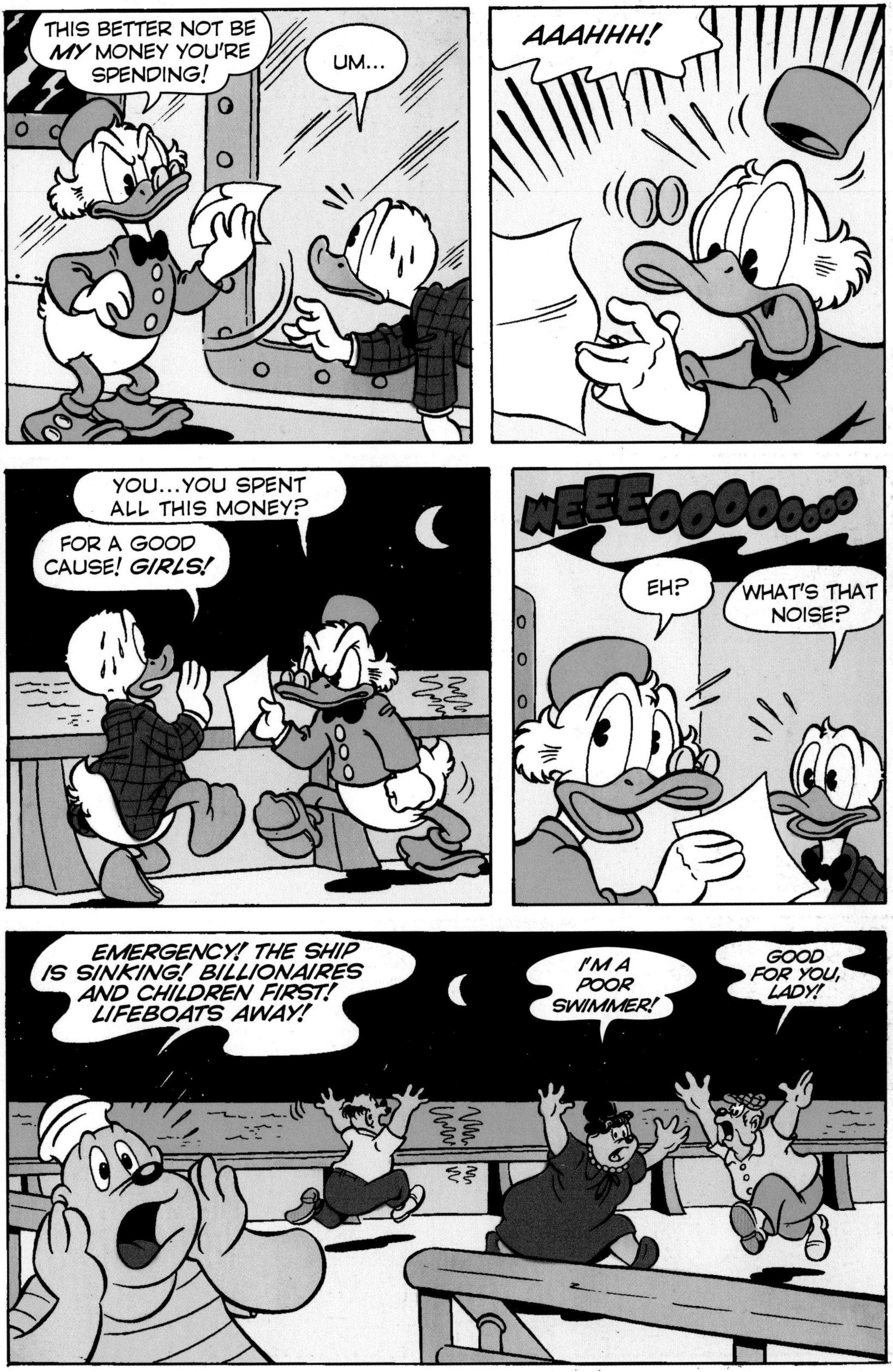
THIS BETTER NOT BE *MY* MONEY YOU'RE SPENDING!
UM...
AAAHHH!
YOU...YOU SPENT ALL THIS MONEY?
FOR A GOOD CAUSE! *GIRLS!*
WEEEOOOOOOooo
EH?
WHAT'S THAT NOISE?
EMERGENCY! THE SHIP IS SINKING! BILLIONAIRES AND CHILDREN FIRST! LIFEBOATS AWAY!
I'M A POOR SWIMMER!
GOOD FOR YOU, LADY!

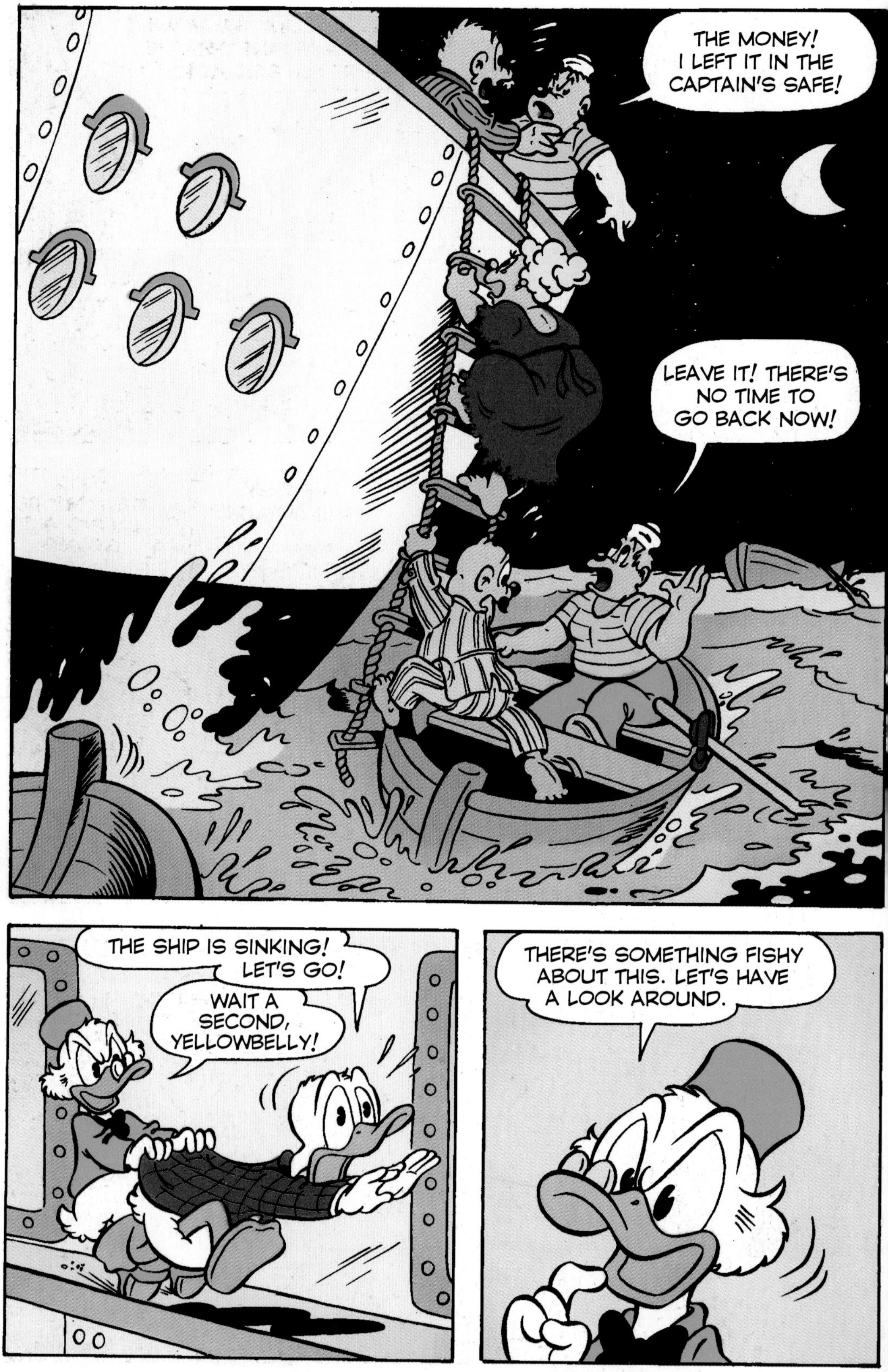
THE MONEY! I LEFT IT IN THE CAPTAIN'S SAFE!
LEAVE IT! THERE'S NO TIME TO GO BACK NOW!
THE SHIP IS SINKING! LET'S GO!
WAIT A SECOND, YELLOWBELLY!
THERE'S SOMETHING FISHY ABOUT THIS. LET'S HAVE A LOOK AROUND.

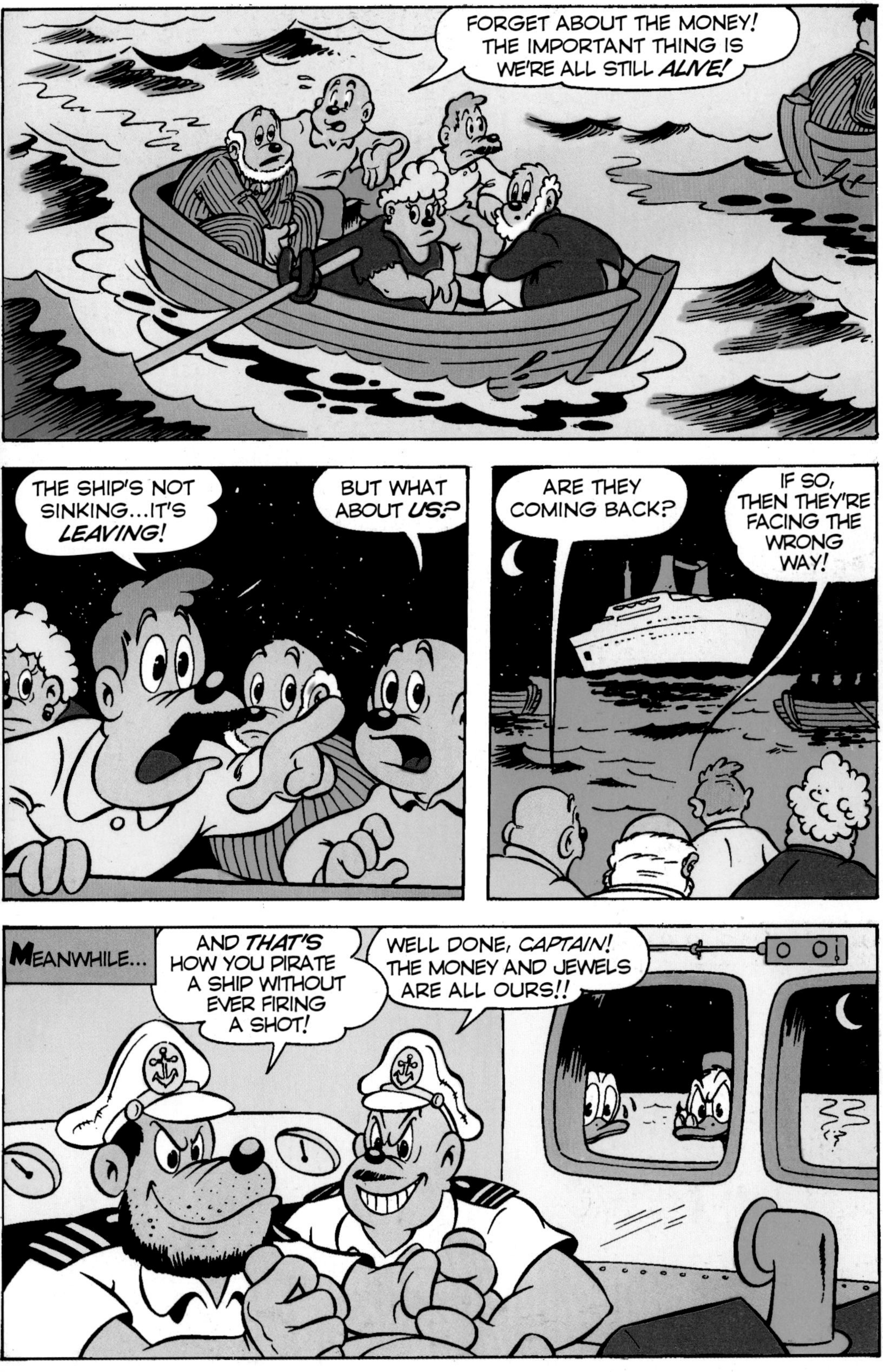
FORGET ABOUT THE MONEY! THE IMPORTANT THING IS WE'RE ALL STILL *ALIVE!*
THE SHIP'S NOT SINKING...IT'S *LEAVING!*
BUT WHAT ABOUT *US?*
ARE THEY COMING BACK?
IF SO, THEN THEY'RE FACING THE WRONG WAY!
MEANWHILE...
AND *THAT'S* HOW YOU PIRATE A SHIP WITHOUT EVER FIRING A SHOT!
WELL DONE, *CAPTAIN!* THE MONEY AND JEWELS ARE ALL OURS!!

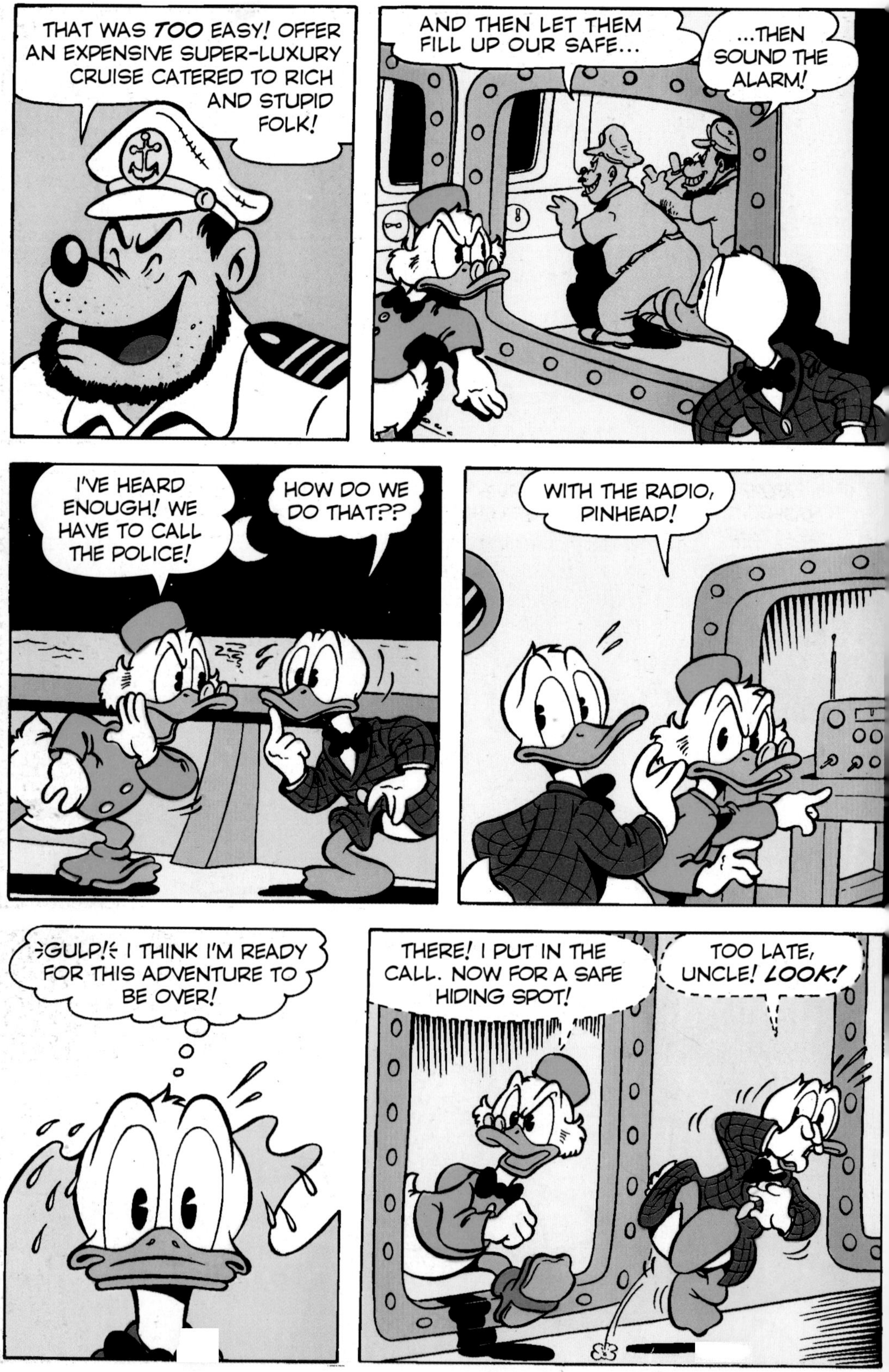
THAT WAS *TOO* EASY! OFFER AN EXPENSIVE SUPER-LUXURY CRUISE CATERED TO RICH AND STUPID FOLK!
AND THEN LET THEM FILL UP OUR SAFE...
...THEN SOUND THE ALARM!
I'VE HEARD ENOUGH! WE HAVE TO CALL THE POLICE!
HOW DO WE DO THAT??
WITH THE RADIO, PINHEAD!
*GULP!* I THINK I'M READY FOR THIS ADVENTURE TO BE OVER!
THERE! I PUT IN THE CALL. NOW FOR A SAFE HIDING SPOT!
TOO LATE, UNCLE! *LOOK!*

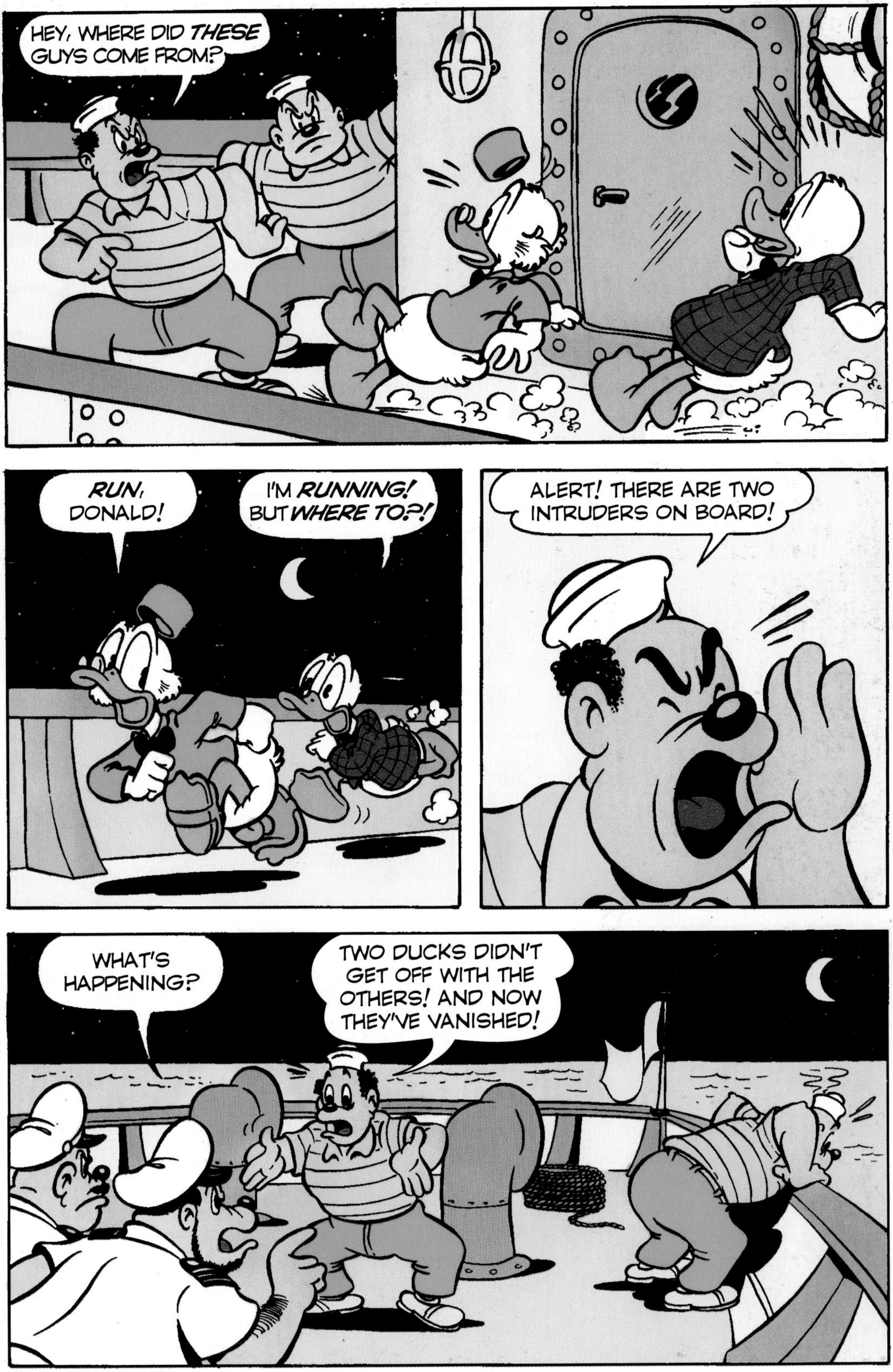
HEY, WHERE DID THESE GUYS COME FROM?
RUN, DONALD!
I'M RUNNING! BUT WHERE TO?!
ALERT! THERE ARE TWO INTRUDERS ON BOARD!
WHAT'S HAPPENING?
TWO DUCKS DIDN'T GET OFF WITH THE OTHERS! AND NOW THEY'VE VANISHED!

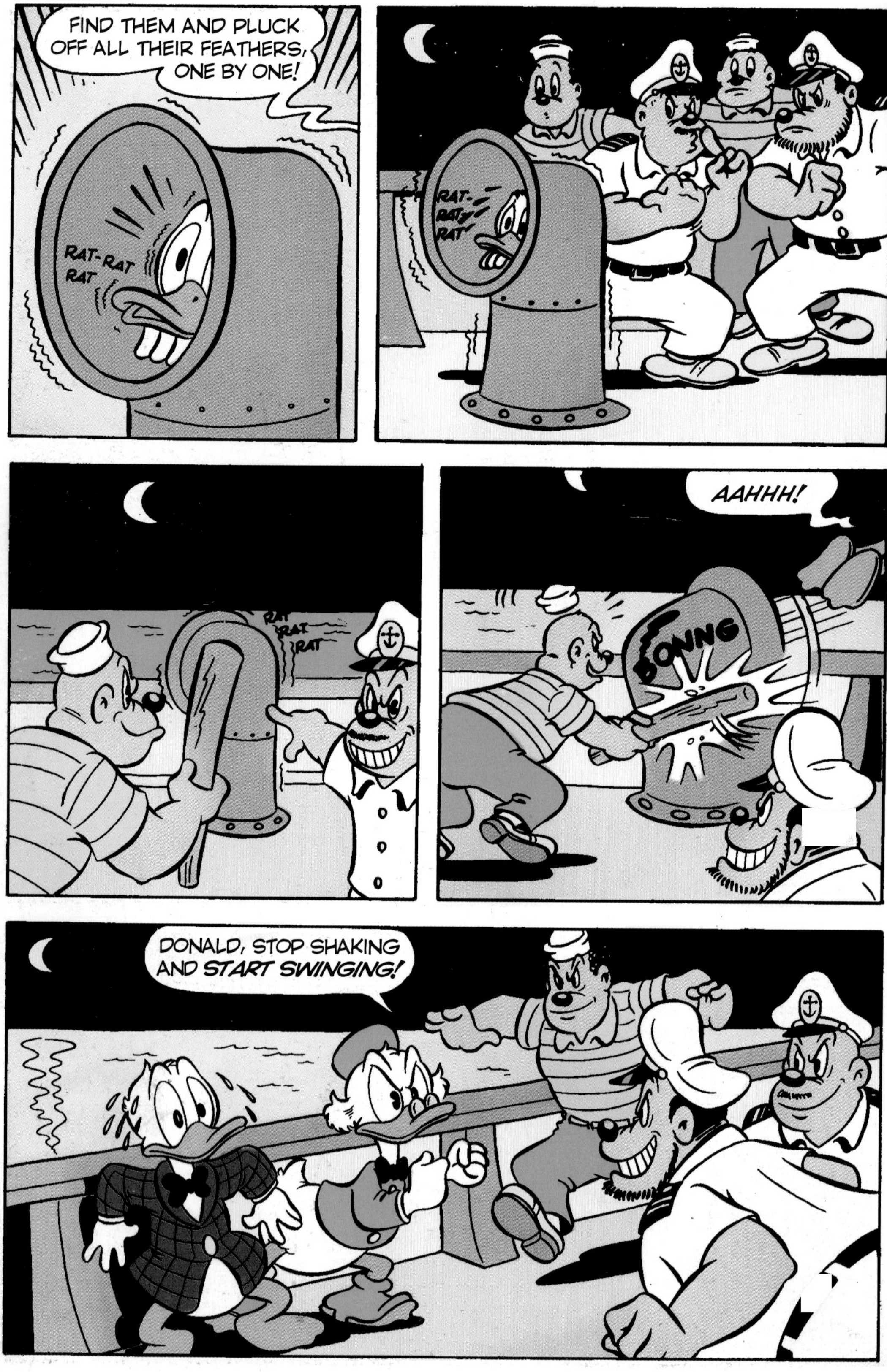
FIND THEM AND PLUCK OFF ALL THEIR FEATHERS, ONE BY ONE!
RAT-RAT RAT
RAT-RAT-RAT
RAT RAT RAT
AAHHH!
BONNG
DONALD, STOP SHAKING AND START SWINGING!

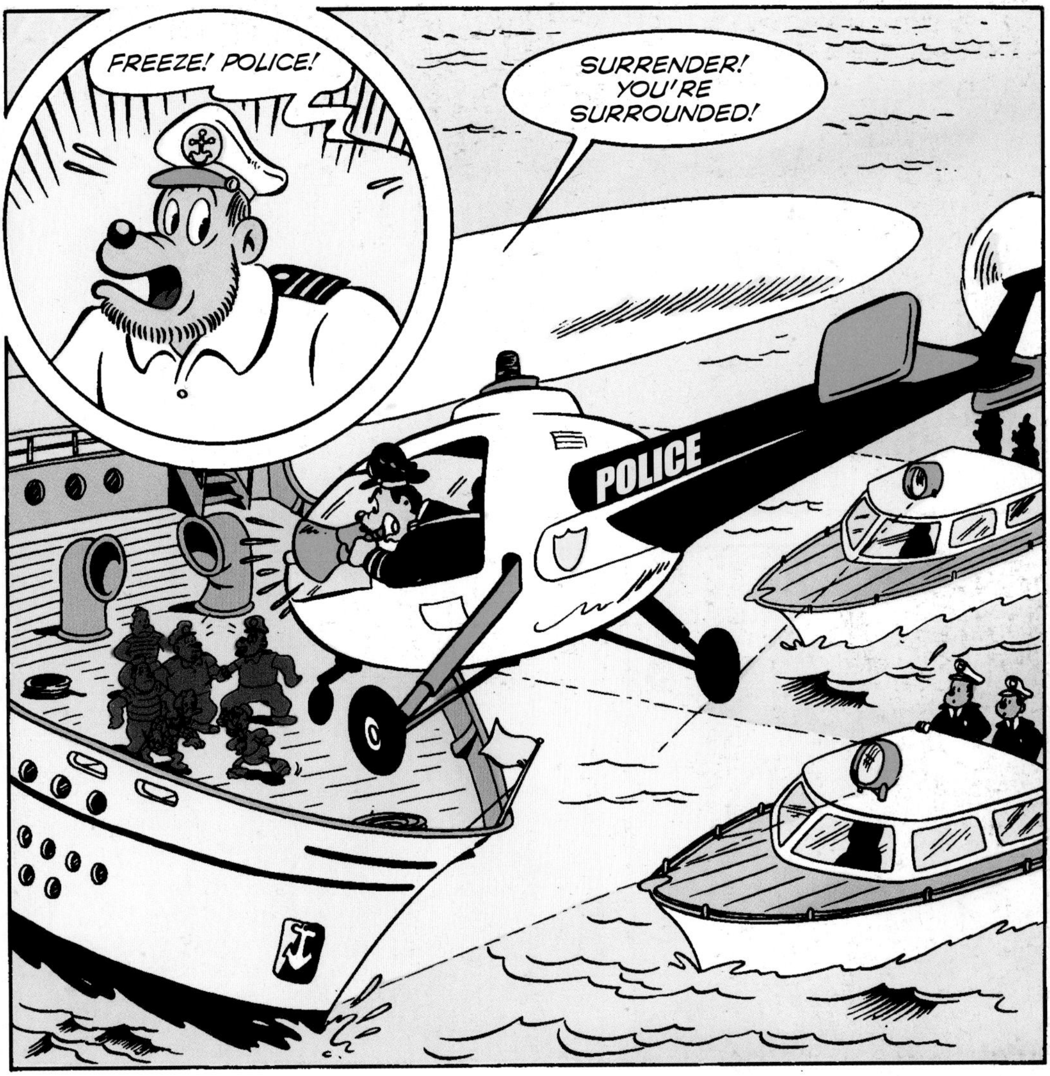
FREEZE! POLICE!
SURRENDER! YOU'RE SURROUNDED!
POLICE

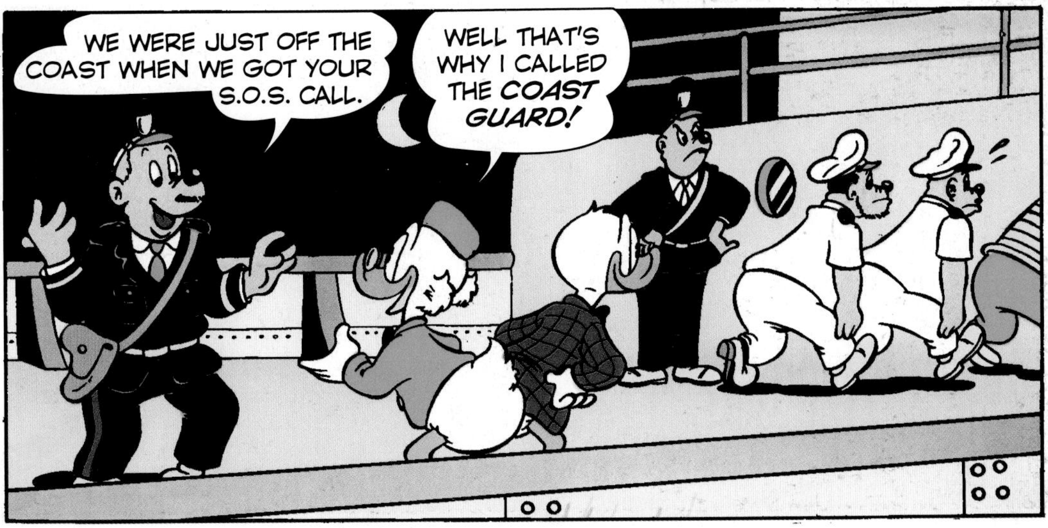
WE WERE JUST OFF THE COAST WHEN WE GOT YOUR S.O.S. CALL.
WELL THAT'S WHY I CALLED THE *COAST GUARD!*

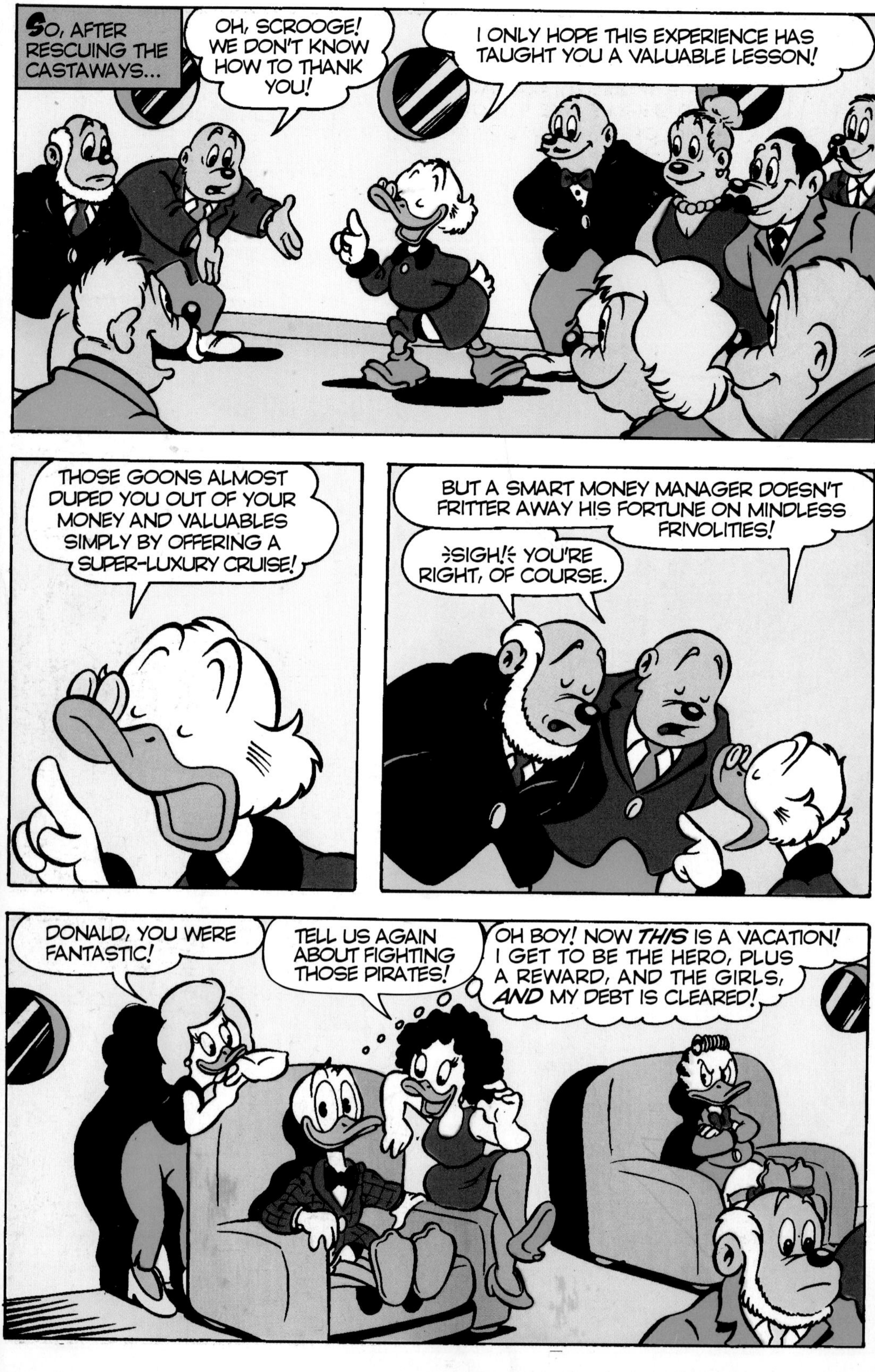
SO, AFTER RESCUING THE CASTAWAYS...
OH, SCROOGE! WE DON'T KNOW HOW TO THANK YOU!
I ONLY HOPE THIS EXPERIENCE HAS TAUGHT YOU A VALUABLE LESSON!
THOSE GOONS ALMOST DUPED YOU OUT OF YOUR MONEY AND VALUABLES SIMPLY BY OFFERING A SUPER-LUXURY CRUISE!
BUT A SMART MONEY MANAGER DOESN'T FRITTER AWAY HIS FORTUNE ON MINDLESS FRIVOLITIES!
SIGH! YOU'RE RIGHT, OF COURSE.
DONALD, YOU WERE FANTASTIC!
TELL US AGAIN ABOUT FIGHTING THOSE PIRATES!
OH BOY! NOW THIS IS A VACATION! I GET TO BE THE HERO, PLUS A REWARD, AND THE GIRLS, AND MY DEBT IS CLEARED!

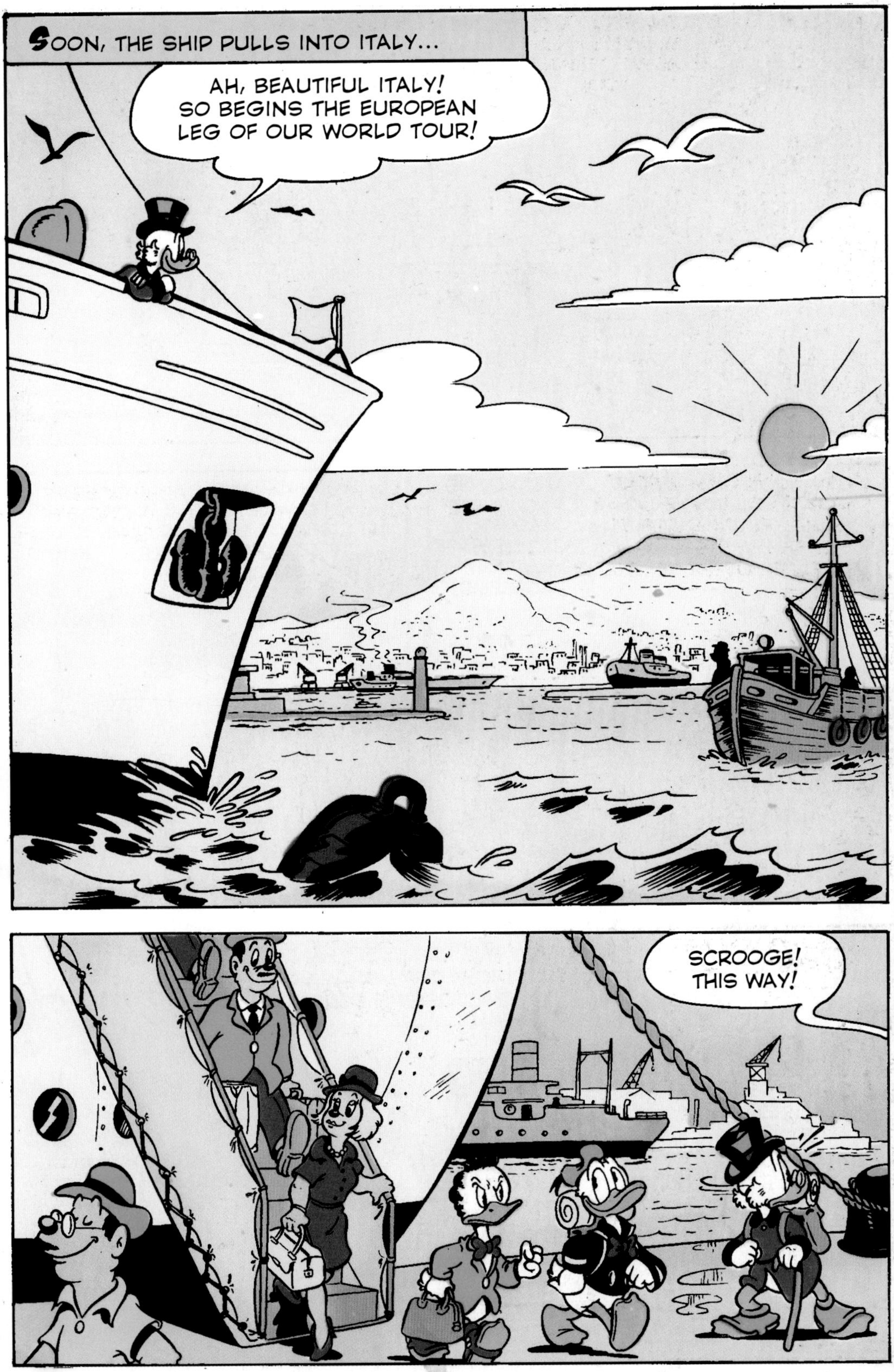
SOON, THE SHIP PULLS INTO ITALY...
AH, BEAUTIFUL ITALY! SO BEGINS THE EUROPEAN LEG OF OUR WORLD TOUR!
SCROOGE! THIS WAY!

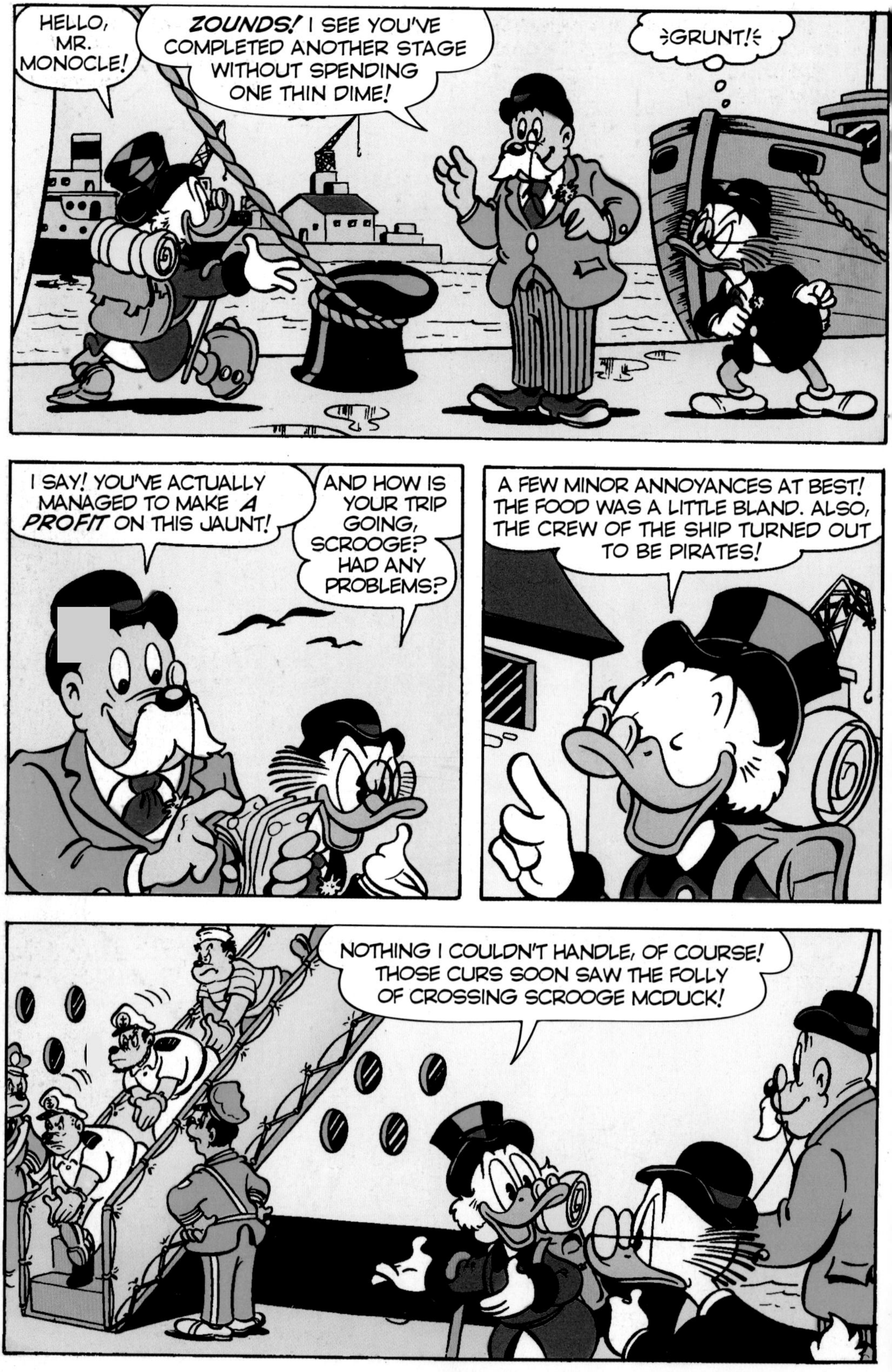
HELLO, MR. MONOCLE!
ZOUNDS! I SEE YOU'VE COMPLETED ANOTHER STAGE WITHOUT SPENDING ONE THIN DIME!
GRUNT!
I SAY! YOU'VE ACTUALLY MANAGED TO MAKE A PROFIT ON THIS JAUNT!
AND HOW IS YOUR TRIP GOING, SCROOGE? HAD ANY PROBLEMS?
A FEW MINOR ANNOYANCES AT BEST! THE FOOD WAS A LITTLE BLAND. ALSO, THE CREW OF THE SHIP TURNED OUT TO BE PIRATES!
NOTHING I COULDN'T HANDLE, OF COURSE! THOSE CURS SOON SAW THE FOLLY OF CROSSING SCROOGE MCDUCK!

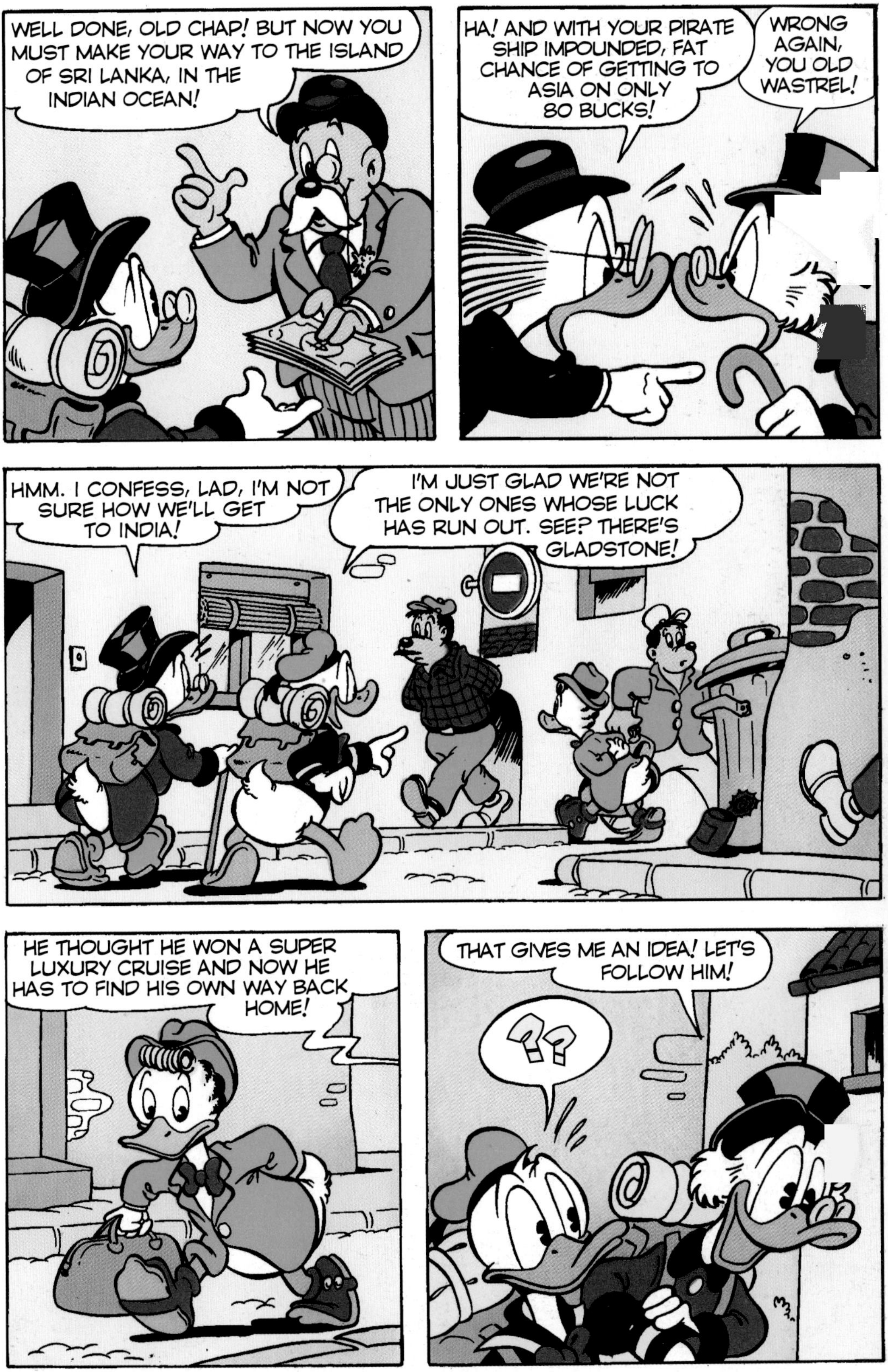
WELL DONE, OLD CHAP! BUT NOW YOU MUST MAKE YOUR WAY TO THE ISLAND OF SRI LANKA, IN THE INDIAN OCEAN!
HA! AND WITH YOUR PIRATE SHIP IMPOUNDED, FAT CHANCE OF GETTING TO ASIA ON ONLY 80 BUCKS!
WRONG AGAIN, YOU OLD WASTREL!
HMM. I CONFESS, LAD, I'M NOT SURE HOW WE'LL GET TO INDIA!
I'M JUST GLAD WE'RE NOT THE ONLY ONES WHOSE LUCK HAS RUN OUT. SEE? THERE'S GLADSTONE!
HE THOUGHT HE WON A SUPER LUXURY CRUISE AND NOW HE HAS TO FIND HIS OWN WAY BACK HOME!
THAT GIVES ME AN IDEA! LET'S FOLLOW HIM!
??

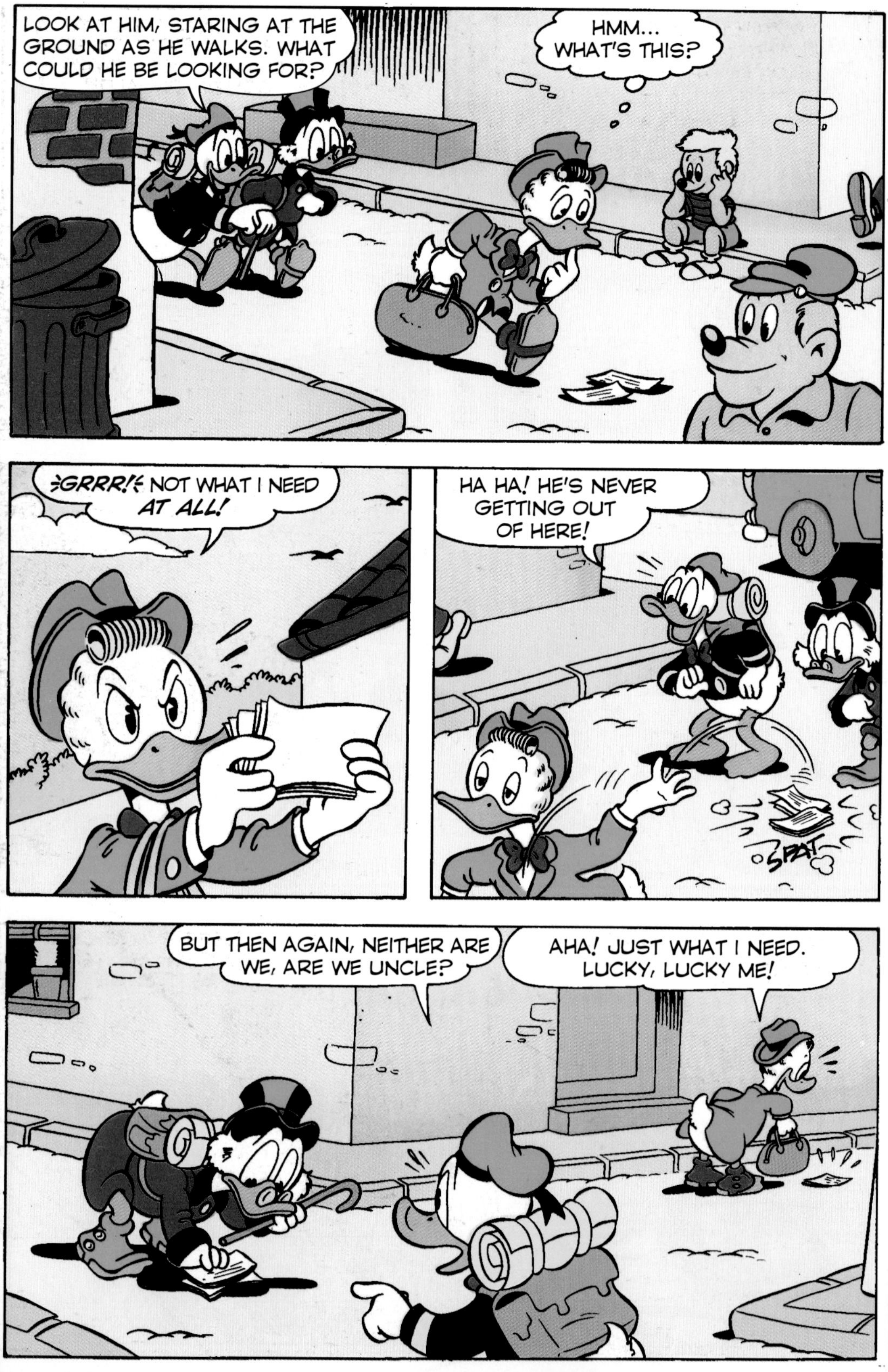
LOOK AT HIM, STARING AT THE GROUND AS HE WALKS. WHAT COULD HE BE LOOKING FOR?
HMM... WHAT'S THIS?
GRRR! NOT WHAT I NEED AT ALL!
HA HA! HE'S NEVER GETTING OUT OF HERE!
SPAT
BUT THEN AGAIN, NEITHER ARE WE, ARE WE UNCLE?
AHA! JUST WHAT I NEED. LUCKY, LUCKY ME!

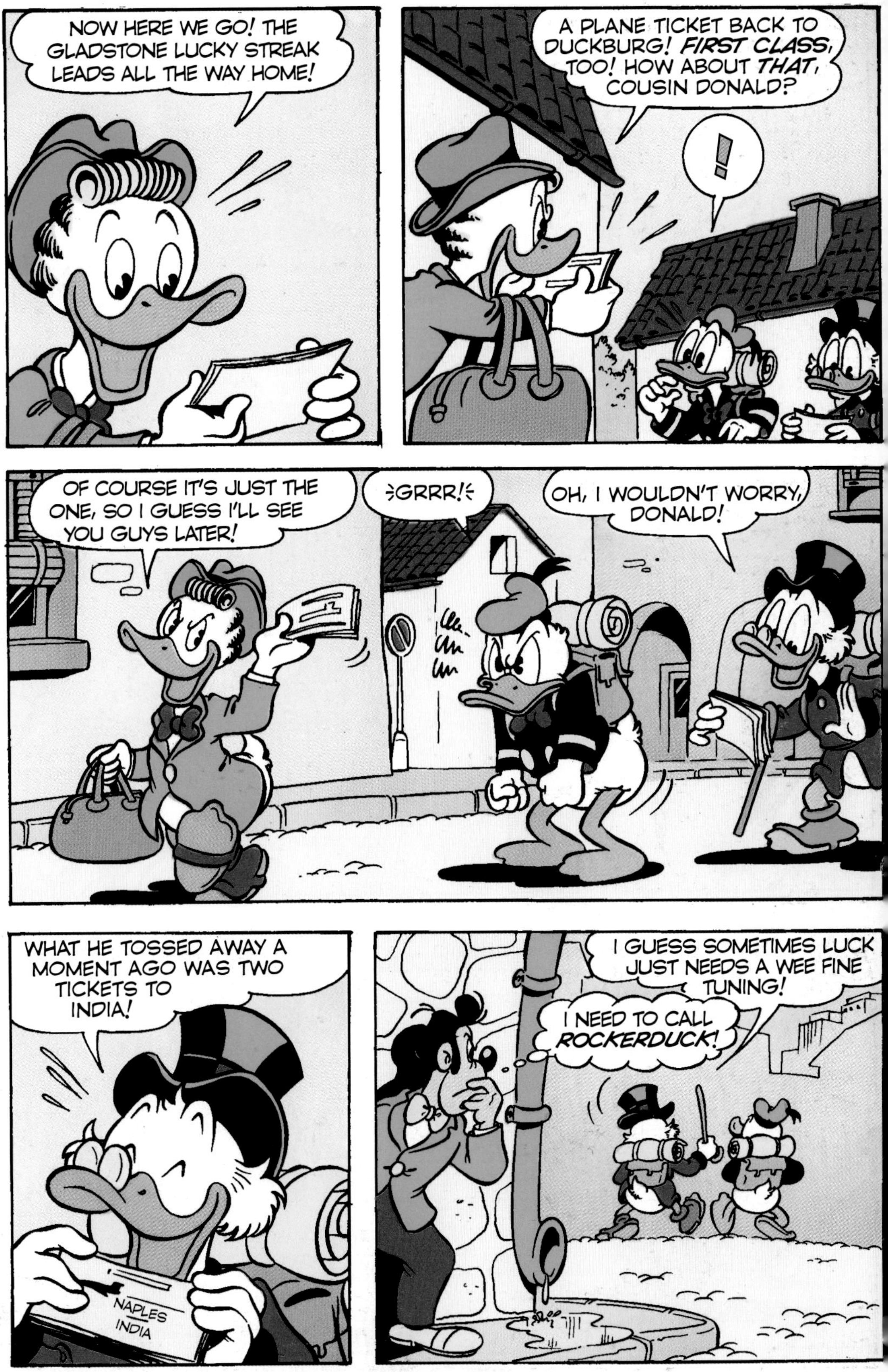
NOW HERE WE GO! THE GLADSTONE LUCKY STREAK LEADS ALL THE WAY HOME!
A PLANE TICKET BACK TO DUCKBURG! *FIRST CLASS,* TOO! HOW ABOUT *THAT,* COUSIN DONALD?
!
OF COURSE IT'S JUST THE ONE, SO I GUESS I'LL SEE YOU GUYS LATER!
GRRR!
OH, I WOULDN'T WORRY, DONALD!
WHAT HE TOSSED AWAY A MOMENT AGO WAS TWO TICKETS TO INDIA!
NAPLES
INDIA
I GUESS SOMETIMES LUCK JUST NEEDS A WEE FINE TUNING!
I NEED TO CALL *ROCKERDUCK!*

LATER...

IF THEY'VE GOT A WAY TO INDIA, YOU NEED TO FIND A WAY TO DRIVE UP THE COST OF THE TRIP!

KEEP A CLOSE EYE ON THEM, AND CALL ME IF YOU SEE *ANY* CHANCE FOR ME TO WIN THIS BET!

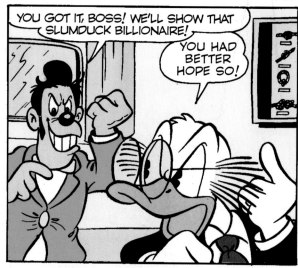

YOU GOT IT, BOSS! WE'LL SHOW THAT SLUMDUCK BILLIONAIRE!

YOU HAD BETTER HOPE SO!

SO FAR YOU'VE COST ME TEN TIMES AS MUCH AS SCROOGE HAS MADE ON THIS TRIP!

⸮GULP!⸮ CHEATING COSTS!

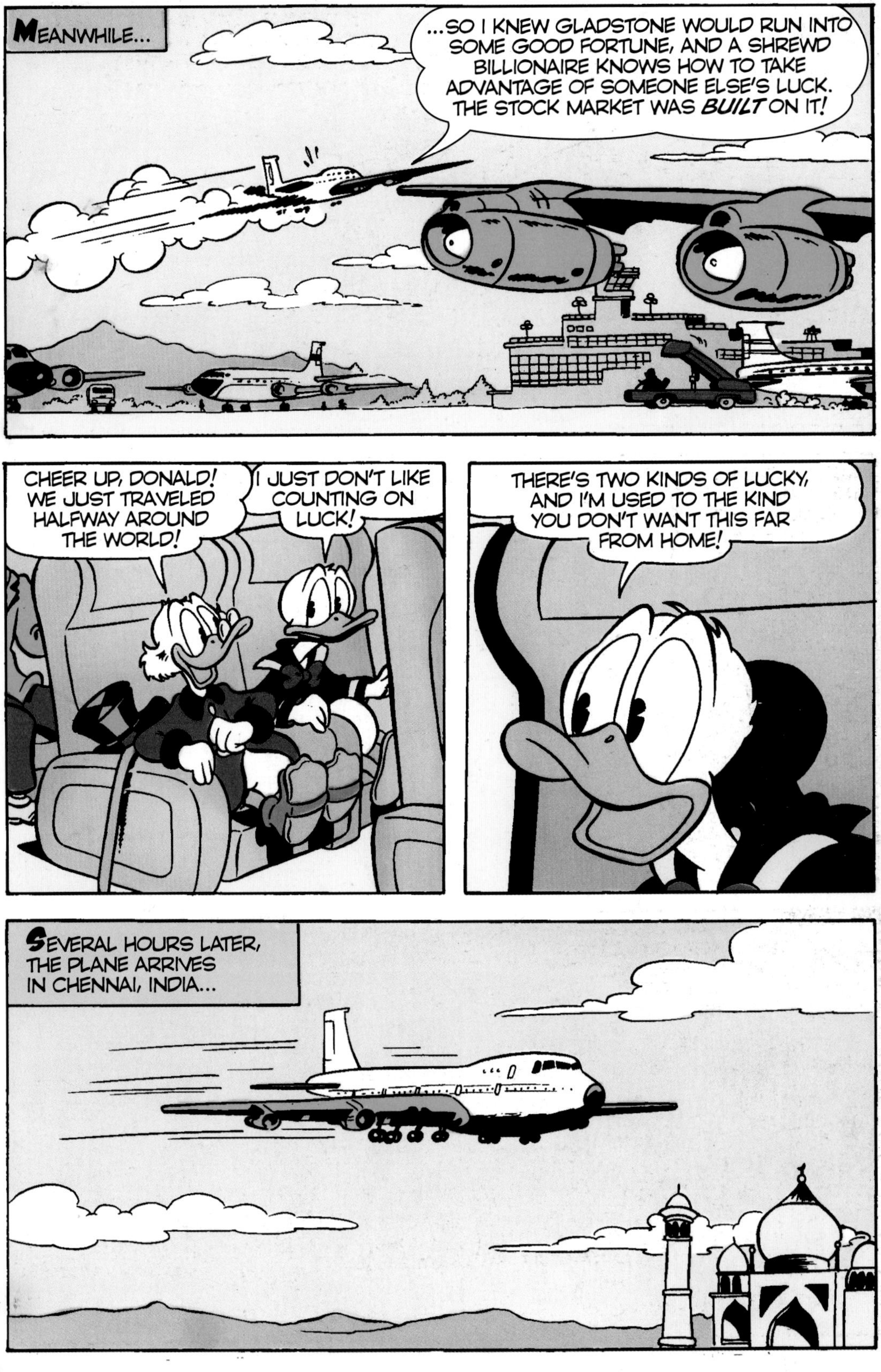
MEANWHILE...
...SO I KNEW GLADSTONE WOULD RUN INTO SOME GOOD FORTUNE, AND A SHREWD BILLIONAIRE KNOWS HOW TO TAKE ADVANTAGE OF SOMEONE ELSE'S LUCK. THE STOCK MARKET WAS BUILT ON IT!
CHEER UP, DONALD! WE JUST TRAVELED HALFWAY AROUND THE WORLD!
I JUST DON'T LIKE COUNTING ON LUCK!
THERE'S TWO KINDS OF LUCKY, AND I'M USED TO THE KIND YOU DON'T WANT THIS FAR FROM HOME!
SEVERAL HOURS LATER, THE PLANE ARRIVES IN CHENNAI, INDIA...

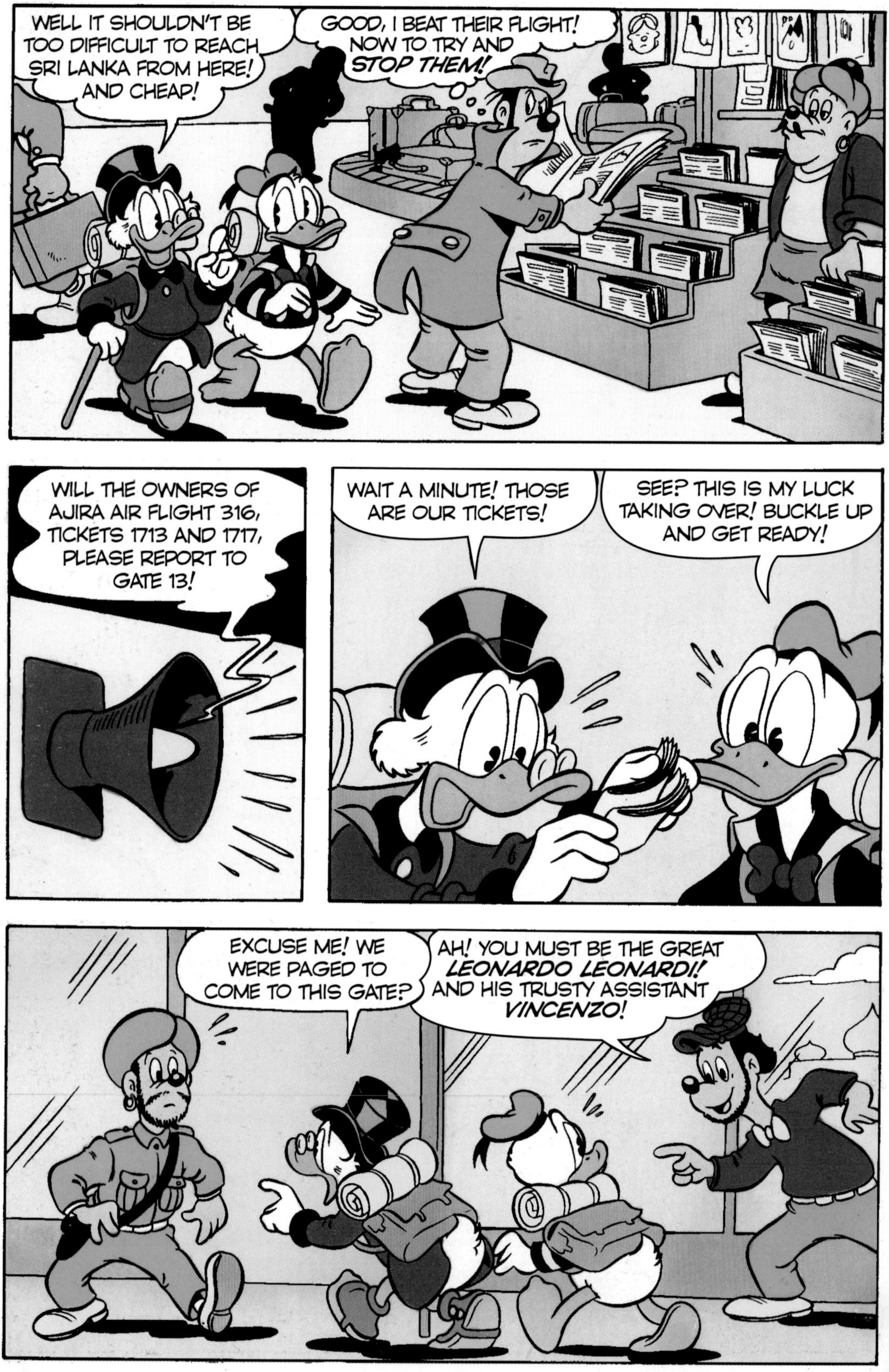

WELL IT SHOULDN'T BE TOO DIFFICULT TO REACH SRI LANKA FROM HERE! AND CHEAP!
GOOD, I BEAT THEIR FLIGHT! NOW TO TRY AND *STOP THEM!*
WILL THE OWNERS OF AJIRA AIR FLIGHT 316, TICKETS 1713 AND 1717, PLEASE REPORT TO GATE 13!
WAIT A MINUTE! THOSE ARE OUR TICKETS!
SEE? THIS IS MY LUCK TAKING OVER! BUCKLE UP AND GET READY!
EXCUSE ME! WE WERE PAGED TO COME TO THIS GATE?
AH! YOU MUST BE THE GREAT *LEONARDO LEONARDI!* AND HIS TRUSTY ASSISTANT *VINCENZO!*

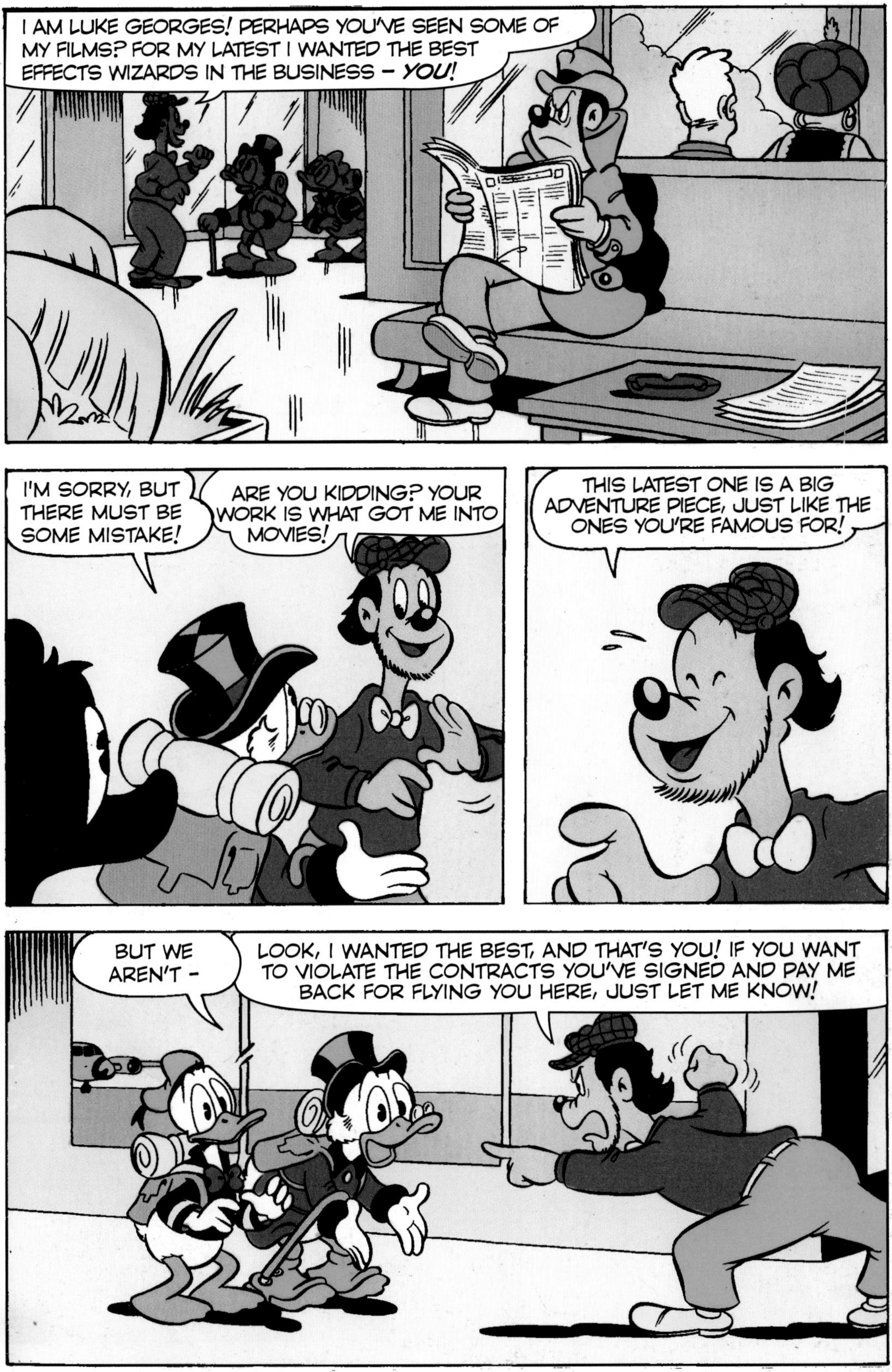
I AM LUKE GEORGES! PERHAPS YOU'VE SEEN SOME OF MY FILMS? FOR MY LATEST I WANTED THE BEST EFFECTS WIZARDS IN THE BUSINESS – YOU!
I'M SORRY, BUT THERE MUST BE SOME MISTAKE!
ARE YOU KIDDING? YOUR WORK IS WHAT GOT ME INTO MOVIES!
THIS LATEST ONE IS A BIG ADVENTURE PIECE, JUST LIKE THE ONES YOU'RE FAMOUS FOR!
BUT WE AREN'T -
LOOK, I WANTED THE BEST, AND THAT'S YOU! IF YOU WANT TO VIOLATE THE CONTRACTS YOU'VE SIGNED AND PAY ME BACK FOR FLYING YOU HERE, JUST LET ME KNOW!

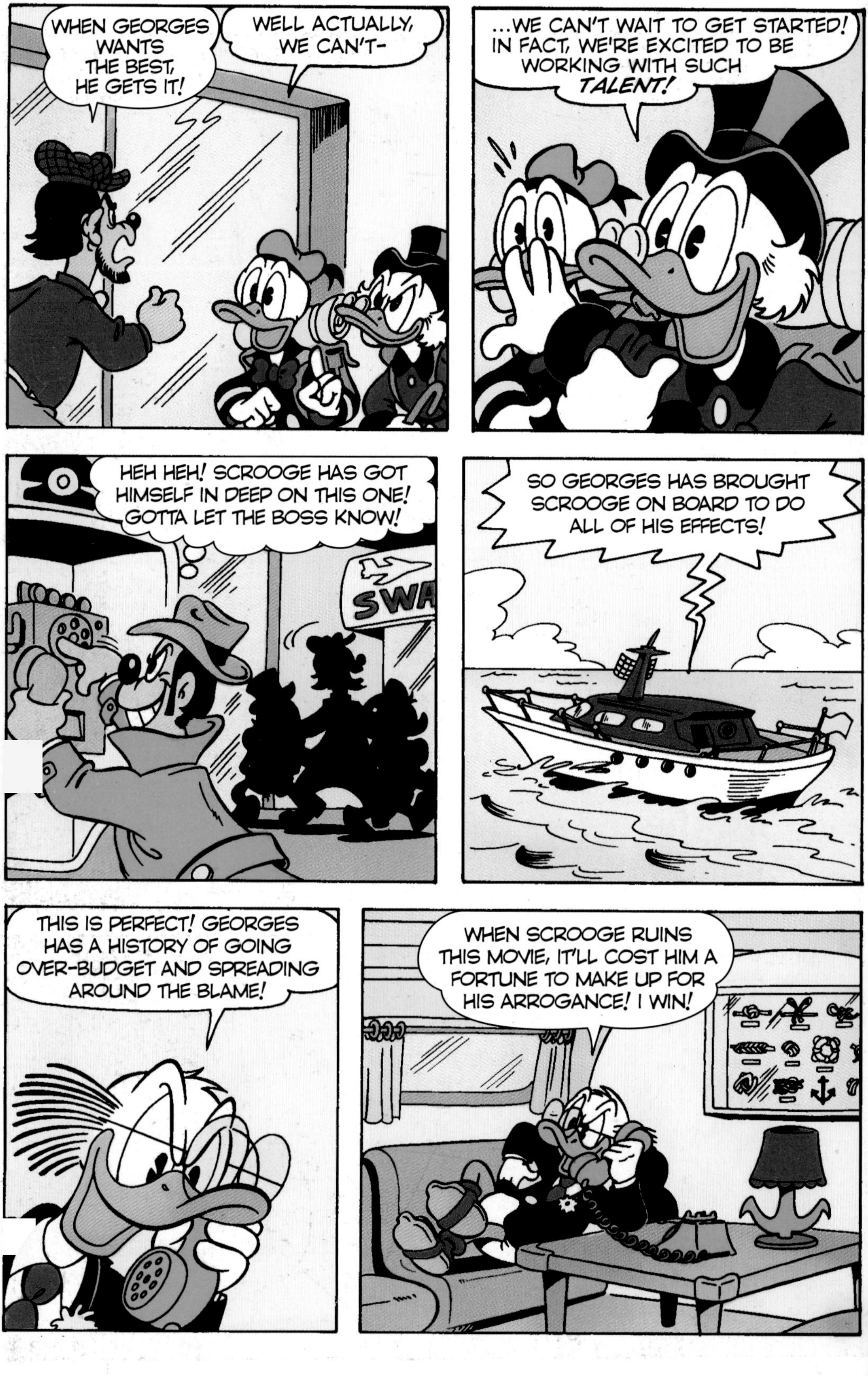
WHEN GEORGES WANTS THE BEST, HE GETS IT!
WELL ACTUALLY, WE CAN'T-
...WE CAN'T WAIT TO GET STARTED! IN FACT, WE'RE EXCITED TO BE WORKING WITH SUCH TALENT!
HEH HEH! SCROOGE HAS GOT HIMSELF IN DEEP ON THIS ONE! GOTTA LET THE BOSS KNOW!
SWA
SO GEORGES HAS BROUGHT SCROOGE ON BOARD TO DO ALL OF HIS EFFECTS!
THIS IS PERFECT! GEORGES HAS A HISTORY OF GOING OVER-BUDGET AND SPREADING AROUND THE BLAME!
WHEN SCROOGE RUINS THIS MOVIE, IT'LL COST HIM A FORTUNE TO MAKE UP FOR HIS ARROGANCE! I WIN!

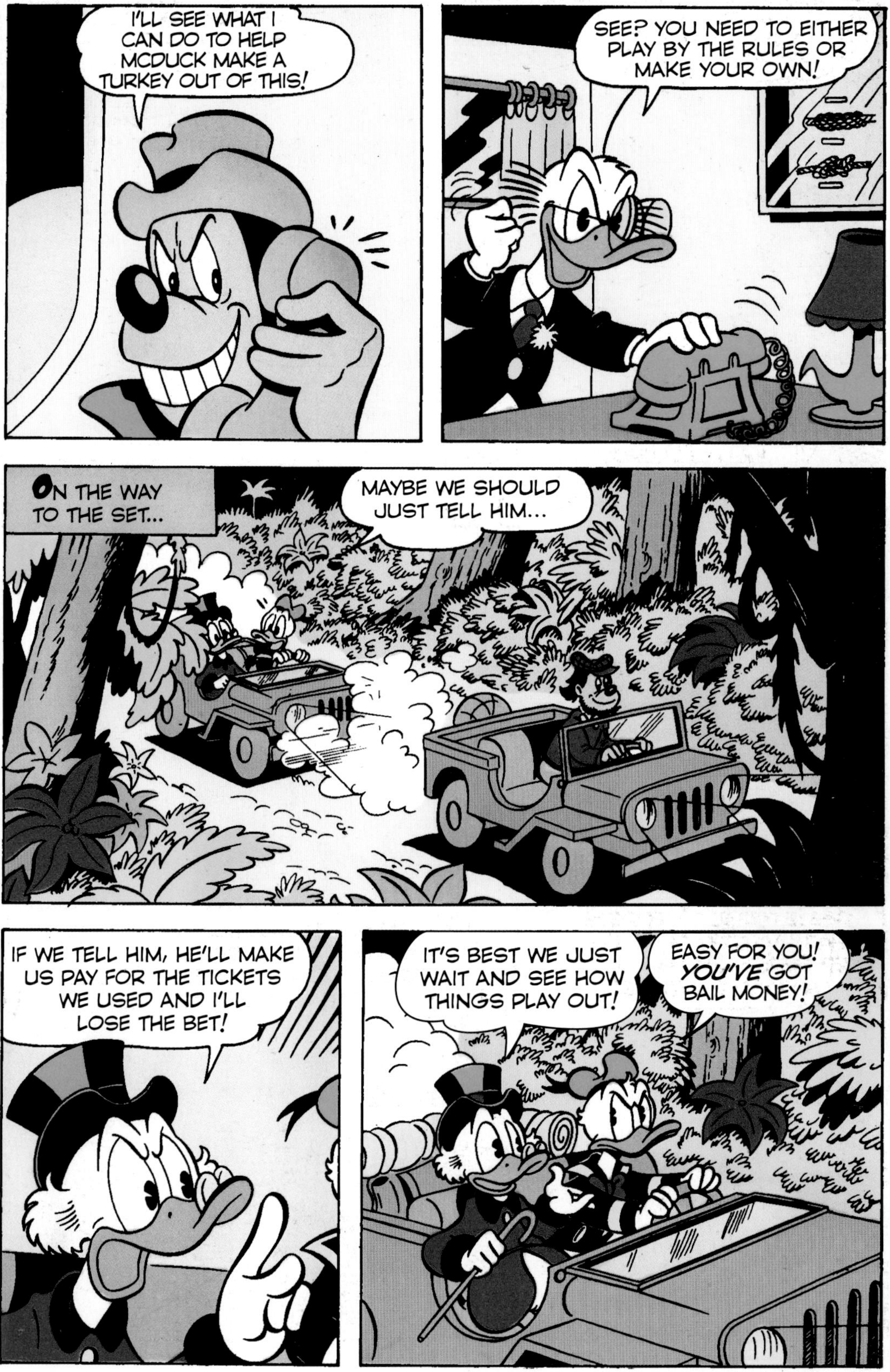
I'LL SEE WHAT I CAN DO TO HELP MCDUCK MAKE A TURKEY OUT OF THIS!
SEE? YOU NEED TO EITHER PLAY BY THE RULES OR MAKE YOUR OWN!
ON THE WAY TO THE SET...
MAYBE WE SHOULD JUST TELL HIM...
IF WE TELL HIM, HE'LL MAKE US PAY FOR THE TICKETS WE USED AND I'LL LOSE THE BET!
IT'S BEST WE JUST WAIT AND SEE HOW THINGS PLAY OUT!
EASY FOR YOU! *YOU'VE* GOT BAIL MONEY!

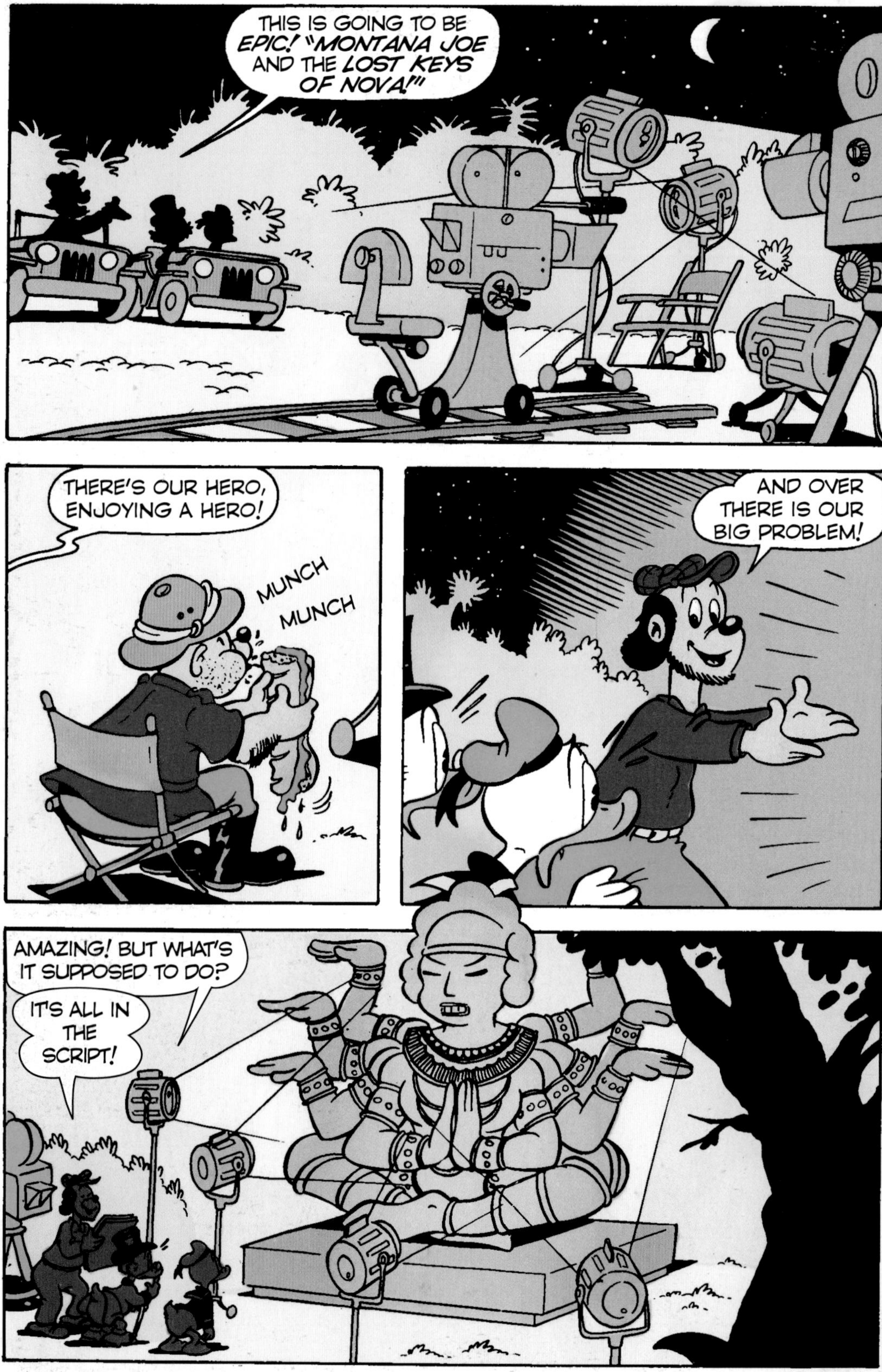
THIS IS GOING TO BE EPIC! "MONTANA JOE AND THE LOST KEYS OF NOVA!"
THERE'S OUR HERO, ENJOYING A HERO!
MUNCH MUNCH
AND OVER THERE IS OUR BIG PROBLEM!
AMAZING! BUT WHAT'S IT SUPPOSED TO DO?
IT'S ALL IN THE SCRIPT!

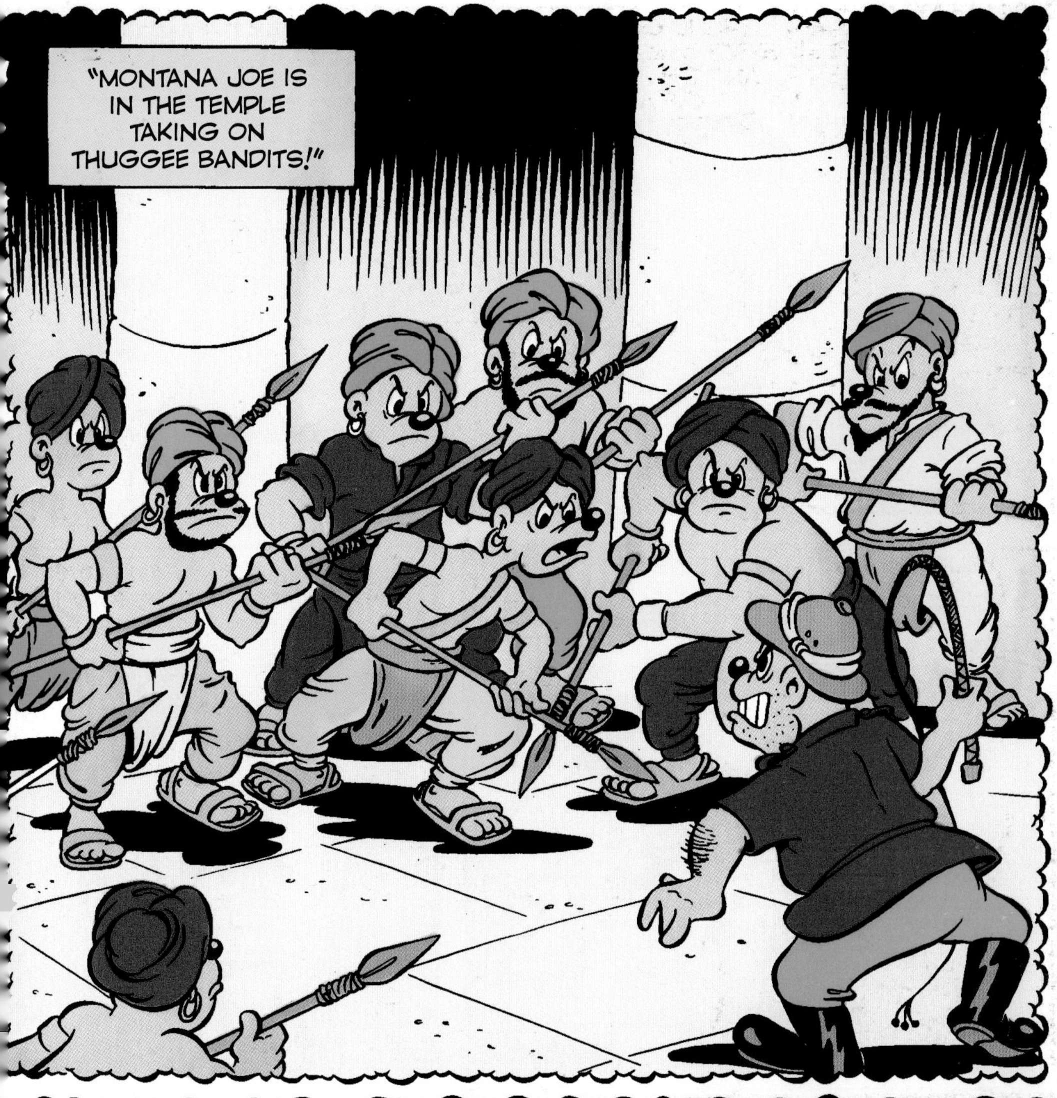
"MONTANA JOE IS IN THE TEMPLE TAKING ON THUGGEE BANDITS!"

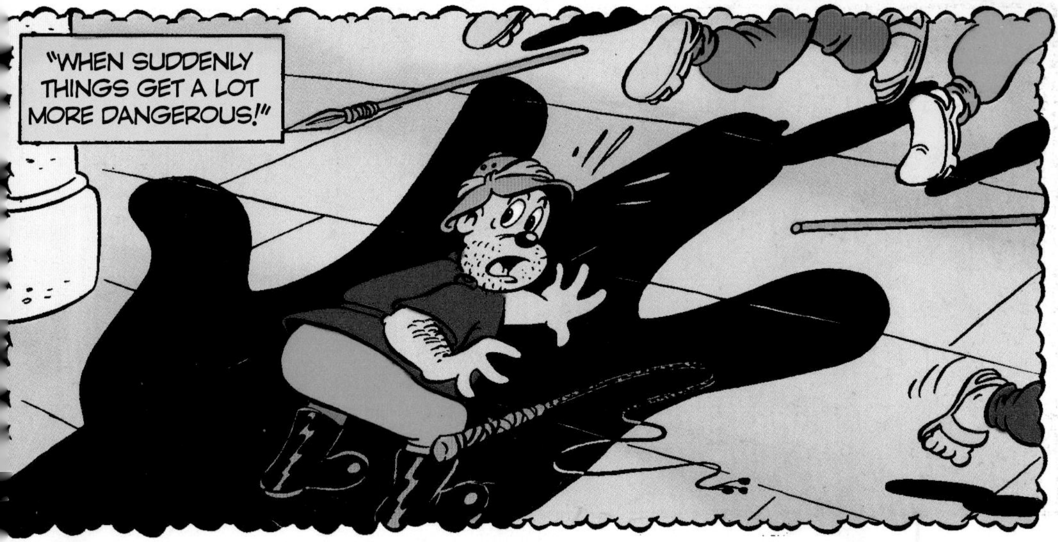
"WHEN SUDDENLY THINGS GET A LOT MORE DANGEROUS!"

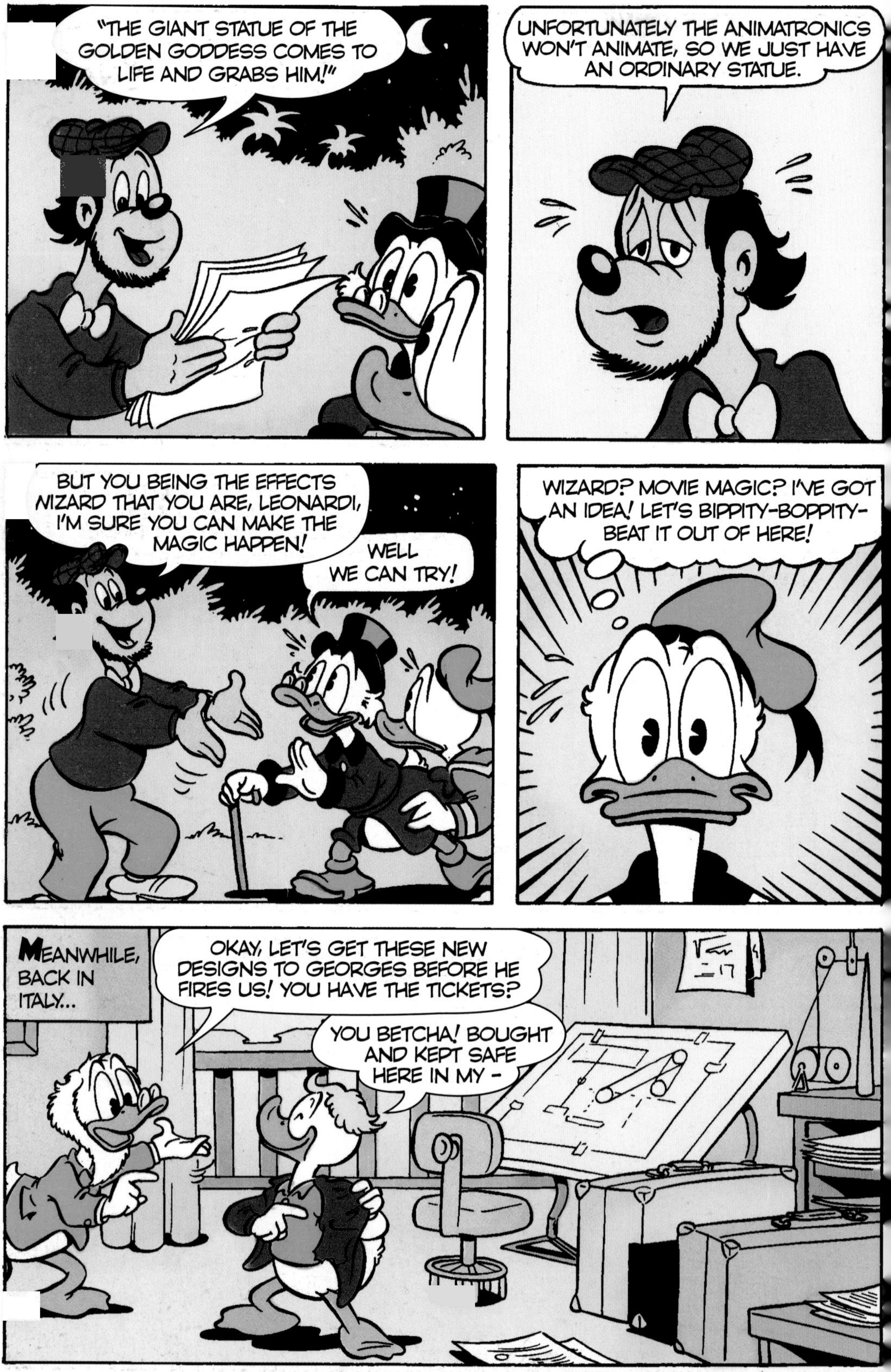
"THE GIANT STATUE OF THE GOLDEN GODDESS COMES TO LIFE AND GRABS HIM!"
UNFORTUNATELY THE ANIMATRONICS WON'T ANIMATE, SO WE JUST HAVE AN ORDINARY STATUE.
BUT YOU BEING THE EFFECTS WIZARD THAT YOU ARE, LEONARDI, I'M SURE YOU CAN MAKE THE MAGIC HAPPEN!
WELL WE CAN TRY!
WIZARD? MOVIE MAGIC? I'VE GOT AN IDEA! LET'S BIPPITY-BOPPITY-BEAT IT OUT OF HERE!
MEANWHILE, BACK IN ITALY...
OKAY, LET'S GET THESE NEW DESIGNS TO GEORGES BEFORE HE FIRES US! YOU HAVE THE TICKETS?
YOU BETCHA! BOUGHT AND KEPT SAFE HERE IN MY -

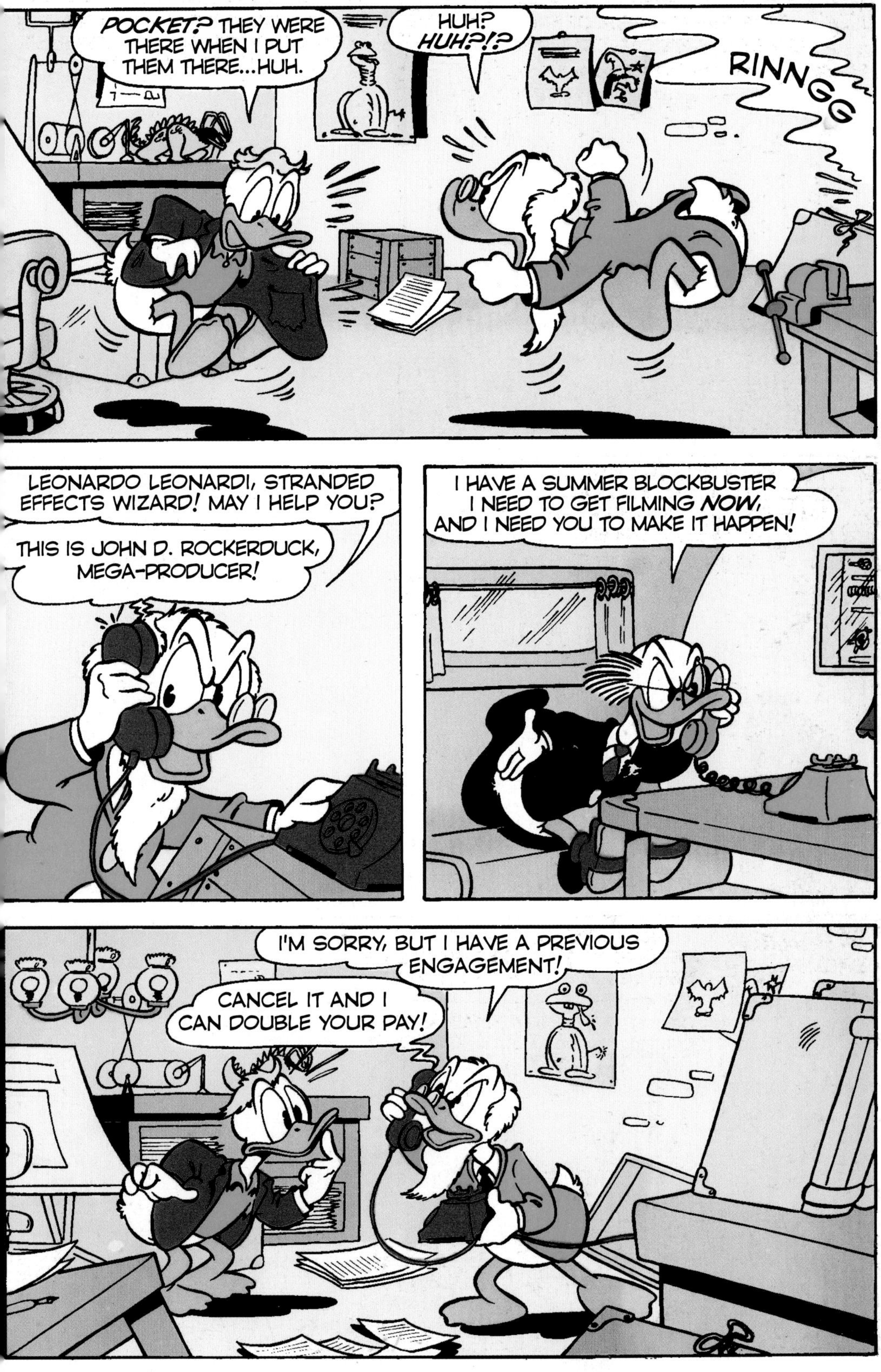
POCKET? THEY WERE THERE WHEN I PUT THEM THERE...HUH.
HUH? HUH?!?
RINNGG
LEONARDO LEONARDI, STRANDED EFFECTS WIZARD! MAY I HELP YOU?
THIS IS JOHN D. ROCKERDUCK, MEGA-PRODUCER!
I HAVE A SUMMER BLOCKBUSTER I NEED TO GET FILMING NOW, AND I NEED YOU TO MAKE IT HAPPEN!
I'M SORRY, BUT I HAVE A PREVIOUS ENGAGEMENT!
CANCEL IT AND I CAN DOUBLE YOUR PAY!

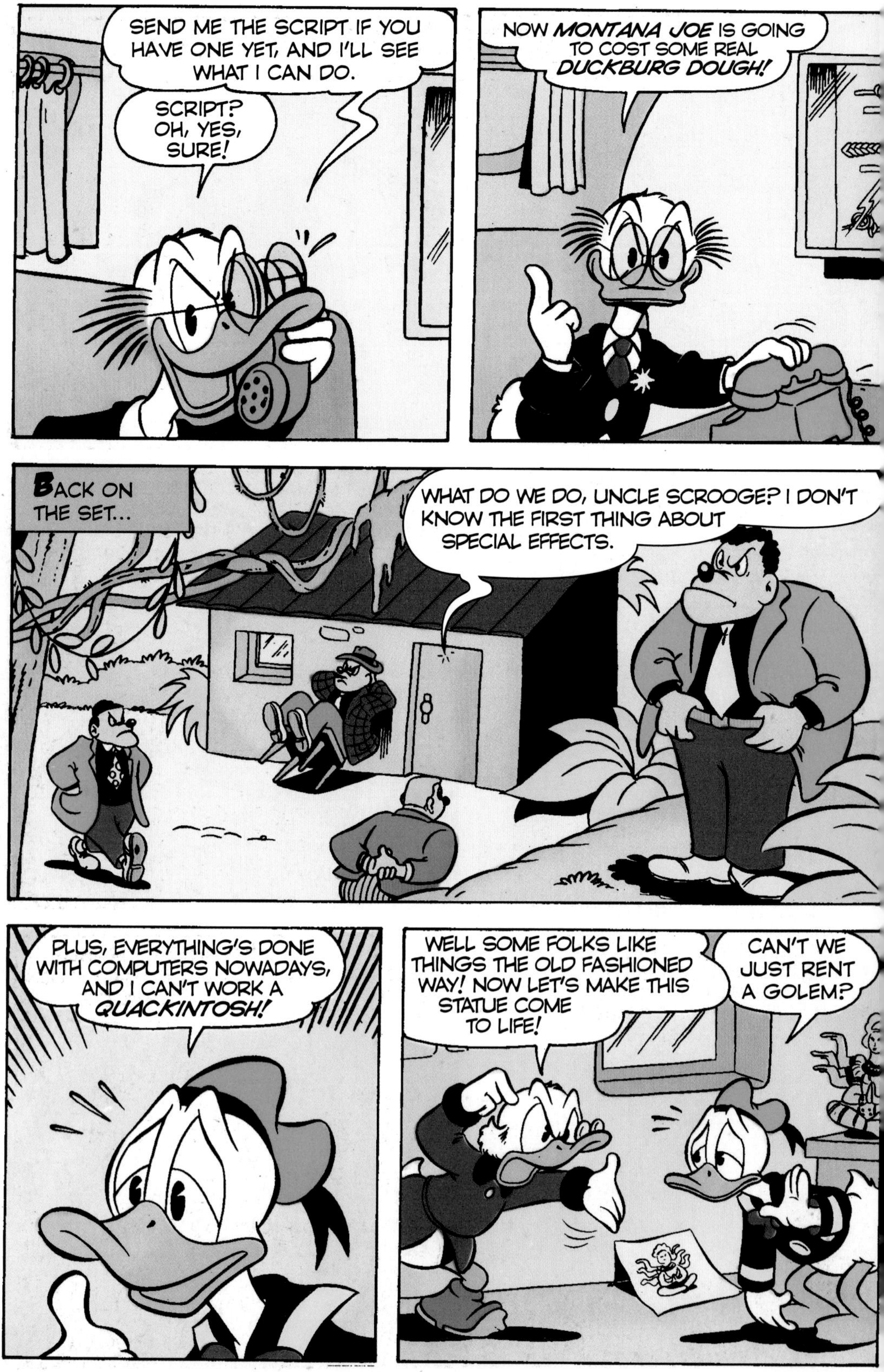
SEND ME THE SCRIPT IF YOU HAVE ONE YET, AND I'LL SEE WHAT I CAN DO.
SCRIPT? OH, YES, SURE!
NOW MONTANA JOE IS GOING TO COST SOME REAL DUCKBURG DOUGH!
BACK ON THE SET...
WHAT DO WE DO, UNCLE SCROOGE? I DON'T KNOW THE FIRST THING ABOUT SPECIAL EFFECTS.
PLUS, EVERYTHING'S DONE WITH COMPUTERS NOWADAYS, AND I CAN'T WORK A QUACKINTOSH!
WELL SOME FOLKS LIKE THINGS THE OLD FASHIONED WAY! NOW LET'S MAKE THIS STATUE COME TO LIFE!
CAN'T WE JUST RENT A GOLEM?

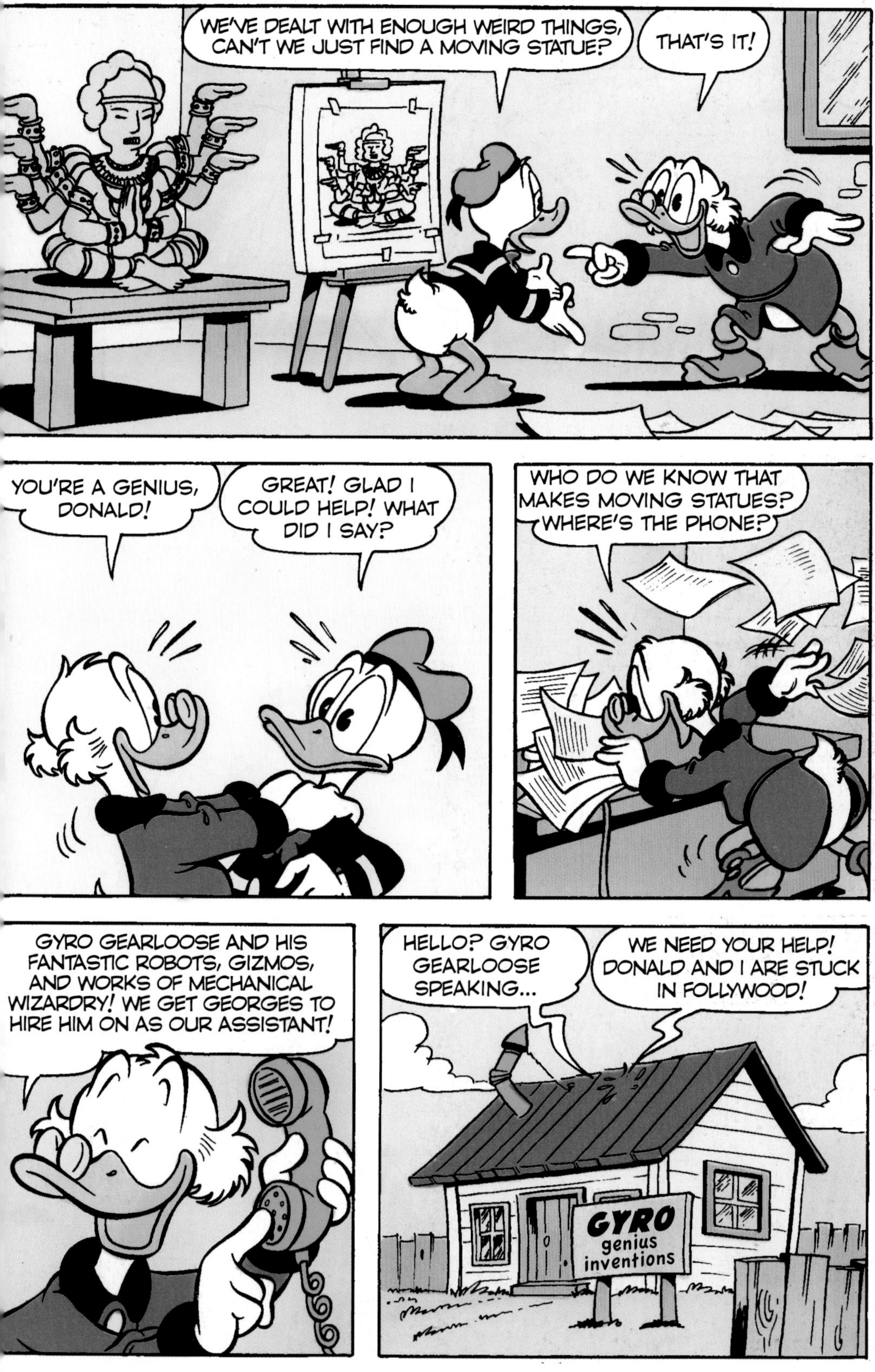
WE'VE DEALT WITH ENOUGH WEIRD THINGS, CAN'T WE JUST FIND A MOVING STATUE?
THAT'S IT!
YOU'RE A GENIUS, DONALD!
GREAT! GLAD I COULD HELP! WHAT DID I SAY?
WHO DO WE KNOW THAT MAKES MOVING STATUES? WHERE'S THE PHONE?
GYRO GEARLOOSE AND HIS FANTASTIC ROBOTS, GIZMOS, AND WORKS OF MECHANICAL WIZARDRY! WE GET GEORGES TO HIRE HIM ON AS OUR ASSISTANT!
HELLO? GYRO GEARLOOSE SPEAKING...
WE NEED YOUR HELP! DONALD AND I ARE STUCK IN FOLLYWOOD!
GYRO genius inventions

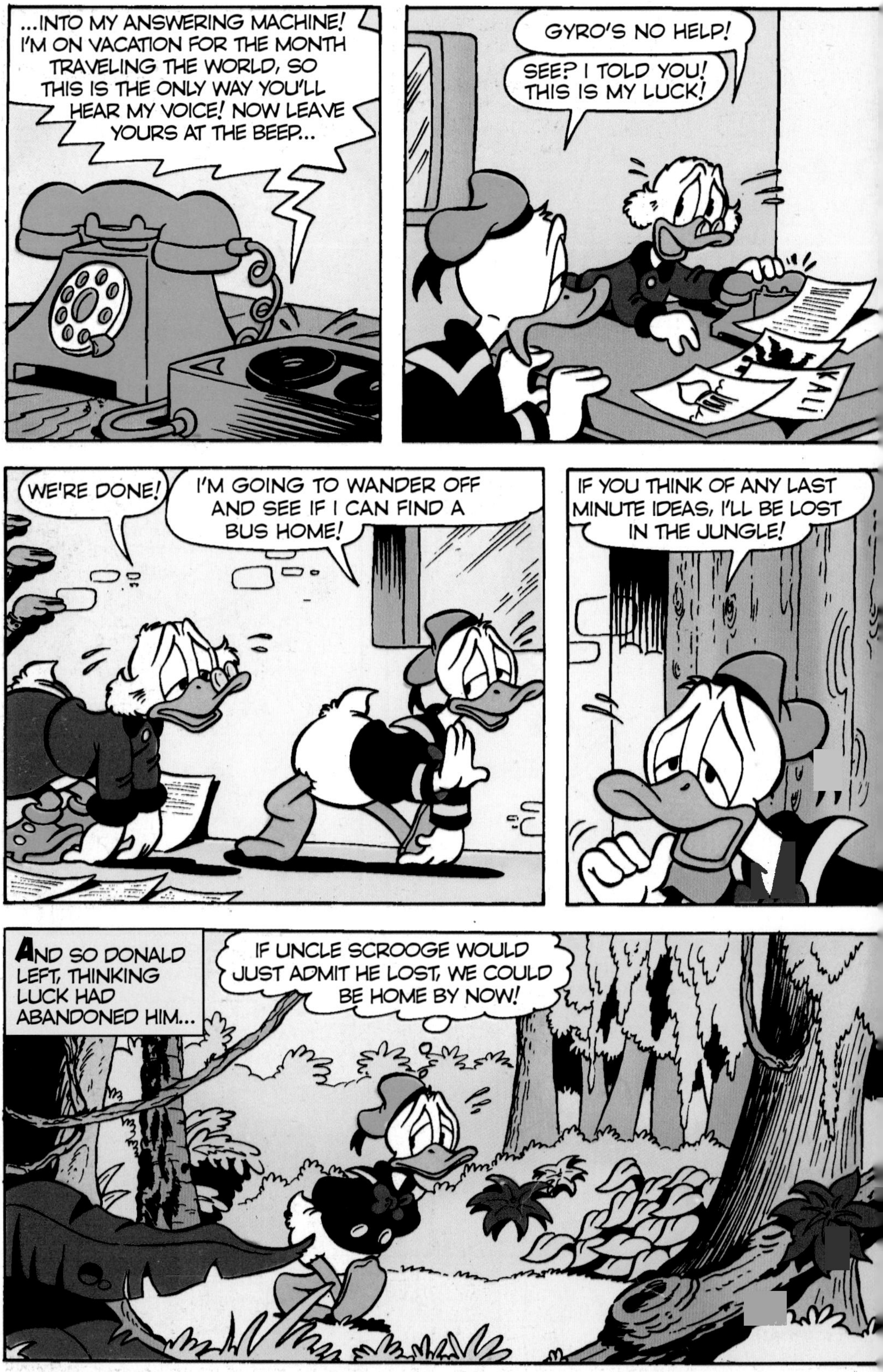
...INTO MY ANSWERING MACHINE! I'M ON VACATION FOR THE MONTH TRAVELING THE WORLD, SO THIS IS THE ONLY WAY YOU'LL HEAR MY VOICE! NOW LEAVE YOURS AT THE BEEP...
GYRO'S NO HELP!
SEE? I TOLD YOU! THIS IS MY LUCK!
WE'RE DONE!
I'M GOING TO WANDER OFF AND SEE IF I CAN FIND A BUS HOME!
IF YOU THINK OF ANY LAST MINUTE IDEAS, I'LL BE LOST IN THE JUNGLE!
AND SO DONALD LEFT, THINKING LUCK HAD ABANDONED HIM...
IF UNCLE SCROOGE WOULD JUST ADMIT HE LOST, WE COULD BE HOME BY NOW!

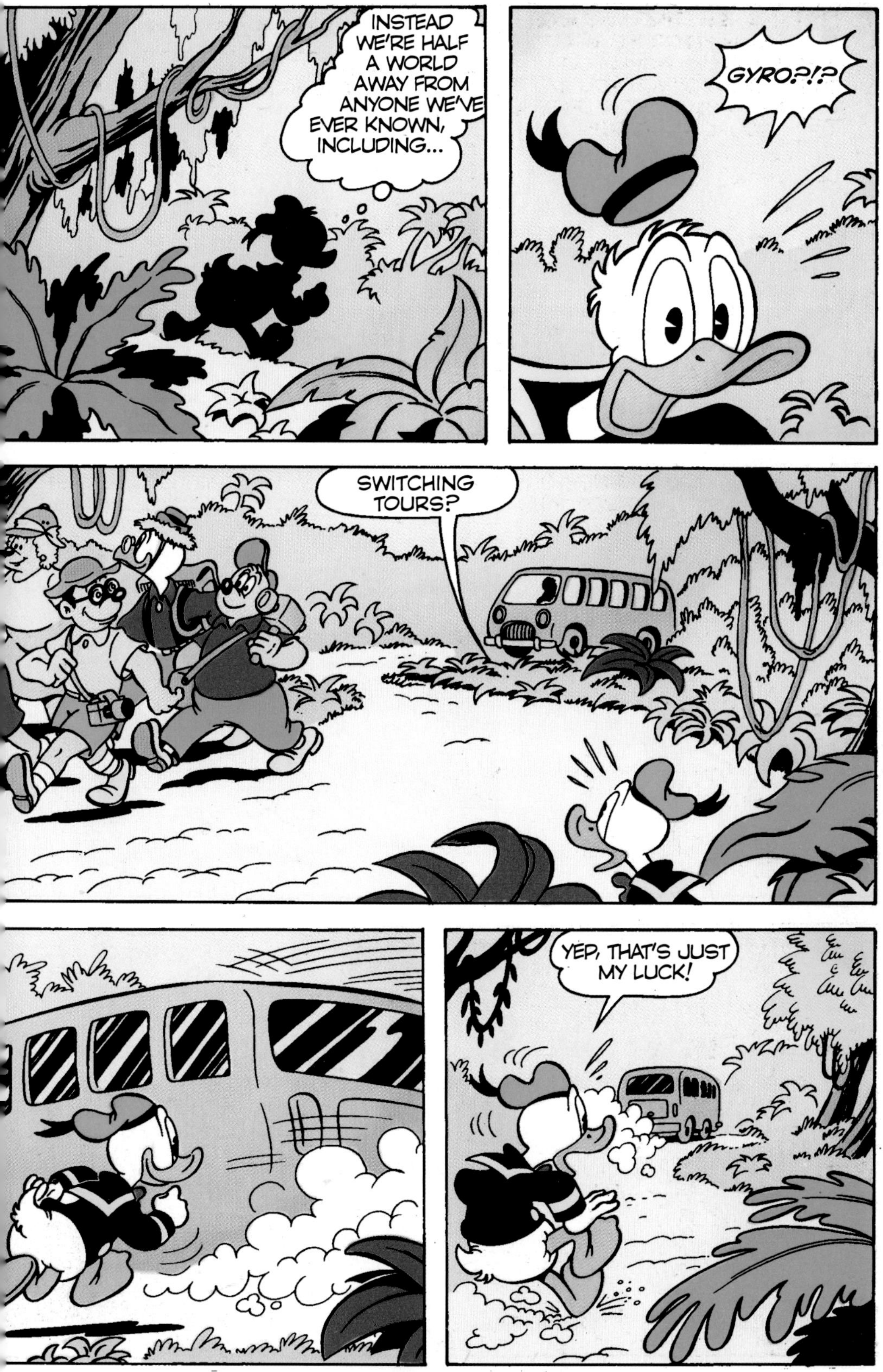
INSTEAD WE'RE HALF A WORLD AWAY FROM ANYONE WE'VE EVER KNOWN, INCLUDING...
GYRO?!?
SWITCHING TOURS?
YEP, THAT'S JUST MY LUCK!

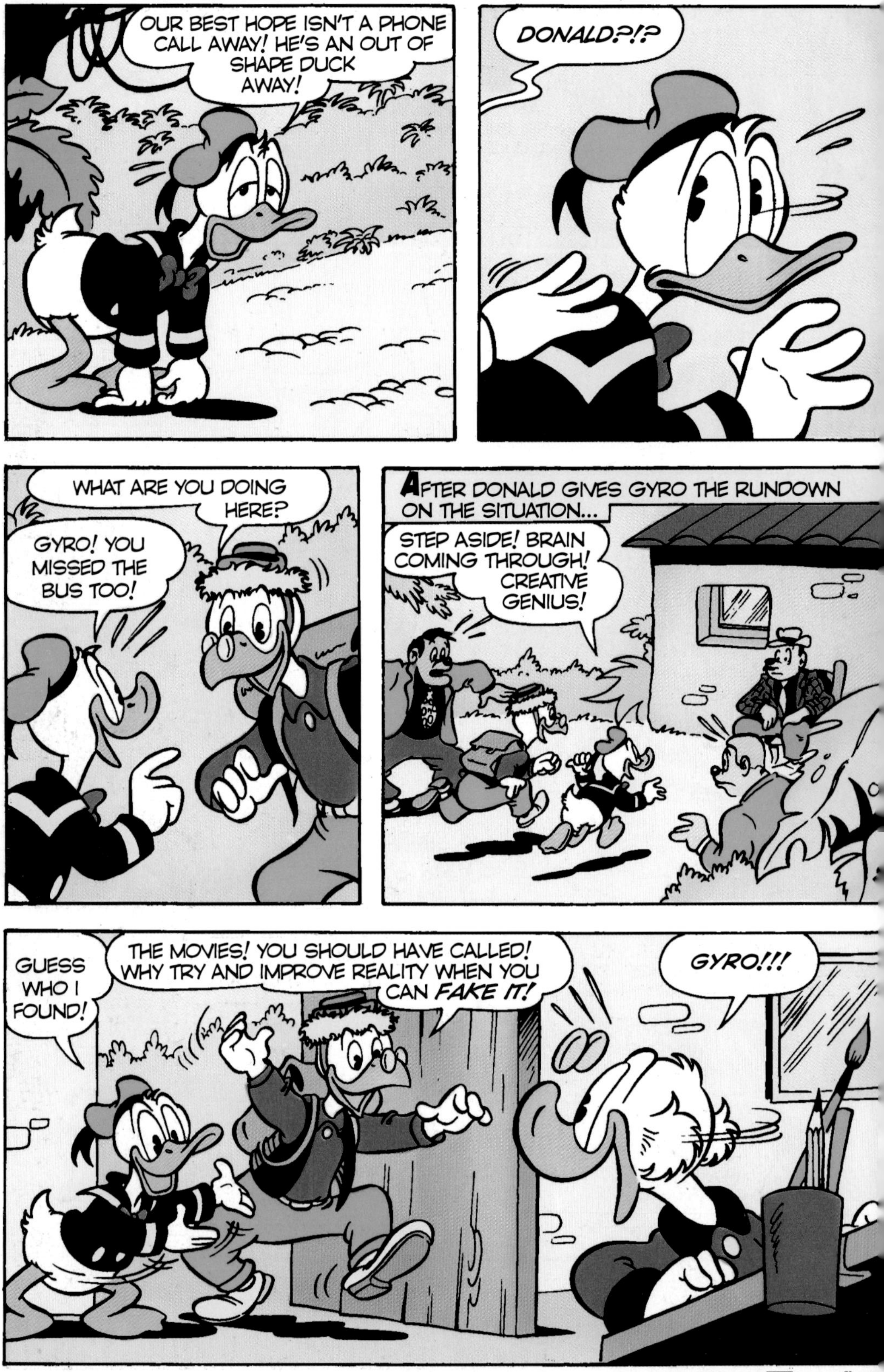
OUR BEST HOPE ISN'T A PHONE CALL AWAY! HE'S AN OUT OF SHAPE DUCK AWAY!
DONALD?!?
WHAT ARE YOU DOING HERE?
GYRO! YOU MISSED THE BUS TOO!
AFTER DONALD GIVES GYRO THE RUNDOWN ON THE SITUATION...
STEP ASIDE! BRAIN COMING THROUGH! CREATIVE GENIUS!
GUESS WHO I FOUND!
THE MOVIES! YOU SHOULD HAVE CALLED! WHY TRY AND IMPROVE REALITY WHEN YOU CAN FAKE IT!
GYRO!!!

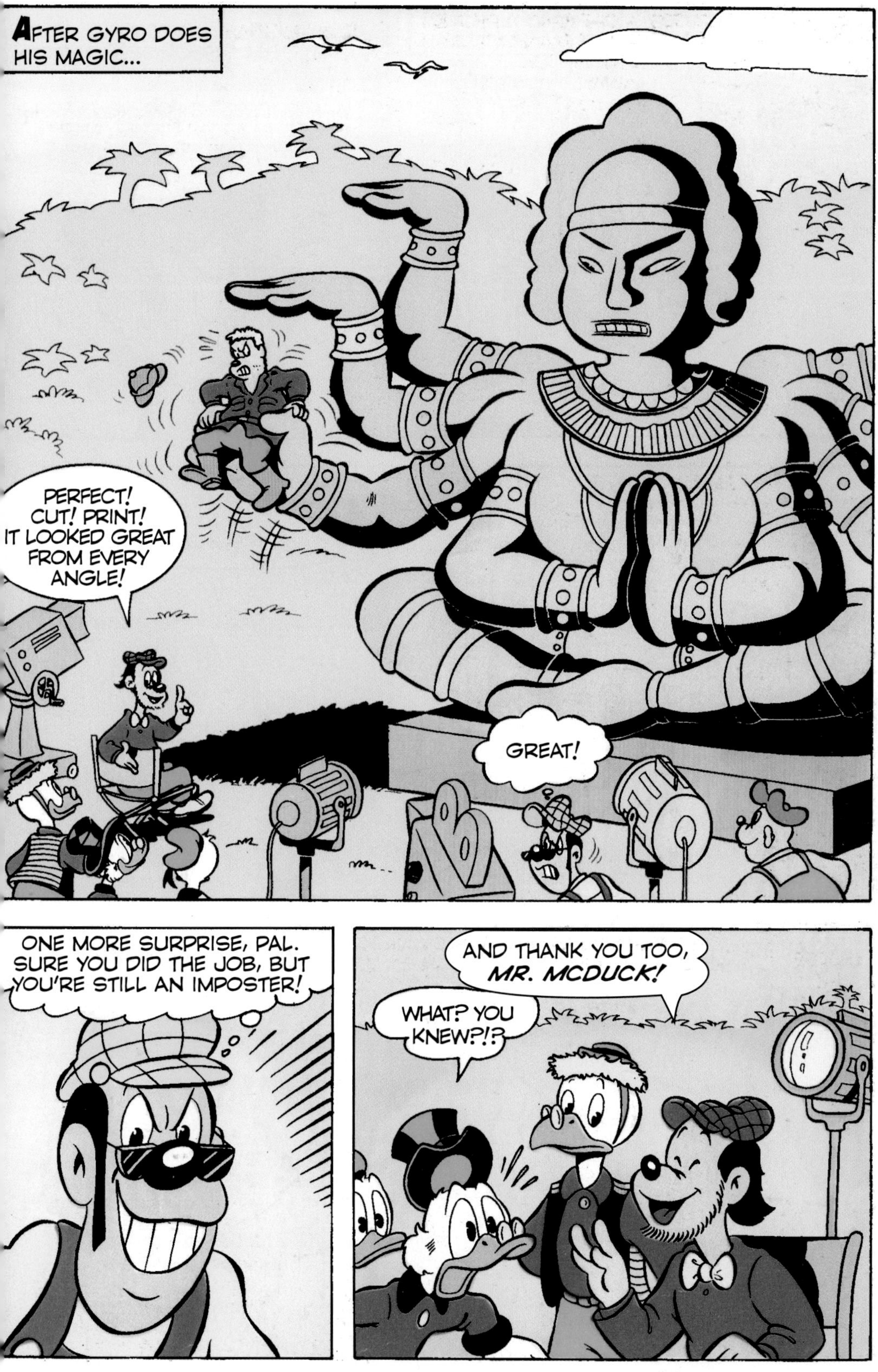
AFTER GYRO DOES HIS MAGIC...
PERFECT! CUT! PRINT! IT LOOKED GREAT FROM EVERY ANGLE!
GREAT!
ONE MORE SURPRISE, PAL. SURE YOU DID THE JOB, BUT YOU'RE STILL AN IMPOSTER!
AND THANK YOU TOO, MR. MCDUCK!
WHAT? YOU KNEW?!?

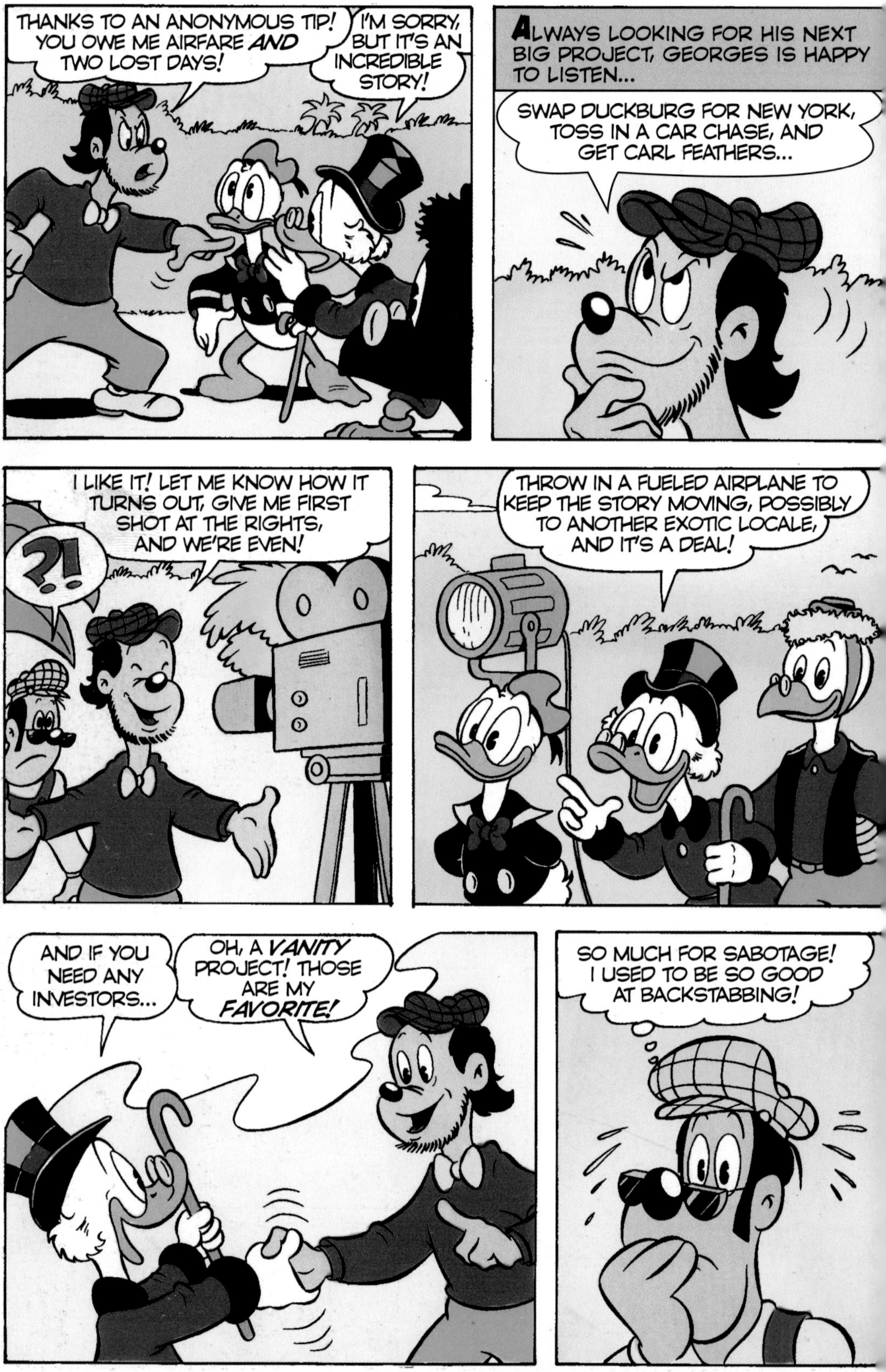
THANKS TO AN ANONYMOUS TIP! YOU OWE ME AIRFARE AND TWO LOST DAYS!
I'M SORRY, BUT IT'S AN INCREDIBLE STORY!
ALWAYS LOOKING FOR HIS NEXT BIG PROJECT, GEORGES IS HAPPY TO LISTEN...
SWAP DUCKBURG FOR NEW YORK, TOSS IN A CAR CHASE, AND GET CARL FEATHERS...
I LIKE IT! LET ME KNOW HOW IT TURNS OUT, GIVE ME FIRST SHOT AT THE RIGHTS, AND WE'RE EVEN!
?!
THROW IN A FUELED AIRPLANE TO KEEP THE STORY MOVING, POSSIBLY TO ANOTHER EXOTIC LOCALE, AND IT'S A DEAL!
AND IF YOU NEED ANY INVESTORS...
OH, A VANITY PROJECT! THOSE ARE MY FAVORITE!
SO MUCH FOR SABOTAGE! I USED TO BE SO GOOD AT BACKSTABBING!

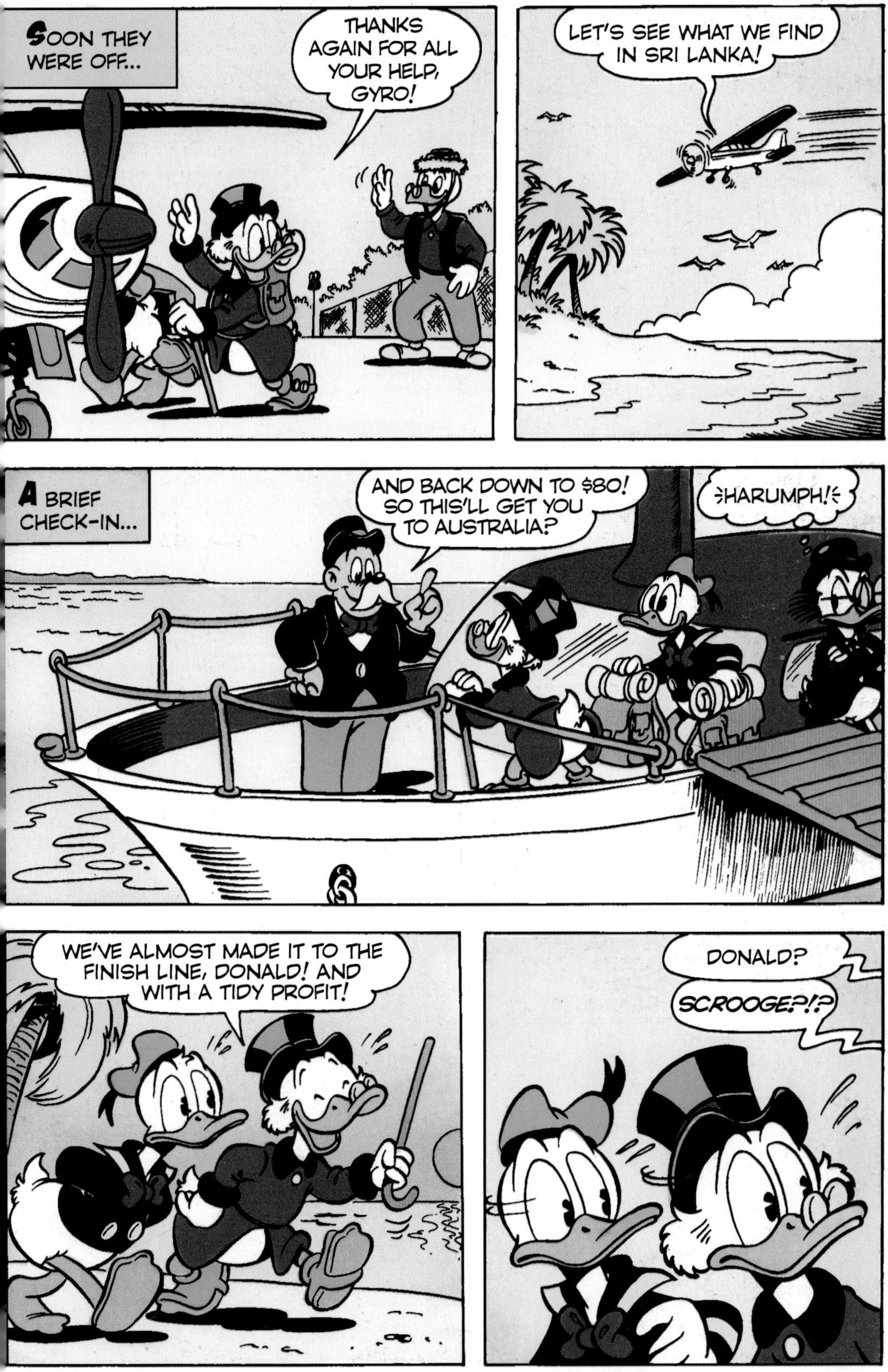
SOON THEY WERE OFF...
THANKS AGAIN FOR ALL YOUR HELP, GYRO!
LET'S SEE WHAT WE FIND IN SRI LANKA!
A BRIEF CHECK-IN...
AND BACK DOWN TO $80! SO THIS'LL GET YOU TO AUSTRALIA?
HARUMPH!
WE'VE ALMOST MADE IT TO THE FINISH LINE, DONALD! AND WITH A TIDY PROFIT!
DONALD?
SCROOGE?!?

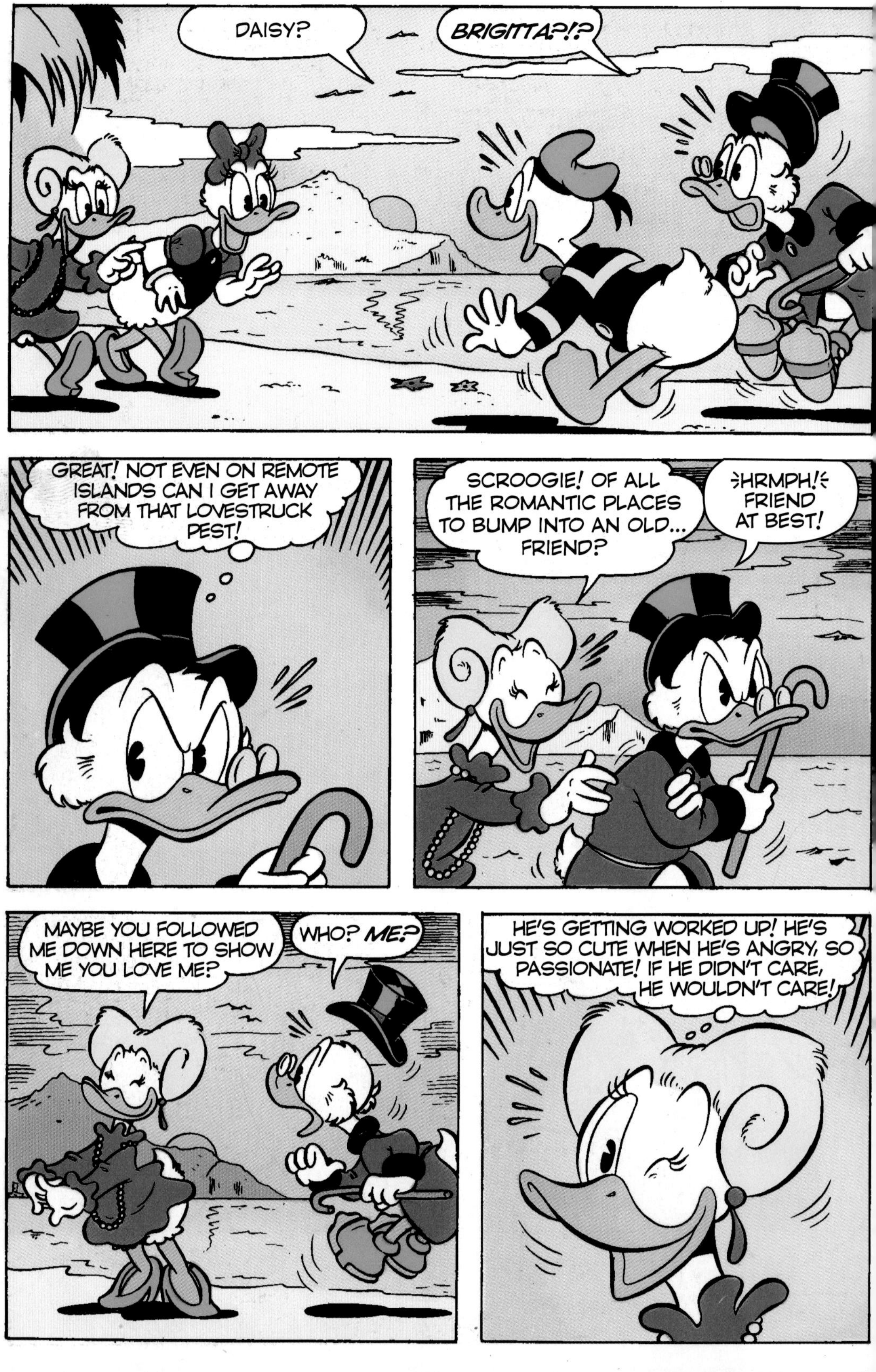
DAISY?
BRIGITTA?!?
GREAT! NOT EVEN ON REMOTE ISLANDS CAN I GET AWAY FROM THAT LOVESTRUCK PEST!
SCROOGIE! OF ALL THE ROMANTIC PLACES TO BUMP INTO AN OLD... FRIEND?
HRMPH! FRIEND AT BEST!
MAYBE YOU FOLLOWED ME DOWN HERE TO SHOW ME YOU LOVE ME?
WHO? ME?
HE'S GETTING WORKED UP! HE'S JUST SO CUTE WHEN HE'S ANGRY, SO PASSIONATE! IF HE DIDN'T CARE, HE WOULDN'T CARE!

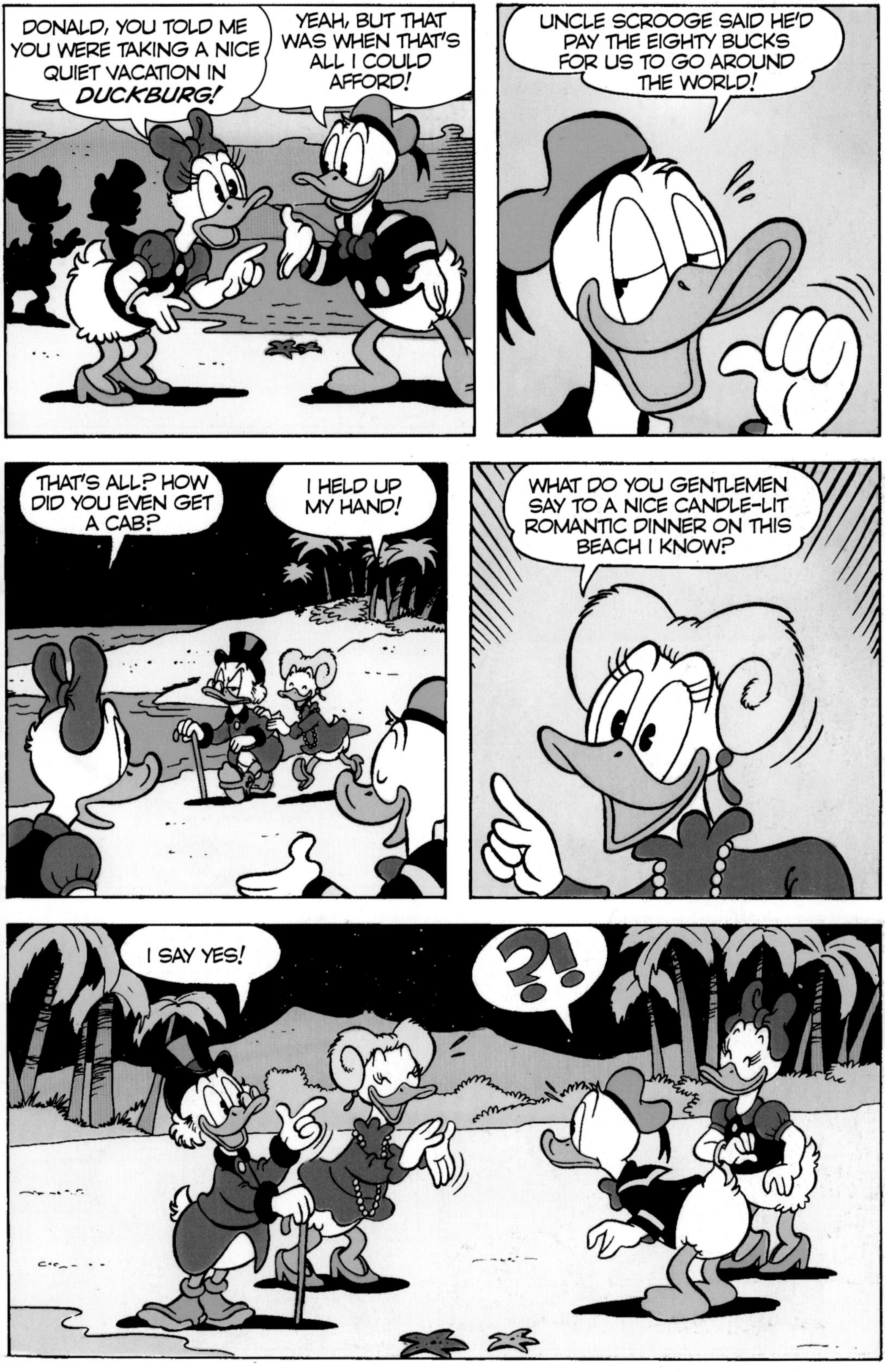
DONALD, YOU TOLD ME YOU WERE TAKING A NICE QUIET VACATION IN DUCKBURG!
YEAH, BUT THAT WAS WHEN THAT'S ALL I COULD AFFORD!
UNCLE SCROOGE SAID HE'D PAY THE EIGHTY BUCKS FOR US TO GO AROUND THE WORLD!
THAT'S ALL? HOW DID YOU EVEN GET A CAB?
I HELD UP MY HAND!
WHAT DO YOU GENTLEMEN SAY TO A NICE CANDLE-LIT ROMANTIC DINNER ON THIS BEACH I KNOW?
I SAY YES!
?!

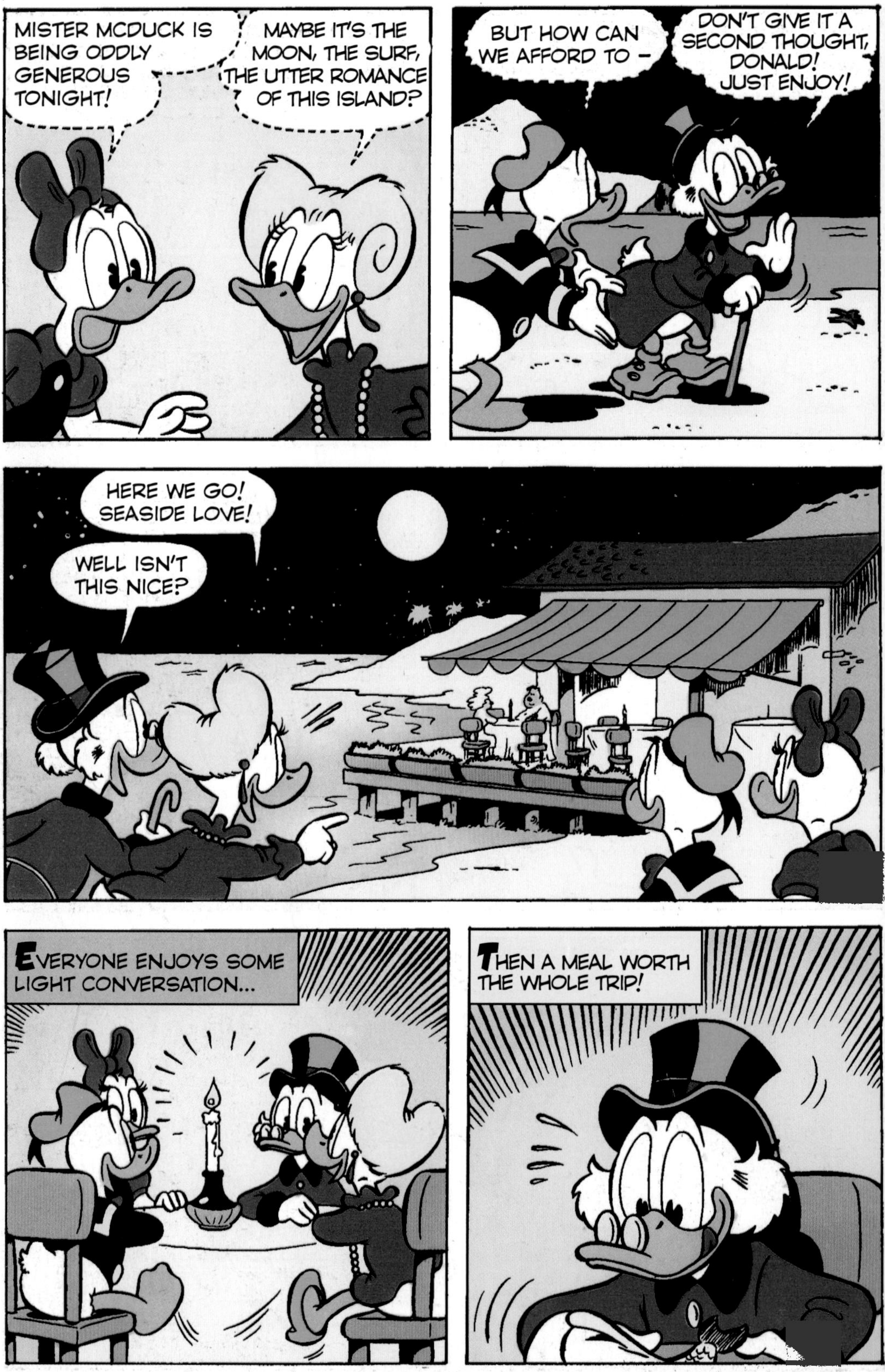
MISTER MCDUCK IS BEING ODDLY GENEROUS TONIGHT!
MAYBE IT'S THE MOON, THE SURF, THE UTTER ROMANCE OF THIS ISLAND?
BUT HOW CAN WE AFFORD TO –
DON'T GIVE IT A SECOND THOUGHT, DONALD! JUST ENJOY!
HERE WE GO! SEASIDE LOVE!
WELL ISN'T THIS NICE?
EVERYONE ENJOYS SOME LIGHT CONVERSATION...
THEN A MEAL WORTH THE WHOLE TRIP!

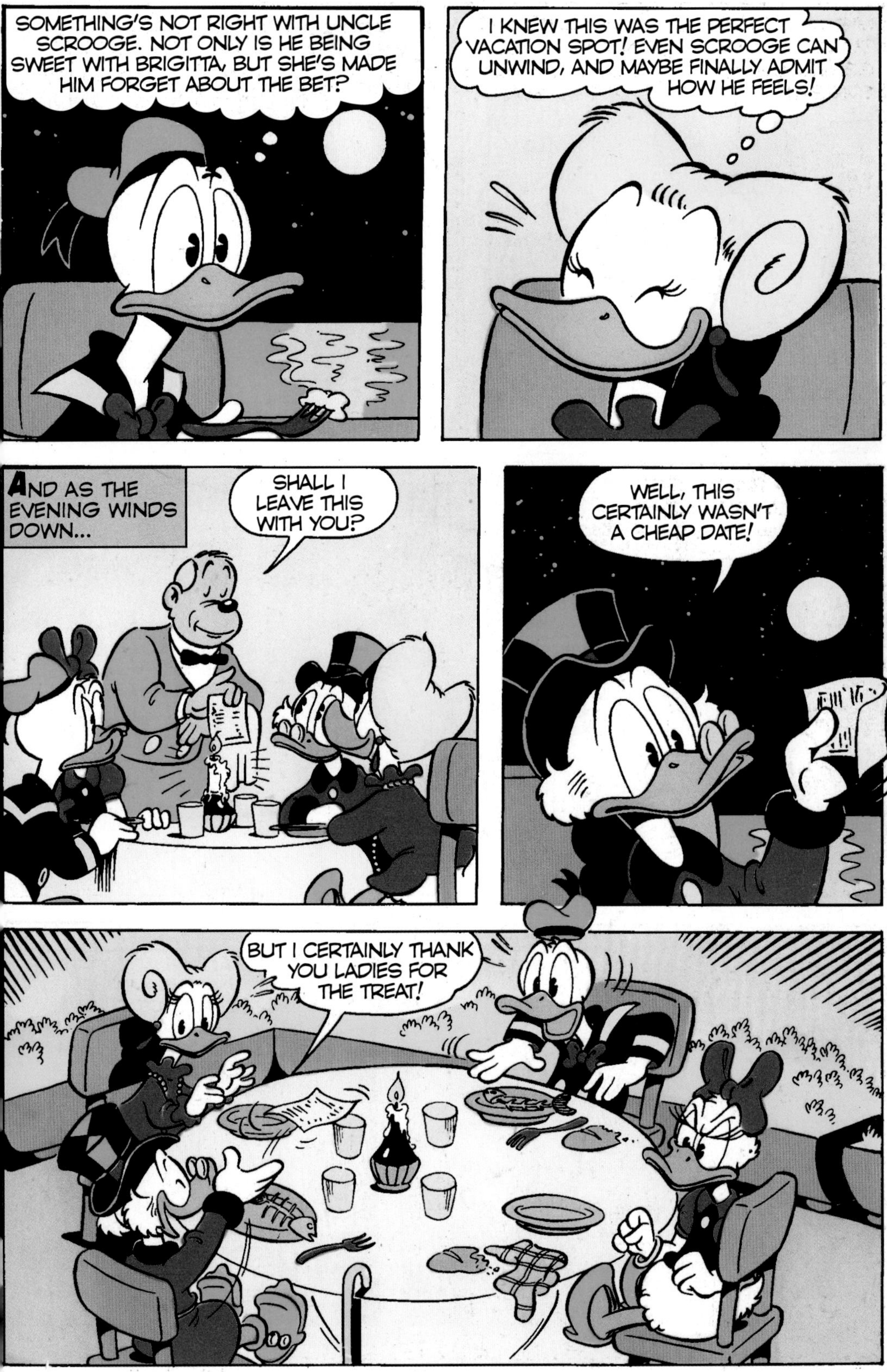
SOMETHING'S NOT RIGHT WITH UNCLE SCROOGE. NOT ONLY IS HE BEING SWEET WITH BRIGITTA, BUT SHE'S MADE HIM FORGET ABOUT THE BET?
I KNEW THIS WAS THE PERFECT VACATION SPOT! EVEN SCROOGE CAN UNWIND, AND MAYBE FINALLY ADMIT HOW HE FEELS!
AND AS THE EVENING WINDS DOWN...
SHALL I LEAVE THIS WITH YOU?
WELL, THIS CERTAINLY WASN'T A CHEAP DATE!
BUT I CERTAINLY THANK YOU LADIES FOR THE TREAT!

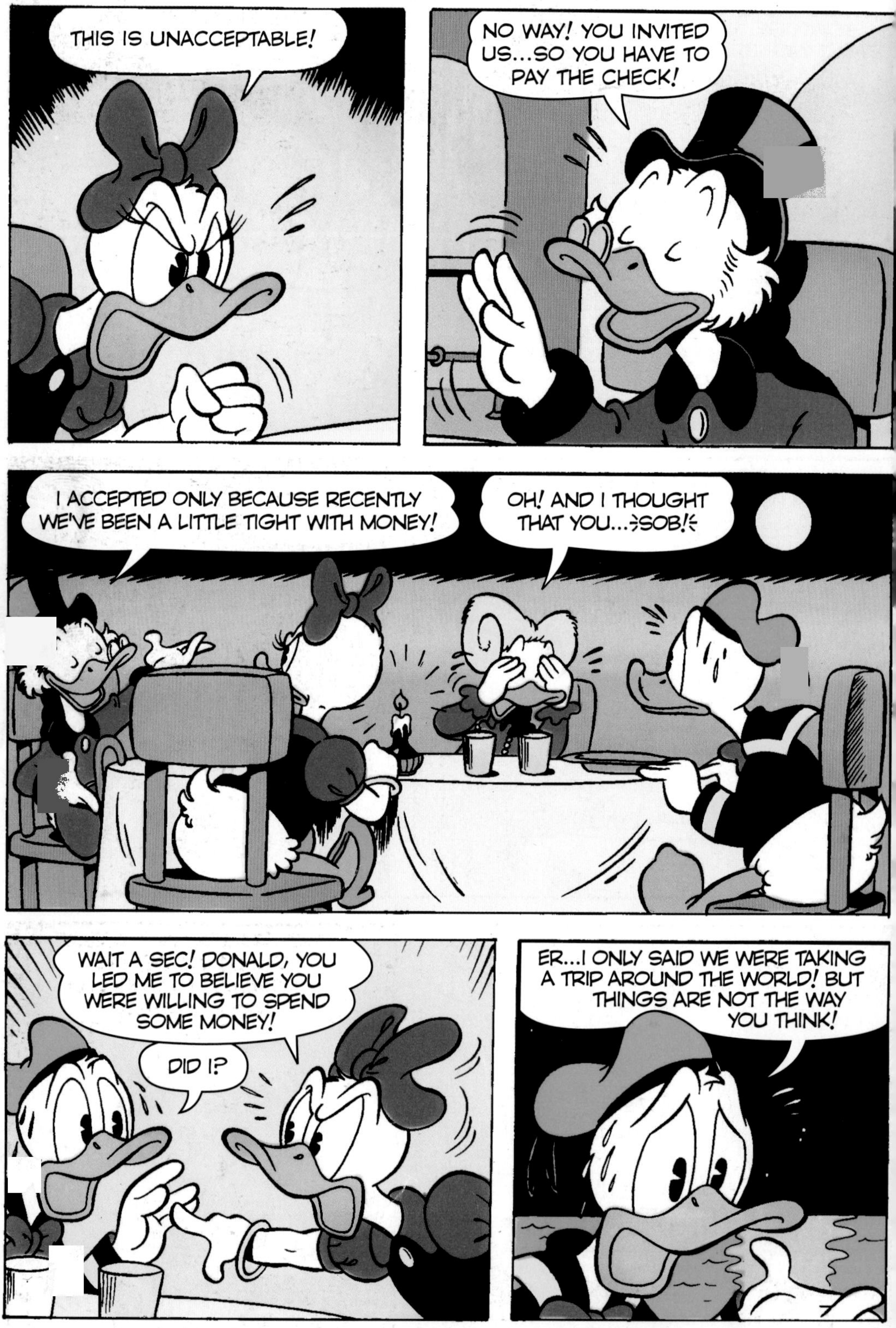

THIS IS UNACCEPTABLE!
NO WAY! YOU INVITED US...SO YOU HAVE TO PAY THE CHECK!
I ACCEPTED ONLY BECAUSE RECENTLY WE'VE BEEN A LITTLE TIGHT WITH MONEY!
OH! AND I THOUGHT THAT YOU... SOB!
WAIT A SEC! DONALD, YOU LED ME TO BELIEVE YOU WERE WILLING TO SPEND SOME MONEY!
DID I?
ER...I ONLY SAID WE WERE TAKING A TRIP AROUND THE WORLD! BUT THINGS ARE NOT THE WAY YOU THINK!

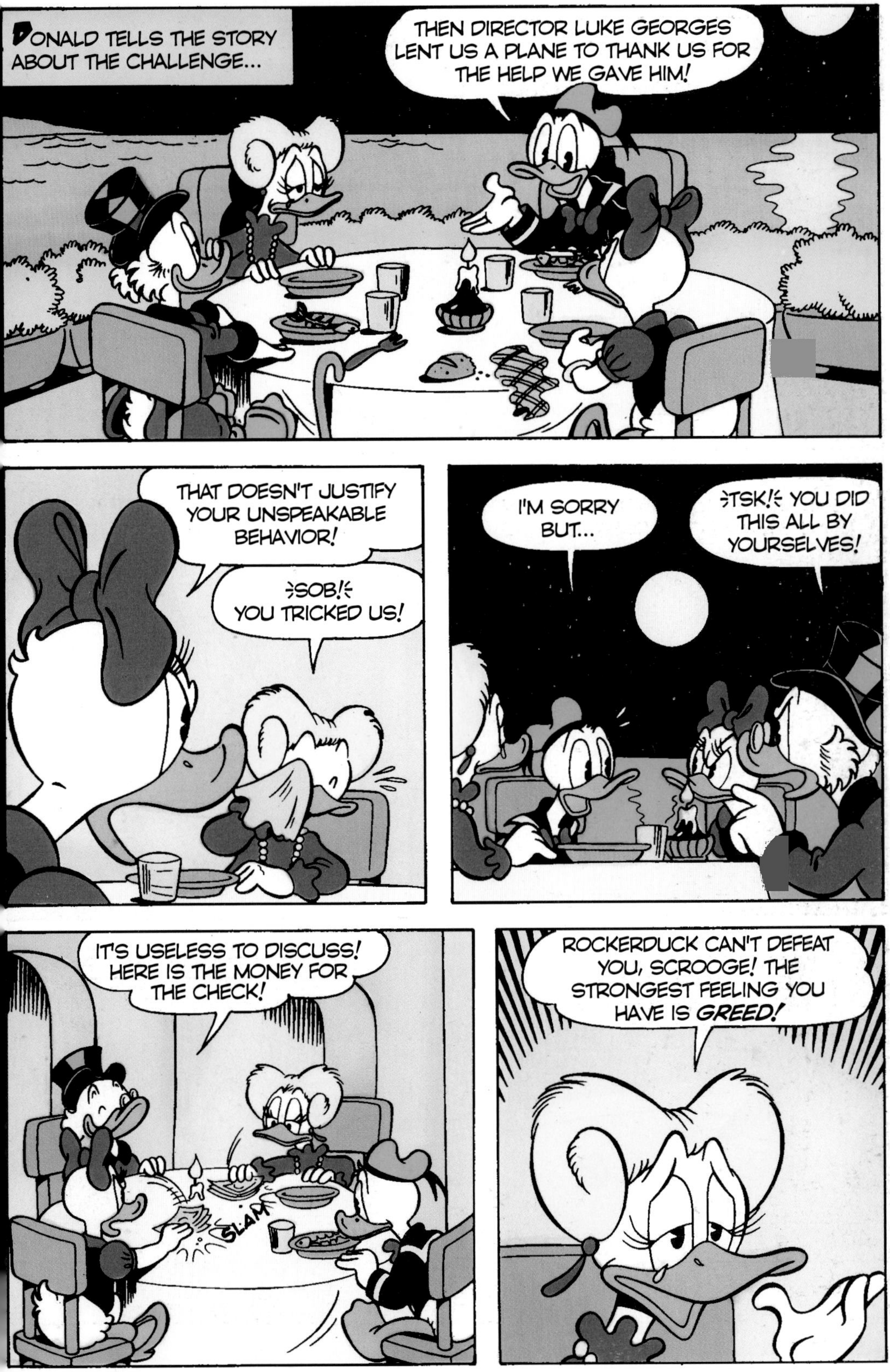
DONALD TELLS THE STORY ABOUT THE CHALLENGE...
THEN DIRECTOR LUKE GEORGES LENT US A PLANE TO THANK US FOR THE HELP WE GAVE HIM!
THAT DOESN'T JUSTIFY YOUR UNSPEAKABLE BEHAVIOR!
SOB! YOU TRICKED US!
I'M SORRY BUT...
TSK! YOU DID THIS ALL BY YOURSELVES!
IT'S USELESS TO DISCUSS! HERE IS THE MONEY FOR THE CHECK!
SLAM
ROCKERDUCK CAN'T DEFEAT YOU, SCROOGE! THE STRONGEST FEELING YOU HAVE IS GREED!

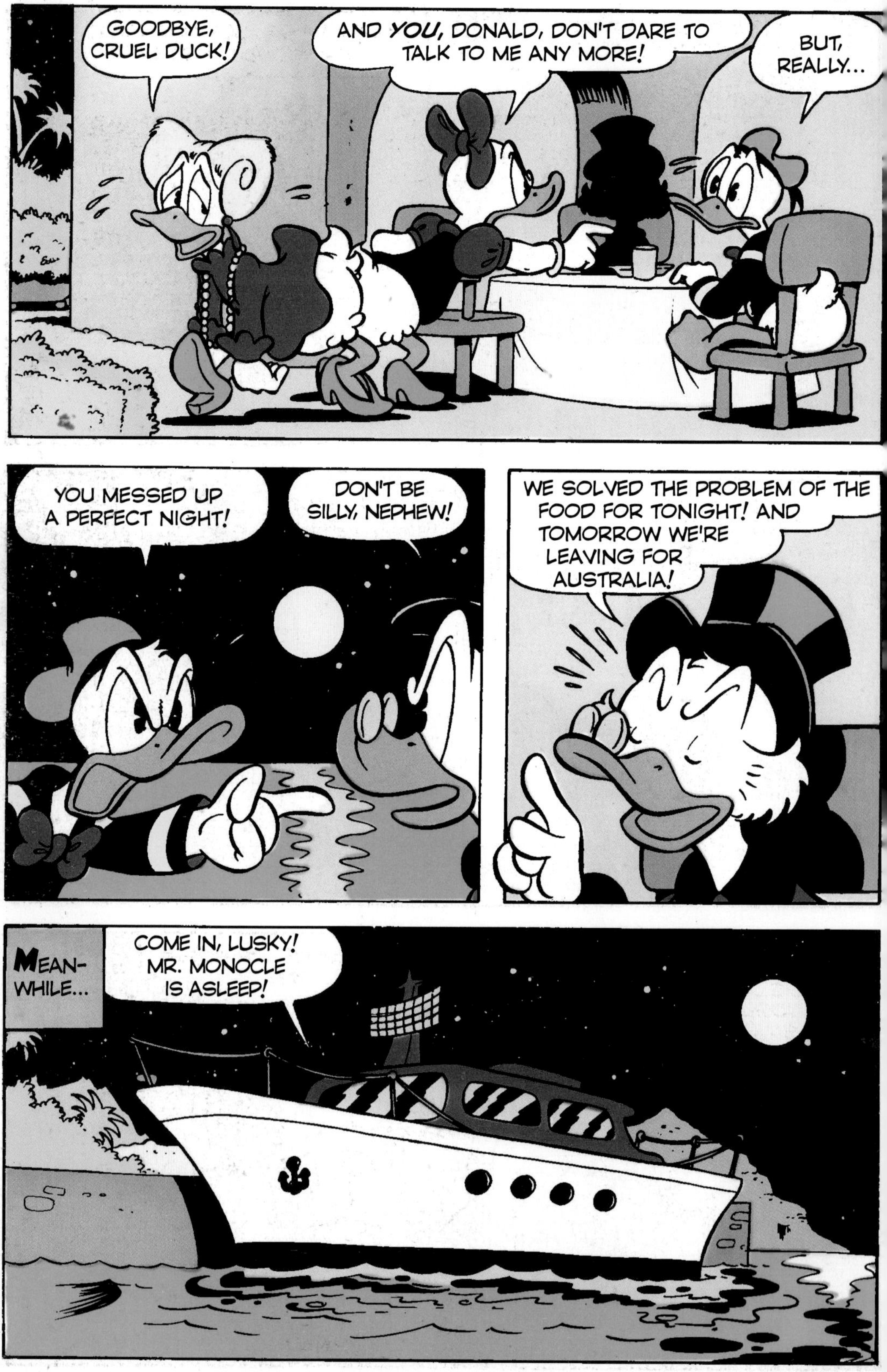
GOODBYE, CRUEL DUCK!
AND *YOU*, DONALD, DON'T DARE TO TALK TO ME ANY MORE!
BUT, REALLY...
YOU MESSED UP A PERFECT NIGHT!
DON'T BE SILLY, NEPHEW!
WE SOLVED THE PROBLEM OF THE FOOD FOR TONIGHT! AND TOMORROW WE'RE LEAVING FOR AUSTRALIA!
MEANWHILE...
COME IN, LUSKY! MR. MONOCLE IS ASLEEP!

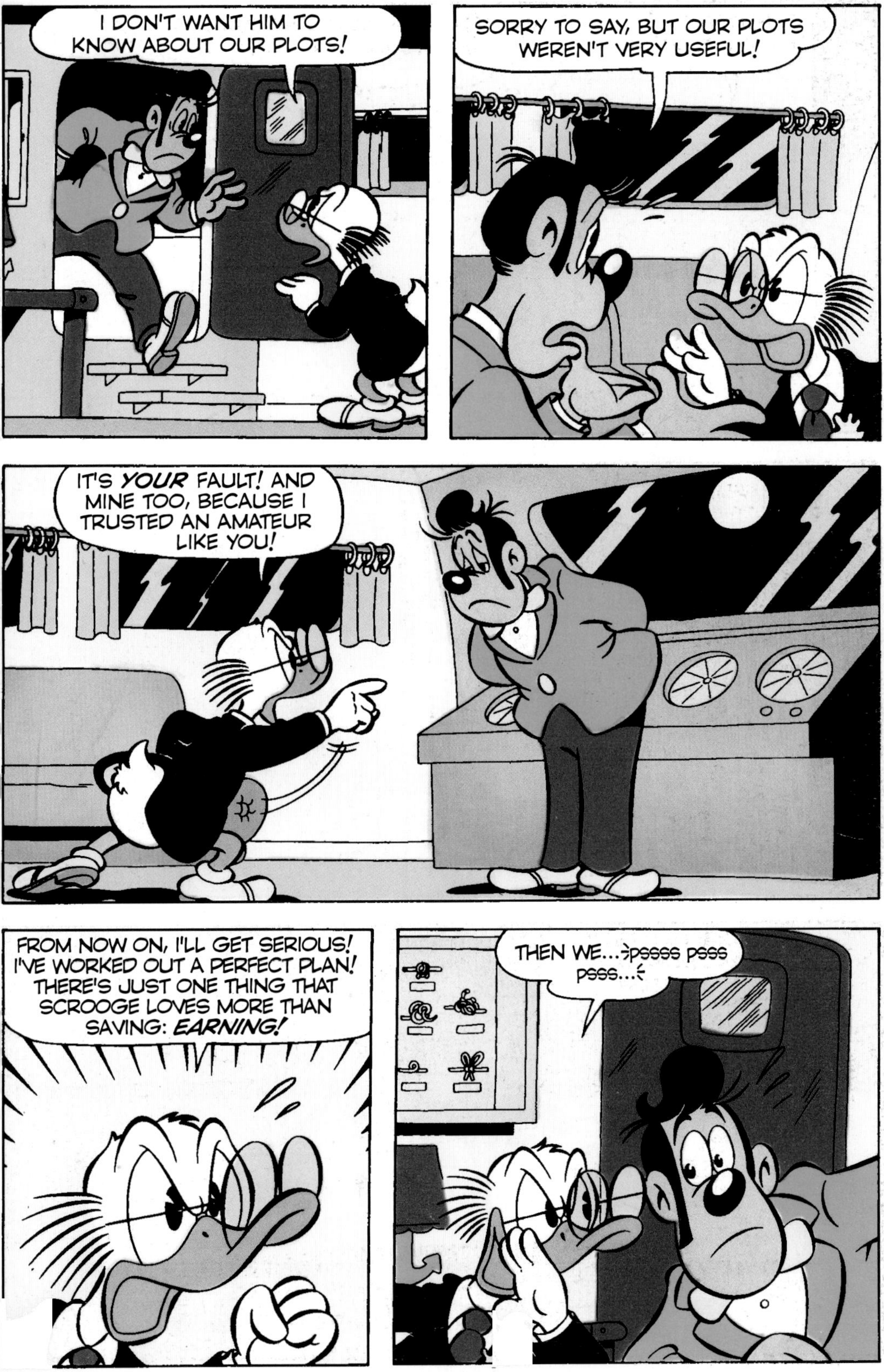
I DON'T WANT HIM TO KNOW ABOUT OUR PLOTS!
SORRY TO SAY, BUT OUR PLOTS WEREN'T VERY USEFUL!
IT'S *YOUR* FAULT! AND MINE TOO, BECAUSE I TRUSTED AN AMATEUR LIKE YOU!
FROM NOW ON, I'LL GET SERIOUS! I'VE WORKED OUT A PERFECT PLAN! THERE'S JUST ONE THING THAT SCROOGE LOVES MORE THAN SAVING: *EARNING!*
THEN WE... pssss psss psss...

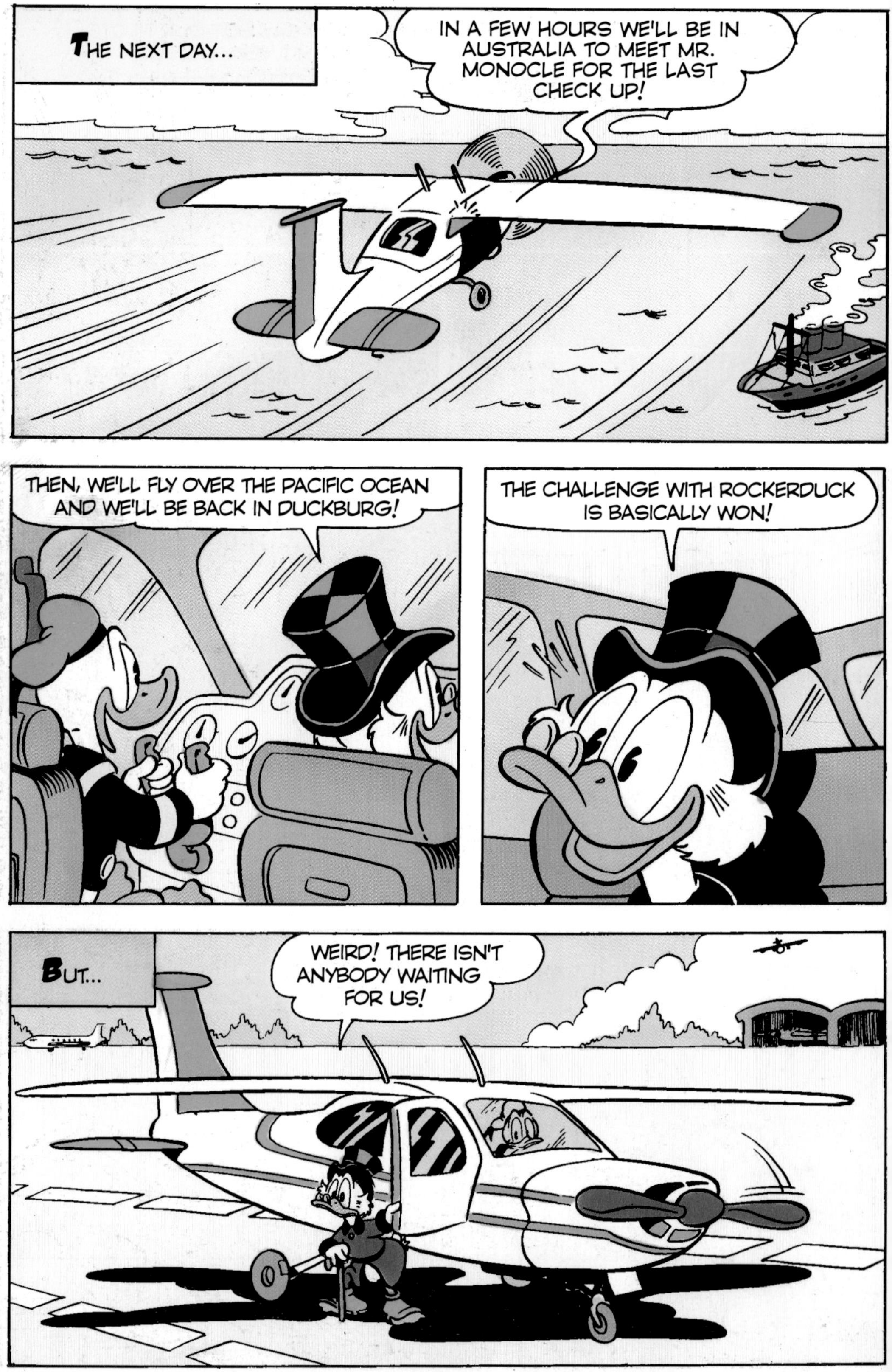
THE NEXT DAY...
IN A FEW HOURS WE'LL BE IN AUSTRALIA TO MEET MR. MONOCLE FOR THE LAST CHECK UP!
THEN, WE'LL FLY OVER THE PACIFIC OCEAN AND WE'LL BE BACK IN DUCKBURG!
THE CHALLENGE WITH ROCKERDUCK IS BASICALLY WON!
BUT...
WEIRD! THERE ISN'T ANYBODY WAITING FOR US!

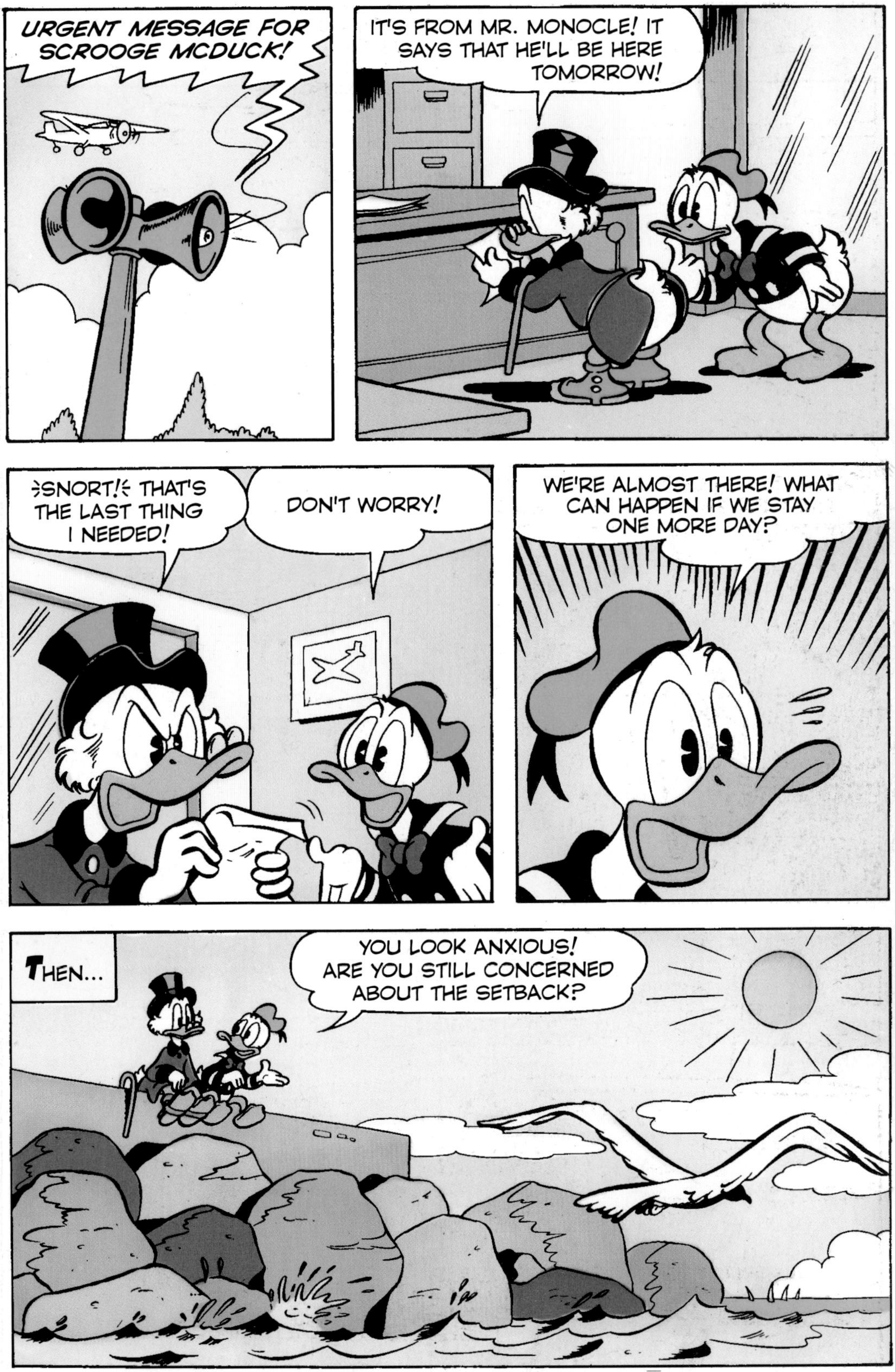
URGENT MESSAGE FOR SCROOGE MCDUCK!
IT'S FROM MR. MONOCLE! IT SAYS THAT HE'LL BE HERE TOMORROW!
*SNORT!* THAT'S THE LAST THING I NEEDED!
DON'T WORRY!
WE'RE ALMOST THERE! WHAT CAN HAPPEN IF WE STAY ONE MORE DAY?
THEN...
YOU LOOK ANXIOUS! ARE YOU STILL CONCERNED ABOUT THE SETBACK?

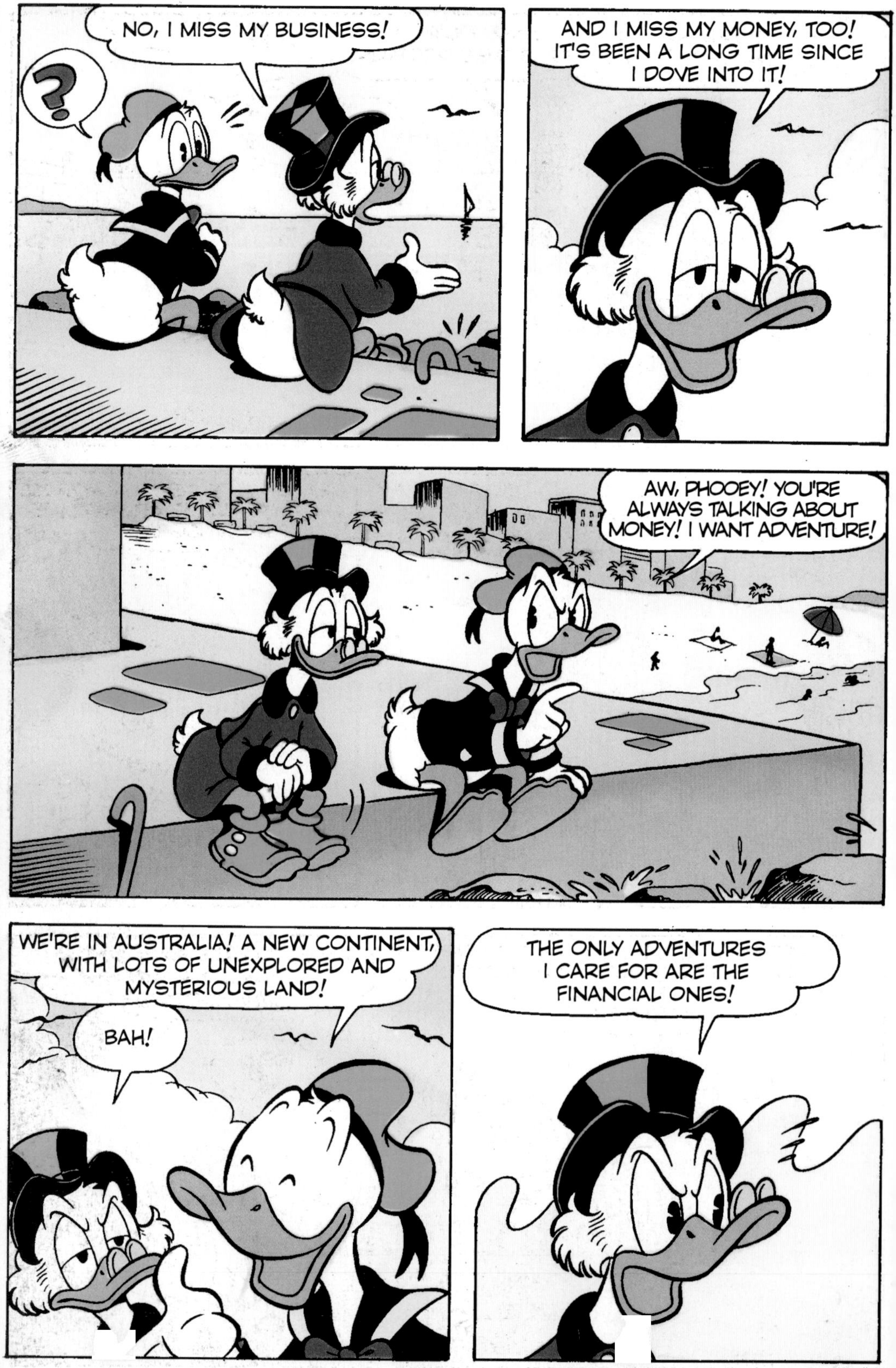
NO, I MISS MY BUSINESS!
?
AND I MISS MY MONEY, TOO! IT'S BEEN A LONG TIME SINCE I DOVE INTO IT!
AW, PHOOEY! YOU'RE ALWAYS TALKING ABOUT MONEY! I WANT ADVENTURE!
WE'RE IN AUSTRALIA! A NEW CONTINENT, WITH LOTS OF UNEXPLORED AND MYSTERIOUS LAND!
BAH!
THE ONLY ADVENTURES I CARE FOR ARE THE FINANCIAL ONES!

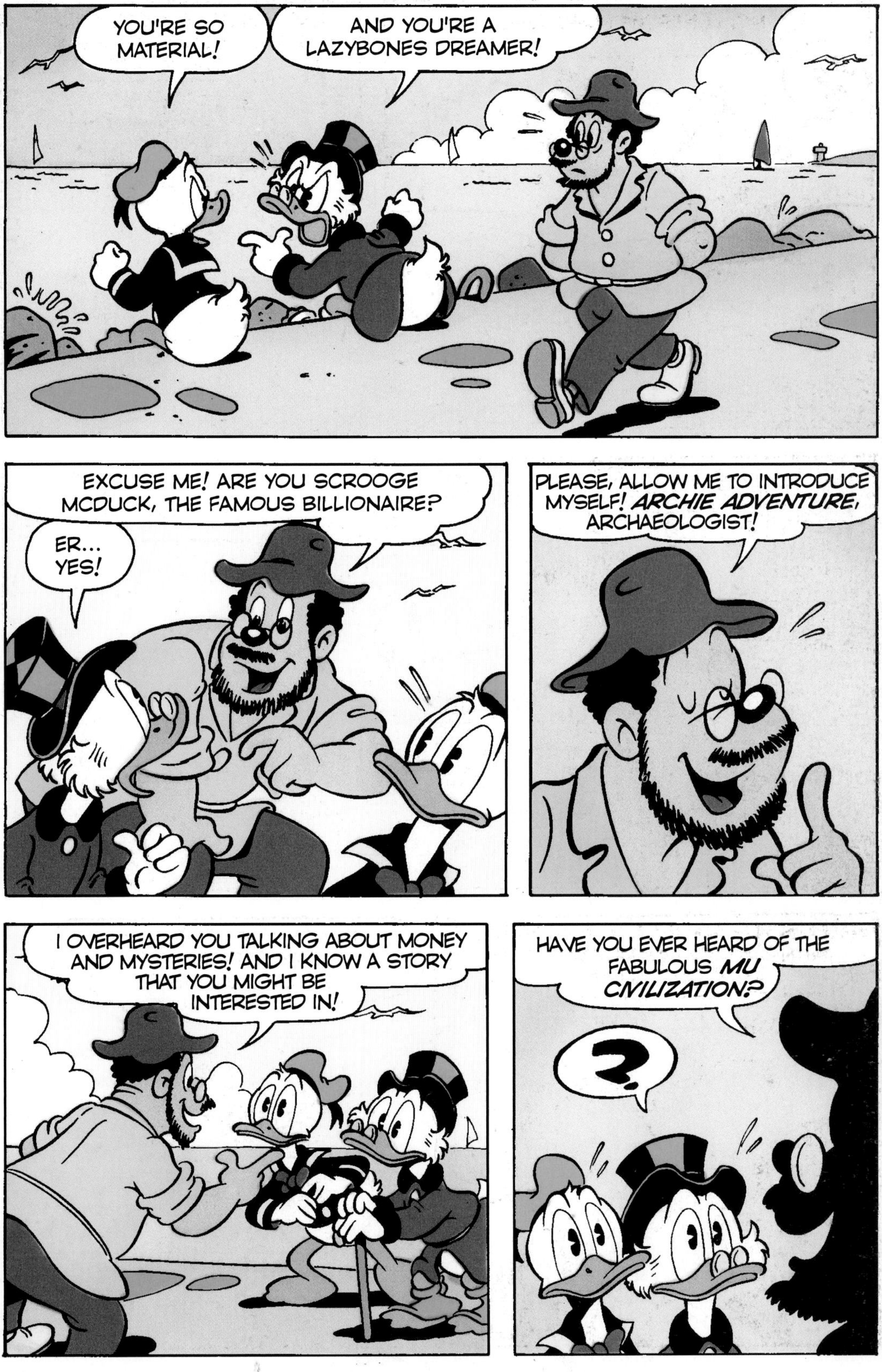
YOU'RE SO MATERIAL!
AND YOU'RE A LAZYBONES DREAMER!
EXCUSE ME! ARE YOU SCROOGE MCDUCK, THE FAMOUS BILLIONAIRE?
ER... YES!
PLEASE, ALLOW ME TO INTRODUCE MYSELF! ARCHIE ADVENTURE, ARCHAEOLOGIST!
I OVERHEARD YOU TALKING ABOUT MONEY AND MYSTERIES! AND I KNOW A STORY THAT YOU MIGHT BE INTERESTED IN!
HAVE YOU EVER HEARD OF THE FABULOUS MU CIVILIZATION?
?

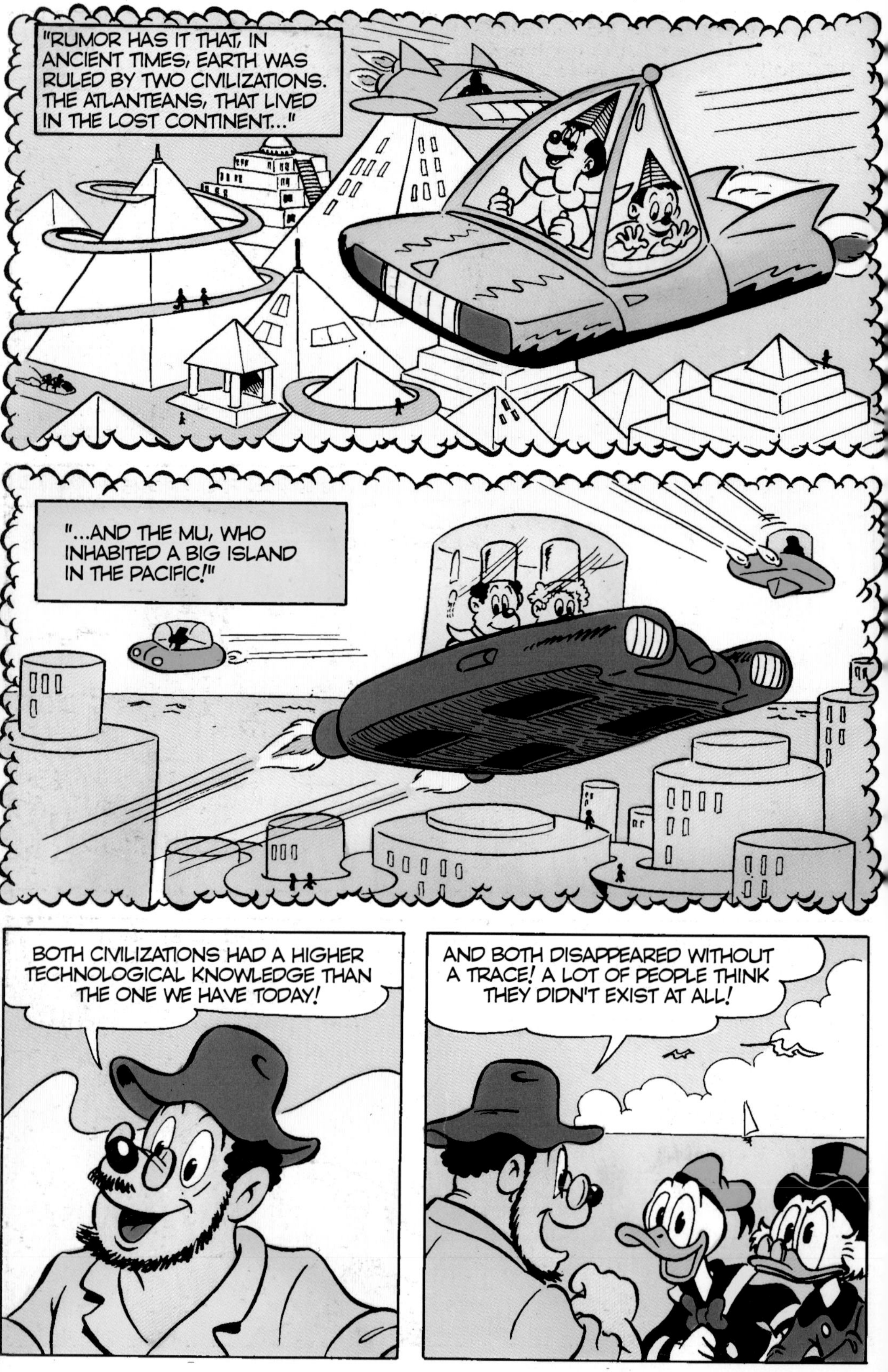
"RUMOR HAS IT THAT, IN ANCIENT TIMES, EARTH WAS RULED BY TWO CIVILIZATIONS. THE ATLANTEANS, THAT LIVED IN THE LOST CONTINENT..."
"...AND THE MU, WHO INHABITED A BIG ISLAND IN THE PACIFIC!"
BOTH CIVILIZATIONS HAD A HIGHER TECHNOLOGICAL KNOWLEDGE THAN THE ONE WE HAVE TODAY!
AND BOTH DISAPPEARED WITHOUT A TRACE! A LOT OF PEOPLE THINK THEY DIDN'T EXIST AT ALL!

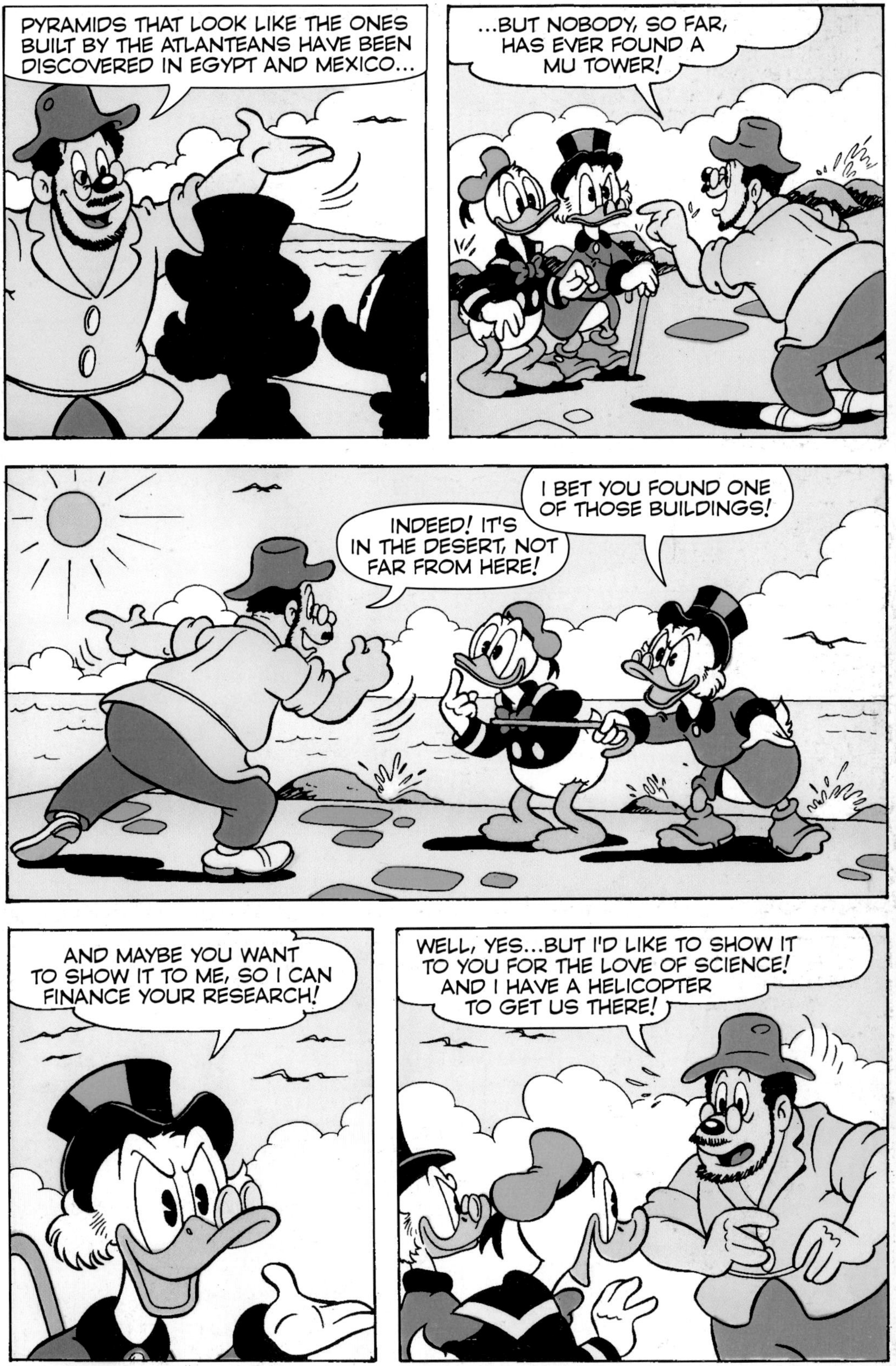
PYRAMIDS THAT LOOK LIKE THE ONES BUILT BY THE ATLANTEANS HAVE BEEN DISCOVERED IN EGYPT AND MEXICO...
...BUT NOBODY, SO FAR, HAS EVER FOUND A MU TOWER!
I BET YOU FOUND ONE OF THOSE BUILDINGS!
INDEED! IT'S IN THE DESERT, NOT FAR FROM HERE!
AND MAYBE YOU WANT TO SHOW IT TO ME, SO I CAN FINANCE YOUR RESEARCH!
WELL, YES...BUT I'D LIKE TO SHOW IT TO YOU FOR THE LOVE OF SCIENCE! AND I HAVE A HELICOPTER TO GET US THERE!

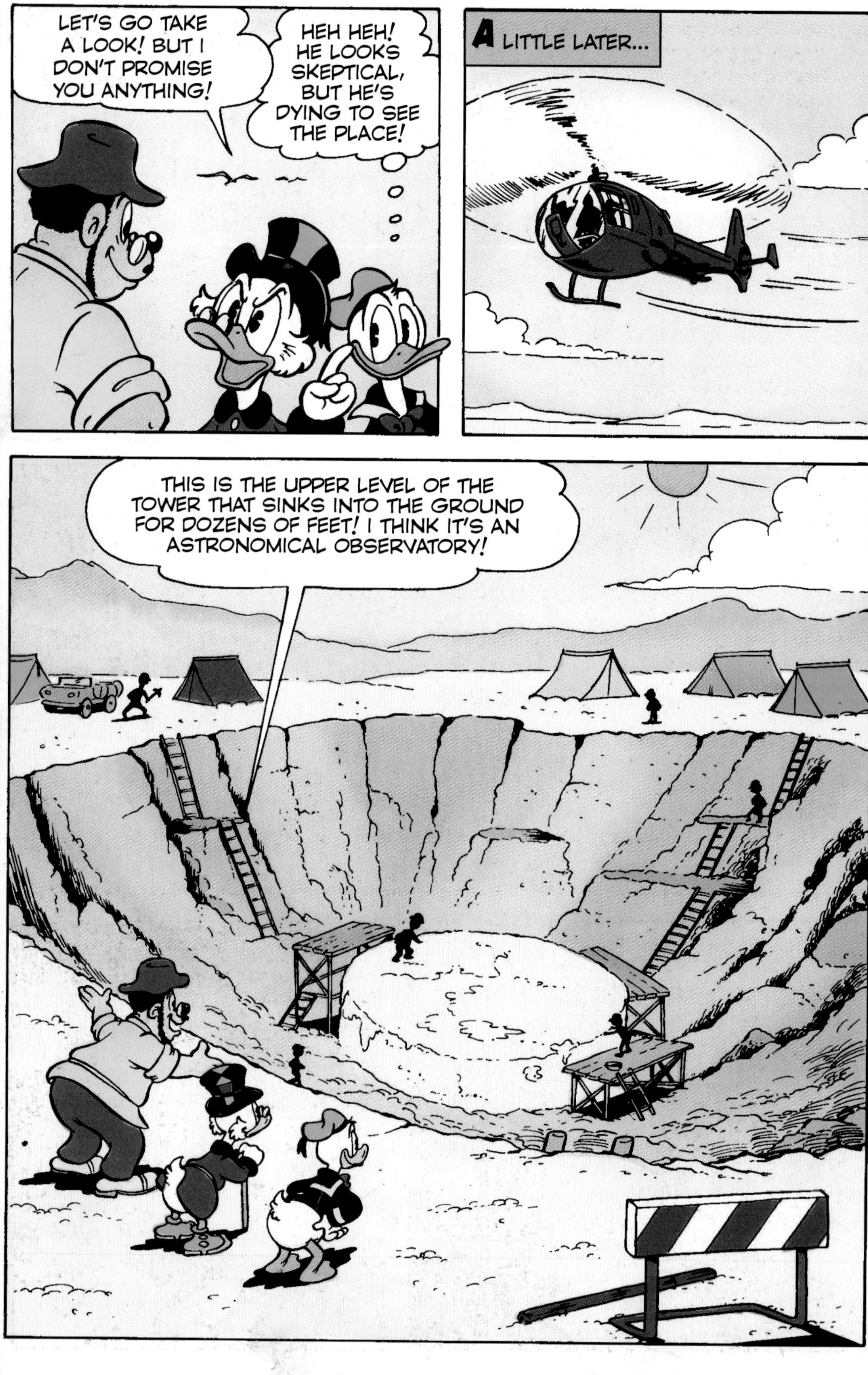
LET'S GO TAKE A LOOK! BUT I DON'T PROMISE YOU ANYTHING!
HEH HEH! HE LOOKS SKEPTICAL, BUT HE'S DYING TO SEE THE PLACE!
A LITTLE LATER...
THIS IS THE UPPER LEVEL OF THE TOWER THAT SINKS INTO THE GROUND FOR DOZENS OF FEET! I THINK IT'S AN ASTRONOMICAL OBSERVATORY!

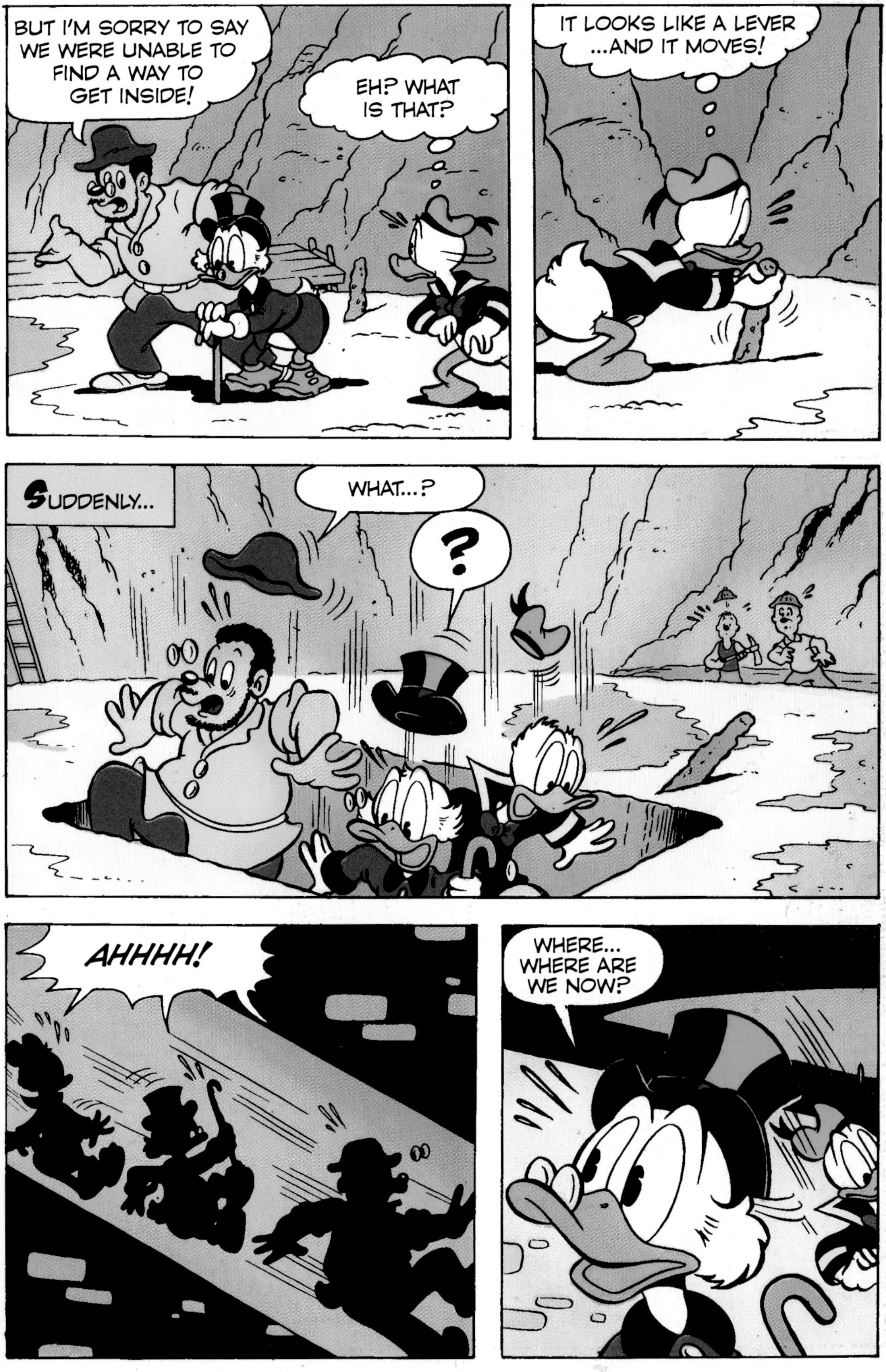
BUT I'M SORRY TO SAY WE WERE UNABLE TO FIND A WAY TO GET INSIDE!
EH? WHAT IS THAT?
IT LOOKS LIKE A LEVER ...AND IT MOVES!
SUDDENLY...
WHAT...?
?
AHHHH!
WHERE... WHERE ARE WE NOW?

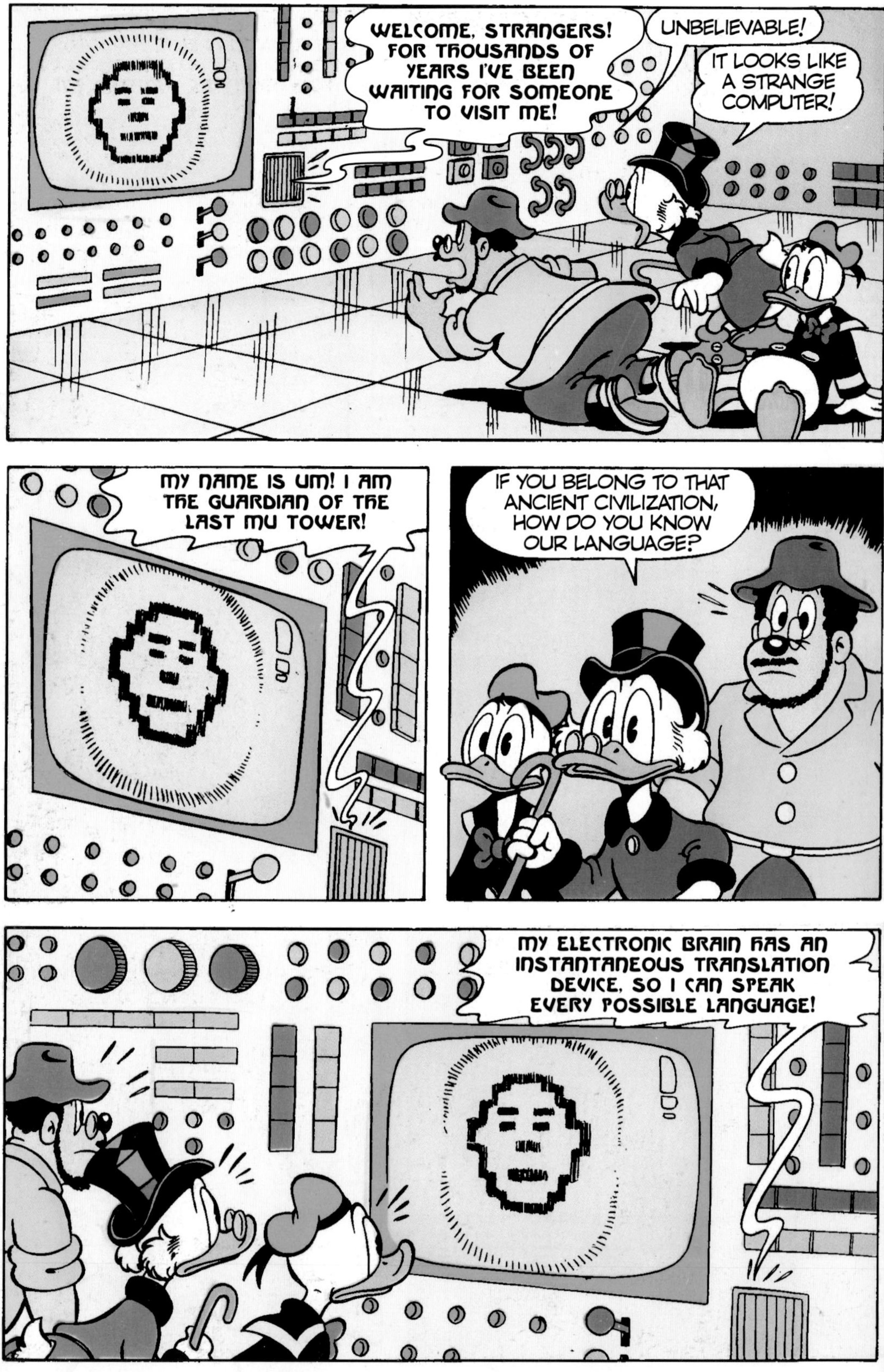
WELCOME, STRANGERS! FOR THOUSANDS OF YEARS I'VE BEEN WAITING FOR SOMEONE TO VISIT ME!
UNBELIEVABLE!
IT LOOKS LIKE A STRANGE COMPUTER!
MY NAME IS UM! I AM THE GUARDIAN OF THE LAST MU TOWER!
IF YOU BELONG TO THAT ANCIENT CIVILIZATION, HOW DO YOU KNOW OUR LANGUAGE?
MY ELECTRONIC BRAIN HAS AN INSTANTANEOUS TRANSLATION DEVICE, SO I CAN SPEAK EVERY POSSIBLE LANGUAGE!

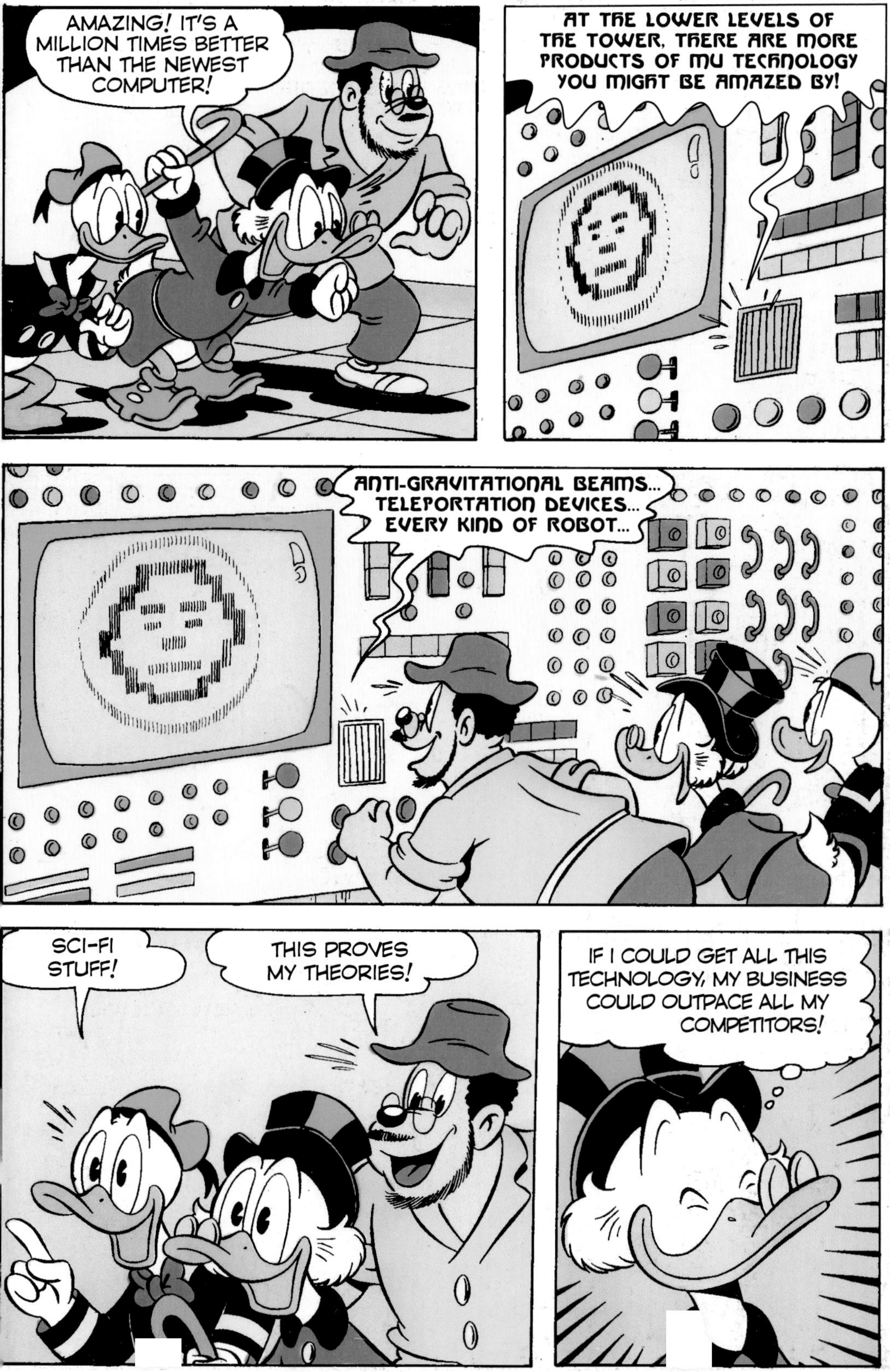
AMAZING! IT'S A MILLION TIMES BETTER THAN THE NEWEST COMPUTER!
AT THE LOWER LEVELS OF THE TOWER, THERE ARE MORE PRODUCTS OF MU TECHNOLOGY YOU MIGHT BE AMAZED BY!
ANTI-GRAVITATIONAL BEAMS... TELEPORTATION DEVICES... EVERY KIND OF ROBOT...
SCI-FI STUFF!
THIS PROVES MY THEORIES!
IF I COULD GET ALL THIS TECHNOLOGY, MY BUSINESS COULD OUTPACE ALL MY COMPETITORS!

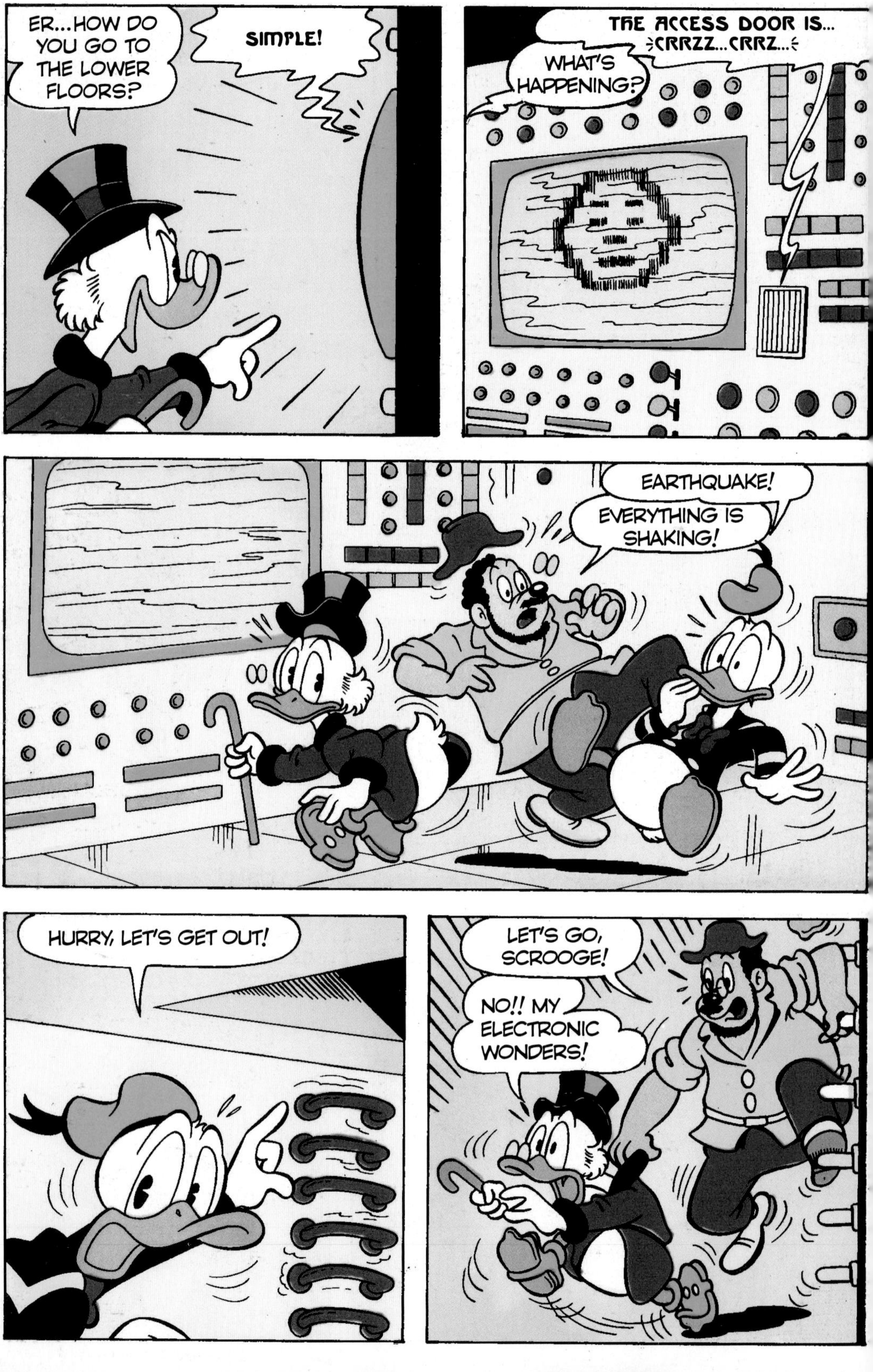
ER...HOW DO YOU GO TO THE LOWER FLOORS?
SIMPLE!
THE ACCESS DOOR IS... CRRZZ...CRRZ...
WHAT'S HAPPENING?
EARTHQUAKE!
EVERYTHING IS SHAKING!
HURRY, LET'S GET OUT!
LET'S GO, SCROOGE!
NO!! MY ELECTRONIC WONDERS!

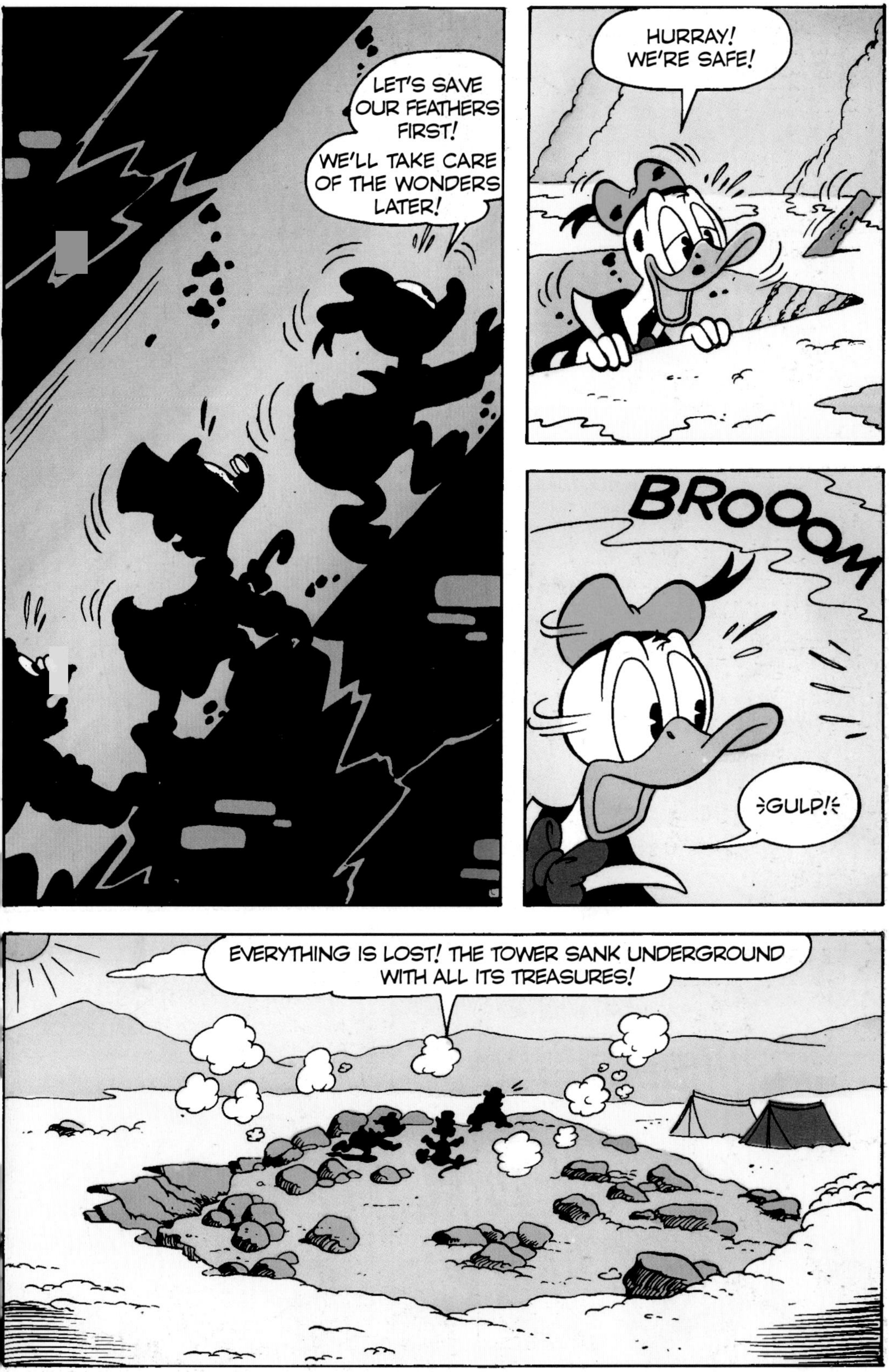
LET'S SAVE OUR FEATHERS FIRST! WE'LL TAKE CARE OF THE WONDERS LATER!
HURRAY! WE'RE SAFE!
BROOOOM
GULP!
EVERYTHING IS LOST! THE TOWER SANK UNDERGROUND WITH ALL ITS TREASURES!

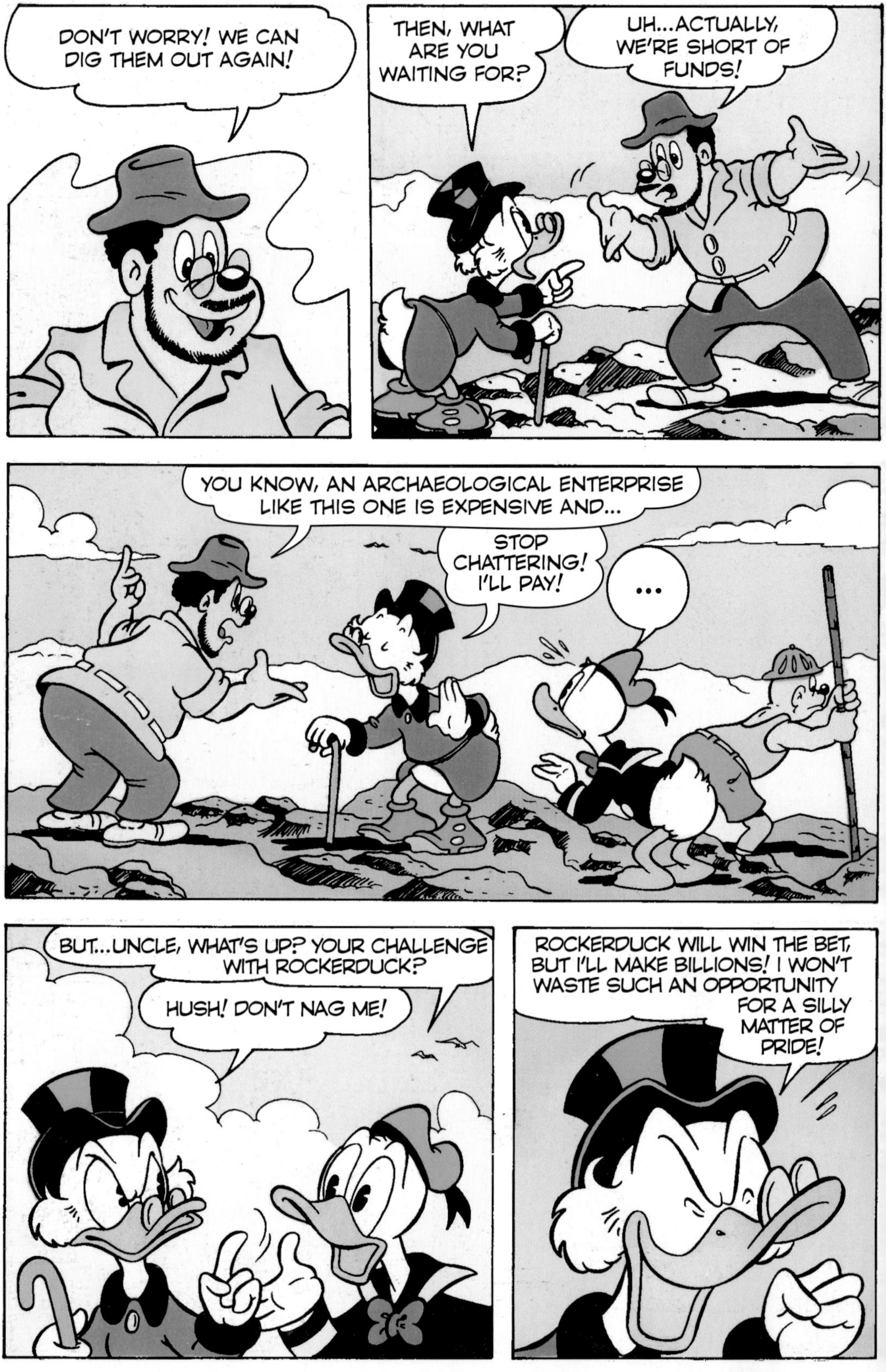
DON'T WORRY! WE CAN DIG THEM OUT AGAIN!
THEN, WHAT ARE YOU WAITING FOR?
UH...ACTUALLY, WE'RE SHORT OF FUNDS!
YOU KNOW, AN ARCHAEOLOGICAL ENTERPRISE LIKE THIS ONE IS EXPENSIVE AND...
STOP CHATTERING! I'LL PAY!
...
BUT...UNCLE, WHAT'S UP? YOUR CHALLENGE WITH ROCKERDUCK?
HUSH! DON'T NAG ME!
ROCKERDUCK WILL WIN THE BET, BUT I'LL MAKE BILLIONS! I WON'T WASTE SUCH AN OPPORTUNITY FOR A SILLY MATTER OF PRIDE!

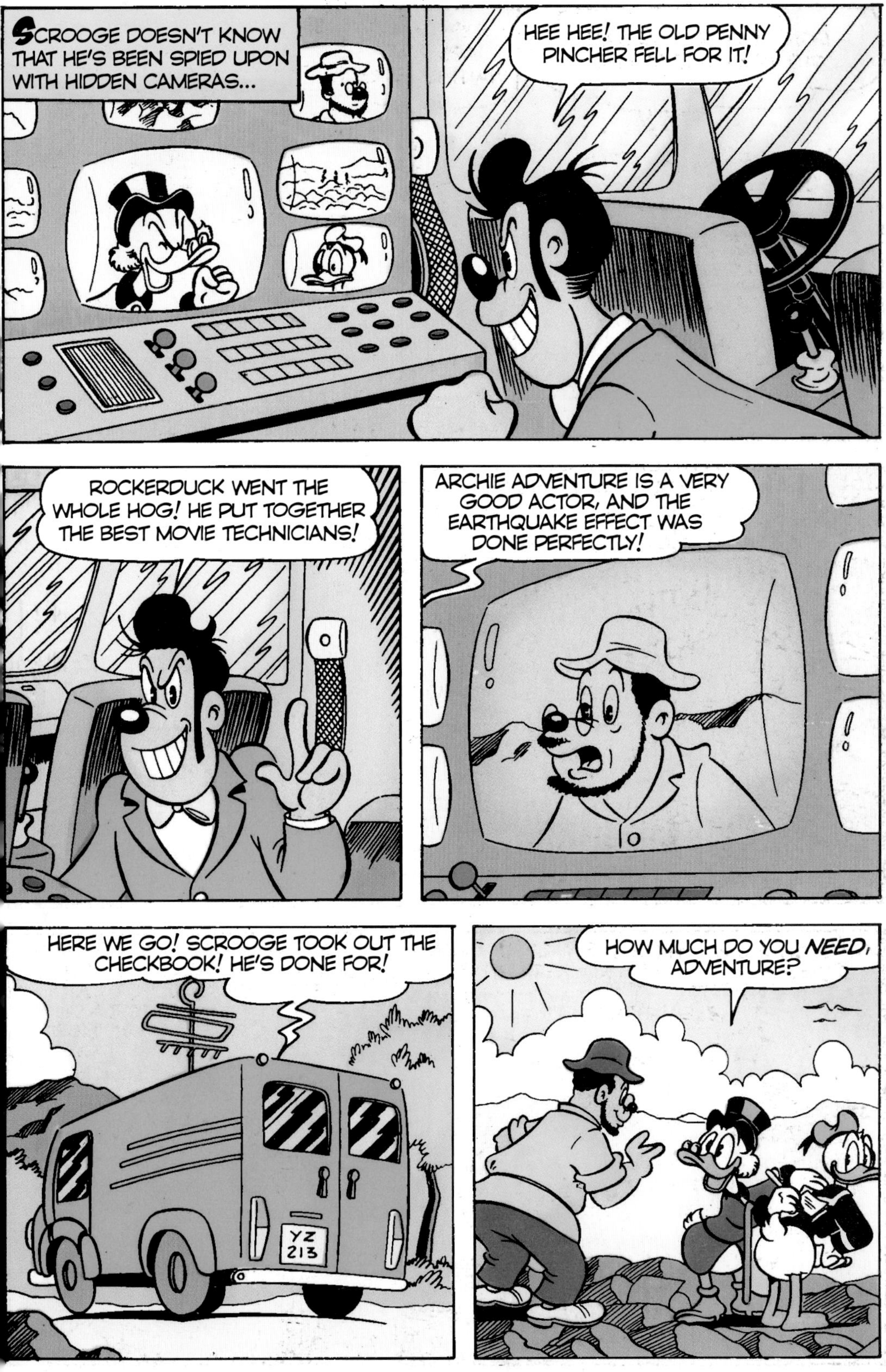
SCROOGE DOESN'T KNOW THAT HE'S BEEN SPIED UPON WITH HIDDEN CAMERAS...
HEE HEE! THE OLD PENNY PINCHER FELL FOR IT!
ROCKERDUCK WENT THE WHOLE HOG! HE PUT TOGETHER THE BEST MOVIE TECHNICIANS!
ARCHIE ADVENTURE IS A VERY GOOD ACTOR, AND THE EARTHQUAKE EFFECT WAS DONE PERFECTLY!
HERE WE GO! SCROOGE TOOK OUT THE CHECKBOOK! HE'S DONE FOR!
YZ 213
HOW MUCH DO YOU *NEED*, ADVENTURE?

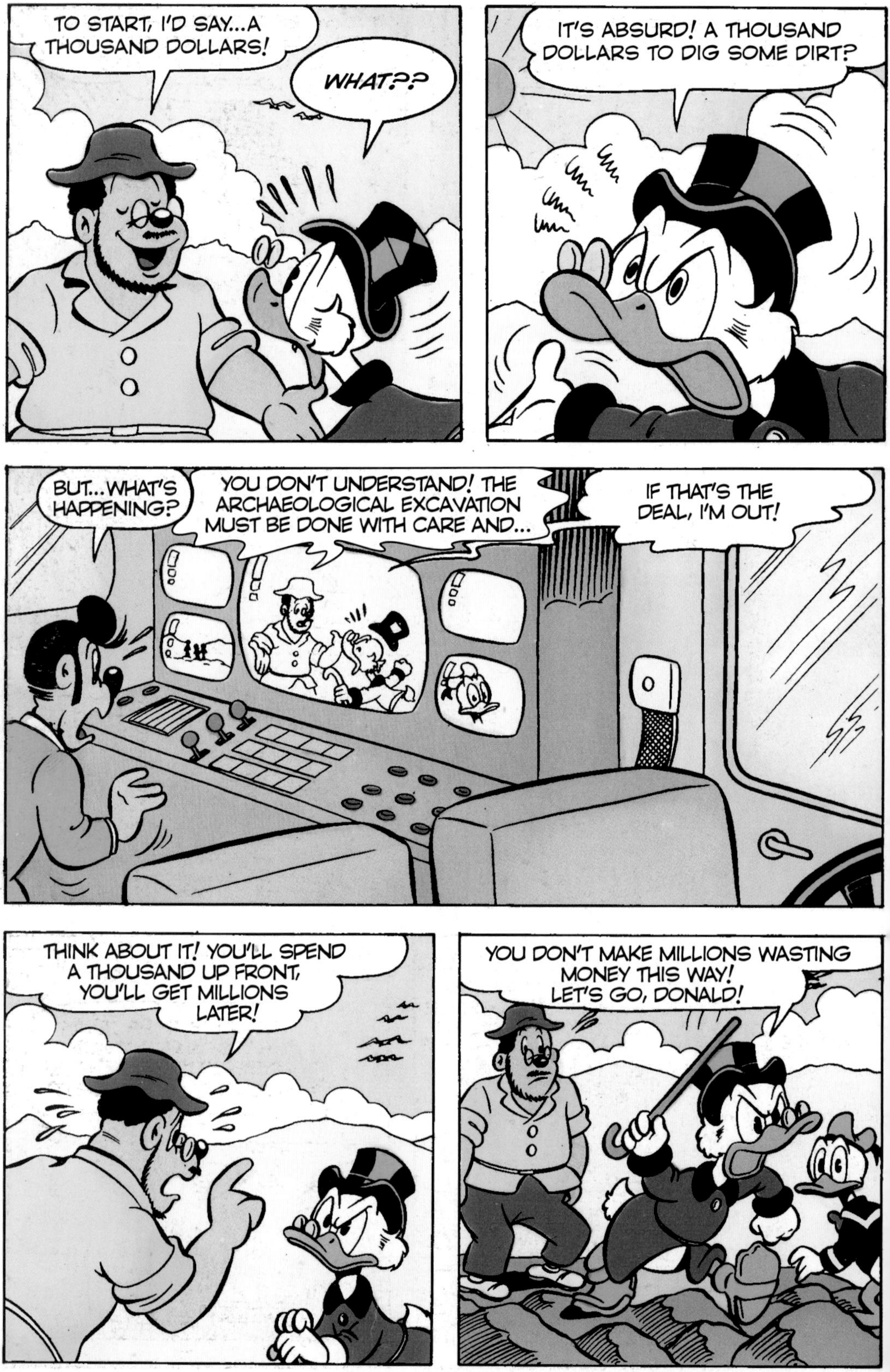
TO START, I'D SAY...A THOUSAND DOLLARS!
WHAT??
IT'S ABSURD! A THOUSAND DOLLARS TO DIG SOME DIRT?
BUT...WHAT'S HAPPENING?
YOU DON'T UNDERSTAND! THE ARCHAEOLOGICAL EXCAVATION MUST BE DONE WITH CARE AND...
IF THAT'S THE DEAL, I'M OUT!
THINK ABOUT IT! YOU'LL SPEND A THOUSAND UP FRONT, YOU'LL GET MILLIONS LATER!
YOU DON'T MAKE MILLIONS WASTING MONEY THIS WAY! LET'S GO, DONALD!

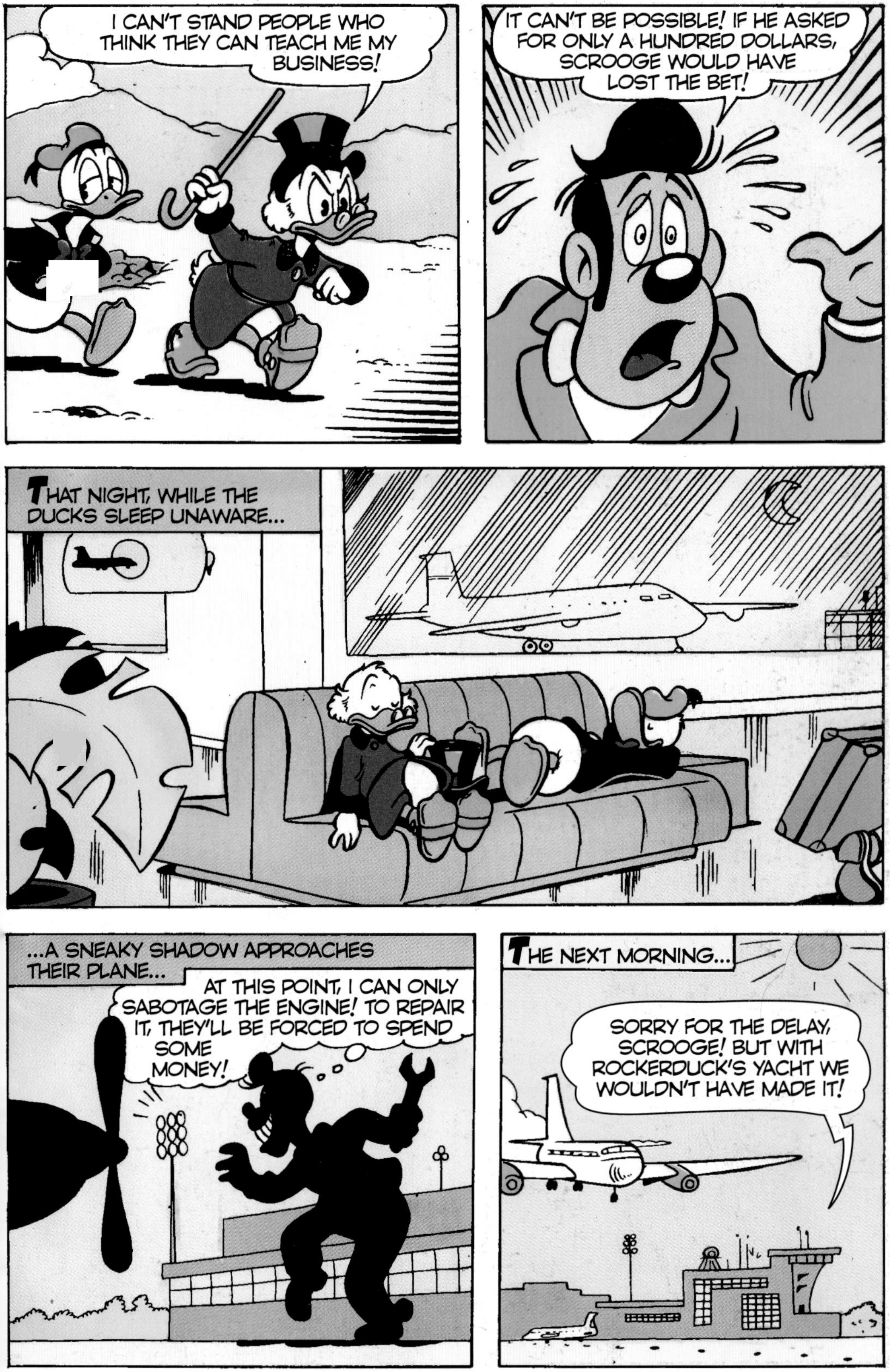
I CAN'T STAND PEOPLE WHO THINK THEY CAN TEACH ME MY BUSINESS!
IT CAN'T BE POSSIBLE! IF HE ASKED FOR ONLY A HUNDRED DOLLARS, SCROOGE WOULD HAVE LOST THE BET!
THAT NIGHT, WHILE THE DUCKS SLEEP UNAWARE...
...A SNEAKY SHADOW APPROACHES THEIR PLANE...
AT THIS POINT, I CAN ONLY SABOTAGE THE ENGINE! TO REPAIR IT, THEY'LL BE FORCED TO SPEND SOME MONEY!
THE NEXT MORNING...
SORRY FOR THE DELAY, SCROOGE! BUT WITH ROCKERDUCK'S YACHT WE WOULDN'T HAVE MADE IT!

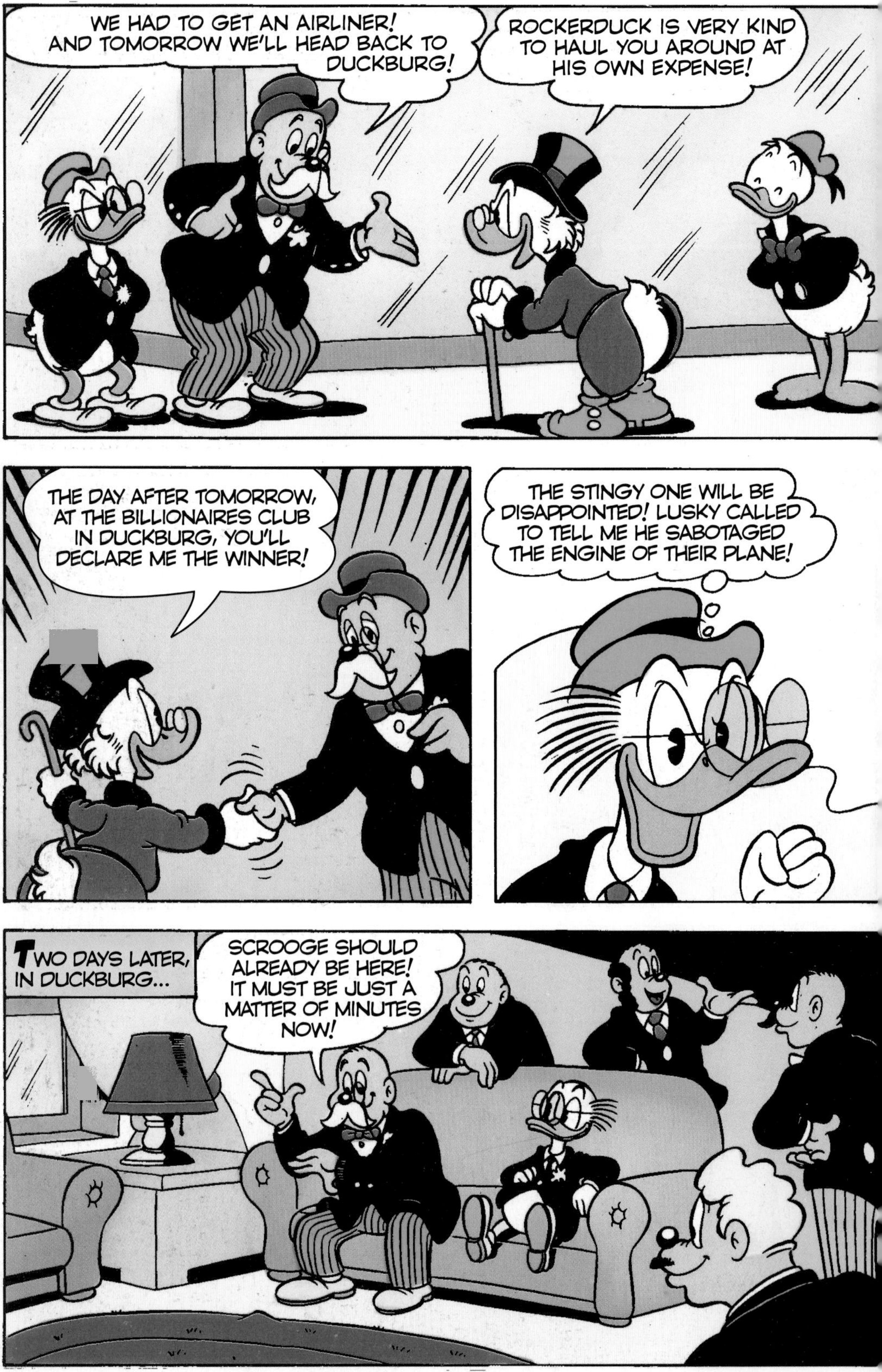
WE HAD TO GET AN AIRLINER! AND TOMORROW WE'LL HEAD BACK TO DUCKBURG!
ROCKERDUCK IS VERY KIND TO HAUL YOU AROUND AT HIS OWN EXPENSE!
THE DAY AFTER TOMORROW, AT THE BILLIONAIRES CLUB IN DUCKBURG, YOU'LL DECLARE ME THE WINNER!
THE STINGY ONE WILL BE DISAPPOINTED! LUSKY CALLED TO TELL ME HE SABOTAGED THE ENGINE OF THEIR PLANE!
TWO DAYS LATER, IN DUCKBURG...
SCROOGE SHOULD ALREADY BE HERE! IT MUST BE JUST A MATTER OF MINUTES NOW!

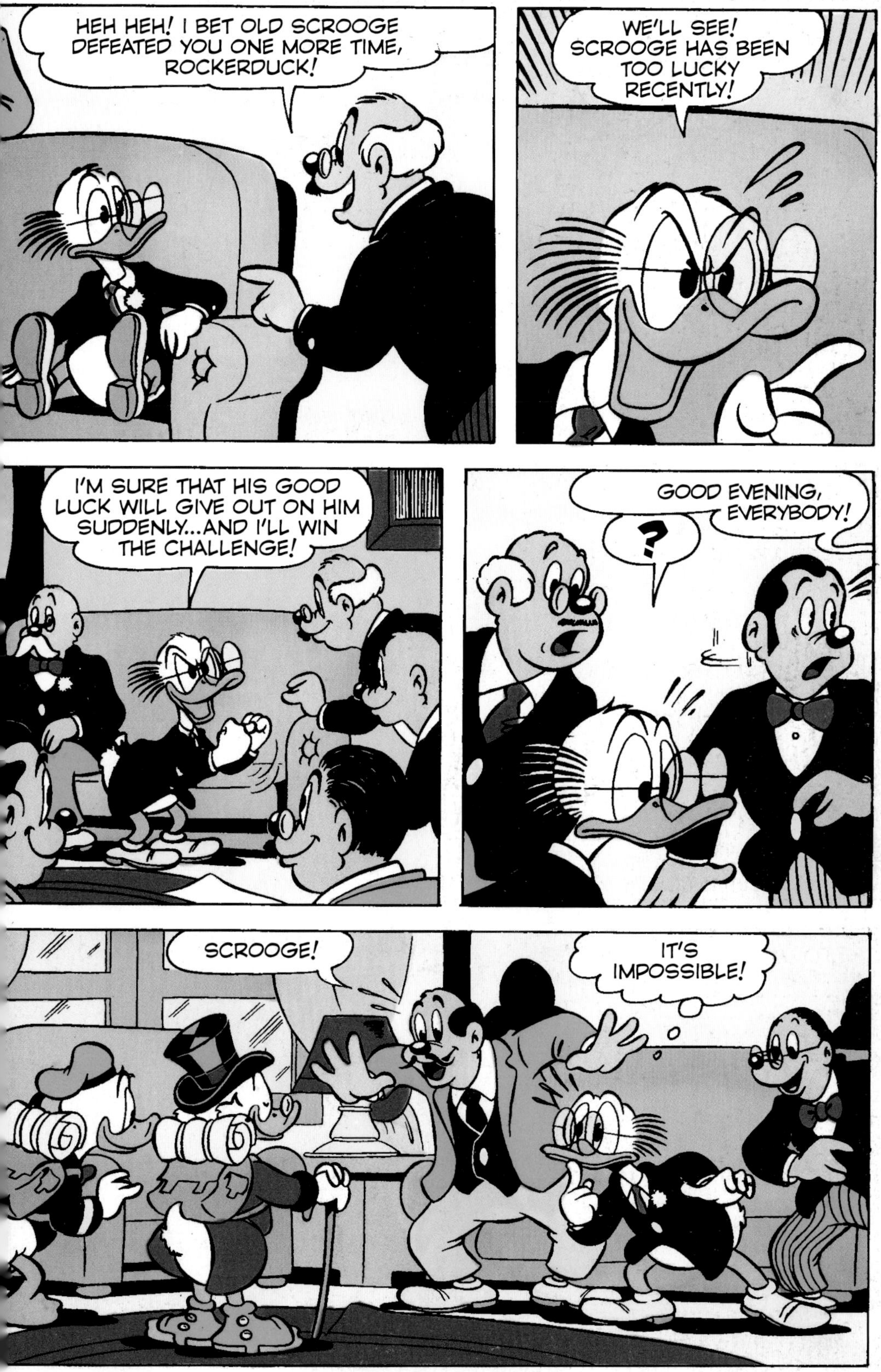
HEH HEH! I BET OLD SCROOGE DEFEATED YOU ONE MORE TIME, ROCKERDUCK!
WE'LL SEE! SCROOGE HAS BEEN TOO LUCKY RECENTLY!
I'M SURE THAT HIS GOOD LUCK WILL GIVE OUT ON HIM SUDDENLY...AND I'LL WIN THE CHALLENGE!
GOOD EVENING, EVERYBODY!
?
SCROOGE!
IT'S IMPOSSIBLE!

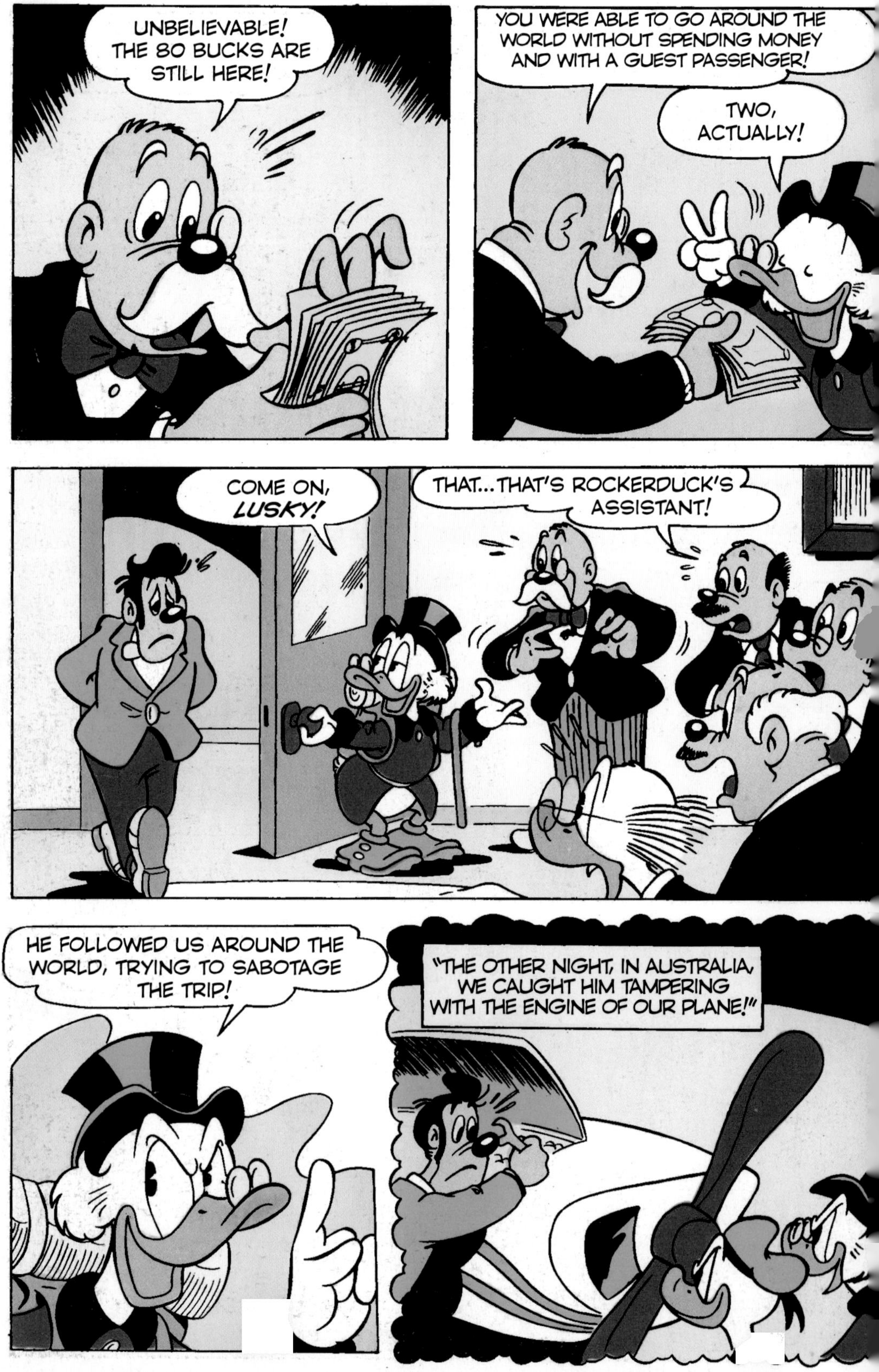
UNBELIEVABLE! THE 80 BUCKS ARE STILL HERE!
YOU WERE ABLE TO GO AROUND THE WORLD WITHOUT SPENDING MONEY AND WITH A GUEST PASSENGER!
TWO, ACTUALLY!
COME ON, LUSKY!
THAT...THAT'S ROCKERDUCK'S ASSISTANT!
HE FOLLOWED US AROUND THE WORLD, TRYING TO SABOTAGE THE TRIP!
"THE OTHER NIGHT, IN AUSTRALIA, WE CAUGHT HIM TAMPERING WITH THE ENGINE OF OUR PLANE!"

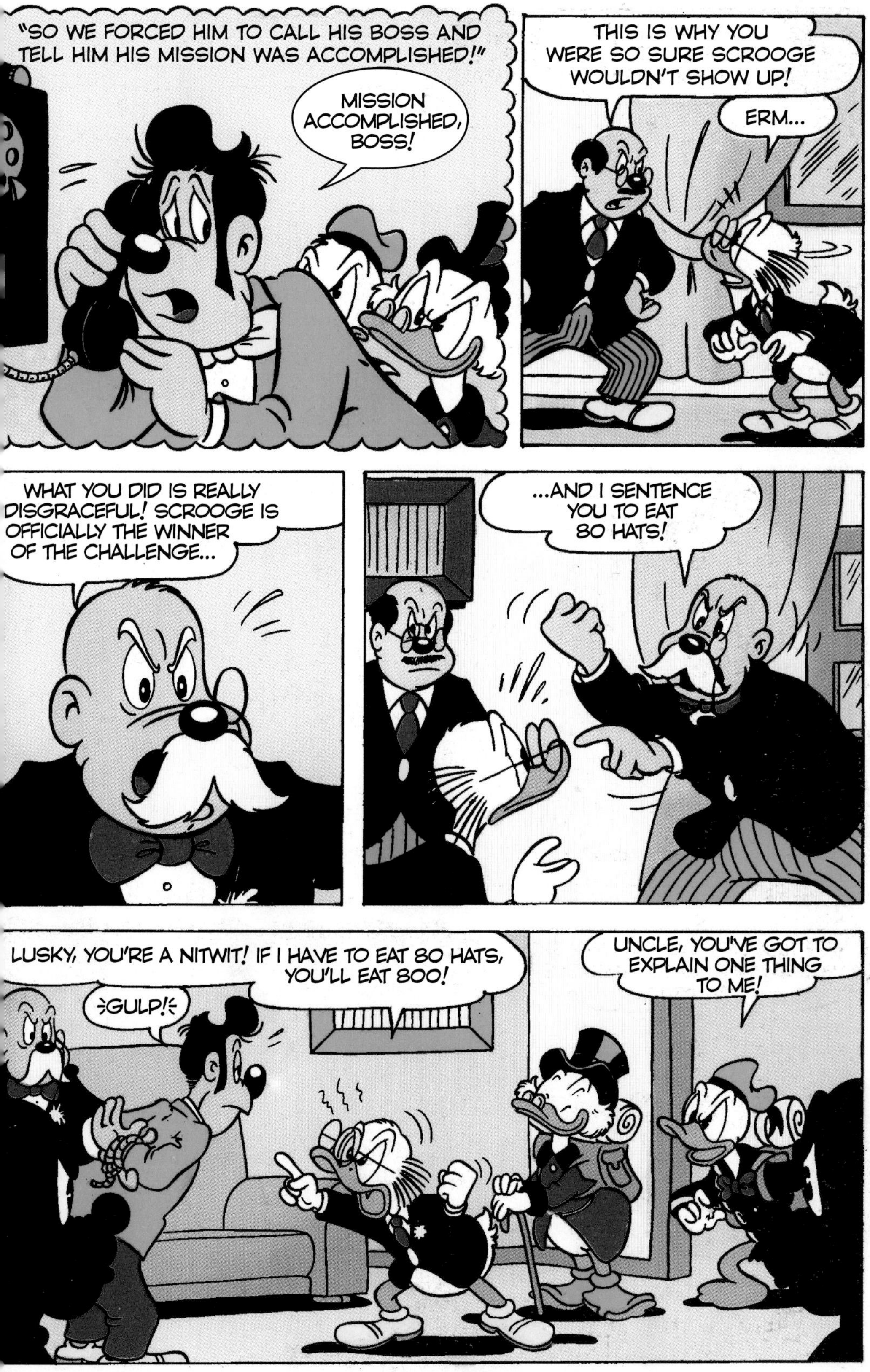
"SO WE FORCED HIM TO CALL HIS BOSS AND TELL HIM HIS MISSION WAS ACCOMPLISHED!"
MISSION ACCOMPLISHED, BOSS!
THIS IS WHY YOU WERE SO SURE SCROOGE WOULDN'T SHOW UP!
ERM...
WHAT YOU DID IS REALLY DISGRACEFUL! SCROOGE IS OFFICIALLY THE WINNER OF THE CHALLENGE...
...AND I SENTENCE YOU TO EAT 80 HATS!
LUSKY, YOU'RE A NITWIT! IF I HAVE TO EAT 80 HATS, YOU'LL EAT 800!
GULP!
UNCLE, YOU'VE GOT TO EXPLAIN ONE THING TO ME!

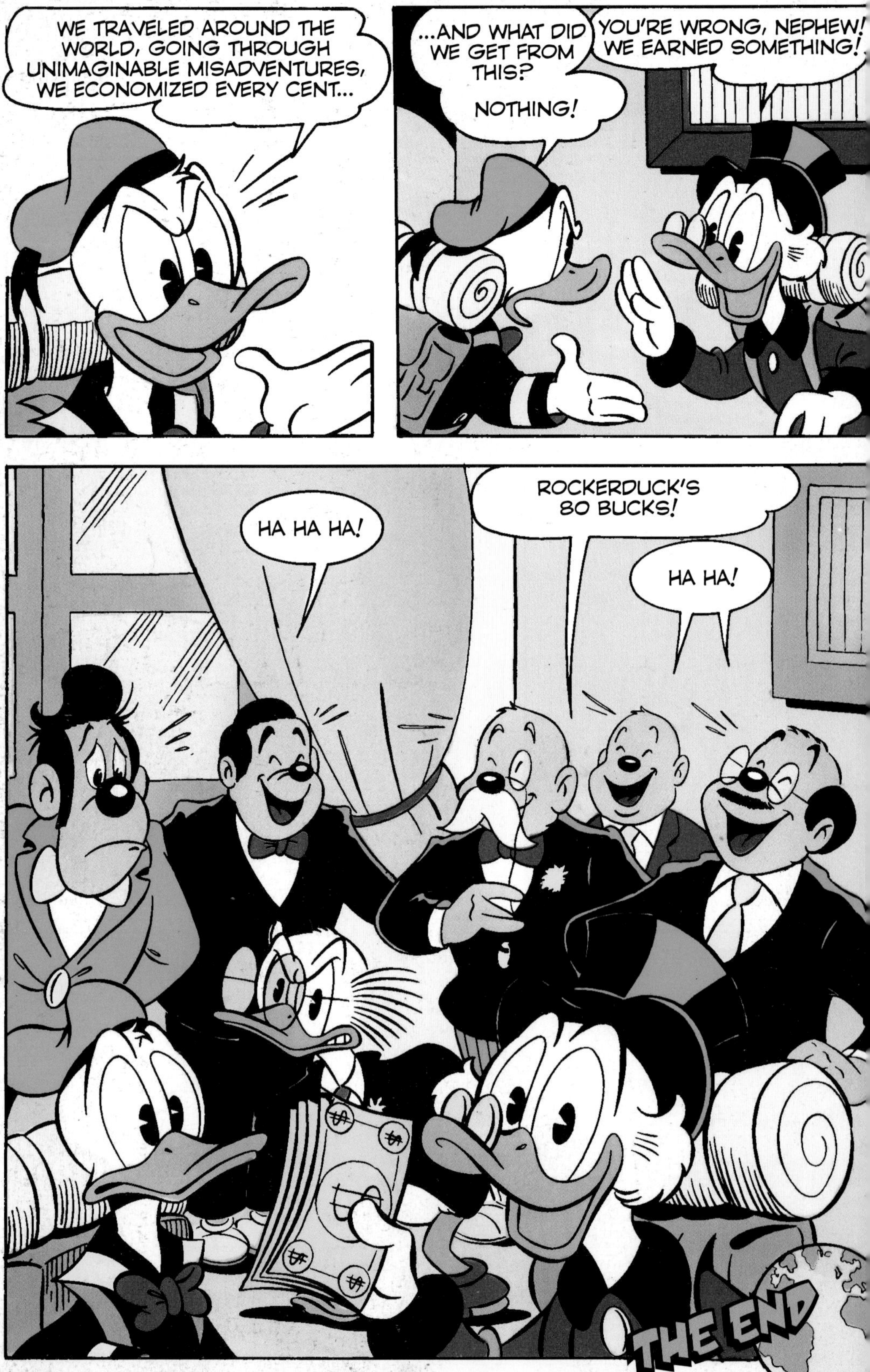
WE TRAVELED AROUND THE WORLD, GOING THROUGH UNIMAGINABLE MISADVENTURES, WE ECONOMIZED EVERY CENT...
...AND WHAT DID WE GET FROM THIS?
NOTHING!
YOU'RE WRONG, NEPHEW! WE EARNED SOMETHING!
ROCKERDUCK'S 80 BUCKS!
HA HA HA!
HA HA!
THE END

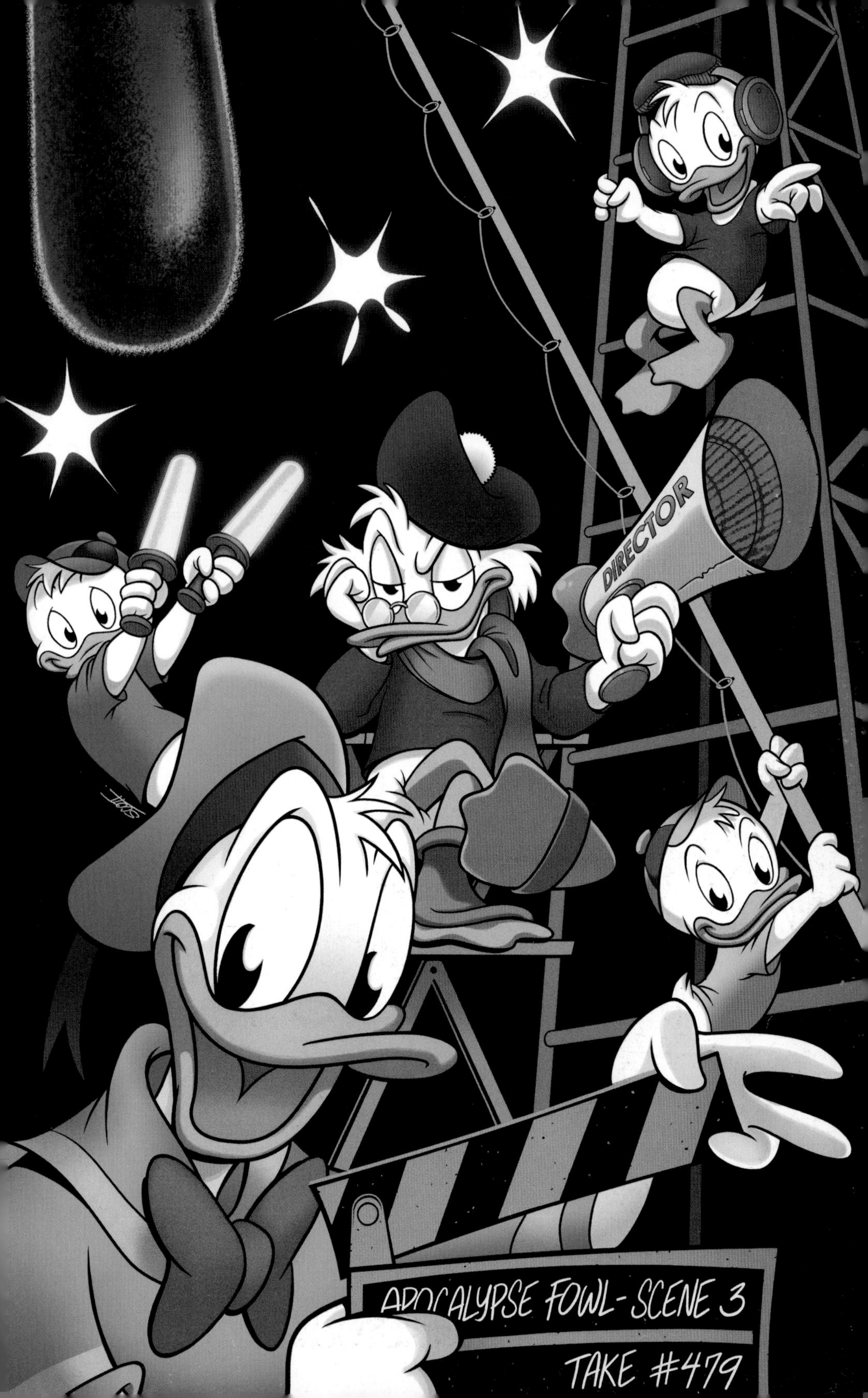
DIRECTOR
APOCALYPSE FOWL - SCENE 3
TAKE #479

# LOOKING FOR MORE FUN WITH YOUR FAVORITE CHARACTERS?

CHECK OUT THESE EXCLUSIVE PREVIEWS OF OTHER GREAT TITLES NOW AVAILABLE FROM

BOOM KIDS!

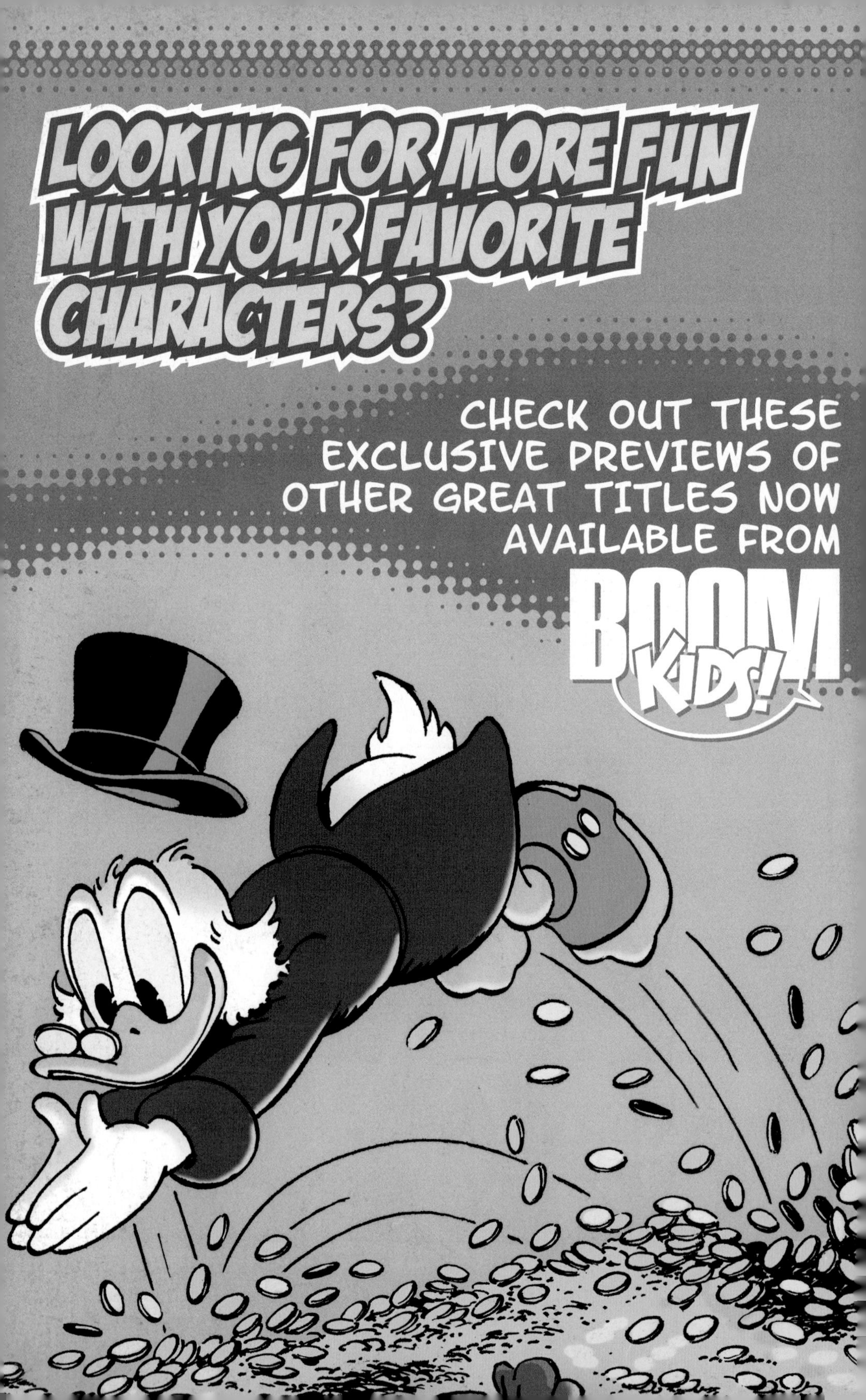

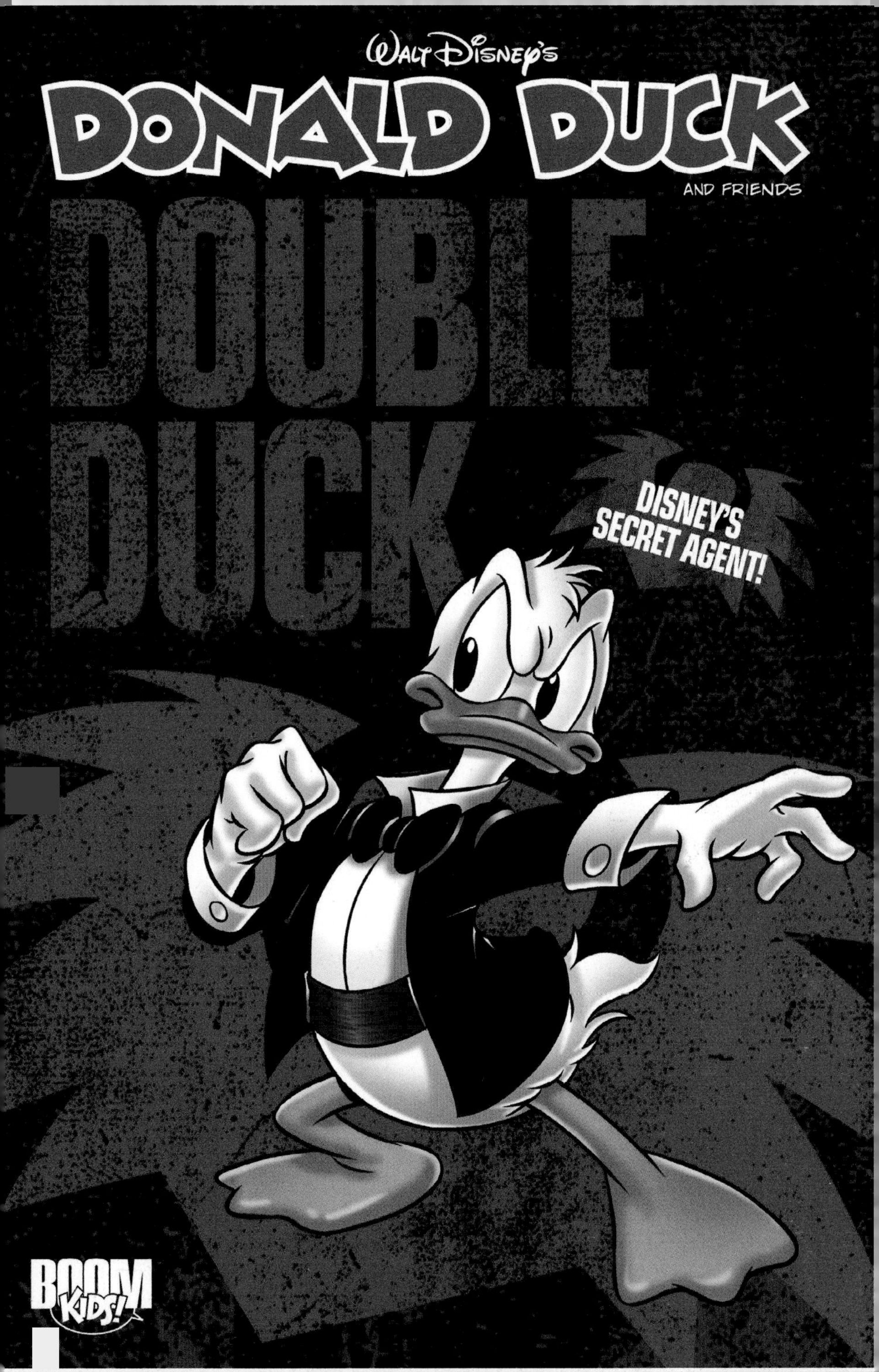

# WALT DISNEY'S
# DONALD DUCK
### AND FRIENDS

# DOUBLE
# DUCK

**DISNEY'S
SECRET AGENT!**

Donald Duck...as a secret agent? Villainous
riends beware as the world of super-sleuthing
and espionage will never be the same! This is
Donald Duck like you've never seen him!

DONALD DUCK AND FRIENDS: DOUBLE DUCK
DIAMOND CODE: DEC090752
SC $9.99 ISBN 978160886545
HC $24.99 ISBN 978160886551

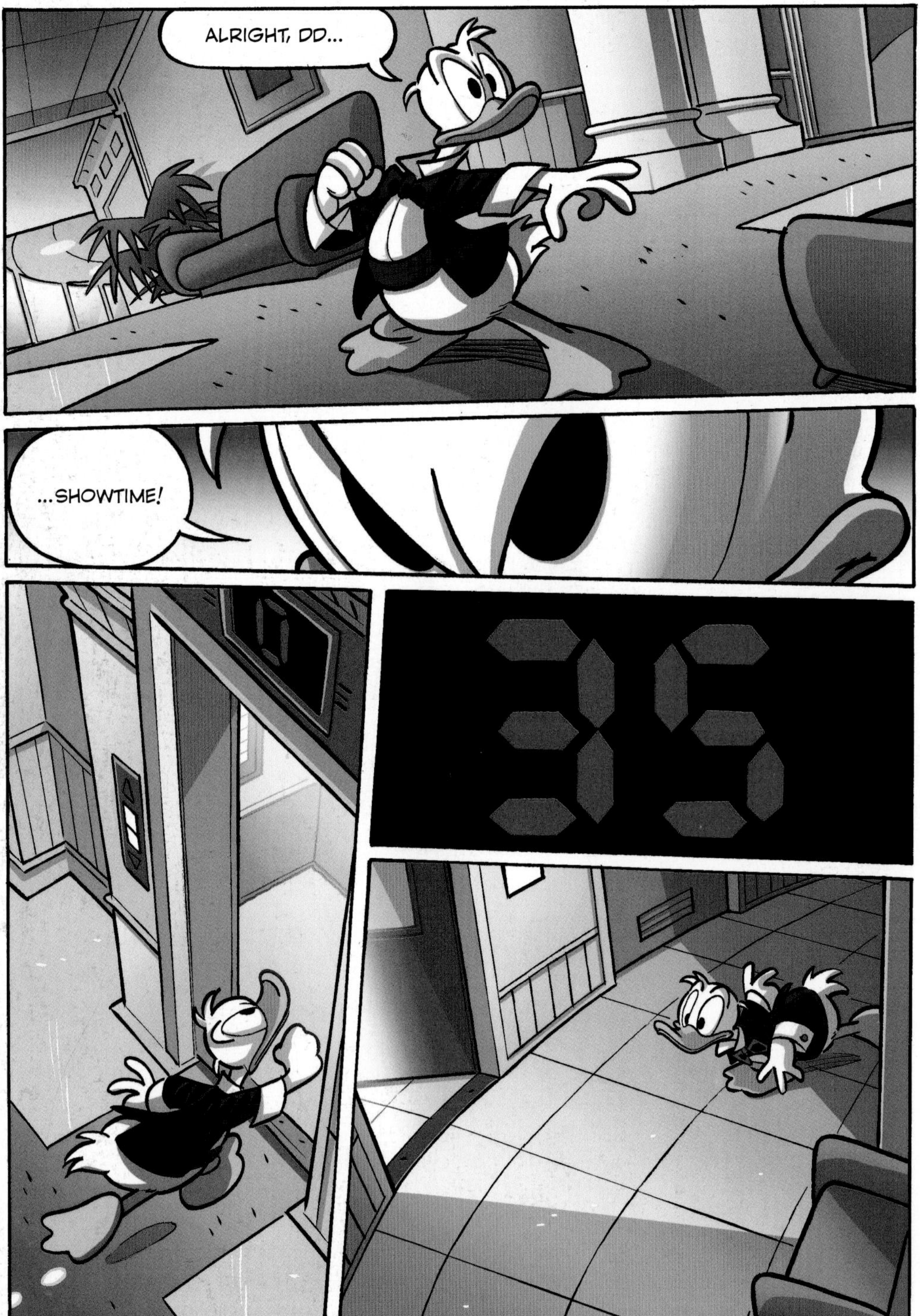
ALRIGHT, DD...
...SHOWTIME!
35

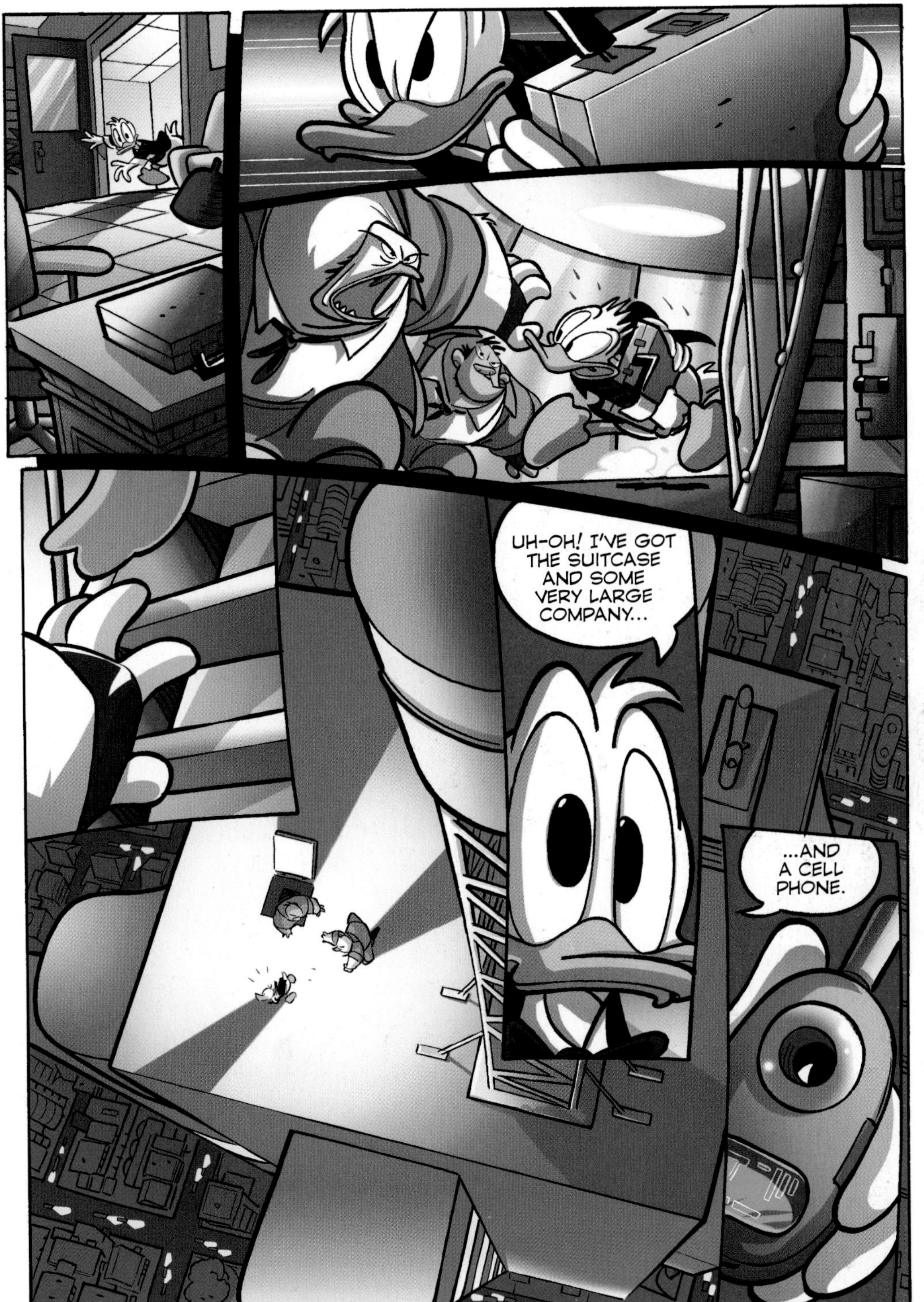
UH-OH! I'VE GOT THE SUITCASE AND SOME VERY LARGE COMPANY...
...AND A CELL PHONE.

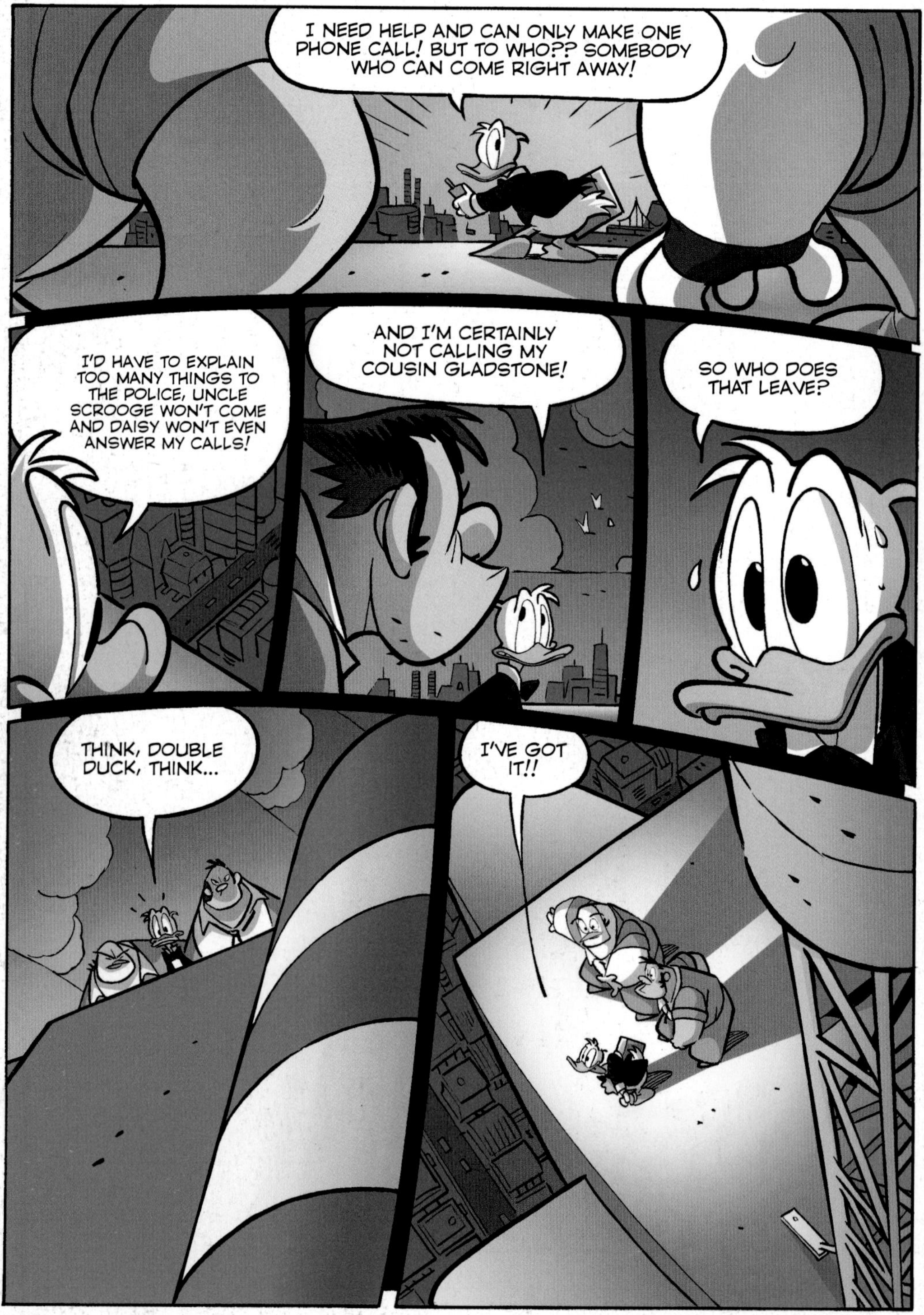
I NEED HELP AND CAN ONLY MAKE ONE PHONE CALL! BUT TO WHO?? SOMEBODY WHO CAN COME RIGHT AWAY!
I'D HAVE TO EXPLAIN TOO MANY THINGS TO THE POLICE, UNCLE SCROOGE WON'T COME AND DAISY WON'T EVEN ANSWER MY CALLS!
AND I'M CERTAINLY NOT CALLING MY COUSIN GLADSTONE!
SO WHO DOES THAT LEAVE?
THINK, DOUBLE DUCK, THINK...
I'VE GOT IT!!

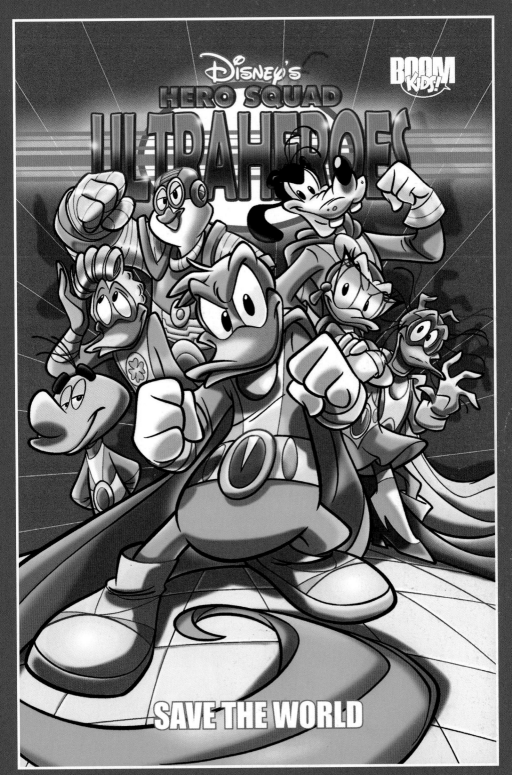

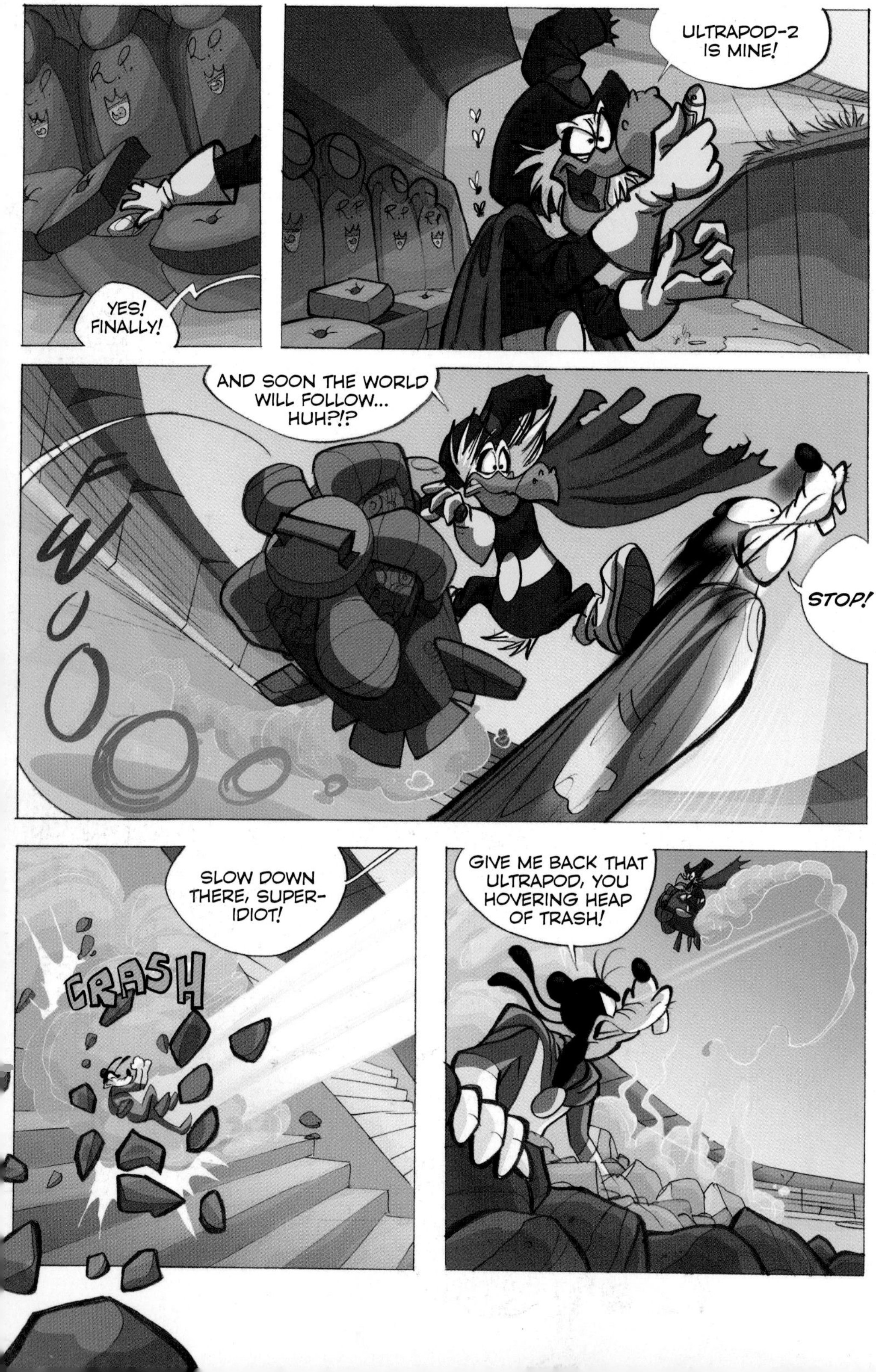
YES! FINALLY!
ULTRAPOD-2 IS MINE!
AND SOON THE WORLD WILL FOLLOW... HUH?!?
FWOOO
STOP!
SLOW DOWN THERE, SUPER-IDIOT!
CRASH
GIVE ME BACK THAT ULTRAPOD, YOU HOVERING HEAP OF TRASH!

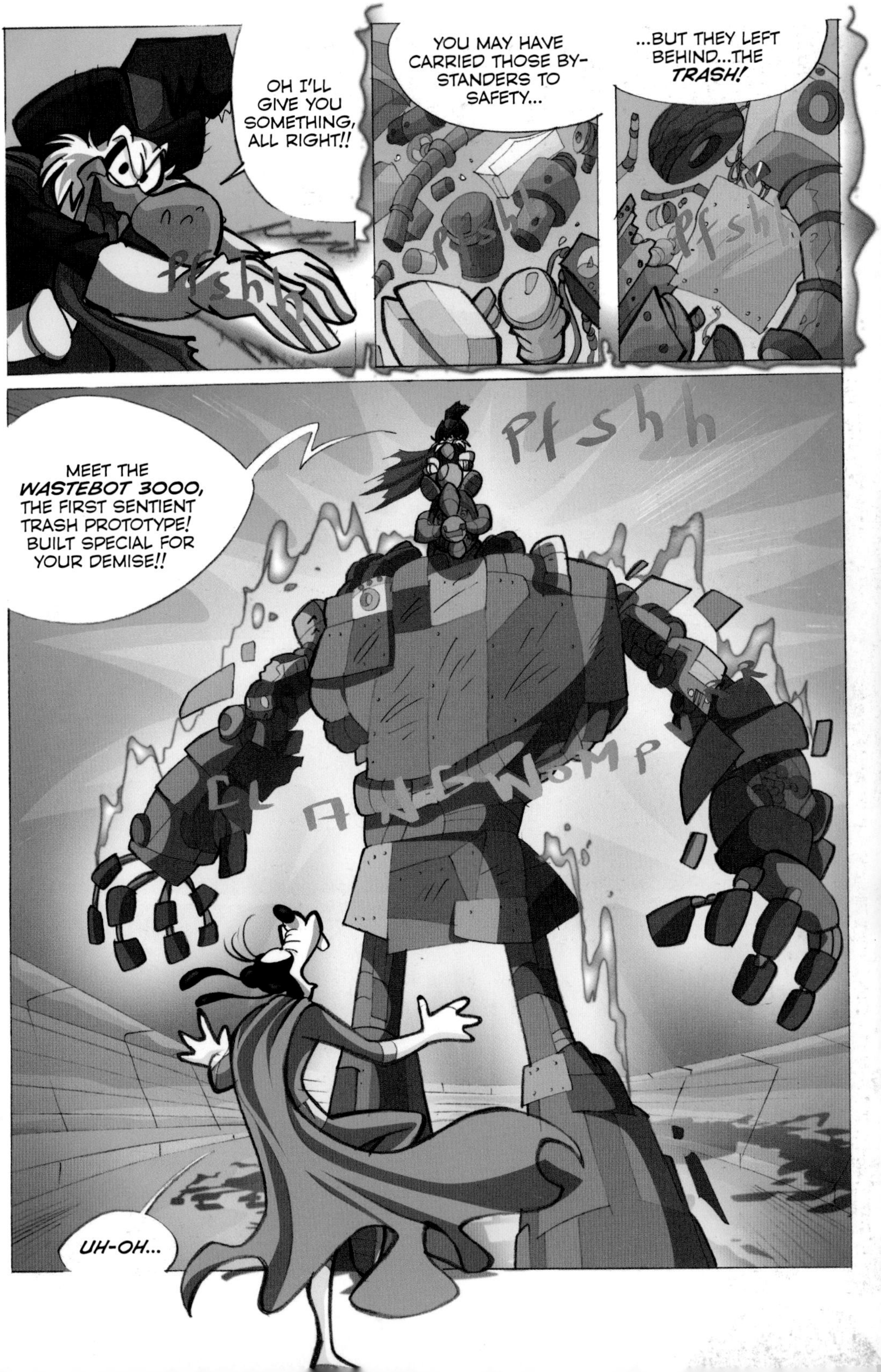
OH I'LL GIVE YOU SOMETHING, ALL RIGHT!!
YOU MAY HAVE CARRIED THOSE BY-STANDERS TO SAFETY...
...BUT THEY LEFT BEHIND...THE *TRASH!*
MEET THE ***WASTEBOT 3000,*** THE FIRST SENTIENT TRASH PROTOTYPE! BUILT SPECIAL FOR YOUR DEMISE!!
*UH-OH...*

YOUR PUNCHES CAN'T HURT *HIM!*

BUT *HIS* CAN HURT YOU...

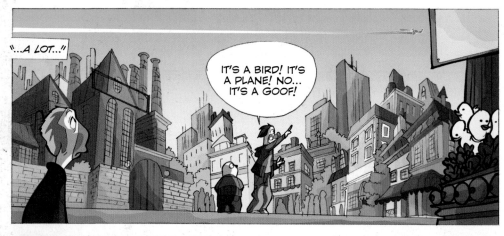

"...A LOT..."

IT'S A BIRD! IT'S A PLANE! NO... IT'S A GOOF!

"...A WHOLE LOT!"

グセコツテバピ マミムピホ ュョヰヱネノ*

*PRETTY MUCH WHAT WAS SAID ABOVE – ABRIDGED AARON

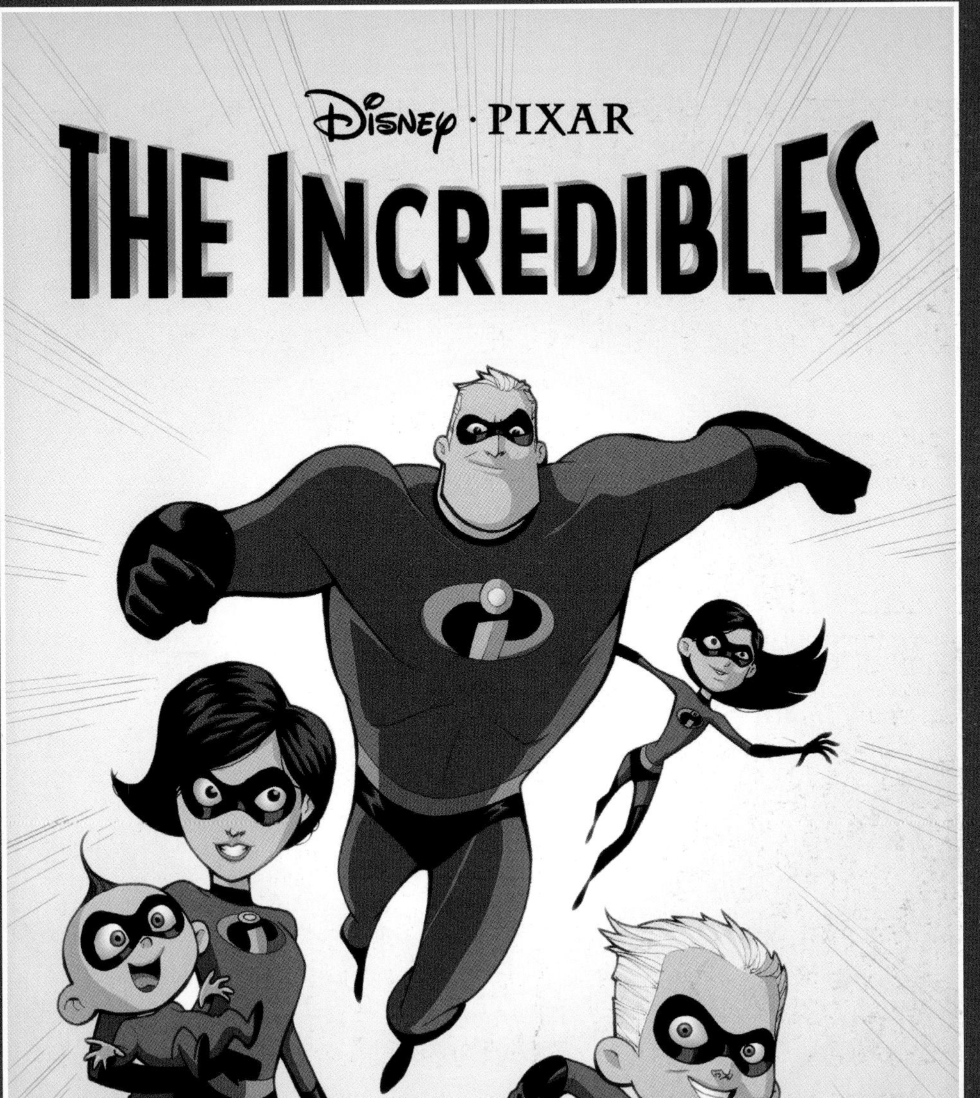

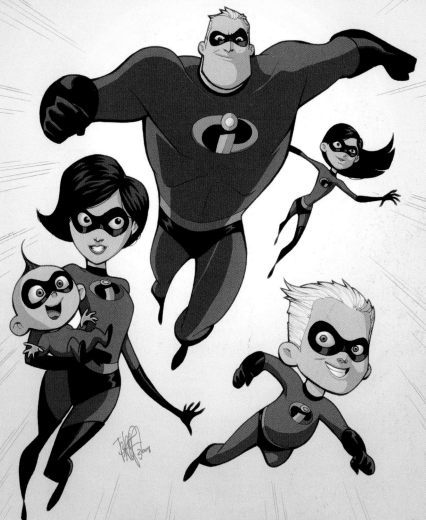

DISNEY · PIXAR
THE INCREDIBLES
FAMILY MATTERS

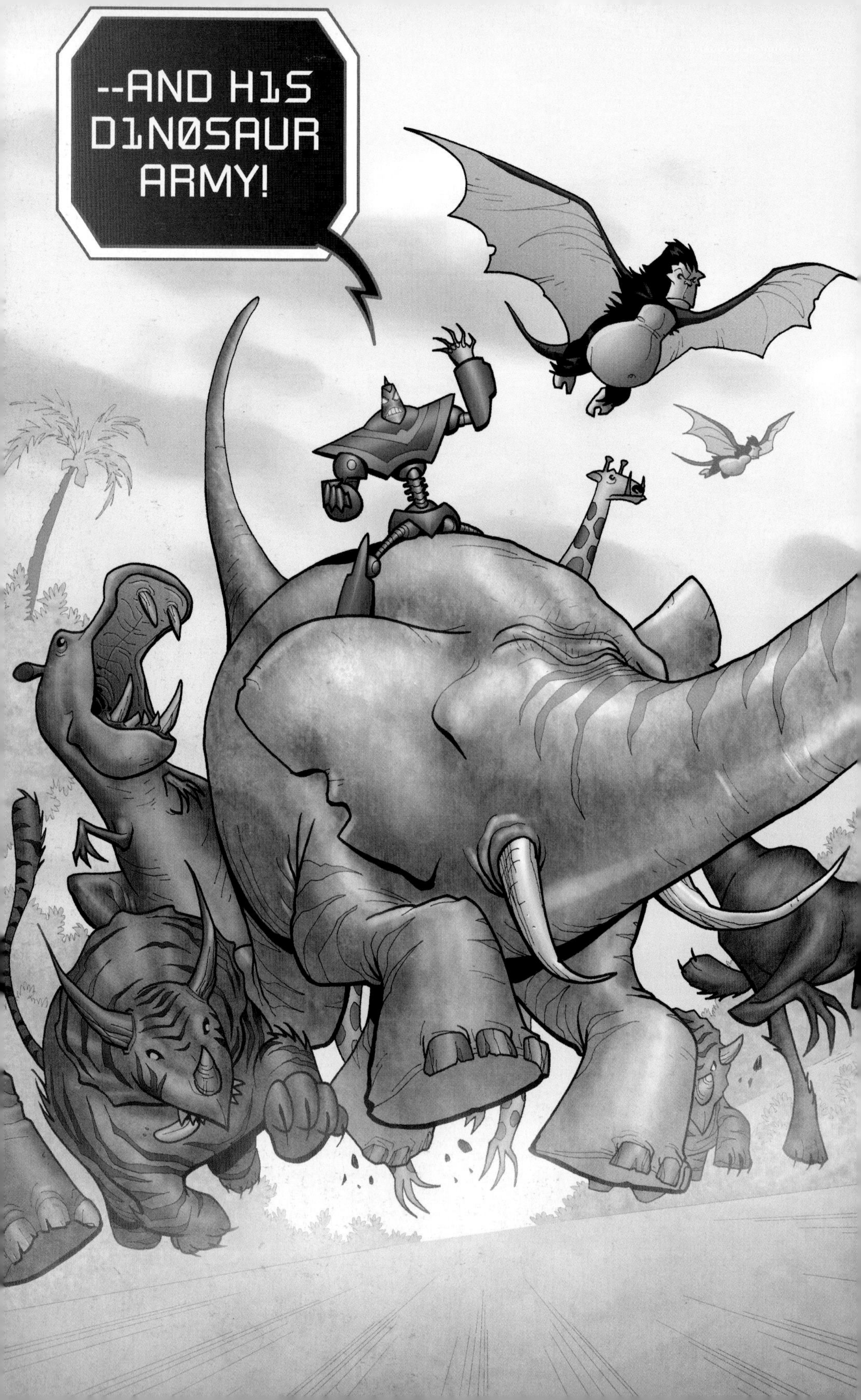
--AND H1S D1N0SAUR ARMY!

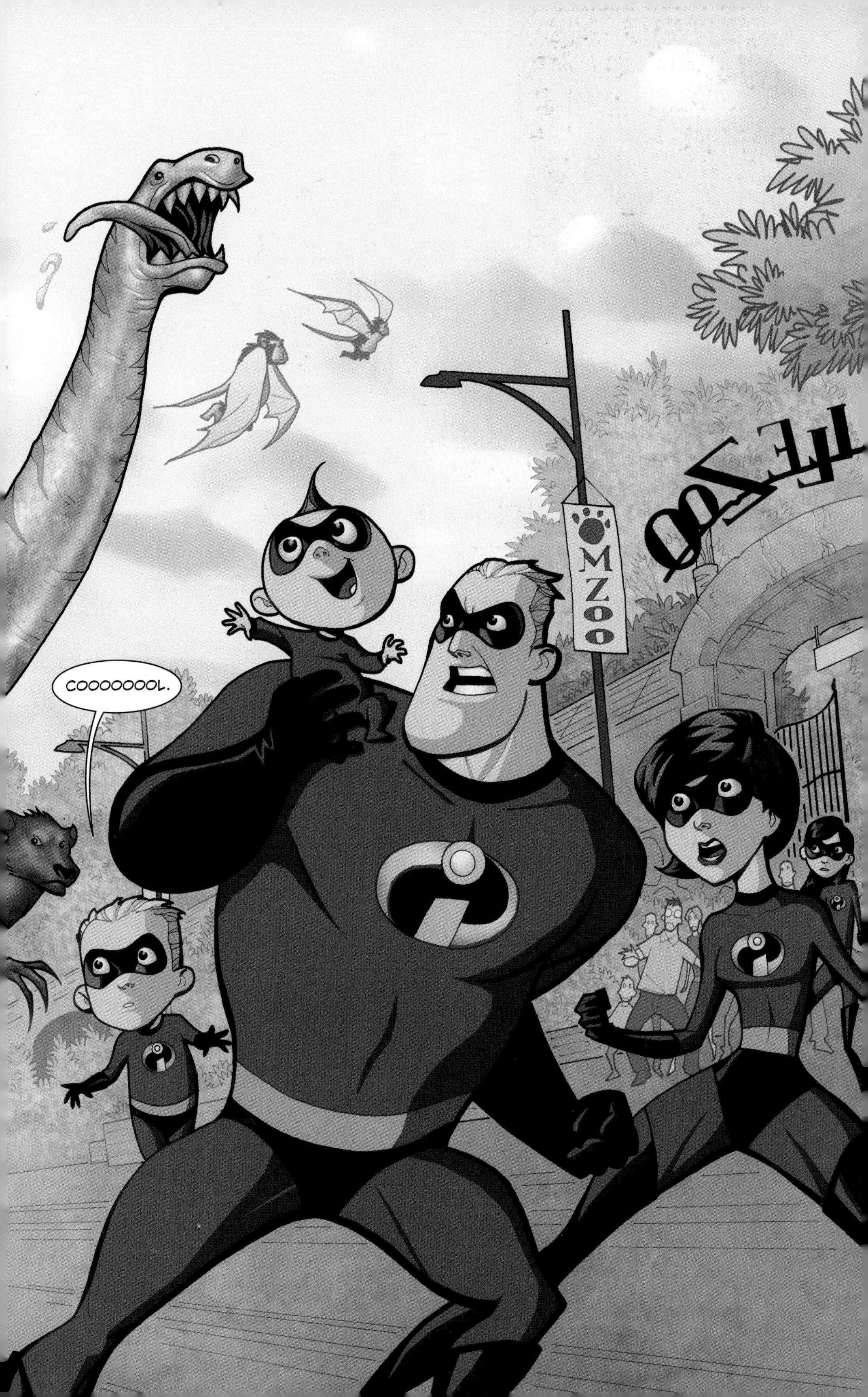
COOOOOOOL.
MZOO

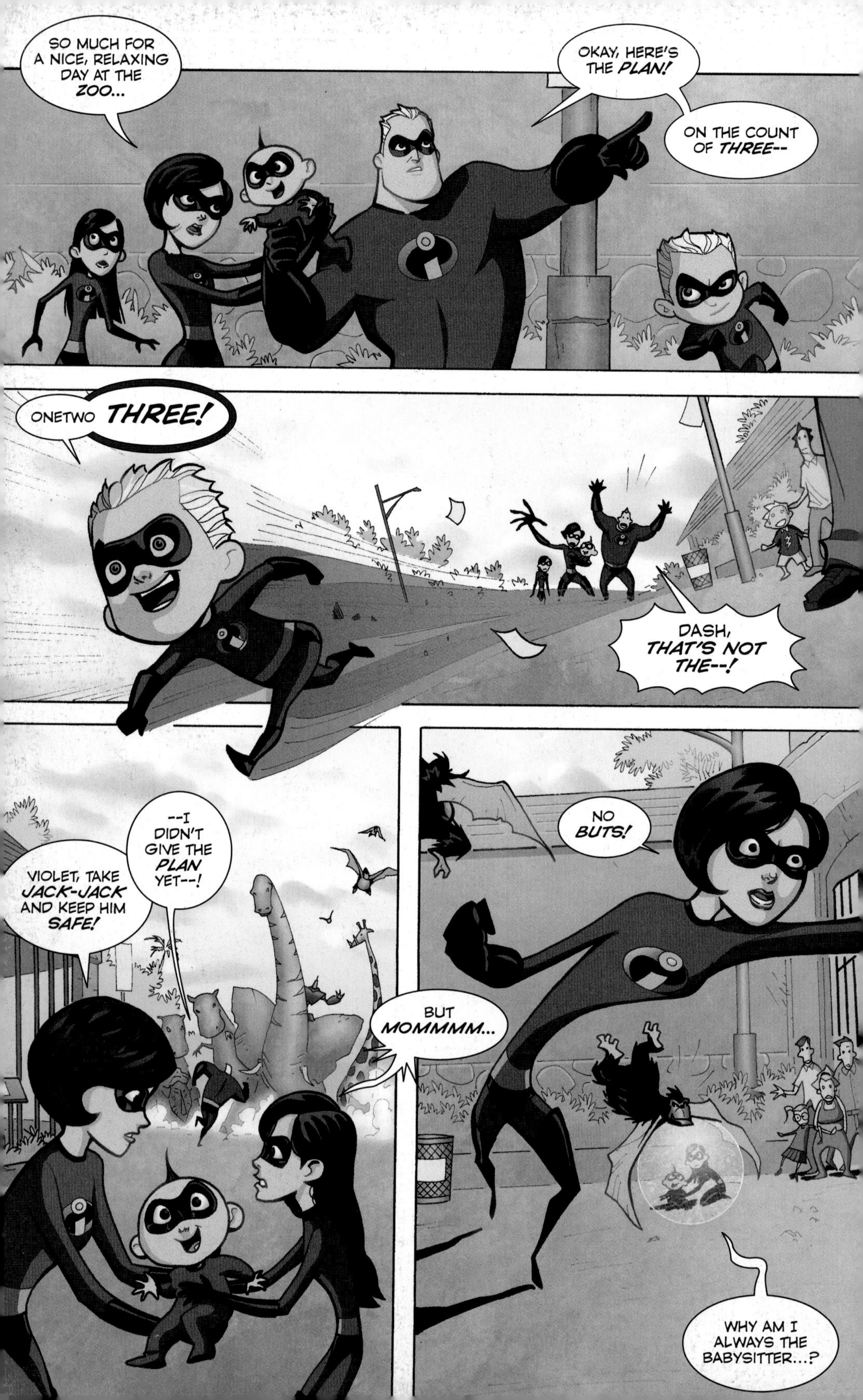
SO MUCH FOR A NICE, RELAXING DAY AT THE ZOO...
OKAY, HERE'S THE *PLAN!*
ON THE COUNT OF *THREE--*
ONETWO **THREE!**
DASH, *THAT'S NOT THE--!*
VIOLET, TAKE *JACK-JACK* AND KEEP HIM *SAFE!*
--I DIDN'T GIVE THE *PLAN* YET--!
BUT *MOMMMM...*
NO *BUTS!*
WHY AM I ALWAYS THE BABYSITTER...?

Disney · PIXAR

# TOY STORY

BOOM Kids!

## THE RETURN OF BUZZ LIGHTYEAR

It's a battle of the Buzzes when Andy gets an unexpected present... another Buzz Lightyear?

TOY STORY: THE RETURN OF BUZZ LIGHTYEAR
DIAMOND CODE: JAN100839
SC $9.99 ISBN 9781608865574
HC $24.99 ISBN 9781608865581

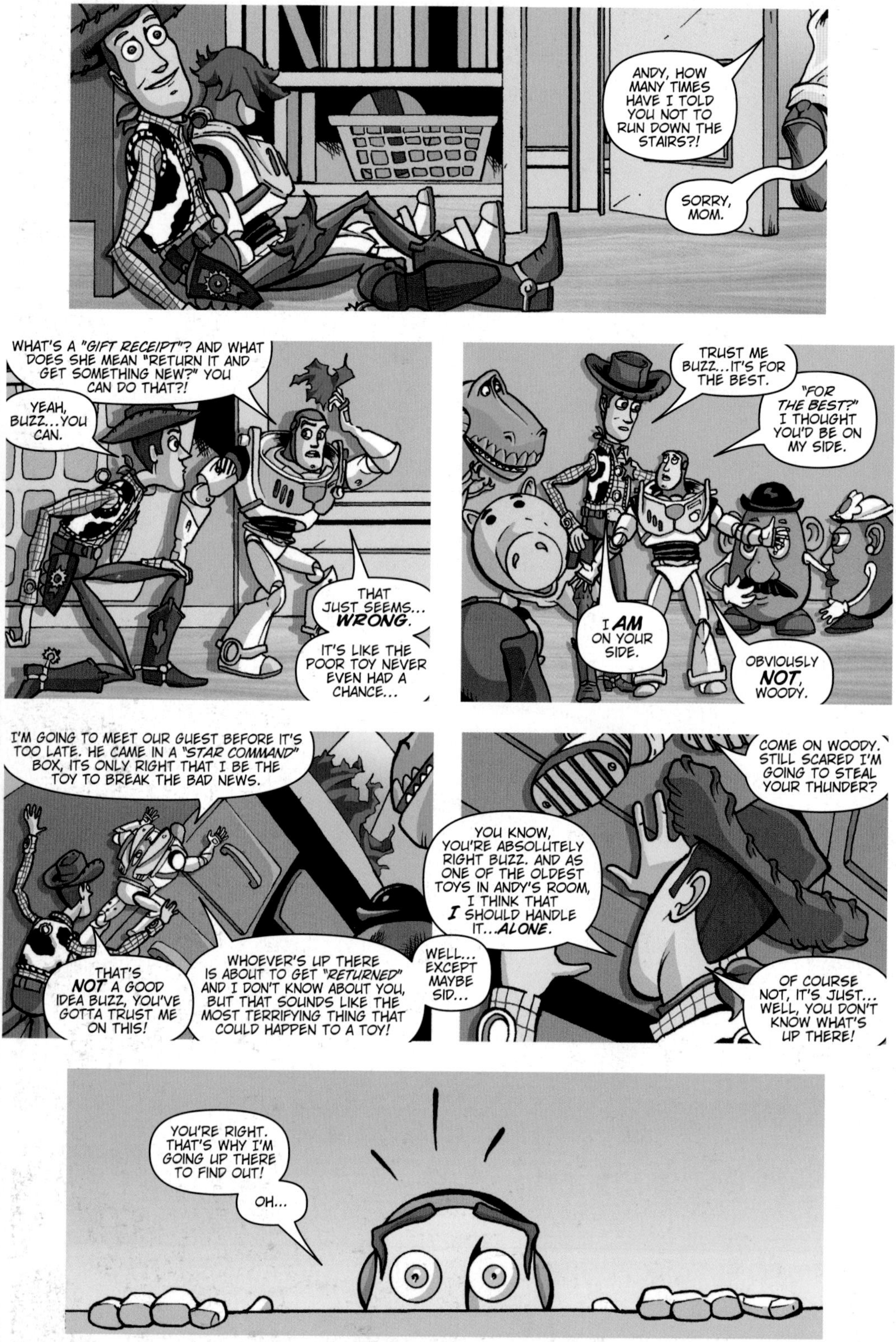
ANDY, HOW MANY TIMES HAVE I TOLD YOU NOT TO RUN DOWN THE STAIRS?!
SORRY, MOM.
WHAT'S A "GIFT RECEIPT"? AND WHAT DOES SHE MEAN "RETURN IT AND GET SOMETHING NEW?" YOU CAN DO THAT?!
YEAH, BUZZ...YOU CAN.
THAT JUST SEEMS... WRONG.
IT'S LIKE THE POOR TOY NEVER EVEN HAD A CHANCE...
TRUST ME BUZZ...IT'S FOR THE BEST.
"FOR THE BEST?" I THOUGHT YOU'D BE ON MY SIDE.
I AM ON YOUR SIDE.
OBVIOUSLY NOT, WOODY.
I'M GOING TO MEET OUR GUEST BEFORE IT'S TOO LATE. HE CAME IN A "STAR COMMAND" BOX, ITS ONLY RIGHT THAT I BE THE TOY TO BREAK THE BAD NEWS.
THAT'S NOT A GOOD IDEA BUZZ, YOU'VE GOTTA TRUST ME ON THIS!
WHOEVER'S UP THERE IS ABOUT TO GET "RETURNED" AND I DON'T KNOW ABOUT YOU, BUT THAT SOUNDS LIKE THE MOST TERRIFYING THING THAT COULD HAPPEN TO A TOY!
WELL... EXCEPT MAYBE SID...
COME ON WOODY. STILL SCARED I'M GOING TO STEAL YOUR THUNDER?
YOU KNOW, YOU'RE ABSOLUTELY RIGHT BUZZ. AND AS ONE OF THE OLDEST TOYS IN ANDY'S ROOM, I THINK THAT I SHOULD HANDLE IT...ALONE.
OF COURSE NOT, IT'S JUST... WELL, YOU DON'T KNOW WHAT'S UP THERE!
YOU'RE RIGHT. THAT'S WHY I'M GOING UP THERE TO FIND OUT!
OH...

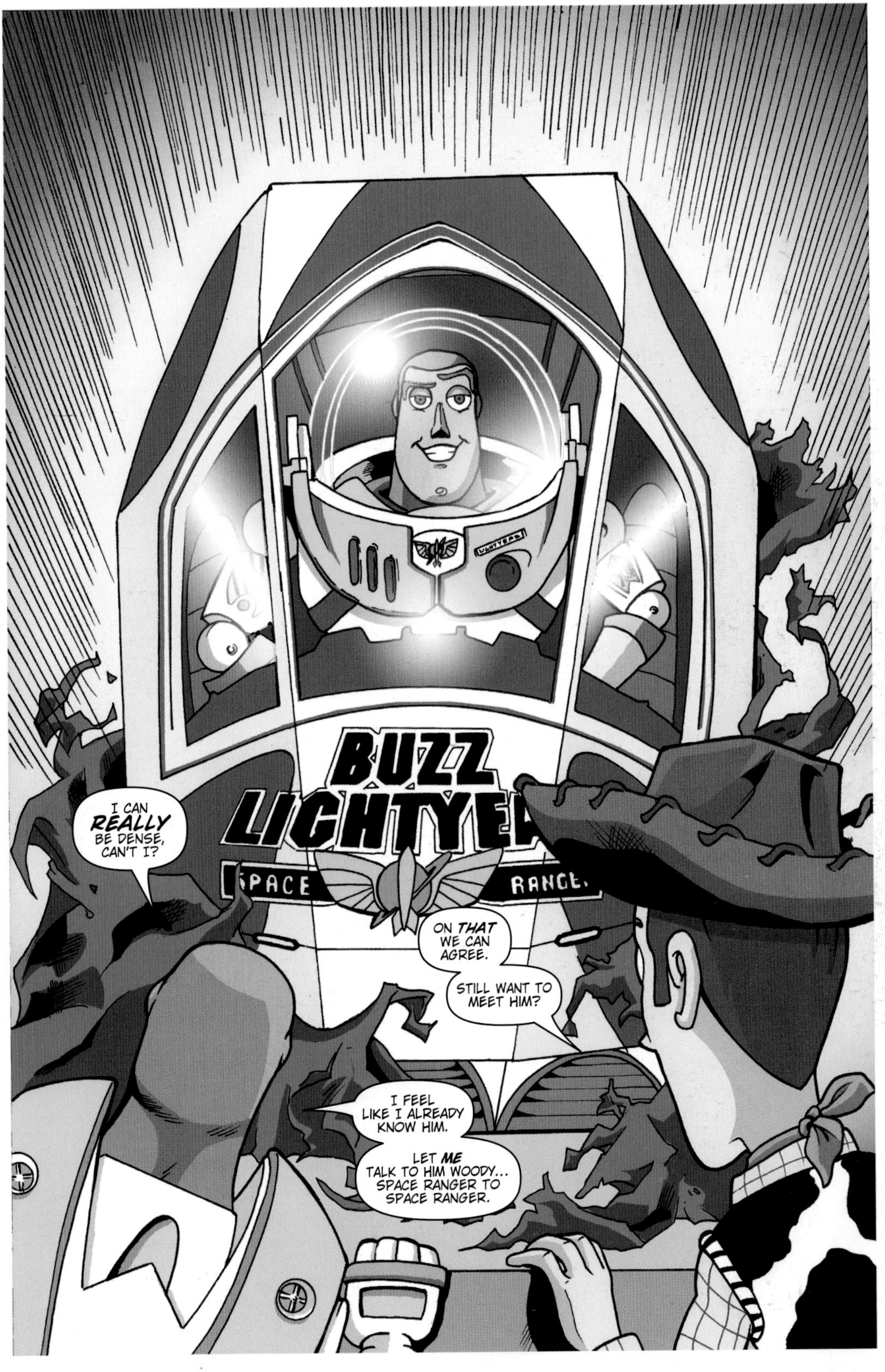
BUZZ LIGHTYEAR
SPACE RANGER
I CAN REALLY BE DENSE, CAN'T I?
ON THAT WE CAN AGREE.
STILL WANT TO MEET HIM?
I FEEL LIKE I ALREADY KNOW HIM.
LET ME TALK TO HIM WOODY... SPACE RANGER TO SPACE RANGER.

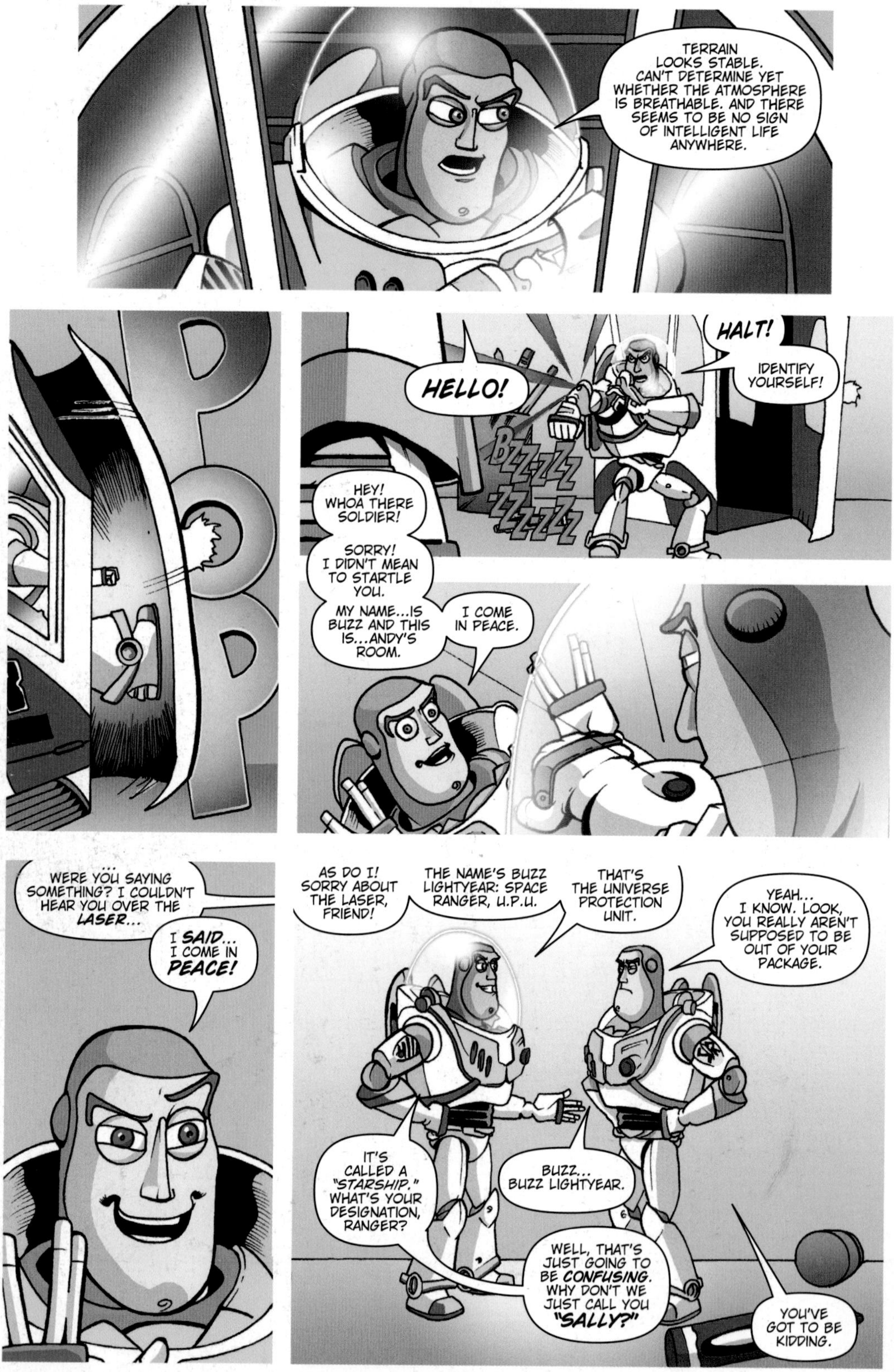
TERRAIN LOOKS STABLE. CAN'T DETERMINE YET WHETHER THE ATMOSPHERE IS BREATHABLE. AND THERE SEEMS TO BE NO SIGN OF INTELLIGENT LIFE ANYWHERE.
POP
HALT!
IDENTIFY YOURSELF!
HELLO!
HEY! WHOA THERE SOLDIER!
SORRY! I DIDN'T MEAN TO STARTLE YOU.
MY NAME...IS BUZZ AND THIS IS...ANDY'S ROOM.
I COME IN PEACE.
...WERE YOU SAYING SOMETHING? I COULDN'T HEAR YOU OVER THE LASER...
I SAID... I COME IN PEACE!
AS DO I! SORRY ABOUT THE LASER, FRIEND!
THE NAME'S BUZZ LIGHTYEAR: SPACE RANGER, U.P.U.
THAT'S THE UNIVERSE PROTECTION UNIT.
YEAH... I KNOW. LOOK, YOU REALLY AREN'T SUPPOSED TO BE OUT OF YOUR PACKAGE.
IT'S CALLED A "STARSHIP." WHAT'S YOUR DESIGNATION, RANGER?
BUZZ... BUZZ LIGHTYEAR.
WELL, THAT'S JUST GOING TO BE CONFUSING. WHY DON'T WE JUST CALL YOU "SALLY?"
YOU'VE GOT TO BE KIDDING.

# WALT DISNEY'S UNCLE $CROOGE

## THE HUNT FOR THE OLD NUMBER ONE

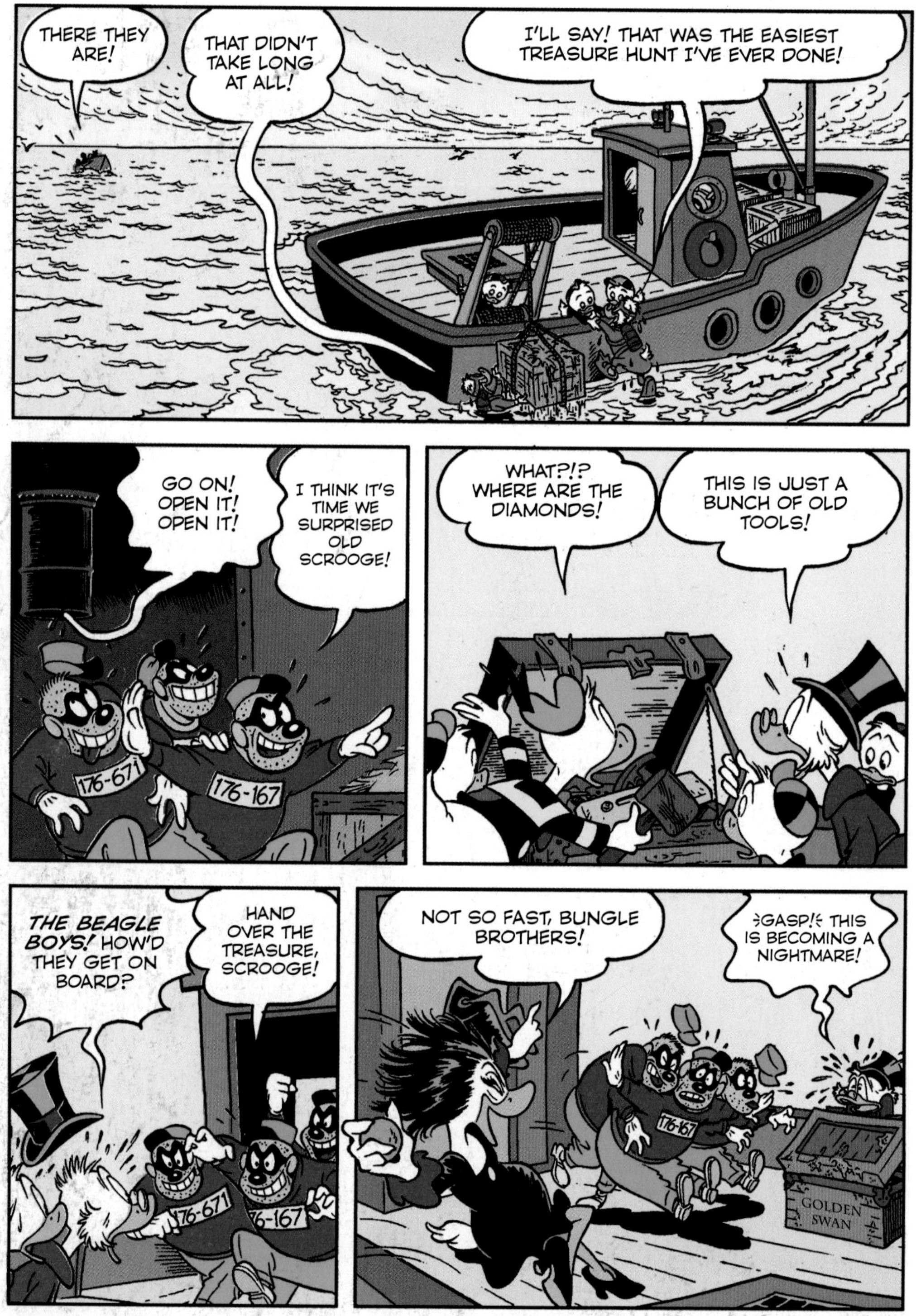
THERE THEY ARE!
THAT DIDN'T TAKE LONG AT ALL!
I'LL SAY! THAT WAS THE EASIEST TREASURE HUNT I'VE EVER DONE!
GO ON! OPEN IT! OPEN IT!
I THINK IT'S TIME WE SURPRISED OLD SCROOGE!
176-671
176-167
WHAT?!? WHERE ARE THE DIAMONDS!
THIS IS JUST A BUNCH OF OLD TOOLS!
THE BEAGLE BOYS! HOW'D THEY GET ON BOARD?
HAND OVER THE TREASURE, SCROOGE!
176-671
76-167
NOT SO FAST, BUNGLE BROTHERS!
GASP! THIS IS BECOMING A NIGHTMARE!
176-167
GOLDEN SWAN

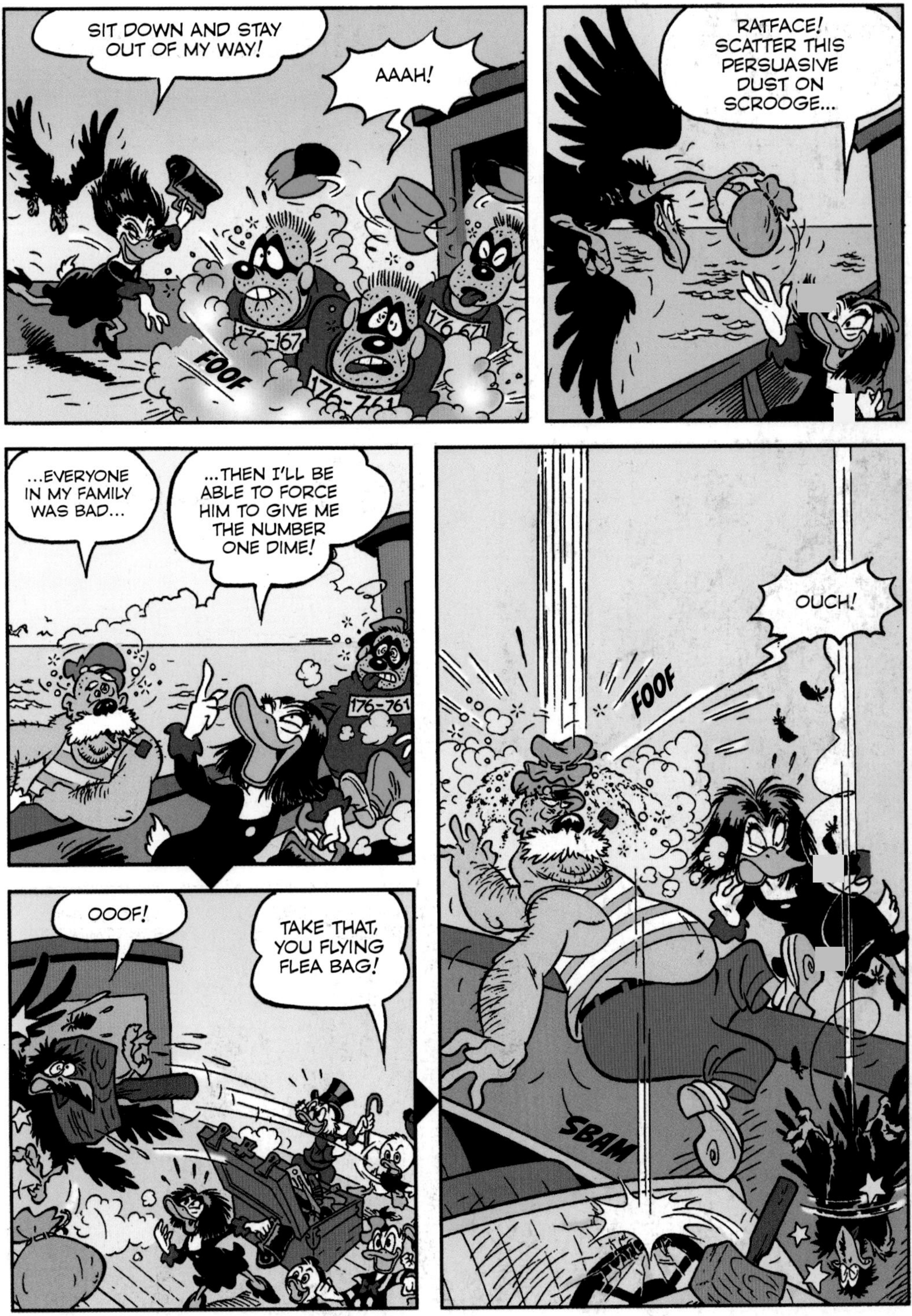
SIT DOWN AND STAY OUT OF MY WAY!
AAAH!
FOOF
176-167
176-761
176-671
RATFACE! SCATTER THIS PERSUASIVE DUST ON SCROOGE...
...EVERYONE IN MY FAMILY WAS BAD...
...THEN I'LL BE ABLE TO FORCE HIM TO GIVE ME THE NUMBER ONE DIME!
176-761
OOOF!
TAKE THAT, YOU FLYING FLEA BAG!
OUCH!
FOOF
SBAM

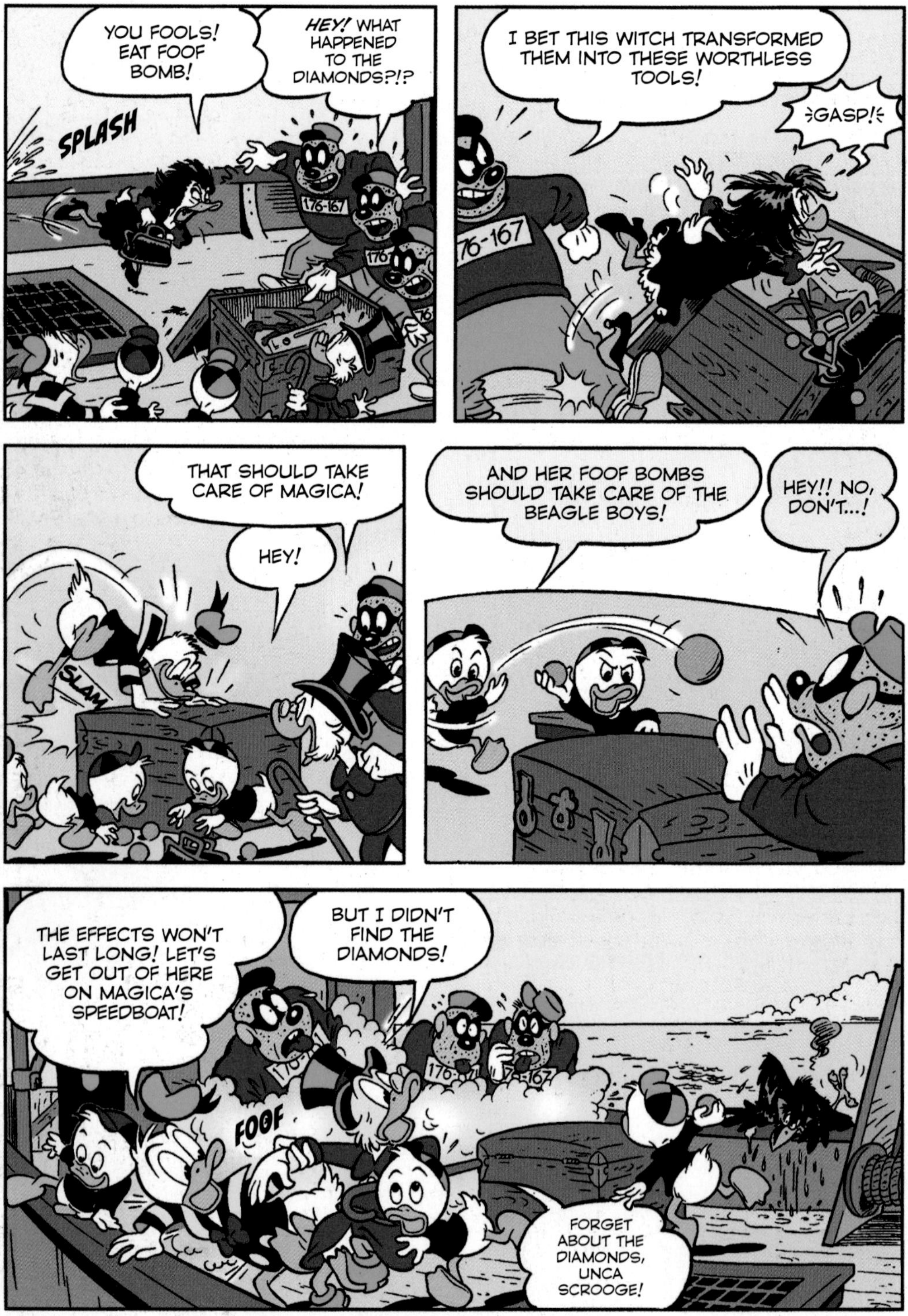

YOU FOOLS! EAT FOOF BOMB!
HEY! WHAT HAPPENED TO THE DIAMONDS?!?
SPLASH
176-167
I BET THIS WITCH TRANSFORMED THEM INTO THESE WORTHLESS TOOLS!
GASP!
176-167
THAT SHOULD TAKE CARE OF MAGICA!
HEY!
SLAM
AND HER FOOF BOMBS SHOULD TAKE CARE OF THE BEAGLE BOYS!
HEY!! NO, DON'T...!
THE EFFECTS WON'T LAST LONG! LET'S GET OUT OF HERE ON MAGICA'S SPEEDBOAT!
BUT I DIDN'T FIND THE DIAMONDS!
FOOF
FORGET ABOUT THE DIAMONDS, UNCA SCROOGE!

# GRAPHIC NOVELS AVAILABLE NOW!

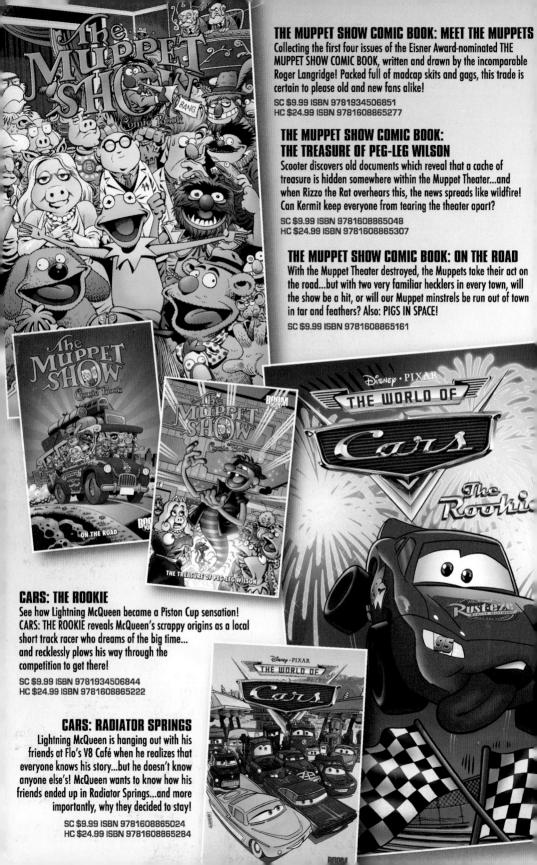

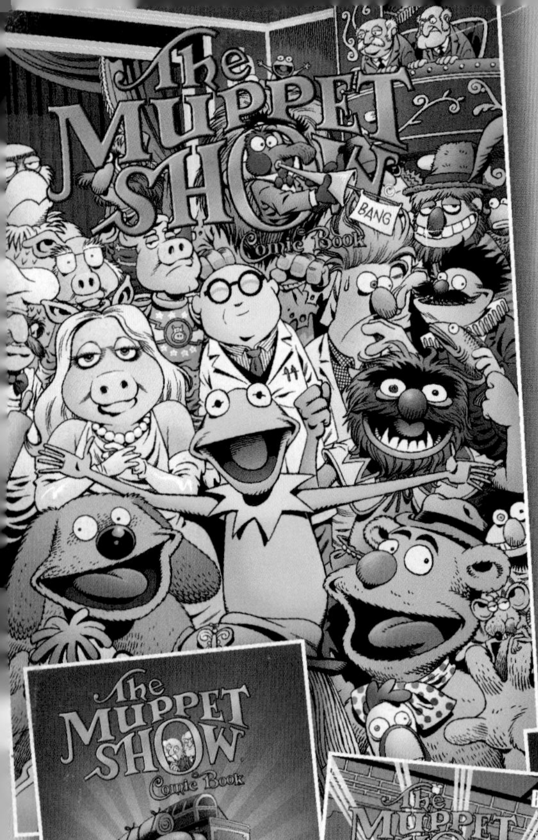
The Muppet Show
Comic Book
BANG

## THE MUPPET SHOW COMIC BOOK: MEET THE MUPPETS

Collecting the first four issues of the Eisner Award-nominated THE MUPPET SHOW COMIC BOOK, written and drawn by the incomparable Roger Langridge! Packed full of madcap skits and gags, this trade is certain to please old and new fans alike!

SC $9.99 ISBN 9781934506851
HC $24.99 ISBN 9781608865277

## THE MUPPET SHOW COMIC BOOK: THE TREASURE OF PEG-LEG WILSON

Scooter discovers old documents which reveal that a cache of treasure is hidden somewhere within the Muppet Theater...and when Rizzo the Rat overhears this, the news spreads like wildfire! Can Kermit keep everyone from tearing the theater apart?

SC $9.99 ISBN 9781608865048
HC $24.99 ISBN 9781608865307

## THE MUPPET SHOW COMIC BOOK: ON THE ROAD

With the Muppet Theater destroyed, the Muppets take their act on the road...but with two very familiar hecklers in every town, will the show be a hit, or will our Muppet minstrels be run out of town in tar and feathers? Also: PIGS IN SPACE!

SC $9.99 ISBN 9781608865161

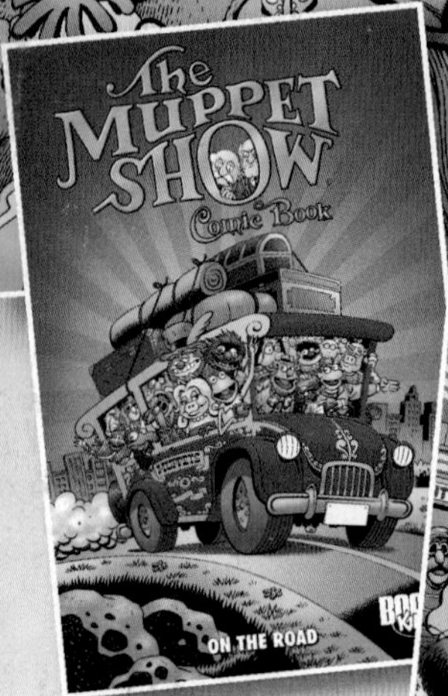
The Muppet Show
Comic Book
ON THE ROAD

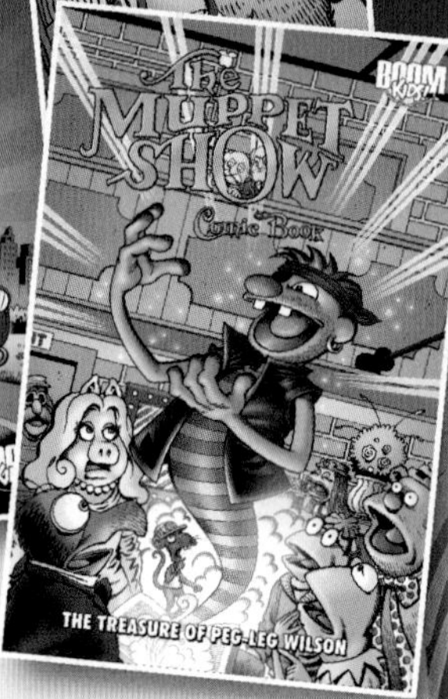
The Muppet Show
Comic Book
BOOM! KIDS!
THE TREASURE OF PEG-LEG WILSON

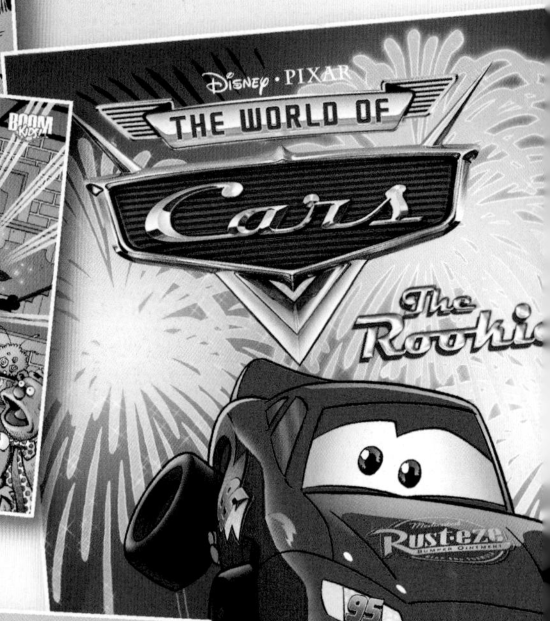
Disney · PIXAR
THE WORLD OF
Cars
The Rookie
Rust-eze
95

## CARS: THE ROOKIE

See how Lightning McQueen became a Piston Cup sensation! CARS: THE ROOKIE reveals McQueen's scrappy origins as a local short track racer who dreams of the big time... and recklessly plows his way through the competition to get there!

SC $9.99 ISBN 9781934506844
HC $24.99 ISBN 9781608865222

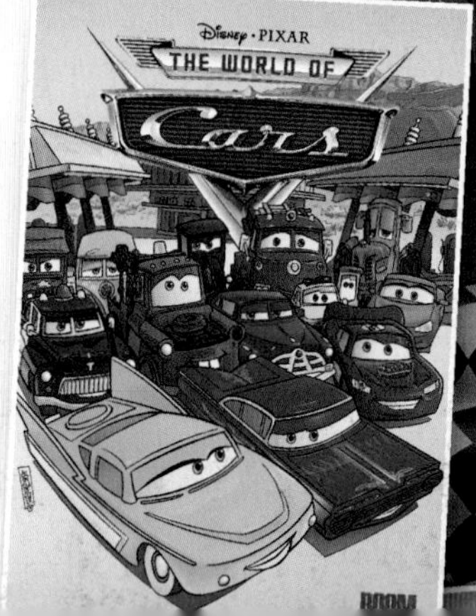
Disney · PIXAR
THE WORLD OF
Cars

## CARS: RADIATOR SPRINGS

Lightning McQueen is hanging out with his friends at Flo's V8 Café when he realizes that everyone knows his story...but he doesn't know anyone else's! McQueen wants to know how his friends ended up in Radiator Springs...and more importantly, why they decided to stay!

SC $9.99 ISBN 9781608865024
HC $24.99 ISBN 9781608865284

## WALL•E: RECHARGE

Before WALL•E becomes the hardworking robot we know and love, he lets the few remaining robots take care of the trash compacting while he collects interesting junk. But when these robots start breaking down, WALL•E must adjust his priorities...or else Earth is doomed!

SC $9.99 ISBN 9781608865123
HC $24.99 ISBN 9781608865543

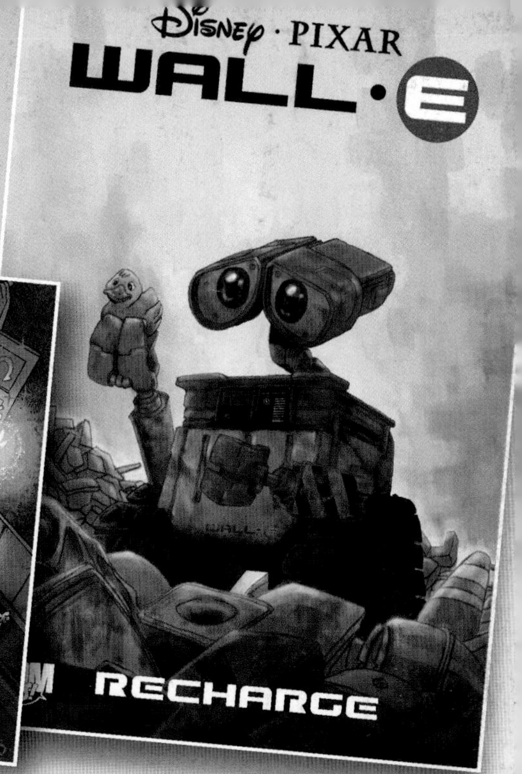
DISNEY · PIXAR
WALL•E
RECHARGE

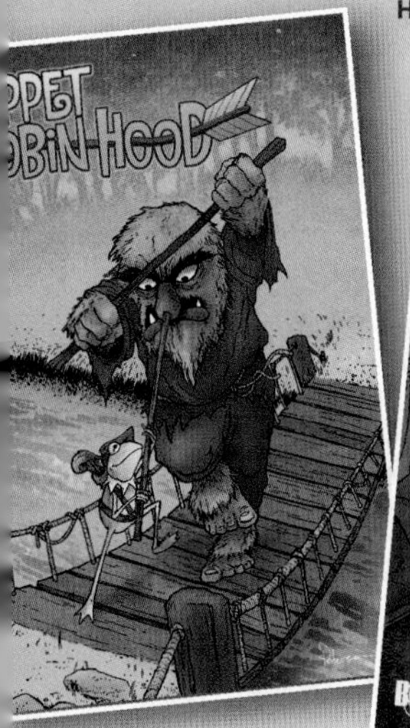

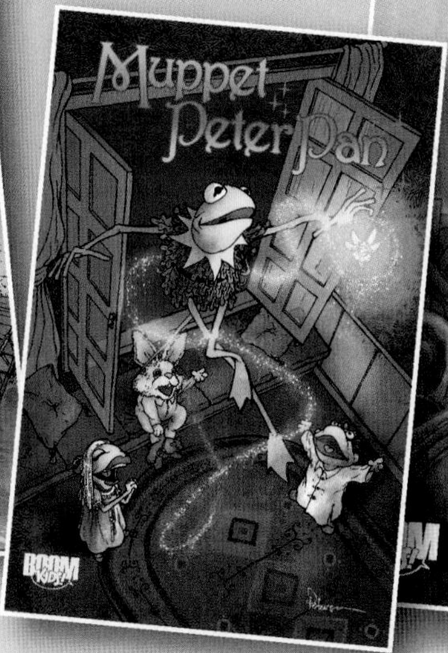
Muppet Peter Pan

## MUPPET ROBIN HOOD

The Muppets tell the Robin Hood legend for laughs, and it's the reader who will be merry! Robin Hood (Kermit the Frog) joins with the Merry Men, Sherwood Forest's infamous gang of misfit outlaws, to take on the Sheriff of Nottingham (Sam the Eagle)!

SC $9.99 ISBN 9781934506790
HC $24.99 ISBN 9781608865260

## MUPPET PETER PAN

When Peter Pan (Kermit) whisks Wendy (Janice) and her brothers to Neverswamp, the adventure begins! With Captain Hook (Gonzo) out for revenge for the loss of his hand, can even the magic of Piggytink (Miss Piggy) save Wendy and her brothers?

SC $9.99 ISBN 9781608865079
HC $24.99 ISBN 9781608865314

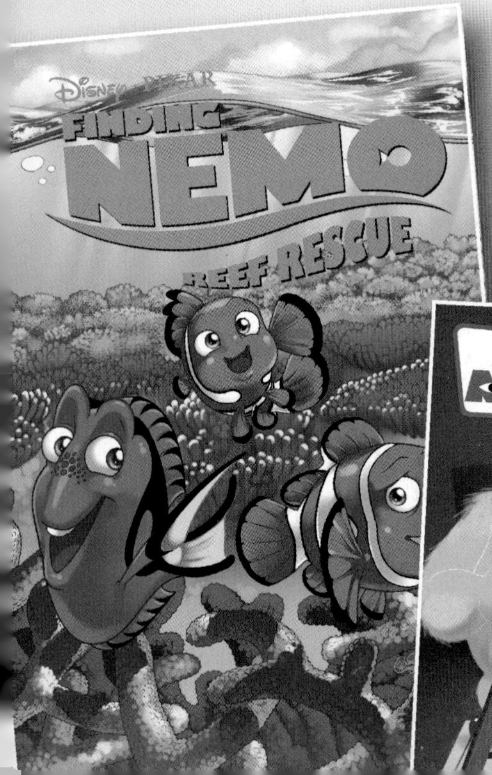
FINDING
NEMO
REEF RESCUE

## FINDING NEMO: REEF RESCUE

Nemo, Dory and Marlin have become local heroes, and are recruited to embark on an all-new adventure in this exciting collection! The reef is mysteriously dying and no one knows why. So Nemo and his friends must travel the great blue sea to save their home!

SC $9.99 ISBN 9781934506882
HC $24.99 ISBN 9781608865246

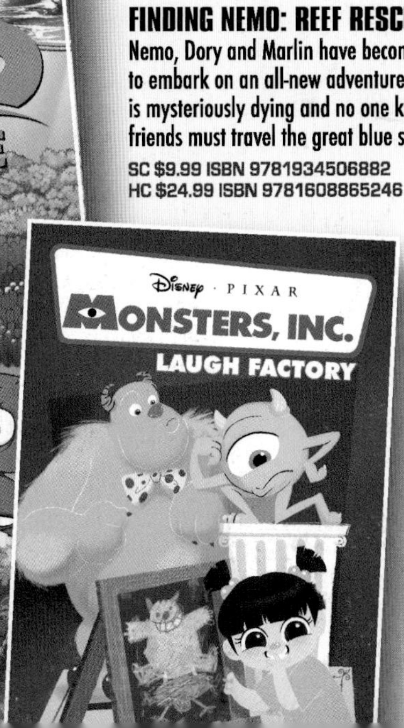
DISNEY · PIXAR
MONSTERS, INC.
LAUGH FACTORY

## MONSTERS, INC.: LAUGH FACTORY

Someone is stealing comedy props from the other employees, making it difficult for them to harvest the laughter they need to power Monstropolis...and all evidence points to Sulley's best friend Mike Wazowski!

SC $9.99 ISBN 9781608865086
HC $24.99 ISBN 9781608865338

## DISNEY'S HERO SQUAD: ULTRAHEROES VOL. 1: SAVE THE WORLD

It's an all-star cast of your favorite Disney characters, as you have never seen them before. Join Donald Duck, Goofy, Daisy, and even Mickey himself as they defend the fate of the planet as the one and only Ultraheroes!

SC $9.99 ISBN 9781608865437
HC $24.99 ISBN 9781608865529

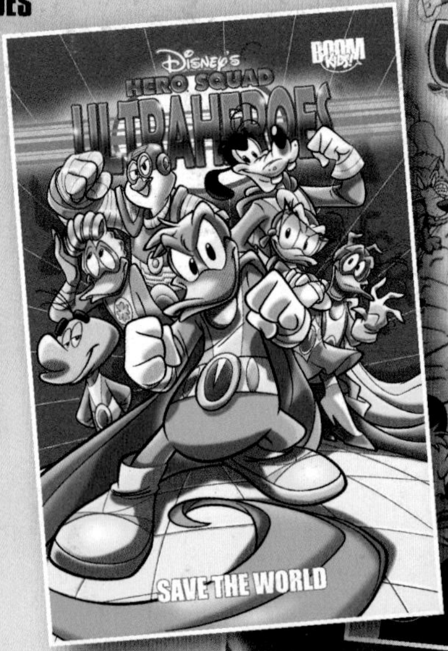
Disney's
Hero Squad
Ultraheroes
BOOM! Kids!
SAVE THE WORLD

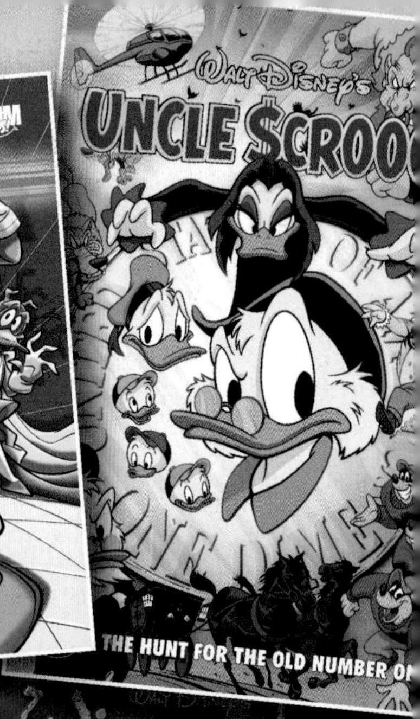
Walt Disney's
THE HUNT FOR THE OLD NUMBER

## UNCLE SCROOGE: THE HUNT FOR THE OLD NUMBER ONE

Join Donald Duck's favorite penny-pinching Uncle Scrooge as he, Donald himself and Huey, Dewey, and Louie embark on a globe-spanning trek to recover treasure and save Scrooge's "number one dime" from the treacherous Magica De Spell.

SC $9.99 ISBN 9781608865475
HC $24.99 ISBN 9781608865536

## WIZARDS OF MICKEY VOL. 1: MOUSE MAGIC

Your favorite Disney characters star in this magical fantasy epic! Student of the great wizard Nereus, Mickey allies himself with Donald and team mate Goofy, in a quest to find a magical crown that will give him mastery over all spells!

SC $9.99 ISBN 9781608865413
HC $24.99 ISBN 9781608865505

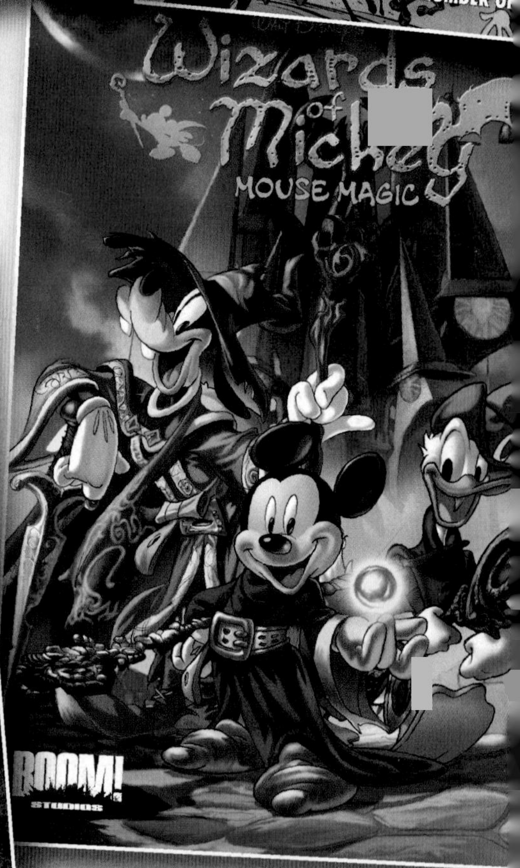
Wizards of Mickey
MOUSE MAGIC
BOOM!
STUDIOS

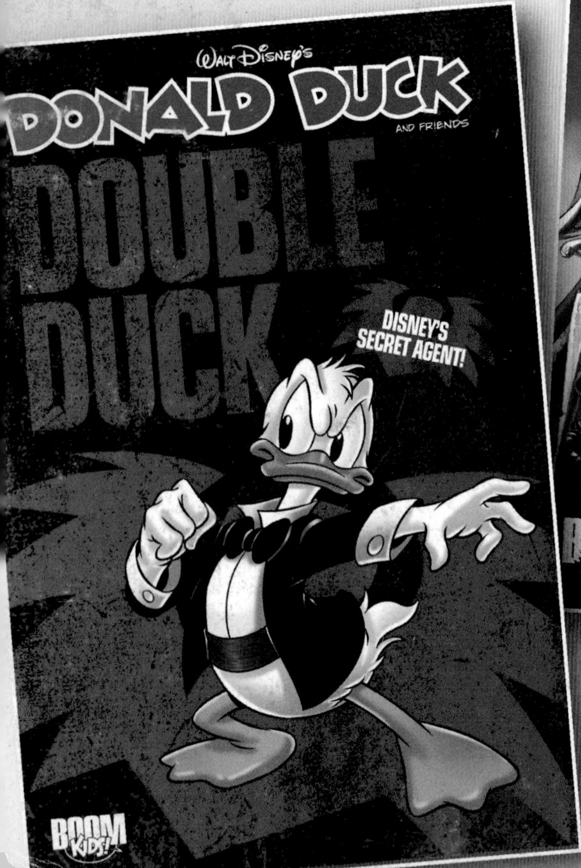
Walt Disney's
DONALD DUCK
AND FRIENDS
DOUBLE DUCK
DISNEY'S SECRET AGENT!
BOOM KIDS!

## DONALD DUCK AND FRIENDS: DOUBLE DUCK VOL. 1

Donald Duck as a secret agent? Villainous fiends beware as the world of super sleuthing and espionage will never be the same! This is Donald Duck like you've never seen him!

SC $9.99 ISBN 9781608865451
HC $24.99 ISBN 9781608865512

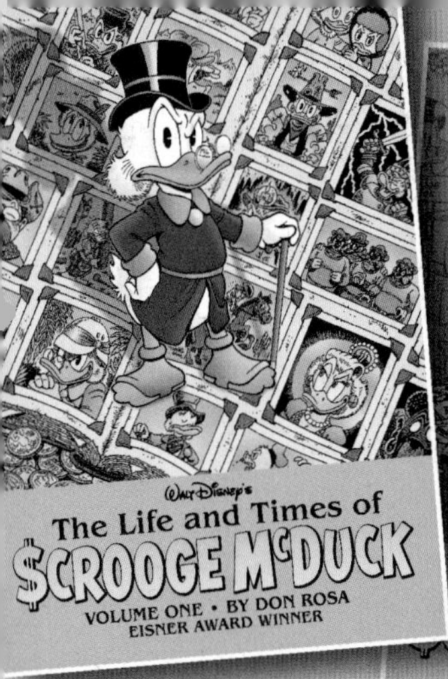
Walt Disney's
The Life and Times of
$CROOGE McDUCK
VOLUME ONE • BY DON ROSA
EISNER AWARD WINNER

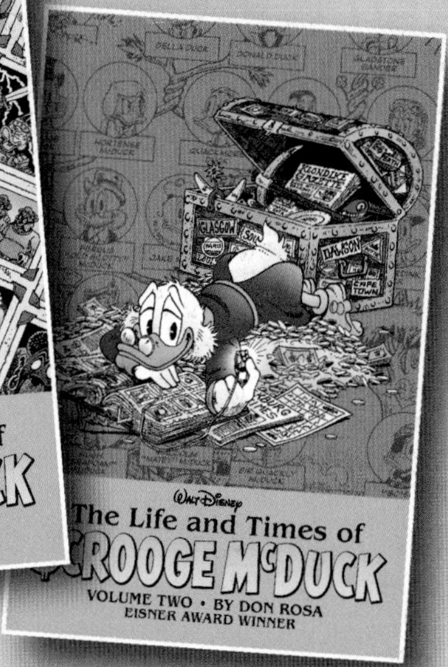
Walt Disney
The Life and Times of
SCROOGE McDUCK
VOLUME TWO • BY DON ROSA
EISNER AWARD WINNER

## THE LIFE AND TIMES OF SCROOGE McDUCK VOL. 1

BOOM Kids! proudly collects the first half of THE LIFE AND TIMES OF SCROOGE MCDUCK in a gorgeous hardcover collection – featuring smyth sewn binding, a gold-on-gold foil-stamped case wrap, and a bookmark ribbon! These stories, written and drawn by legendary cartoonist Don Rosa, chronicle Scrooge McDuck's fascinating life.

HC $24.99 ISBN 9781608865383

## THE LIFE AND TIMES OF SCROOGE McDUCK VOL. 2

BOOM Kids! proudly presents volume two of THE LIFE AND TIMES OF SCROOGE MCDUCK in a gorgeous hardcover collection in a beautiful, deluxe package featuring smyth sewn binding and a foil-stamped case wrap! These stories, written and drawn by legendary cartoonist Don Rosa, chronicle Scrooge McDuck's fascinating life.

HC $24.99 ISBN 9781608865420

## MICKEY MOUSE CLASSICS: MOUSE TAILS

See Mickey Mouse as he was meant to be seen! Solving mysteries, fighting off pirates, and generally saving the day! These classic stories comprise a "Greatest Hits" series for the mouse, including a story produced by seminal Disney creator Carl Barks!

HC $24.99 ISBN 9781608865390

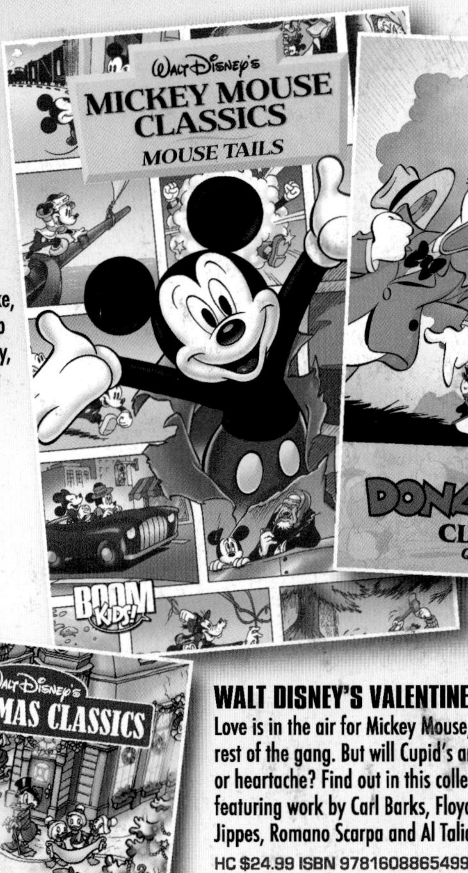
Walt Disney's
MICKEY MOUSE CLASSICS
MOUSE TAILS
BOOM KIDS!

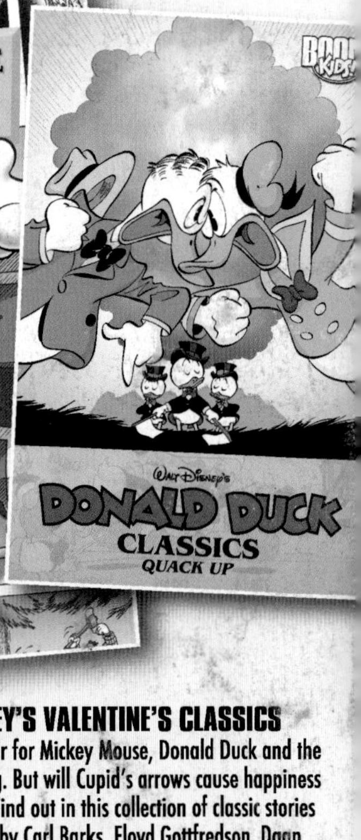
BOOM KIDS!
Walt Disney's
DONALD DUCK
CLASSICS
QUACK UP

## DONALD DUCK CLASSICS: QUACK UP

Whether it's finding gold, journeying to the Klondike, or fighting ghosts, Donald will always have the help of his much more prepared nephews – Huey, Dewey, and Louie – by his side. Featuring some of the best Donald Duck stories Carl Barks ever produced!

HC $24.99 ISBN 9781608865406

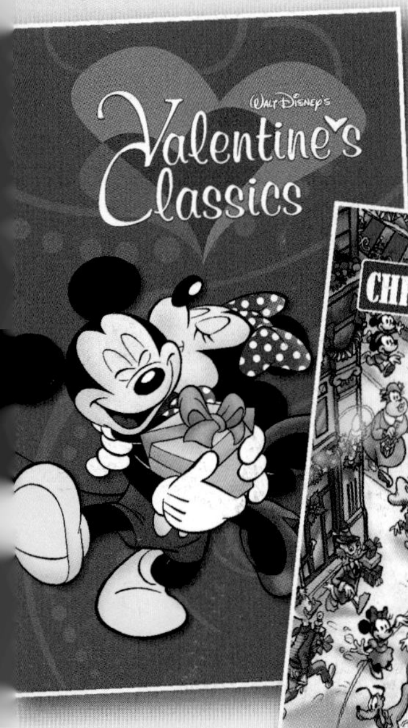
Walt Disney's
Valentine's
Classics

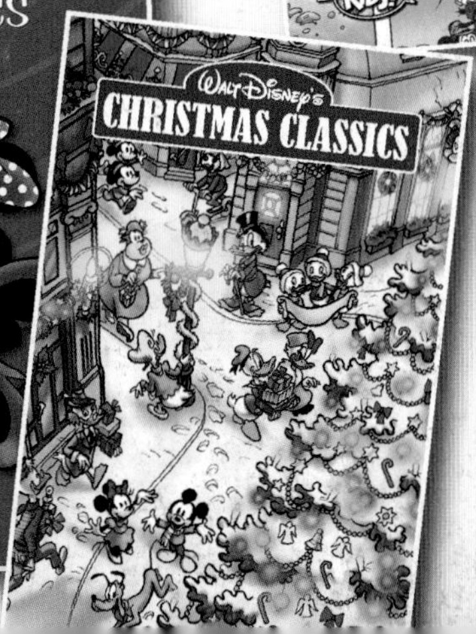
Walt Disney's
CHRISTMAS CLASSICS

## WALT DISNEY'S VALENTINE'S CLASSICS

Love is in the air for Mickey Mouse, Donald Duck and the rest of the gang. But will Cupid's arrows cause happiness or heartache? Find out in this collection of classic stories featuring work by Carl Barks, Floyd Gottfredson, Daan Jippes, Romano Scarpa and Al Taliaferro.

HC $24.99 ISBN 9781608865499

## WALT DISNEY'S CHRISTMAS CLASSICS

BOOM Kids! has raided the Disney publishing archives and searched every nook and cranny to find the best and the greatest Christmas stories from Disney's vast comic book publishing history for this "best of" compilation.

HC $24.99 ISBN 9781608865482

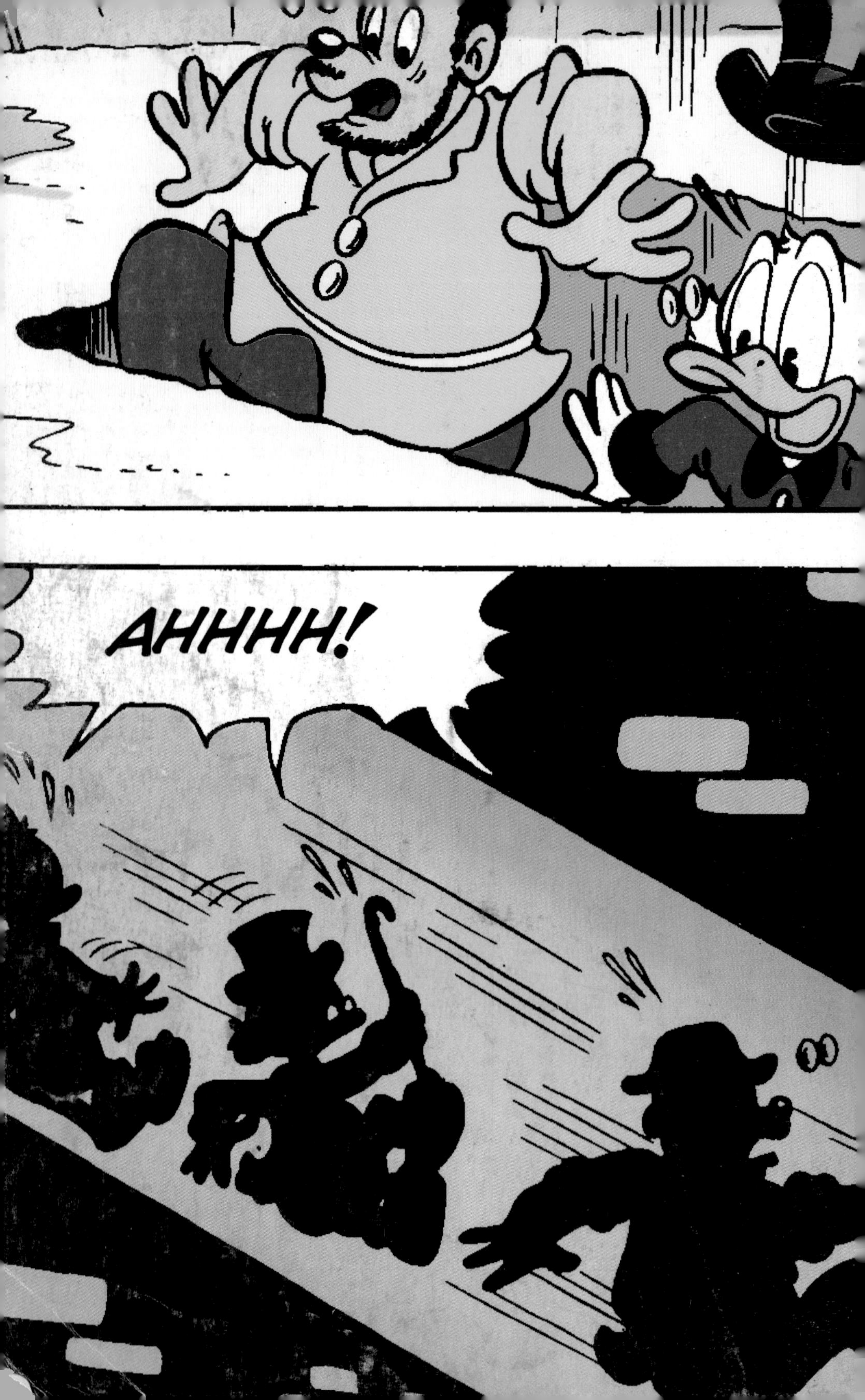
AHHHH!